THE
PROMISE

"The pleasure of *The Promise* is in its nostalgic simplicity, the wholesome goodness of its characters, and the fierce concern with moral righteousness."
　　　　　　　　—Christopher Lehmann-Haupt,
　　　　　　　　The New York Times

"It will bring tears to your eyes, knowledge to your mind, warmth to your heart."
　　　　　　　　—*Phillipsburg, N. J., Free Press*

"A superb mirror of a place, a time, and a group of people who capture our immediate interest and hold it tightly."
　　　　　　　　—*The Philadelphia Inquirer*

"Moves quickly to a powerful climax. . . . Potok has become a master of the story-teller's art."
　　　　　　　　—*St. Louis Globe-Democrat*

"What Potok really writes about is the love and respect that people have for themselves and for others."
　　　　　　　　—*Miami Herald*

Fawcett Crest Books
by Chaim Potok:

THE CHOSEN
THE PROMISE
MY NAME IS ASHER LEV
IN THE BEGINNING

THE
PROMISE

by Chaim Potok

A FAWCETT CREST BOOK • NEW YORK

THE PROMISE

**THIS BOOK CONTAINS THE COMPLETE TEXT
OF THE ORIGINAL HARDCOVER EDITION.**

Published by Fawcett Crest Books, a unit of CBS Publications,
the Consumer Publishing Division of CBS Inc.,
by arrangement with Alfred A. Knopf, Inc.

Copyright © 1969 by Chaim Potok

ISBN: 0-449-23500-9

Printed in the United States of America

' 22 21 20 19 18 17 16 15 14 13

TO
THE CHILDREN

Rena, Naama, Akiva

This is a work of fiction, one man's vision of things. No correspondence between the people, places, and events in this book and people, places, and events in the real world is intended. What correspondence might exist is the result of coincidence.

My deepest thanks to Professors Herbert Callen, David Halivni (Weiss), and Solomon Zeitlin, Drs. Israel Charny and Bernard Shuman, and Adena, my wife, for helping with the research.

C. P.

If the book we are reading does not wake us, as with a fist hammering on our skull, why then do we read it? Good God, we would also be happy if we had no books, and such books as make us happy we could, if need be, write ourselves. But what we must have are those books which come upon us like ill-fortune, and distress us deeply, like the death of one we love better than ourselves, like suicide. A book must be an ice-axe to break the sea frozen inside us.

FRANZ KAFKA

Master of the Universe, send us our Messiah, for we have no more strength to suffer. Show me a sign, O God. Otherwise . . . otherwise . . . I rebel against Thee. If Thou dost not keep Thy Covenant, then neither will I keep that Promise, and it is all over, we are through being Thy chosen people, Thy peculiar treasure.

THE REBBE OF KOTZK

THE
PROMISE

All around us everything was changing in the order of things we had fashioned for ourselves.

The neighborhood changed. In the years before the Second World War, the Williamsburg section of Brooklyn had been inhabited by only a few Hasidic sects. By the fifth year after the war, the neighborhood seemed dark with their presence. They had come from the sulfurous chaos of the concentration camps, remnants, one from a hamlet, two from a village, three from a town, dark, somber figures in long black coats and black hats and long beards, earlocks hanging alongside gaunt faces, eyes brooding, like balls of black flame turned inward upon private visions of the demonic. Here, in Williamsburg, they set about rebuilding their burned-out world. Families had been destroyed; they remarried and created new families. Dynasties had been shattered; elders met and formed new dynasties. Children had been killed; their women now seemed forever pregnant. And by the fifth year after the war, Lee Avenue, the main street of the neighborhood, was filled with their bookstores and bookbinderies, butcher shops and restaurants, beeswax candle stores, dry-cleaning stores, grocery stores and vegetable stores, appliance stores and hardware stores—the signs in Yiddish and English, the storekeepers bearded and in skullcaps, the gentiles gone now from behind the counters, the Italians and Irish and Germans and the few Spanish

Civil War refugee families all gone now too from the neighborhood.

The street I lived on changed. It was a quiet sycamore-lined street directly off Lee Avenue, and I had lived on it all my life with my father and Manya, the Russian woman who had come in to care for me when my mother died suddenly soon after I was born. The row houses on the street were all three-story brownstones, with small grassy back yards and neatly kept areaways in front where hydrangeas flowered and shone in the sunlight like huge snowballs. Then the newcomers moved into the street. They lived in a dimension of reality that made trees and grass and flowers irrelevant to their needs. So the street began to sag with neglect. The grassy back yards went slowly bald, the hydrangeas were left to fade and die, and the brownstones became old and worn. Soon even the musky odor of the ailanthus trees in the back yards was gone from the street.

The school I attended changed. The Samson Raphael Hirsch Seminary and College stood on Bedford Avenue near Eastern Parkway in the Crown Heights section of Brooklyn. It had been a small Orthodox rabbinical school and secular college during the war, the only one of its kind in the United States. In the years after the war it had begun to expand. Adjoining homes and buildings were acquired, college departments were enlarged, additional faculty was hired, and in the final months of my senior year a graduate school was started. Sometime during the summer after my graduation from the college in the fifth year after the war, the name of the school was changed to Hirsch University. I continued to attend the rabbinical school for my ordination.

The winter came late that year. There was a long Indian summer and the sycamores on my block turned slowly in the gentle winds. The leaves remained on the trees until early November, and then began to fall. Soon the street was covered with them and I felt them beneath my feet, thin, brittle, papery things that had once been green with life. The sycamores stood bare against the sky

and seemed to be waiting for the winter. In late December
the air turned suddenly cold and bitter. And on a day in
early January I walked beneath the naked sycamores on
my way home from school and saw the sky dull gray and
heavy with clouds and felt the first flakes of snow against
my face, and the winter was here.

All through that winter my father was writing his book
on the Talmud. He wrote during those afternoons when he
did not have to teach and every evening and night, except
the nights of Shabbat and festivals. He left the apartment
only to go to his school or occasionally to meet with a
colleague or to do research in the rare-manuscript room at
the Zechariah Frankel Seminary, the non-Orthodox rabbinical school and teachers institute on Eastern Parkway.

In the late spring of that year I met Rachel Gordon at a
party. She was a junior at Brooklyn College and majored
in English literature, and when I first met her I found
myself intrigued by the fact that she was the niece of
Professor Abraham Gordon, who taught Jewish philosophy at the Zechariah Frankel Seminary and whose books
were scorned and despised by the rabbis in my very
Orthodox school. I began to date her. Both of us were
surprised and pleased when we discovered we would be
together for part of the coming summer in a resort area
near Peekskill, a small town about thirty miles from New
York, where her parents had a lakeside home and where
my father and I vacationed every August in a cottage we
rented.

In the first week of June the spring weather ended
abruptly with a stifling heat wave. On Lee Avenue the
dark-clothed Hasidim sweated in the fierce heat, but the
sycamores on my block shaded the street and there was a
breeze in the nights and I could hear it in the leaves
through the open window of my room.

Rachel and her parents left for their summer home in
the last week of June. I went up to visit her on a Sunday
morning in the middle of July and met her cousin Michael,
who was with them that summer. He was a sad-faced,
precocious fourteen-year-old boy and he spent the morn-

ing roaming along the shore collecting frogs and salamanders and the afternoon reading an astronomy book
while Rachel and I swam and sailed on the lake. New
York seemed dazed with heat when I returned that night.

In the first week of August my father and I packed
some bags and left for the cottage on a day when the heat
reached to just over one hundred degrees and even Lee
Avenue surrendered to the summer and stood empty and
deserted, a stagnant pool of shimmering asphalt burning in
the sun.

BOOK ONE

*Yes; but you must wager. It is not optional.
You are embarked.*

PASCAL

One

The county fair was Rachel's idea. She had a passion for the theater, James Joyce, and county fairs, and she could be quite persuasive when it came to those three passions. We would go on the Sunday in the third week of August, the closing night of the fair, when there would be a fireworks display. We would have a splendid time, she said. It was also her idea that we take her cousin Michael.

It was warm that Sunday night and the sky was clear and filled with stars. We sat in the front seat of the DeSoto and Rachel drove carefully along the dark asphalt country roads. Michael sat quietly between us, staring out the windshield. A moment after we reached the highway he suddenly became quite talkative. He chatted about his frogs and salamanders. He talked about Andromeda, white dwarfs, and red giants. He seemed to know a great deal about astronomy. He had a high, thin voice and he spoke animatedly and in a rushing flow of technical words. I saw Rachel smiling. She wore a yellow sleeveless summer dress and her short auburn hair blew in the warm wind that came through the open windows of the car.

We came to a crossroads, bright with the neon life of a night highway, then went around a sharp curve. Set into the darkness about an eighth of a mile away, and looking as though it had carved itself into the night, was the county fair. Michael abruptly ceased talking and leaned forward in the seat.

The fair lay stretched out upon a huge field alongside

the highway, bathed in a blaze of electric lights and neon signs, with strings of bulbs across an entrance arch spelling out the word PARKING, and floodlights poking bright fingers into the black sky, and blurred gashes of colored lights from a moving Ferris wheel and parachute jump. The brightness formed a pale, smoky, faintly pink arc-shaped cloud over the entire area, sealing it off from the darkness beyond. In the center of the field was a roller coaster with strings of lighted bulbs following its tortuous contour.

Rachel parked the car and we came out onto the graveled surface of the parking lot and to a chain-link fence with a gate. We went through the gate and into the country fair.

The three of us were standing on an asphalt road that was jammed with people. Teen-agers jostled roughly through the crowd, children ran about wildly, young and old couples moved along or stood near booths playing carnival games. A thick din choked the air. I heard gongs, bells, rifle shots from a nearby shooting gallery, the music of a calliope, the whooshing roar of the roller coaster, and a steady waterfall of human noise. It seemed as if all the noise of the world's wide night had descended upon this one stretch of lighted earth.

"We're in the wrong place," I said to Rachel.

She stood alongside me on 'the asphalt road, her face pale in the garish lights. Michael was staring around wide-eyed at the booths.

"What did you do, take a wrong turn somewhere?" I was annoyed and I let my voice show it.

"No, I did not take a wrong turn somewhere."

"What happened to your county fair?"

"It was advertised as a fair. You saw the poster. Annual county fair. In big red letters. You saw it too."

"I don't like carnivals," I said.

"Neither do I."

"What do you want to do?"

She looked around indecisively, chewing her lip. I saw

her glance at Michael, who stood nearby staring at the roller coaster.

"Why don't we call up James Joyce and find out what he would do?" I said, feeling irritated and annoyed and wanting to get away from the noise and the wildness.

She gave me an angry look. "Don't be nasty," she said. "It isn't my fault."

"What do you want to do?"

"We'll see the exhibits and go right home."

"They've probably got three cows and two horses in a tent somewhere."

"We'll look and go right home. So it won't be a total waste. What gall to advertise this as a fair."

We found the tent. There were cows, horses, calves, pigs, roosters, hens, awkward paintings by local artists, and some prize-winning home-baked pies. The wooden floor of the tent was covered with sawdust, and the smell of animal droppings was very strong.

"I'm thrilled," I said. "You have no idea how thrilled I am to see rural America at its creative best."

"Don't be mean," Rachel said. But she was as angry as I was.

"I'm not mean. I'm thrilled."

"I've seen beautiful fairs."

"Let's go home," I said.

Michael stood a few feet away from us, looking curiously at a prize calf. He wore a rumpled white sport shirt, tan shorts, and an old pair of tennis sneakers with the laces untied. He had wild dark-brown hair that badly needed trimming and dreamy blue eyes behind shell-rimmed glasses that were too large for his narrow face.

We came out of the tent onto the black asphalt road of the carnival. Michael wanted to know where the other exhibits were.

"That's all there is," I told him. "We just saw the whole fair. It's a carnival. They stuck some animals in and called it a fair. But it's a carnival."

"We're going home now," Rachel said.

Michael stared at her, his mouth dropping open.

"Reuven and I don't like carnivals," Rachel said.

But Michael did not want to go home. Why should we go home just because it was a carnival? he wanted to know. What was wrong with carnivals? He and Rachel stood on the road, arguing. It seemed to me they argued a long time. Michael had a strong, stubborn, aggressive streak. In the end, Rachel yielded.

We walked along the crowded asphalt road through the litter of pop bottles, ice-cream wrappers, soiled paper bags, popsicle sticks, beer cans, discarded newspapers. The carnival booths lined both sides of the road, and from inside the booths pitchmen shouted their games to the crowd. Some booths were large, with expensive-looking prizes on their shelves; most were small shantylike affairs, with gambling games or tossing games operated by hard-voiced carnival people some of whom wore derbies or straw hats. The booths were on wheels and were scarred and blotched from travel. The carnival had been set up in the form of a circle, with the booths lining both sides of the curving asphalt road, and the Ferris wheel, parachute jump, and roller coaster in the center.

We approached a ring-toss game operated by a short, double-chinned pitchman in a straw hat. He was chewing on a dead cigar and shouting automatically at the crowd. He took off the straw hat and wiped his bald head with a red handkerchief. There was no one at his booth. He put the handkerchief away and saw me looking at him. His voice focused itself directly upon us, and we were drawn reluctantly to the booth.

We played the ring-toss game twice. Then we went to another booth and played a pitching game. Michael played awkwardly. His glasses kept slipping down the bridge of his nose and he kept pushing them back up with abrupt motions of his hand. After the pitching game Rachel told him again that she wanted to go home but he ignored her and went on ahead, moving restlessly along the asphalt road. He was a thin, narrow-shouldered, gawky boy, about five inches shorter than my own five feet ten inches, and he seemed all caught up in the tumult around us.

So we continued along the asphalt road, playing the games and ignoring the freak shows. Even Michael did not want to see the freak shows. We fired rifles at wooden ducks, threw pennies into flat plates, tossed baseballs at fat-nosed clowns. Rachel won a charm bracelet from the penny-tossing game, and Michael came away from the fat nose of a clown with a pen and pencil set which he stuck away in his shirt pocket with a triumphant grin. Now he wanted to go on the roller coaster, he said.

Rachel told him she did not like roller coasters.

"Then I'll go with Reuven," he said.

I told him I did not like roller coasters either.

"Then I'll go alone," he said, and started by himself toward the ticket booth.

Rachel looked at me helplessly.

"Your cousin is a first-class brat," I said. "Come on. We can't let him go up there by himself."

Michael grinned delightedly as he watched us purchase our tickets. We came through the turnstile and climbed into the front seat of a car. The remaining seats filled rapidly. The teen-age boy who had taken our tickets shouted something to the man behind the ticket counter and pushed down a long lever set near the tracks. There was a faint hum of machinery. The car moved forward. Michael sat to my left, talking excitedly about the last time he had been on a roller coaster years ago in Coney Island. He had been scared half to death, he said, grinning at me and pushing the glasses back up on the bridge of his nose. Rachel sat to my right, looking a little frightened. The car climbed slowly up a steep incline. Then we were at the crest and with a suddenness that pushed me back against the seat and took the air from my lungs we dropped wildly into the night.

The car hurtled downward on roaring wheels between lights that blurred into quivering lines. Michael held on tightly to the support rod, his body rigid, his teeth clenched. Rachel gave me a resigned look. We rose and fell

and rose again and fell again. On the ground below, the
carnival heaved and undulated like a garish blanket in a
windstorm. There were screams and shouts from the other
passengers and the fierce crescendo of racing steel wheels.
Michael sat with his eyes narrow against the whipping of
the wind and his mouth open as though gulping the air
that beat against him. Then, with an abrupt motion, he
stood up in the car.

Immediately Rachel shouted at him to sit down.

He stood there, holding tightly to the rod, his body
swaying with the wild motions of the car, and ignored her.

"Sit down!" Rachel screamed.

He turned his head and looked at her and laughed.

Rachel gave me a frightened, pleading look. I struggled
to my feet and stood next to him, holding on to the rod
and feeling my arms strain and pull against the sudden
force of a drop that almost lifted me from the floor of the
car. Then we were out of it and the tracks leveled and
slanted off to the right and we seemed to be on our sides
as we hurtled along the rim of the coaster over the booths
and the lights and the asphalt road below. I heard Rachel
shout at Michael again to sit down. He ignored her. We
were climbing again. I turned my head to glance at Rachel.
She was white-faced. I started to reach for Michael's
shoulder to pull him into the seat, but we had climbed
to another crest and were falling again and I needed both
hands on the rod. We fell a long time and I saw Michael
release one hand from the rod and brush at his nose, then
clutch quickly at the rod as the drop curved into a wildly
slanting turn. I looked at his face. There was a faint dark
smear on his upper lip. I saw him brush again at his nose,
and now the smear was darker, moving liquidly across his
face, and the wind lifted it and blew it against his cheeks
and onto his shirt and out behind him into the night. We
came out of the turn and straightened and dropped again
down a long straight slope that looked like a ski jump,
then looped upward into another climb. Michael stared at
his hand. It had come away from his nose stained with
blood. He sat down quickly.

"He's got a nosebleed," I shouted to Rachel above the noise of the wheels. I turned to Michael. "Lean back. Put your head back." I took out my handkerchief and wiped away some of the blood. It trickled strongly from his left nostril, a dark stream against the whiteness of his narrow face.

"Press down on his upper lip," Rachel said, shouting into the wind.

I put my forefinger across his upper lip and pressed down hard. Michael stared up at me. The next drop lifted my finger from his face and threw me against him, and I felt him squirming beneath my weight. Then I was sitting next to him, holding him and pushing down hard on his upper lip. He reached up and put both his hands on my arm and I thought he was using my arm to support himself in the seat, but he was pushing against me instead, pushing my finger away from his face. He took out his own handkerchief and held it to his nose, looking at me intently, a strange calm in his eyes. The car slowed, ran level for a moment, then came to a stop.

We climbed out. Michael held the handkerchief to his nose. Some of the passengers looked at him as they passed by. We moved away from the car and stood on the asphalt road near the roller coaster ticket booth.

"Are you all right?" Rachel asked him. Her voice was faint and she looked very frightened.

He took the handkerchief away from his nose. The bleeding had stopped. The handkerchief hung limply from his hand, stained with blood. He stuffed it into a pocket.

"What was that all about?" I said.

He grinned at me. There was a strange sly look on his narrow face.

"That was a stupid thing to do. What were you trying to prove?"

"I wasn't scared," he said, grinning. "I enjoyed it."

"You scared hell out of me and Rachel."

"Let's play some more games," he said.

Rachel said she wanted to go home.

"In a little while," Michael said.

Rachel said she wanted to go home right now.

Michael ignored her. He was looking at the booths alongside the road beyond the roller coaster. Then he started on up the road, walking quickly, as if he were by himself now.

"He's turning into a royal pain in the neck," I said.

Rachel stood there, looking a little dazed and watching Michael go up the road.

"We should have gone home right away," she said.

"Come on," I said. "We'll lose him in a minute."

"We should have gone home right away," she said again. Then she started quickly along the road. I walked beside her.

Up ahead, Michael had stopped in front of a small booth and was peering at it curiously. We came alongside him. The booth was about seven feet high and five feet deep and was built of wide planks. A single bare electric bulb hung by a black wire from the wooden ceiling. The shelves lining the back and side walls were filled with expensive, brightly colored radios, which had been carefully lacquered. On a shelf in the center of the rear wall was a large, brown-leather AM-FM short-wave radio trimmed in gold and with a gleaming silver antenna jutting upward from its side like a regal finger. It was a magnificent radio, and it sat as though enthroned amidst the smaller radios on the shelves.

The counter that fronted the booth was painted gold. Upon it lay a white wooden board and a brown-leather dice cup. The board contained ten rows of holes, ten holes in each row, one hundred holes in all. A number ranging from one to ten had been painted in black beneath each hole. The numbers appeared to be in random sequence and stood out sharp and black beneath the holes, the insides of which were bright red. The board glittered brightly in the harsh light of the electric bulb.

The three of us stood there, listening to the pitchman behind the counter. He was tall and thin, with skeletal features and dark, shiny hair brushed flat on top of his head. His dark eyes were narrow and lay in deep sockets beneath arching black brows. His fingers were long and white and thin, with bony knuckles and joints, and nails that looked manicured. He wore sharply pressed dark trousers, a white long-sleeved silk shirt, a red vest, and a red bow tie. His voice was strong, smooth, caressing. I saw him watching our faces intently as he explained the game.

It was a gambling game. The dice cup contained eight silver balls. The balls were tossed onto the board. The numbers below the holes into which they fell were added together. A card, which he now brought out and placed on the counter next to the board, was then consulted to determine the value of the total. As soon as the player's separate throws added up to ten, he was given a radio.

"Can't be simpler than that," the pitchman said.

Michael stared at the large, brown-leather, gold-trimmed radio. He stood there, staring at the radio, his white shirt spotted with blood, his brown hair wild, his thin body taut. I saw him push his glasses up along the bridge of his nose and wet his lips.

"Look at it, Reuven," he said.

"I'm looking," I told him.

Rachel chewed her lip.

"I want to play," Michael said.

Rachel looked at him in dismay.

The pitchman smiled and ran his fingers over his red bow tie.

"It's a gambling game," Rachel said.

Michael ignored her.

"I don't like gambling games," she said.

"Then don't play," Michael said.

The pitchman leaned forward inside the booth and smiled at Michael. "I'll tell you what I'll do," he said. "You like that big radio, right? It goes for twelve points. I'll give it to you for ten. Same amount of points as a small radio." His long fingers moved slowly across the gleaming leather and gold surface of the radio. "I don't do that for everyone," he said, still smiling. "But you look like a good kid. Ten points. How about it?"

"I don't want you to play," Rachel said.

Michael gave her an annoyed glance. He turned back to the pitchman, hesitated a moment, then looked at me and grinned.

"Reuven will play," he said.

Rachel and I stared at him.

"It'll be with my money. But I want Reuven to play."

"No, thanks," I said. "It's your money, you play."

"Is it all right if my friend plays with my money?" Michael asked the pitchman.

"Makes no difference who plays," said the pitchman.

"You see?" Michael said. "It's all right."

"It's not all right," I told him.

"Look," said the pitchman. "I'll give you a free first throw. How about that?"

I did not say anything.

"What've you got to lose?" the pitchman asked. "A free first throw. You might even win it on that throw." He had the dice cup in his hand now and was clicking the balls together softly. "Why don't you go ahead and make the kid happy?" He clicked the balls together with his right hand and ran his left hand over his smoothly brushed black hair.

"I want you to play," Michael said.

"I don't gamble," I said.

"I want you to play," Michael said again. There was a hard, aggressive tone to his thin voice.

Rachel chewed her lip and said nothing.

"Play," Michael said. I had the feeling I was being manipulated by him for some reason.

"It's a free first throw," the pitchman said.

"Play," Michael said, his voice hard, almost ugly.

Rachel looked grim-faced but said nothing.

I took the dice cup from the pitchman and held it in my hand. I thought I would throw it once and get it over with. I had never held a dice cup in my hand before. I turned it over quickly. The balls scattered across the white board, five of them landing in holes, the remaining three coming to rest against the outer frame of the board.

The pitchman's fingers moved swiftly over the board as

he tallied up the numbers and nudged each ball from its hole. I had made a total of forty-three. The pitchman consulted the card. Number forty-three was worth five points.

"That's pretty good," the pitchman said. "You need five more points."

"How much is it to play?" I heard Michael ask.

"Twenty-five cents a toss."

I put the dice cup down on the counter. Michael dug into a pocket, came up with a crumpled dollar bill, and put it on the counter next to the board. The pitchman took the dollar bill and replaced it with three quarters. He put the balls back into the dice cup and looked at me.

"We're going home," I said.

"No we're not," Michael said. "We made five points for free."

"Come on," I said. "Let's go."

"I want you to play."

"I told you I don't—"

"I want that radio," he said.

"Play by yourself then."

"No," he said. "I want you to play."

I looked at Rachel. She seemed helpless.

"Play," Michael said, picking up the dice cup and offering it to me.

"Go ahead," the pitchman said. "Make the kid happy."

"I want you to play," Michael said, and pushed the dice cup into my hand.

"Why don't you—"

"Play," he said, his voice suddenly rising. "Dammit, play!"

I stared at him in surprise and felt him closing my fingers around the dice cup. For a moment I thought of simply turning and walking away, but I didn't want to leave Rachel there alone with him. I glanced at her. She looked quite frightened now. I held the dice cup in my hand and with an abrupt and angry gesture spilled the balls onto the board.

"Thirty-five," the pitchman counted swiftly, nudging

the balls from the holes. He consulted the card and looked unhappy.

"What's wrong?" I heard Michael ask.

"You make ten points, you get the radio and a fiver," the pitchman said. He took a five-dollar bill from a cigar box on a shelf and put it on top of the leather and gold radio.

I stared at him. All of us stared at him.

"That's the game," he said, looking very unhappy.

"You mean we win the radio and the five dollars if we make five more points?" Michael asked.

"Yeah," said the pitchman.

"You hear that, Reuven?"

"I hear."

"It's half a buck a throw now," the pitchman said. "When it goes up like that, the toss goes up too." He looked at me. "You playing?" He seemed quite willing to let the game end.

"He's playing," Michael said excitedly.

I tossed the balls onto the board.

The pitchman counted, nudging the balls from the holes, and consulted the card. I had made two more points.

Michael laughed. Rachel gave me an uncertain smile.

I tossed the balls again and made half a point. On the next toss, the five dollars Michael stood to win with the radio became ten dollars, and the cost of each toss went up from fifty cents to one dollar. I felt my annoyance at Michael begin to disappear, and I tossed the balls once again. The ten dollars became twenty dollars, and the one dollar became two dollars.

Michael put two dollars on the counter next to the lacquered board. I was playing seriously now and I clicked the balls together inside the dice cup and tossed them onto the board, then leaned forward, watching the swift count of the pitchman.

"Twenty-two," he announced, nudging the last ball from its hole. He consulted the card, touched his tie, and ran his hand over his black hair. "One point," he said. He glanced at the radio on top of which there now lay a new twenty-dollar bill. "You got a point and a half to go," he added unhappily.

I saw Michael put two more dollars on the counter. There was a flush on his cheeks and his eyes burned hungrily. Glancing at Michael, I noticed a man standing near the booth, looking at us curiously. He appeared to be in his late sixties or early seventies, and he stood a few feet behind Michael, leaning on a cane and watching us. I clicked the balls together and tossed them onto the board. They scattered wildly across the lacquered surface, some finding holes, some falling against the frame. The pitchman nudged the balls from the holes as he counted, then consulted the card.

I had made an additional one-half point.

Michael laughed triumphantly and put two dollars on the counter. I had lost track of how much money he had spent so far, but I did not think it could be anywhere near what he stood to win.

I tossed the balls again. They added up to nineteen. The pitchman looked at the card.

"No credit," he said, looking relieved.

The three of us stared at him.

"What do you mean, no credit?" I heard myself say.

"You want to look at the card?"

We looked at the card.

"All right," I said.

Rachel put her hand on my arm and shook her head. I put the dice cup on the counter.

"You quitting?" the pitchman said.

Rachel ignored him. She looked at Michael. "You are going to stop playing," she said very quietly in Sephardic Hebrew.

I saw the old man give her a sudden sharp look.

"Rachel is right," I said to Michael, also in Sephardic Hebrew. "You're spending too much money."

"It's my money," Michael responded in Hebrew. He put two dollars on the counter.

"Michael," Rachel said, very quietly.

"It's only one more point," Michael said, in English now. There was a frantic edge to his thin voice.

Rachel took her hand from my arm. I had never seen her look so helpless. She was quite a strong-minded girl and I wondered why she didn't simply grab Michael by the arm and drag him away from there. Instead she looked at the pitchman, as if pleading with him to stop the game. He stood very still behind the the counter, saying nothing.

"Play," Michael said loudly.

I had had enough. I put the dice cup on the counter.

"Reuven," he said slowly.

"Play by yourself," I told him. "And stop glaring. You look silly."

He stared at me for a long moment. I saw his fists clenching and unclenching. I just stood there, staring back at him. Then, abruptly, he grabbed the dice cup and turned it over.

The twenty dollars became forty dollars, and the cost of each toss went up to four dollars.

Michael stared at the two twenty-dollar bills on top of the radio. He seemed dazed. Rachel said nothing. I felt myself beginning to sweat, felt beads of sweat on my back and beneath my arms. Michael took a five-dollar bill from his pocket and put it on the counter. The pitchman replaced it with a new one-dollar bill which he took from the cigar box on the shelf.

I looked at Rachel. She seemed unable to speak.

Michael picked up the dice cup and tossed the balls. The pitchman consulted the card.

"Double again," he said, sounding surprised and very unhappy. "You two got a lucky streak going." He put two more twenty-dollar bills on top of the radio. "That's eight bucks a throw now. One more point, you win the radio and eighty bucks."

The old man stood behind Michael, watching us curiously.

"I spent all my money," I heard Michael say in Hebrew.

Rachel drew in her breath sharply.

"Please lend me some money," Michael asked me quietly.

A crimson flush spread swiftly across Rachel's face.

"It's only one more point," Michael said.

"That's enough!" Rachel said loudly in Hebrew. She was angry now. She was finally angry. "You may not play any more!"

"Lend me some money," Michael said. He put his right hand out to me, palm up. "I'll pay you back."

"You are not to play!" Rachel ordered. "I should not have let you play this long."

He ignored her. "Lend me some money, Reuven."

Behind Michael, the old man lifted his cane and came toward us to the booth. I thought he wanted to play and I moved aside. Instead he walked past me, raised the drop-leaf attached to the counter, went into the booth, and let the drop-leaf fall behind him. He put the cane on the counter alongside the lacquered board. The cane was made of wood and had a curved handle and a metal tip. The pitchman stepped back. The old man stood behind the counter and put his hands on the board.

He seemed an aged duplicate of the pitchman. He had sparse gray hair and dark eyes set in deep sockets. His cheekbones were more pronounced than those of the pitchman, the cheeks hollower, the skin sallow on his face, dry and papery on his hands, and like wrinkled cloth on his neck. He wore a white long-sleeved silk shirt, sharply pressed trousers, a red bow tie, and a red vest.

Standing side by side inside the small booth, the two of them looked to be father and son.

The old man peered at me out of his deep-socketed eyes and tapped a long, thin finger against the lacquered board.

"I am the owner," he announced.

His voice was hoarse, almost hollow, as if burned out from shouting into the noise of too many carnival nights.

He looked at me a moment longer. Then he looked at Rachel.

"This is your wife?" he said, turning to me and indicating Rachel.

I saw Rachel blush fiercely. Michael was watching him carefully, his eyes narrow, his face expressionless.

"No," I said.

"Your girl friend?" the old man asked.

I nodded.

"You are fortunate. A beautiful girl." He smiled then, showing two rows of uneven, tobacco-stained teeth. He peered at me intently. "Young man," he said, smiling and tapping a finger against the lacquered board, "you have a friend here." He pointed to himself. "You understand? You have a friend here. Go ahead. Schmeiss!" His hand struck the counter with a light, slapping sound.

I stared at him in amazement and disbelief. The tension of the game was suddenly gone. I felt it drain swiftly out of me and it was suddenly gone and I had to restrain myself to keep from laughing aloud with joy. "Schmeiss" means to strike, to hit. It is a Yiddish word borrowed from German.

"Schmeiss," the old man said again, smiling paternally. "I am telling you you are in good hands here." Then he said in Yiddish, "Do not worry yourselves. Everything will be good." And he winked his right eye and nodded his head.

I saw Rachel's face flood with relief. But Michael continued to regard him narrowly, his eyes strangely suspicious.

A moist night wind blew along the asphalt road, carrying the odors of hot popcorn and broiling meat. I heard the roar of the roller coaster and turned and saw a car hurtle down a grade, then move slowly up a steep incline and disappear over the crest. A man laden with prizes bumped heavily into Rachel, almost knocking her down. Clutching his prizes, he muttered an apology and went on up the road. I heard a gong and the crack of a rifle and shouts, and then the roller coaster again, racing downward in a rush of sound.

The three of us were standing right up against the counter now, looking at the old man. The pitchman stood behind him, staring gloomily at the four twenty-dollar bills that lay on the radio.

"From where are you all?" the old man asked pleasantly in Yiddish.

"New York," I told him.

"From where in New York?"

"Brooklyn."

"Ah," he said. "Where in Brooklyn do you live?"

"I live in Williamsburg. Rachel here, and Michael, live in Crown Heights." I spoke slowly, using my halting Yiddish.

"In Williamsburg," he said, and smiled deeply. "With all the Hasidim?"

"That's right."

"There are many Hasidim?"

"It's filled with Hasidim. From the concentration camps."

His face darkened. He was silent a moment. Behind him the pitchman shifted uncomfortably on his feet and ran his hand over his black hair.

"You go to school in Brooklyn?" the old man asked quietly.

"I go to the Hirsch Yeshiva. For smicha." "Smicha" is the Hebrew word for Orthodox rabbinic ordination.

"Smicha?" His deep-socketed eyes widened respectfully. "Very nice. I once studied for smicha, in Russia. And the girl? What is the girl studying?"

"English literature," Rachel said. Her eyes were still bright with the look of delight and relief they had taken on at the old man's first words in Yiddish.

"English literature." He echoed the words mechanically.

"Where in Russia are you from?" Rachel asked in English. She understood Yiddish but could not speak it.

"Mogilev," he said. "You have heard of Kishinev?"

Rachel and I nodded.

"In Mogilev and Shipola there were pogroms like the pogrom in Kishinev. It was terrible. Terrible. After the pogroms I joined a Zionist youth organization. That was illegal. Did you know that was illegal in Russia?"

I stared at him. "Yes," I heard myself say.

"I ran from the Czarist police and came to America."

"Through the underground relay network?" I asked in English.

He looked at me in surprise. "You know about that," he said quietly, still speaking Yiddish.

"That's how my father came to America. For the same reason."

"Thousands came that way," he said in Yiddish. "Thousands." He was quiet for a moment. "I found work in a carnival. In Russia I went to a great yeshiva, and in America I work in a carnival." He shrugged. "One must make a living," he said sadly. "Here you cannot live off others." He looked at me. "What does your father do?"

"He teaches Talmud."

"Talmud. Very nice. Where does he teach?"

"In a yeshiva high school in Crown Heights."

"In a high school. Very nice. He is fortunate. And the girl's father? He is also a teacher?"

"He's a professor of English literature at Brooklyn College," I said. "And her mother is a professor of art at Brooklyn College."

"Professors." He seemed amazed. "And you will tell me the boy's father is also a professor?"

I laughed. Michael's face broke into a proud smile. "He is," Michael said in Yiddish.

"He teaches Jewish philosophy at the Zechariah Frankel Seminary," I said.

"Have you heard of my father?" Michael asked, still speaking in Yiddish.

"What is his name?"

"Abraham Gordon. Professor Abraham Gordon."

"I do not think so."

"He's very famous," Michael said. "Everyone knows about him."

The old man shrugged apologetically. "I live and travel with the carnival. I know only the carnival. I do not know what goes on outside. Here and there I hear a little and read a little. But I was not so fortunate as you." He lapsed into silence. Behind him the pitchman stood very still, staring down at the gleaming radio. The old man was quiet a long time, his eyes moist and sad. He shook his head slowly. "Nu," he said. "Back to business. You are in good hands here now." He had reverted to English. "Schmeiss," he said, smiling. "See how much you will win from me."

I felt calm and protected. The tension and fear were gone now from the game. I put seven dollars on the counter next to the one-dollar bill.

"Go ahead and play," I said to Michael. "I'll pay and you'll play. All right?"

Michael grinned eagerly and picked up the cup. Rachel nodded, her eyes very bright.

"Go ahead," I said. "Play."

Michael clicked the balls together, his hands trembling faintly with excitement, then turned the cup over. The balls spilled onto the lacquered board and the fingers of the old man's right hand poked the balls from the holes as he counted aloud in Yiddish, "Nine, seventeen, twenty-one, thirty-one, thirty-five, forty-one." He looked at the card, smiled at Michael, and said in English, "Half a point."

I felt my heart racing wildly and put eight dollars down on the counter. Michael spilled the balls onto the board.

The old man counted swiftly and consulted the card. His face fell.

"Ah," he said sadly. "That is a shame." He was talking in Yiddish again and seemed quite upset. "There is no credit for thirty-eight. Such a shame."

We stared at him.

"So it goes," he said in Yiddish, smiling at us sadly. "It is a game, and you do not win every time. But it is only another half a point."

I put eight more dollars down on the counter. Michael did not bother clicking the balls together this time. He simply turned the cup over and let the balls spill out onto the lacquered board.

They added up to twenty-nine. On the card, twenty-nine had printed next to it the word "Double."

The old man smiled and shook his head happily. "You see?" he said. "I promised you are in good hands." He removed one of the twenty-dollar bills and replaced it with a new one-hundred-dollar bill. On top of the radio there now lay one hundred and sixty dollars.

"Is it sixteen dollars a toss?" I heard Rachel ask in a faint voice.

"Sixteen dollars," the old man said, nodding.

I felt myself sweating. Michael stood very still, holding the dice cup limply in his hand.

"I have eleven dollars left," I said to Rachel. My voice was dry.

She hesitated, looked for a long moment at the old man, then put a hand into the pocket of her dress and came up with five dollars. I put the money on the counter.

"This is our last try," I said to the old man.

He smiled reassuringly. "This time how can you lose?" he said.

"Go ahead," I said to Michael.

Michael blinked nervously. Very slowly, as if it no longer mattered to him whether he won or lost, he raised the dice cup and turned it over on top of the board. The balls dribbled from the cup almost one by one, rolling across the lacquered surface, only three finding their way into the red holes, the rest falling against the frame. The hand of the old man moved swiftly, knocking the balls from their holes. "Nineteen," he said. He looked at the card. Then he looked at Michael. "Ah," he said, smiling sympathetically. "That is a terrible shame. Nineteen is no credit."

Michael stood frozen, staring at the old man, the dice cup gripped tightly in his hand.

The balls had rolled into the holes very slowly this time, slowly enough for me to have been able to see the black numbers beneath the holes into which they had fallen. There had been a one, a three, and a six. On the card, the number ten offered two points.

I looked at Michael and realized that he too had been able to count the numbers. I saw Rachel stare at Michael. Her eyes were filled with fear again.

"That was a ten," Michael said, his voice trembling. "I counted ten."

The pitchman came forward and stood next to the old man behind the counter.

The old man blinked his deep-socketed eyes and smiled pleasantly.

"Ten is two points," Michael said. "I won the radio and the money."

"Excuse me," the old man said quietly, still smiling. "It was nineteen."

"No, it wasn't," Michael said, his knuckles white around the dice cup. "It couldn't have been."

The old man shook his head and smiled. "Young man, I know my business," he said pleasantly. "Believe me, I know my business."

"I think you miscounted," I said. "The numbers were one, three, and six."

The old man looked at me. He was suddenly no longer smiling. "Ah," he said, "you are a mathematician too. From a rabbi you became a mathematician. Very nice. It was a *ten*, a three, and a six. Not a one, but a ten."

"It was a one," I said.

"Reuven," Rachel said very quietly.

"Just a minute," I told her. I looked at the old man. "Which hole did it land in?"

"Listen," the old man said. "You want to play again? If you want to play again, then play. If you don't want to play again, the game is over."

"That was a ten," Michael repeated, his thin voice rising.

"Young man, don't cause trouble. I know how to count. You think I don't know how to count?"

"You're damn right you know how to count," I said, beginning to feel the anger rise up inside me.

The old man shook his head and sighed sadly. "Always it ends like this. Always. Who likes to lose? But I did not expect it from you."

"That was a one, a three, and a six," I said again. "It landed in that hole right there, and that's a one, not a ten."

The old man sighed again and turned to the pitchman. "What was it?" he asked. "What did you count?"

"Nineteen," the pitchman said.

"You see?" said the old man.

"Sure, I see," I told him.

"It was a one," Michael said. "I saw it. It was a one."

The old man looked at him narrowly from across the counter.

"I want the radio," Michael said.

"He wants the radio," the old man said to the pitchman. "You hear? He wants the radio. Just like that. He lost, but still he wants the radio." He looked intently at Michael. "Young man, you can play again if you want. If not, move away from the counter."

"I won that radio," Michael said defiantly.

"You won nothing. You are missing half a point. Are you playing?"

"I haven't any more money," Rachel said faintly.

"So you are not playing. So move away from the counter. You hear? Move away from the counter. You are keeping away other customers."

The three of us stood there, staring at him.

"You hear me?" the old man shouted suddenly. "Play or get out. Are you playing? No? Then get out! You hear me? *Get out of here*!" He reached for the cane, lifted it high over his head, and brought it down with a crash upon the counter.

Rachel gasped. Michael's hand rose as if to protect his

face from a blow. I felt the blood rush to my head. My legs were trembling.

"Out!" the old man shouted, waving the cane. "Out! Play or get out!"

"Let him play it again," I said, swallowing the rage in my voice. "Call it a miscount and let him play it once more."

"Listen to the rabbi," the old man shouted. He turned to the pitchman. "Did you ever hear such a thing? For free he should play." He turned back to me. "I'm in business," he shouted. "I make a living from this. You want me to give you something for nothing? Go away! Take your friends away! Don't start trouble here. Get out, all of you!"

I took a deep, tremulous breath.

"Reuven, please let's go," Rachel said.

"Come on," I said to Michael, taking his arm. "Let's get out of here."

Michael pulled his arm away. His face was ashen. There was a strange dead look in his eyes.

"I wasn't watching," he said very quietly, his lips trembling. "Usually I'm watching and I can tell when——" He broke off. "I trusted you and I wasn't watching."

I stared at him.

"Why did you do that?" Michael asked, staring at the old man.

The old man looked at him out of narrowed eyes and said nothing.

"You're like all the others," Michael said. There was a flat, toneless quality to his voice. It seemed almost as if someone else were talking from inside him. "You're no different from the others."

I saw Rachel put her hands to her mouth.

"What is he talking about?" the old man asked loudly.

"You hate us," Michael said. "You're just like the others."

"What is he saying?" the old man asked. "He sounds crazy. Look at him. He *looks* crazy. Take him home. All of you, go home!"

Michael stiffened. His eyes widened, bulged. A sudden cry of rage burst from his throat. He raised the dice cup over his head. Rachel gasped loudly. The old man took a step backward into the booth. The pitchman moved in front of him.

"You hate us!" Michael screamed, holding the empty dice cup over his head.

I lunged for his arm. He fought me for a moment, trying to twist away. *"You hate us!"* he screamed again, his mouth close to my ear. The sound echoed painfully inside my head. I grabbed the cup from his hand. He went suddenly limp and sagged heavily against me. I held him with my left arm and tossed the dice cup to the pitchman with my right.

The old man looked out from behind the shoulders of the pitchman. "He's crazy," he said. "Take him home. He's—"

"Go to hell," I said, and led Michael away from the booth. Rachel followed alongside me. Her face was white.

We walked quickly along the asphalt road. I had my arm around Michael's shoulders. He moved mechanically, his face empty of expression, his eyes wide and dead-looking.

"Schmeiss," I said bitterly. "That miserable—" I was in a trembling rage, but I broke off my words.

"Michael, are you all right?" Rachel asked. She was walking alongside him now, looking into his face.

Michael leaned heavily against me. I could feel his bony shoulder beneath my hand. He did not look at Rachel. His eyes were very wide. He stared straight ahead and was quiet.

"I'm frightened of the way he looks," Rachel said.

"He'll be all right," I said, a little frightened now myself.

"We should have gone right home," Rachel said.

We came off the asphalt road onto the parking lot. I helped Michael into the car. He sat between me and Rachel, staring through the windshield.

Rachel started the engine. The car moved slowly off the parking lot onto the dark highway. Driving along the highway, she accelerated swiftly. Inside my head I could still hear the shouts and rifle shots and laughter and roller coaster noise of the carnival. I kept hearing it all as we drove along and was still hearing it when we turned off the highway onto the asphalt country road.

When we were a short distance from Rachel's house I felt Michael slump down on the seat. I looked at him quickly. He was staring through the windshield, paying no attention to the dark trickle that moved across his lips and down onto his chin.

"His nose is bleeding again," I said.

I put my hand under his elbow as he climbed out of the car. He walked limply between me and Rachel. I held my handkerchief to his nose. He had not said a word since we had left the gambling booth.

A yellow light burned dimly over the front door of the house. Wide-winged moths beat against the light with soft thudding sounds. The lights were on in the kitchen and the living room. Beyond the steep slope of the shoreline, the lake moved gently against the rowboat and the dock. It stretched off into the distance like a mass of black stone, darker than the darkness of the night.

We came up the front walk into the house. Rachel's parents were at the kitchen table over tall glasses of iced coffee. Joseph Gordon looked at Michael and slowly took the pipe out of his mouth. Sarah Gordon stared.

"He's got a nosebleed," I told them, and before they could respond I put my hand against Michael's back and steered him to his room. I snapped on the ceiling light and removed the pillow from the bed but did not bother to pull back the spread. I helped Michael onto the bed. He lay on the bed, his head drawn back, his chin jutting upward. I sat on the edge of the bed, put the forefinger of my right hand over his upper lip, and pressed down. He lay very still, breathing softly, his eyes closed. He seemed unaware of what was happening.

The door to the room opened and closed. Joseph Gordon came up to the foot of the bed. He was a tall man in his late forties, with broad shoulders, thinning brown hair, sharp blue eyes, a square jaw, and deeply tanned features. He stared at Michael, his teeth clamped tight around his pipe.

"You had quite a time. Rachel told me."

"Yes, we did. A splendid time."

"I ought to go over there tomorrow and break his neck."

"He won't be there tomorrow. This was the last night."

He took the pipe from his mouth and leaned over the foot of the bed. Michael lay very still, his eyes closed.

"That vulturous bastard," Joseph Gordon said under his breath. He looked at me. "I'm going to call a doctor."

My finger was still on Michael's upper lip. I felt him stir. He opened his eyes.

"I don't need a doctor," he said very quietly.

Joseph Gordon looked down at him. "I want someone to check that bleeding." His voice was suddenly gentle.

"I don't want any doctor," Michael said. He pushed my hand away from his lip.

"Did you have to play that stupid game?" Joseph Gordon asked.

"It wasn't stupid."

Joseph Gordon put the pipe back into his mouth. "All right," he said. He gave me an angry look and seemed about to say something. Then he glanced at Michael. He turned abruptly and went from the room.

I looked down at Michael. He lay very still on the bed. I saw him put his arm across his eyes.

"I really trusted him," he said.

"We all trusted him."

"I hated him." His voice was flat, without emotion. "I could have killed him."

I felt cold listening to him talk like that.

"I should never have trusted him." His eyes were covered by his arm. His voice was rising. Below the small straight nose, his lips opened and closed stiffly, mouthing the words. "You can't trust any of them. They're all the same. They're—" and a long scalding torrent of vile and hate-filled words began pouring out of him.

I told him to stop it.

He took his arm away from his eyes and raised his head slightly and looked at me.

"Go away," he said.

"We gambled and were cheated. Don't make it worse than it was."

"What do you know about it?" He put his head back and covered his eyes with his arm. "They're all the same," he said. "Only he didn't have a beard."

I heard the door open. Sarah Gordon came into the room. She was a slender, fine-looking woman with oval features and auburn hair and gray eyes. Her voice had a quality of forced calm to it as she told Michael she had brought him a glass of milk.

Michael said he didn't want any milk.

She came over to the bed and put the glass down on the night table.

"Look at your shirt," she said.

"It's blood," Michael said. His voice had lapsed into its flat, unemotional tone.

"Shouldn't you change your shirt?" She spoke very gently.

Michael sat up slowly on the edge of the bed.

"Shall I get one for you?"

"No," Michael said.

She looked at him for a long moment. "Please drink the milk, Michael." She went out of the room.

Michael lay back on the bed and put his arm over his eyes.

"Is it bleeding again?" I asked.

"No."

"Drink your milk."

"Why don't you mind your own business?"

I looked at him and did not say anything.

"Everyone is always hovering over me."

"I'm trying to help."

"Who asked you to? Stop hovering and go away."

"All right," I said.

I went out of the room and through the hall and into the kitchen. Rachel and her parents were sitting around the table.

"How is he?" Rachel asked. Her face was still very pale.

"Angry."

"That was a stupid thing to do," Joseph Gordon said. "Letting him play that kind of game."

I thought I heard a door open and close somewhere inside the house. "He wanted the radio," I said.

"Was that a door?" Joseph Gordon said.

Rachel rose quickly and rushed from the kitchen.

"You should have brought him home immediately you saw it was a carnival," Sarah Gordon said.

"Rachel should have brought him home," Joseph Gordon said. "What the hell is going on out there?" Doors were being opened and closed all through the house. He was getting to his feet when Rachel came into the kitchen. Michael wasn't in the house, she said.

"Oh my God," Sarah Gordon said.

"I just left him in his room," I said.

"He isn't anywhere in the house, I tell you."

"He could have gone through the patio to the road," Sarah Gordon said faintly.

Joseph Gordon put his pipe down on the table and went from the kitchen. Rachel followed him. I heard the front door open and close.

Sarah Gordon sat at the table, looking at me. "You should have brought him home immediately you saw it was a carnival," she said. "You should have brought him home immediately."

I got to my feet. "I'll have a look at the dock," I said, and could feel her staring at me as I went through the kitchen to the wooden stairway outside. The sky was black and dotted with stars. There was a faint breeze. A sliver of moon hung over the lake like a curved lantern. I had forgotten to turn on the outside lights but I could see him on the dock outlined against the lake.

I went quickly down the stairs and up to the end of the dock. He did not look at me. He was staring up at the sky.

"Michael," I said softly.

He stared up at the sky and said nothing.

"You had better come back inside."

Still he said nothing. He was wearing the soiled shirt and the shorts and tennis sneakers. His hair was disheveled and his arms hung limply at his sides.

I put a hand on his shoulder. "Come on," I said.

He stood there, staring up at the sky. "Look at it," he said. "Look at it for a minute." His voice had a soft, dreamy quality to it now. "It's like every star in the universe is out tonight."

I stood alongside him, my hand on his shoulder, thinking of Rachel and her father on the road searching for him.

"Just look at it," he said. "I didn't think to bring the viewer. But look at it."

I was quiet.

"Did you know our galaxy is a hundred thousand light-years in diameter?" he asked softly.

I looked at him.

"And the visible universe is ten billion light-years?" He was silent a moment. Then he inclined his head slightly and looked at me. "Do you know the distance of the Andromeda galaxy?"

"No," I said.

"Almost four hundred and fifty thousand parsecs. Do you know what that is in miles?"

"No," I said again.

"Take the number ten and add eighteen zeroes. That's how many miles it is." He looked back up at the sky. "There are ten billion galaxies in the universe," he said. "Ten billion galaxies."

"Michael, let's go back," I said softly.

"Why did he do that?" he said.

I felt a coldness on the back of my neck and took my hand from his shoulder.

"He's nothing," he said. "He's smoke." He used the Hebrew word "hevel" for smoke. "I can prove he's smoke." He turned to me slowly. "Do you know how easily I can prove he's smoke?" he asked.

"Sure," I said.

He turned back to the sky. "He can't hurt you," he said. "Why do you keep thinking he can hurt you when he really can't?" He seemed to be talking to the sky. "He can't hurt you one bit," he said.

"Come on," I urged. "You've got everyone all upset. Let's go back inside."

I put my hand back on his shoulder. He let me turn him around and take him along the dock. At the foot of the wooden stairway he stopped and looked at me.

"I can't get him out of my mind," he said faintly.

I did not say anything.

We were halfway up the stairway when the outside floodlights suddenly came on, throwing bright blinding light onto the stairs and the dock. Rachel and her father came from the kitchen and stood at the head of the stairs looking down at us. Michael stopped and stared up at them, blinking. A moment later, Rachel's mother appeared at the head of the stairs. The three of them stood there, staring down at us and saying nothing. I prodded Michael gently and we went up to them. I shook my head at them and we passed them by and I took Michael through the kitchen into his room. He walked slowly, heavily, the laces of his sneakers trailing behind him. He lay down on the bed and closed his eyes.

"You ought to go to sleep," I told him.

"Go away," he said, putting his arm across his eyes. "Just go away."

I went from the room. Rachel and her parents were in the hallway right outside the door.

"What was he doing out there?" Joseph Gordon asked in a tight whisper.

I told him. Rachel bit her lip. Her mother looked panicky.

"Let's go into the kitchen," Joseph Gordon said.

"I've got to get back. It's late."

He seemed to want me to stay. But I was feeling dull-headed with fatigue.

"Walk me to the door," I said to Rachel.

We came out of the house. The floodlights had been turned off. A moist breeze blew in from the lake. I could hear the water lapping softly against the dock and the shore.

"How do you feel?" I asked.

"Fragile," she said. Her face was faintly luminous in the darkness. "And raped."

I did not say anything.

She stared across the lawn at the black expanse of the lake.

"I think I had better get back. Is the flashlight in the car?"

"Yes. I'll drive you if you'd like."

"I want to walk."

We went to the car. She took the flashlight from the glove compartment and handed it to me. She gave me a dark, uneasy look.

"Are you bringing Danny over next week?" she asked. Danny Saunders was my oldest and closest friend.

"I don't know," I said. "It depends upon Danny."

She bit her lip.

"Do you want me to ask him?"

"Yes."

"All right. It would be nice to have him meet you finally."

She did not say anything. I leaned forward and kissed her cheek. Her face felt hot and dry.

"I'll call you in the morning," I said.

I left her standing near the car and went up the asphalt

road, walking quietly past summer homes and sloping
lawns. To my left was the lake, dark and silent beyond the
houses and the lawns. From the dense woods along the
right side of the road came the soft pulsating sounds of
crickets and frogs. The sky was filled with stars. But the
road was dark and I could see almost nothing beyond the
beam of the flashlight. Then the road curved to the right
and the houses and lawns were gone and there were woods
on both sides. I walked on the gravel shoulder on the left
side of the road, letting the light play on the brush and the
trees. The path through the woods was narrow, a barely
visible break in the dense brush. I came off the road and
entered the woods.

The path twisted narrowly, thick with dead leaves and
fallen branches and the tangled roots of elms and oaks
and sycamores, then straightened and ran through a small
clearing of tall grass. Beyond the clearing it curved between giant trees and led downward and curved again,
and the air was dense now with the odor of the lake and
the smell of damp dead leaves and wet black earth.

I stood near the edge of the lake. The water was black
and motionless, wedged stonelike against the shore. In the
beam of the flashlight a long-legged spider skated soundlessly across the surface of the water. I followed the
curve of the shore. A small white animal crouched on the
path, frozen by the light. I moved the light away and
heard it scampering into the woods. The beam slanted
upward toward the stars, a pale unsteady finger of light
burrowing through the darkness, and it was a moment
before I realized my hands were trembling.

I turned off the light and stood very still. In the abrupt,
total darkness of the night the odor of moist decay was
suddenly overpowering.

I snapped the light back on and continued walking. The
shoreline straightened, curved sharply, and straightened
again, forming a tiny inlet. The smooth surface of the lake
reflected the stars, stone speckled with tiny quivering
pinpoints of light. I stepped over dead trees and thick

branches. Then the path angled sharply away from the lake and I was in the woods again, walking very quickly between thick-trunked trees, and there was the maple and the back lawn and the cottage, dark except for the single yellow light that burned over the door of the screened-in porch. My father was asleep.

I lay awake in my bed and listened to the trees outside the open window. I lay awake a long time and saw myself staring out the window at the black asphalt-paved street that was Bedford Avenue and listening to a short, intense, thick-shouldered, black-bearded man explain a passage of Talmud. I lay very still in the darkness.

Two

The wind woke me. It blew through the open window and stirred the curtains. I could feel it cool and moist on my face. I lay in the bed and remembered the night.

When I came out to the screened-in porch I saw my father already there, praying the Morning Service, the fringes of his long tallith reaching nearly to the floor, the straps of his tefillin wound carefully around his arm and head. The porch faced eastward and the sun shone above the trees of the woods and came through the screening, and my father stood facing the sun, praying from memory, his eyes closed behind their steel-rimmed spectacles, the sun bright on his thin features and gray hair. I put on my tefillin and prayed quietly and afterward I prepared a light breakfast and we sat in the kitchen and ate. The branches on the maple near the edge of the woods swayed heavily in the wind. But it was a warm wind now and would not keep me from the lake.

I told my father about last night. "He scares me a little," I said when I was done. "I've never seen anyone so angry."

"He had reason to be angry. You are certain that old man deliberately cheated you?"

"That old man was the vilest person I've ever met."

Later, I went into the living room and dialed the phone. I heard it ring for quite some time before it was answered.

"Hello," I said.

"Reuven?" Rachel said.

"Where's Michael?"

"He's around somewhere."

"How are you feeling?"

"Very, very fragile."

I asked her if she was working on her paper. She was spending her mornings that summer writing a long paper on the Ithaca section of James Joyce's *Ulysses* for an English honors course.

Yes, she was working on the paper, she said.

"Would Michael want to go sailing?"

She hesitated. I could feel her hesitating.

"Ask your father if it's okay."

The phone went silent. She had evidently cupped her hand over it. I waited for what seemed to me to be a long time.

"My father thinks it's all right," she said finally.

"Give a yell for Michael."

She cupped her hand over the phone again.

"Yes?" Michael said after another long pause. His voice sounded thin and distant.

"Hello," I said. "How are you?"

"All right."

"Would you like to go sailing?"

"Now?"

"Yes."

"I don't know. It's very windy."

"It's the best time for it."

There was a brief silence. "All right," he said. "But I don't know too much about sailing."

"I'll teach you. Find yourself a piece of string and tie it to the earpieces of your glasses and put it tight around your head so the glasses won't fall off. And wear a bathing suit and some kind of shirt. Okay?"

"Yes," he said, very hesitantly.

"I'll see you soon."

I changed into swim trunks, a T shirt, and thongs, went into the kitchen, found some string, and tied my glasses tightly to my head. Through the screen door of the kitchen I saw my father seated at the wooden table on the back porch, working on his book. I told him I was going over to Rachel and would be back in time for lunch. He nodded vaguely, without looking up. I went out to the street and walked quickly beneath the trees to the beach.

Some early bathers were lounging about on the sand and splashing in the water. The wind blew stiffly across the lake. I walked across the beach to the boat-rental concession, which was operated by a white-haired man in his early sixties and his seventeen-year-old son. The man was not there. The boy was sitting on the edge of the dock, his legs dangling in the water, his eyes closed. He turned when he heard me coming up the dock and gave me a sleepy look.

"Rough night?" I said, to make conversation.

"Yeah," he said, and grinned.

I wondered for a moment if I ought to take a sailboat instead of a Sailfish, then decided against it. A Sailfish was less complicated, despite the possibility of its turning over, and I did not think I wanted to trust Michael with the jib sheet of a sailboat. Serving as ballast for a Sailfish would be enough for him.

I asked for a Sailfish.

He stared sleepily at the boats tied to the dock and bobbing in the waves. "Take any one you want." He yawned noisily.

I took off my thongs and handed them to him, then pulled a Sailfish parallel to the dock, climbed on board, and put up the mainsail. The Sailfish was painted red and the mainsail was white with narrow red stripes. I let the sheet hang loose and the sail flapped noisily in the wind.

"Where's the center board?" I asked.

He looked at the boat, grinned sheepishly, then went with the thongs to the shed on the beach near the dock and came back with the board. I balanced myself carefully on the Sailfish and inserted the board. It went in with difficulty.

"Is this the right board?"

"They're all the same. How long you going to be gone?"

"About two hours."

"You got a great wind," he said with obvious uninterest, and yawned again.

"Untie me," I said.

He loosened the rope from the metal ring on the dock and dropped it into the water. I worked the mainsail sheet with my right hand and the tiller with my left. The sail caught the wind. I hauled in on the sheet and the sail billowed out and went taut. The Sailfish moved swiftly away from the dock. I tacked toward the middle of the lake, bouncing on the waves and sliding into troughs. The wind blew steadily and the waves were big and dark and crested with foam. There were clouds in the sky now but they were nowhere near the sun. I felt the Sailfish begin to slide and I put the sheet between my teeth and pushed the center board all the way down. The Sailfish lurched to starboard in a gust of wind, the port side lifting up out of the water. I transferred the sheet to my hand and leaned out backward over the edge, feeling the exhilaration of fighting the wind and riding the waves. The Sailfish raced across the water, leaving behind a white foamy wake, and for a long time I forgot about the old man and the carnival and Michael waiting for me in the house on the other side of the lake, and felt only the wind and the sun and the spraying of the water and the sheet tight in my hand against the gusting air.

The dock was deserted. I pulled up alongside it and tied the Sailfish to a support beam and climbed up the ladder. The planks were hot beneath my bare feet. I shouted Michael's name. A moment later, the door at the head of the wooden stairway opened and Michael came outside. Behind him came Sarah and Joseph Gordon, and Rachel. They followed him down the stairway. Michael wore a dark swimsuit and a T shirt. He had tied his glasses to his head with a piece of string. He looked a little nervous.

They came up to the edge of the dock and stared down at the bobbing Sailfish. The water surged against the support beams of the dock and rolled onto the shore. On the other side of the dock, the rowboat bounced on the waves.

Michael was looking at the Sailfish.

"I've never been out in one of those," he said.

"They're a lot of fun."

"You've got a rough wind for a Sailfish," Joseph Gordon said.

"It goes like a motorboat." I was trying to sound cheerful.

"I thought you would bring a boat," Sarah Gordon said. She wore a light-green summer dress that blew out behind her in the wind.

"The Sailfish is simpler."

"Please be careful," Rachel said. She had on her reading glasses and was holding her hands against the sides of her head to keep her hair from blowing about.

They stood there, hovering protectively around Michael.

I climbed down onto the Sailfish and, balancing myself carefully, helped Michael aboard and sat him down alongside the center board. I untied the rope and pushed us off and scrambled for the sheet. I hauled in on the sheet and the sail billowed out with a sudden puffing sound, and the Sailfish responded to the rudder and slid swiftly away from the dock. I looked over my shoulder. Rachel and her parents stood stiffly on the dock, looking as though they were witnessing a departure for an ocean voyage.

I looked at Michael. He sat near the center board, gripping the rail behind him with both hands, tense, tight, wide-eyed. The Sailfish lurched to port in a sudden gust of wind and Michael gasped as the starboard side tilted up out of the water.

"Lean back," I told him. "All the way back. That's right." The Sailfish straightened, responding immediately to Michael's weight. "Good. Very good. Now come in slowly toward the center." He wriggled forward a little, his hands pushing on the flat surface of the boat. "That's right," I said, and gave him an encouraging smile. "You'll balance the boat with your weight. Okay?" He nodded hesitantly. "You move back and forth to keep us straight in the water. But move slowly." We lurched again to port. "Now!" I said. "That's right. Move back. Slowly. All the way back. Lean out as far as you can." The boat straightened and Michael slid forward again toward the center. "Very good. You're doing fine. Just fine." He gave me a brief, tentative smile.

We sailed toward the middle of the lake. There were many clouds now in the sky but they were off in the west and not blocking the sun. Far off in the distance there was a sheen of gold across the water and beyond it was the blue line of the horizon. We sailed swiftly in the wind, and the waves were dark and choppy and the troughs were deep and we dropped into them and came steeply up, crashing into the waves and sliding somewhat despite the center board. The mainsail sheet was around my hand and I felt it biting into the flesh but I held it tight and the sail held the wind and we moved like a motorboat across the water. We sailed for a very long time and I watched Michael moving his body back and forth and he had the feel of it now and at one point he leaned way out across the rail in response to a wild gust of wind, half his body over the side, arching tightly, grasping the rail and leaning out backward, and suddenly he laughed and it was the same laugh I had heard from him on the roller coaster the night before. Then he looked at me and there was spray on his face and a brightness in his eyes. There were many boats on the lake now and veering away from one of them we took a strong gust of wind and the boom went down toward the water and Michael leaned way out over the rail, throwing his head and shoulders back. We tilted sharply to port and the boom skimmed the water and I braced myself and felt spray on my face and hands, and the boom went under and then the sail, and we came to a dead stop. Michael was sitting on the upended edge of the Sailfish and I saw him let go of the rail and slide slowly into the water and disappear. I slid off the Sailfish. The water was warm. I did not go under. Michael reappeared alongside me, still wearing his glasses. He shook water from his face. His dark-brown hair looked pasted to his head. I heard him laugh and watched him tread water.

"Too much wind," I told him, and grinned.

"I wasn't scared," he said. "I went in and wasn't scared at all."

"You were okay."

"What do we do?"

He helped me right the Sailfish. Then we were back on it and I was tacking toward the house and the dock. Michael lay near the center board, his eyes closed now, his wet face to the sun. He was smiling to himself. His lips smiled and then went straight and then they smiled again and then went straight again. He kept smiling on and off as he shifted his weight on the Sailfish. He lay like that a long time, and then he opened his eyes and raised his head and looked around.

"Are we going back?"

"No."

"There's the dock. Why are we going toward the dock?"

"There's a cove beyond the house."

He looked at me.

"There won't be the wind there. We can tie up the boat. It'll be shallow but the water will be smooth."

He looked at me and his eyes narrowed with suspicion.

"We can lie around and relax and swim. It's a very nice cove."

He lay back on the Sailfish and closed his eyes.

"We can do some more sailing later on if you want."

He did not say anything. We sailed toward the cove.

"I'll need you to raise the center board soon."

He opened his eyes. We were coming in very fast. He sat up and put his hands on top of the board.

We were about fifty yards from the shoreline, the water deep and dark and very choppy. We sailed past the house. The dock was deserted. There were huge boulders along the shore, and tall trees and dense brush. I could see the trees swaying in the wind. A few hundred yards beyond the house was the cove, a shallow inlet protected from the wind by steep banks and towering trees. I tacked toward the cove and we moved along a zigzag course, and then the water was suddenly shallow and I saw the lake bed, and I said, "Okay. Raise it halfway."

Michael pulled up on the center board. It did not move.

"Pull up hard," I said.

He was on his knees alongside it, pulling, and it would not move and I felt it scrape against the bottom of the lake and the Sailfish bucked.

"Pull!" I yelled.

He pulled with all his strength, the muscles of his thin arms bulging. I felt the center board scrape again along the lake bed. I put the mainsail sheet between my teeth and leaned forward and put my right hand on the center board. Michael looked at me. His hair lay across his forehead. His face was tight. He pried my hand from the board. I felt his thin fingers prying my hand from the board. He pulled furiously on the board. The wind gusted against the sail and the sheet tugged hard on my teeth. I transferred the sheet to my hand and held the sail taut. The center board moved up slowly.

"Halfway," I said. "Okay. Now leave it. We'll need it up all the way in a minute. Wait. All right. Pull it up. Can you manage it?"

The center board came up without difficulty. Michael sat back on the Sailfish. His face was pale.

I collapsed the sail. The prow scraped against the bank. I tied up to the branch of a fallen tree that lay in the water.

Michael sat stiffly near the center board.

"It was stuck," he said. "I couldn't get it up."

"I had trouble with that board myself before."

"Why was it stuck?"

"The water warps them sometimes."

"I got it up by myself though."

"You did all right."

A smile flickered across his face. He lay back on the Sailfish and closed his eyes.

We were in about two feet of water. The cove was narrow, with tall banks of dark moist earth that broke the force of the wind and huge trees and water lilies that grew along the shoreline. The sun shone through the water to the bottom of the lake and I could see schools of small fish and the dark mud of the lake bed. Tiny waves lapped with soft sounds against the Sailfish and the shore.

We lay on the Sailfish and rested. Then we swam for a while, stirring up the muddy bottom of the cove with our feet. Michael did the crawl and back stroke and side stroke and tried very hard to show me he was a good swimmer. With his glasses off, his eyes had a dreamy, distant look to them. We swam around and had a fine time and when we came back to the Sailfish I smiled at him and he smiled back tentatively and I said he was all right as a swimmer but he needed to put on some weight, he was too skinny. He put his glasses back on and lay on the Sailfish with his face to the sun.

"I'm chronically underweight. My mother keeps taking me to doctors and they all say I'm chronically underweight."

"You'll outgrow it. I used to be a little underweight."

"That's what the doctors say about my nosebleeds. I have nosebleeds when I exert myself too much or get too excited. Did you used to have nosebleeds?"

"No."

"I have them all the time."

"Like last night."

He opened his eyes and looked at me. He did not say anything. He looked away and placed the palms of his hands under his head and stared up at the sky. His arms formed sharp angles on each side of his head, the elbows jutting upward.

"Your nose isn't bleeding today. You did plenty of hard work out there on the lake and your nose didn't bleed at all."

"That's right," he said.

"How do you explain that?"

"I don't know. It doesn't bleed every time."

"I'm glad it didn't bleed out there."

He turned his head and looked at me. "Let's not talk about that any more. Okay? Let's just not talk about that."

"All right."

"I don't like to talk about it."

"All right, Michael."

I lay back on the Sailfish. We were silent. I could hear the wind in the trees. The boat lay still in the water.

"It's very nice out here," I heard Michael say quietly.

"I'm glad you like it."

"I really enjoyed the sailing. I was a little afraid at the beginning. I had to get used to it." He was silent for a long time. I saw him staring intently at the sky. Then he said, very quietly, "Can you read clouds?"

"How do you mean?"

"It's a game I play sometimes." He gave me a sidelong glance, then looked back up at the sky. "It shows you how you see things."

"How do you play it?"

"You look at the clouds and you say what their shapes remind you of. See that big cloud over there? What does it look like?"

He was pointing to a large fleecy cloud that lay above the high line of trees along the northern side of the shoreline.

I told him it looked like a large fleecy cloud.

He looked disappointed. "Don't you want to play? It's really a serious game, Reuven."

"I'm sorry."

"Sometimes I feel better after I play if I tell myself the truth about how they look. You have to tell yourself the truth."

"All right. Let me try again."

I looked at the cloud. "It looks like a camel with a lot of humps on its back."

He was quiet for a moment, his face turned to the sky. "It looks like a roller coaster," he said, very quietly.

I looked up at the cloud and didn't say anything.

"The one near it, the one that's a little above it and to the right, that one looks like the face of an old man." He paused. "Does it look like that to you, Reuven?"

"A little," I said, still keeping my face turned to the sky.

We lay on the Sailfish and were quiet. A flock of birds soared high overhead, heading west away from the sun. The Sailfish floated smoothly in the calm water of the cove.

Michael broke the silence. "Look at how the roller coaster is changing shape," he said, his voice very soft. "It's becoming round. You see that? It looks round now. Does that remind you of anything?"

"Yes," I said.

"What does it remind you of?"

"A ball."

He looked at me slowly.

"A giant of a ball. Like the balls we played with last night multiplied thousands of times."

He looked at me and nodded and was silent.

I scanned the sky. The cloud Michael had said resembled the old man was changing now, moving slowly along its edges, parts of it drifting off, other parts flowing and re-forming.

"The old man is smiling," I said. "Can you see him smiling?"

"Yes," Michael said as if from very far away.

"But he has a mean look. I don't like him."

"Neither do I."

"He reminds me of the old man at the carnival."

Michael did not speak for a long time. He lay very still, staring up at the cloud. Then he said, in a low voice, "I like Rachel. I like her a lot."

I did not say anything.

"Are you and Rachel in love?"

"I don't know."

"Are you going to ask her to marry you?"

"It isn't anywhere near that yet."

"Do you and your father come here every summer?"

"Yes. In August."

"It's strange you didn't meet her before. She's been coming here every summer since the end of the war."

I did not respond. He was quiet again. Then he said, looking up at the cloud, "It reminds me of the old man too. The cloud, I mean. It reminds me of the old man at the carnival and of others like him."

"Which others?"

He was silent.

"Which others, Michael?"

"You won't be angry? I don't want you to be angry."

"Why should I be angry? Which others?"

"Some of the rabbis in your school." He glanced at me, then looked quickly away.

"Which rabbis?"

"Rav Kalman."

"Why does it remind you of Rav Kalman?"

"Because he's vicious and deceitful like that old man."

"Why do you say that?"

"Because he is."

"I don't think he's vicious and deceitful."

"Do you know Rav Kalman?"

"I'm in his Talmud class."

He looked startled. "I didn't know that," he murmured. He sounded afraid and very apologetic. He was quiet for a moment. "Is he a good scholar?"

"He's a great scholar. Why do you say he's vicious and deceitful?"

"You won't be angry at me? He's your teacher and I don't want to talk about him if it will make you angry at me."

"Well, I might get a little angry at you, Michael. But that doesn't mean I won't like you."

He looked at me and a peculiar questioning frown came across his face, as if he were trying to understand what I had just said. After a long moment, I heard him say, "Rav Kalman is very religious. Isn't he fanatically religious?"

"He's very religious. Yes."

"Then why does he go around using slander against

people who disagree with him?" He used the Talmudic term "lashon hara" for slander.

"Where did you ever hear Rav Kalman use slander?"

"He uses it all the time."

"You're talking about the way he attacks your father and his school. Is that what you're talking about?"

His face darkened and turned sullen. "You know what the Talmud says is the punishment for lashon hara? Leprosy. There's a rabbi in the Talmud who even says there's no atonement for lashon hara. How can Rav Kalman be so religious and use lashon hara?"

"How do you know so much about Rav Kalman?"

"I know. I read what he writes in those Orthodox magazines and newspapers."

"He writes about your father and his school?"

"He writes about them all the time. Don't you read those newspapers?"

"No. They're not too interesting."

"You're a funny kind of yeshiva student. You swim and you sail and you're tanned and you don't read your own Orthodox newspapers. I've never met a yeshiva student like you."

"How many have you met?"

"I meet them all the time. I go to a yeshiva."

"I thought that was a very modern yeshiva."

"There are a lot of Orthodox students in that yeshiva."

"You don't like Orthodox students?"

"They're vicious."

"The Orthodox students in your yeshiva are vicious?"

"I hate them."

"Why?"

"I hate them," he said.

I was silent.

"They're vicious and I hate them."

"They can't all be vicious, Michael."

"What do you know about it?"

"I know you can't call a whole group of people vicious."

"You don't know anything about it. I go to that school."

"Why do you go if they're vicious?"

"My parents want me to. Especially my mother. She says it's a good school."

"It's one of the best yeshivas in the country."

"I hate it. I can't wait to get out of it."

"Because the Orthodox students are vicious?"

"You don't believe me."

"I don't understand what you mean by vicious."

"You're Orthodox. What do you know about it? You can't even see it. You have to be outside to see it."

"Outside what?"

"Let's drop the subject. I don't want to talk about it. Let's just drop the whole subject."

"All right."

"I feel very tired when I talk about it."

"We won't talk about it any more. What are you going to study in college?"

"Astronomy."

"I would never have guessed."

"I had a telescope in my room once. My father helped me build it. I used to be able to look up at the sky at night when there weren't any clouds. I really liked that telescope."

"What happened to it?"

"I—broke it. It was an accident. My father said he would help me build another one as soon as he comes back from the trip. He's on this trip to Europe and Israel now. You know about that. He had to go to a big conference and my mother always goes with him when he takes long trips. That's why I'm staying with Rachel and her parents."

"Couldn't you go?"

"No."

"Because of the nosebleeds?"

"Our doctor said I shouldn't go. Have you ever read any of my father's books?"

"All of them."

"He writes all the time. Mostly at night. He's probably even writing now while he's traveling. My mother helps him. She keeps encouraging him. He gets pretty sad sometimes because of the way he's attacked. But she keeps encouraging him."

"Is he writing another book?"

"Yes. He's always writing books."

"What is this one about?"

"I don't know. God and revelation and things like that. I don't understand his books too well."

"I used to have that problem with my father's writing. Why don't you ask your father to explain some of it to you?"

"He does sometimes. But it's very complicated. I'm not really interested in that stuff."

"Is your father religious?"

"What do you mean religious?"

"Does he keep the Commandments? Does he put on tefillin every day?"

"Of course he puts on tefillin. I put on tefillin. We're pretty religious. We keep kosher and everything."

"Do you observe the Shabbat?"

"Sure. Can we sail some more now?"

"In a little while."

"Did you take me out sailing so we could talk?"

"Yes."

"Why do you want to talk?"

"Why not?"

"I thought you just wanted us to have a good time."

"Aren't you having a good time?"

"I don't like being asked questions."

"Why?"

"I don't like it, that's all."

"All right. I won't ask you any more questions."

He lay back on the Sailfish and was quiet a very long time. Then he said, "I should have listened to Rachel last night."

"We both should have listened to Rachel."

"I wanted that radio."

"Yes, you certainly did."

"I was terrible last night. Did I throw anything at that old man?"

"No."

"I remember I wanted to throw something."

"You were going to throw the dice cup."

"I didn't throw it?"

"No. I stopped you."

"I remember wanting to throw something and then I can't remember anything until my uncle said he was calling a doctor."

"You don't remember anything at all?"

"No. But I remember that old man. I remember thinking he was like Rav Kalman and some of the others. You trust them because they're supposed to be decent and very religious and then they turn out to be vicious. They have crazy ideas, especially the ones who came here after the war. They think they're God over Judaism. They stamp on you like you're a bug if you don't agree with them. They're going to poison all of us with their crazy ideas."

"They're fighting for what they believe in."

"They're vicious. I really hate them. They're disgusting."

"All right, Michael."

Again, he was quiet a very long time. He lay with his eyes closed and I thought he had fallen asleep and then I saw him open his eyes and look up at the sky.

"It's beautiful out here. Look at the trees and the sky. It's really beautiful. I don't mind it so much talking out here."

"Sailing and talking. What could be better?"

"I wish it were night. Then I could see the stars."

"We couldn't sail if it were night."

"I wish it were night and we could sail anyway and I could see the stars."

"You could give me a lesson in astronomy."

"Do you know anything about astronomy?"

"I know how to find the Big Dipper."

"That isn't very much."

"That isn't anything at all."

"I wish it were night. It's easier to talk at night with the stars."

"You haven't done so badly talking now."

"No," he murmured. "It's easy to talk to you."

"And I'm a yeshiva boy."

"Yes . . ."

"I'm of the nonvicious variety."

He smiled.

"Would you like to swim?"

"Yes."

"Then we'll get in some more sailing."

"I'd like that."

"Okay," I said. "I'll race you to that rock."

We raced and I won and we swam a while in the cove and then sailed back out toward the middle of the lake and Michael lay on the Sailfish, moving back and forth with the thrusting of the wind. His eyes were narrow and his face was to the sun and he kept his hands tight around the rail of the craft—and he talked. "Can you feel the sun, Reuven? Can you feel how hot it is? Did you know Giordano Bruno was burned alive in Rome in 1600 for writing that the stars were suns? Did you know the gases in the interior of the sun are more than ten million degrees Kelvin? That's hot. They burned him alive because he wrote that the stars were suns. I wonder what it's like to be burned alive. Fire on your feet and around your legs and the pain as the fire creeps up. When do you die when you're burned alive? I think about that sometimes. They cheated Bruno. They killed him for the truth. But he didn't cheat. He wrote the truth. You have to get killed sometimes but you can't cheat. The cheating never hurts the stars but your eyes get clouded. I really believe that. Your eyes get clouded and you can't see through the telescope, any kind of telescope. There are different kinds of telescopes. Did you know that? There are refracting telescopes and reflecting telescopes and there's the Schmidt telescope. I read about them in a book. Refracting telescopes are okay but you have to watch out for chromatic aberration. Reflecting telescopes don't have that problem. But they have other problems, lots of other different problems. God, listen to me talking. I can't stop talking. Why can't I stop talking? What was I saying? Problems. The Schmidt telescope has problems too. Everything has problems. There's nothing anywhere without problems. There's no one without problems. Look at the clouds. They're beautiful. God, they're beautiful. There's one that looks like someone burning. Yes. Someone is burning. Who doesn't have problems?" We sailed and he talked and then we were near the shoreline and he talked and I could make out clearly the trees and the boulders and summer homes and people on the lawns and a deer at the edge of the woods and still he talked. Then, quite suddenly, he was silent. We sailed in that silence the rest of the way to the dock.

I collapsed the sail and tied up to the dock. I climbed the ladder and put out my hand to help Michael but he went up by himself, moving carefully from the Sailfish to the ladder and then up the rungs, and he stood next to me on the dock looking out across the lake, his hair blowing in the wind, his eyes blue and dreamy and moist behind his large glasses. He did not look at me. He looked out at the lake and his voice was soft.

"I wanted the radio for my parents. I wanted to give it to them as a coming-home present."

"You'll find something else to give them."

"Our old radio keeps breaking down. My parents like to listen to radio broadcasts from Europe. Especially my mother. She understands and speaks a lot of languages. French, Spanish, Italian, German, Hebrew. Then there are other languages she can only read but can't speak."

"That's a lot of languages, all right."

"Reuven." He was looking at me now.

"Yes."

"Did we lose much money last night?"

"Yes."

"My father will pay you back what you loaned me."

I did not say anything.

"I wish we had never gone."

"Well, we went."

"I wouldn't have minded it so much if we had gambled and just lost."

"It doesn't do much good to keep talking about it, Michael."

"We gambled and were cheated. You have to fight when you're cheated. But I can't fight."

"Come on. I'll walk you to the house."

"You don't have to come in with me. We've been out a long time. The boat will cost you a lot of money."

"All right. Tell everyone I said hello."

"I wish it had been night. I could have shown you the constellations."

"Another time."

"Clouds have strange shapes sometimes. That one looks like Rachel. But if it had been night there would have been no clouds . . . Reuven?"

"Yes, Michael."

"I gambled I would enjoy sailing with you. I didn't really know you at all until today. I gambled."

"Did you win?"

"Yes," he said. Then he turned and I watched him go slowly along the dock and up the stairway and into the house.

I climbed back down onto the Sailfish. The wind moved me away from the shoreline. I sailed alone on the Sailfish. There were clouds in the sky. The sun felt hot. I sailed alone and looked back at the dock and saw it off in the distance, a deserted sliver of white-painted wood thrust into the heaving darkness of the lake. The clouds were mountainous. The sun felt very hot. I sailed alone on the Sailfish and moved back and forth to keep the boat level in the water. The wind took me swiftly across the lake.

Three

I called Rachel the next morning. She was in a bad mood. Her passion for James Joyce was undergoing a severe test as she made her way through Ithaca. Michael was in a splendid mood, she said. He had gone swimming earlier and was now buried in an astronomy book. Yes, he had loved the sailing. His parents had cabled from Jerusalem. They were flying in from Israel on Thursday and would be up for the weekend. She had to get back to her Ithaca catechism. She was working on an idea in connection with Bloom's thoughts about Stephen's thoughts about Bloom and Bloom's thoughts about Stephen's thoughts about Bloom's thoughts about Stephen. It was a splendid idea, she said. I wished her luck. It rained all of Wednesday.

I spent most of Tuesday and Wednesday alone, studying Talmud. I had brought along Quine's *Methods of Logic* and used my evenings to go over the sections on polyadic problems and Löwenheim's Theorem. My father continued working on his book. On Thursday morning the galley proofs arrived for the revised part of the manuscript, which he had sent to his publisher some weeks ago. His hands trembled as he opened the package. He looked at the galleys and his eyes shone and he seemed to be looking at a newborn child.

That afternoon I took a sailboat out on the lake. There was a strong wind and I sailed toward the dock of Rachel's house. I wanted to surprise Michael and take him sailing again. The dock was deserted. The house seemed empty.

There were tall white clouds in the sky. I tied up to the dock and climbed the stairway and knocked on the door to the kitchen. No one answered. The door was locked. I realized they had probably all gone to the airport. I took the sailboat back across the lake.

Later that evening I called Rachel. The phone rang a long time before I hung up. I came out to the back porch. My father had completed his revisions of the last part of the manuscript that afternoon and had sent it off to his publisher. Now he was checking the galleys. The wind moved loudly through the branches of the maple near the edge of the back lawn. I sat for a while and watched him. Then I went inside to my room.

I talked to Rachel early the next morning. They had gone into New York to meet Michael's parents at the airport. The plane had been an hour late. Yes, Michael's parents were at the house now. They were resting. No, it wasn't a good idea for me to come over on Shabbat. The family wanted to be alone. They had a lot to talk about. Her voice sounded subdued. How were Bloom's thoughts about Stephen's thoughts about Bloom? I wanted to know. Bloom was alone in the cold of interstellar space, she said. "That's cold," I told her.

She was about to hang up. Then she asked me to wait a moment. The phone went silent. Then I heard a loud, deep voice. I had been holding the phone close to my ear. The voice made my ear tingle.

"Reuven Malter," the voice said.

"Yes."

"This is Abraham Gordon."

A lot more than just my ear began to tingle. I gripped the phone tightly.

"Yes, sir," I said.

"Is your father in?"

"Yes."

"Let me talk to him."

I called my father in from the porch. He took the phone. They talked briefly. "Sunday morning at ten," my father said. "Yes. It will be good to see you again, Abraham. You were shown the Dead Sea Scrolls? We must talk about that. How is Kaufmann? I am glad to hear it. Yes. Sunday. Fine. Shabbat shalom."

He handed me the phone and went from the room.

"Reuven," I heard Abraham Gordon say.

"Yes, sir."

" 'Verbal fraud is worse than monetary fraud.' " The words came out in a rapid Sephardic Hebrew. "Is that statement familiar to you?"

"Shimon ben Yochai in *Baba Metzia*," I said, giving the Talmudic source of the quote he had used.

"You are David Malter's son, no doubt of that. You experienced both kinds of fraud last Sunday night, I understand. We'll discuss it on Sunday. Michael enjoyed sailing with you. Shabbat shalom. What?" He spoke away from the phone. "Yes." He came back on the phone. "Michael says to tell you Shabbat shalom for him."

His voice echoed inside my head for quite a while after I hung up the phone.

The next morning my father and I prayed at the small synagogue a few blocks from the cottage, then returned to the cottage for our Shabbat meal. We studied Talmud together for a while after the meal, and then my father went into his bedroom to rest. I took a blanket out to the back lawn and lay in the sun reading an Agnon novel in Hebrew. Clouds drifted overhead, huge balls of white cotton moving against the brilliant blue of the sky. A cardinal disappeared into the maple and for a while it seemed the leaves were singing. I fell asleep on the blanket in the sun. I thought I heard a deep voice call my name. I opened my eyes. The grass shivered faintly in the warm breeze. I was alone on the lawn.

Rachel called that night a few minutes after the end of Shabbat. They had had a good Shabbat, she said, sounding very subdued. They had talked last night until two in the morning and all of today. Was Danny still due up tomorrow? Yes, I said. He hadn't called to say he wasn't coming and I hadn't called to withdraw the invitation.

How had James Joyce fared during Shabbat? I asked her.
"He rested," she said.

The call from Danny woke me at seven thirty the next
morning. His slightly nasal voice was thin and metallic
over the phone. He had just been called by the treatment
center. There was an emergency with one of the boys. He
had to run. He would not be over today. He could come
up tomorrow. They were giving him the day off tomorrow. Was it all right for him to come up tomorrow? I told
him tomorrow would be fine. He was doing his pre-
doctoral fieldwork in psychology at a residential treatment
center in the Flatbush section of Brooklyn and that was
his third emergency that summer.

I waited until nine o'clock and called Rachel. She listened and put her hand over the phone. Then she took her
hand away. "My uncle will be over in an hour. He'll talk
to you."

I sat on the back porch reading the Sunday *New York
Times* and waiting for Abraham Gordon. There were
accounts of the truce negotiations in Korea and the latest
doings of Senator Joseph McCarthy. Outside two squirrels
played on the lawn for a while, then scampered up the
trunk of the maple and disappeared into the leaves. It was
warm and the sky was blue and cloudless. A bird sang
somewhere nearby. My father sat at the wooden table
reading his galleys. I put down the newspaper and sat very
still and looked at the sunlight on the leaves of the maple
and listened to the bird. It sang a very long time. Then it
was silent. I thought I could still hear it singing.

Back in January, I had found a copy of Abraham
Gordon's first book on a shelf in the Brooklyn Public
Library and had taken it home to read. The book was
worn and had obviously been read by many people before
me. One of those people had scribbled in Hebrew across
the half-title page: "This is the book of an apostate. Those
who fear God are forbidden to read it."

When I was done reading it, I brought it back to the
library. I checked the catalogue for the most recent book

by Abraham Gordon and found that one of the books listed in the catalogue had been published a year ago. I assumed that was his most recent book. I searched for it but it was out. All his other books were out too. I came back to the library a few days later and found the book. It contained a list of all his previously published titles. I checked the catalogue again and discovered that the library had all his books.

I began to reserve the books in the order in which they had been published. I would reserve a book and after a week or so I would be informed that it was in and I would take it out and reserve the next book. All through the rest of the winter and into the early spring I read the books of Abraham Gordon. I read them only at home. I would not dare bring them to school. Occasionally I would discuss the books with my father, who had read them but did not have them in his study library, which was comprised almost entirely of works that had to do with the Talmud.

"There is more to religion than sociology and anthropology," he said to me once as we sat around the kitchen table talking about Abraham Gordon's second book. "You are attracted to Abraham Gordon's ideas, Reuven? They are very radical ideas."

"I'm only curious."

"Yes, I can see you are."

"He asks very good questions. I don't like his answers. But he asks some very important questions."

He smiled. "I will tell him when I see him that my son likes his questions."

The book we were discussing was on the table. I turned to the half-title page. It contained the same scrawled Hebrew warning I had found in the previous book: "This is the book of an apostate. Those who fear God are forbidden to read it." I showed it to my father.

He became angry. "It should read 'those who fear ideas,' not 'those who fear God.' There are times when those who fear God make themselves very unpleasant as human beings."

Abraham Gordon had published five books. Each of

those books had the same words written on the half-title page: "This is the book of an apostate. Those who fear God are forbidden to read it." I grew to loathe the writer of those words.

It was a long and lonely winter. My father was writing. Danny was off at Columbia, working for his doctorate in clinical psychology. In September three new rabbis had come onto the Talmud faculty in Hirsch. They had been in concentration camps. They were great Talmudists. They valued nothing but Talmud and knew nothing but Talmud. The greatest scholar of the three was Rav Jacob Kalman. He was given the class in the Talmud tractate *Chullin*. The knowledge of that tracate was a prerequisite for ordination. I was put into his class. I spent the winter studying *Chullin* and reading the works of Abraham Gordon. The day after Passover I finished the last of his published books.

I found myself intrigued by those books. They were written in a clear and on occasion almost exquisite prose style, the kind of style one rarely finds in works of philosophy and theology. And they were filled with blunt questions: Do you believe the world was created in six days? Do you believe in the order of creation given in the Bible? Do you believe Eve was created from Adam's rib? Do you believe in angels? Do you believe in the biblical account of the Revelation at Sinai? Do you believe in miracles? Do you believe that God guides the destiny of every living creature? Do you believe that God talked, actually talked, in the manner described in the Bible? How is one to react to the findings of archeology and anthropology and biology and astronomy and physics? How is one to react to the discoveries of modern biblical scholarship? How might one not believe literally in the Bible and still remain a traditional Jew? Are total belief or complete abandonment the only available choices, or is it possible to reinterpret ancient beliefs in a way that will make them relevant to the modern world and at the same time not cause one to abandon the tradition? The problems he raised fascinated me.

But Abraham Gordon was a humanist, a naturalist. For him supernaturalism and mysticism were irrelevant to modern thought. Revelation was a fiction, believed in by the ancients but no longer believable today. Religion was the creation of man; its purpose was to make meaningful certain aspects of human existence. Religious rituals heightened the routinized activities of man. God was a lofty human idea, a goal, a man-created aspiration, an abstract guarantor of the intrinsic meaningfulness of the universe. None of this was I able to accept—yet, I remained intrigued by Abraham Gordon.

The dust jackets of his books had no biographical information on him beyond the brief statement that he was professor of Jewish philosophy at the Zechariah Frankel Seminary. Nor had there been any photographs. But I found him listed in *Who's Who*: born forty-five years ago in Chicago; raised there; B.A., University of Chicago; doctorate, in philosophy, from Harvard; the next two years in Europe; the following four years studying for the rabbinate at the Zechariah Frankel Seminary, whose faculty he joined, at the age of thirty-two, immediately on being ordained. He published his first book at thirty-four. He belonged to some half-dozen national and international scholarly organizations. His wife's name was Ruth, and he had one child, a son, Michael.

That was all I learned about Abraham Gordon from *Who's Who*. The biographical data gave no indication as to how his books had been received over the years by the very Orthodox. There was no allusion to the loathing and hatred with which certain people pronounced Abraham Gordon's name. But I did not need *Who's Who* to tell me about that.

On a night in the first week of May I took a subway to Danny's apartment near Columbia and we talked about Abraham Gordon. I had seen Danny only a few times during the winter. Before entering Columbia he had removed the visible indicators of his Hasidic origin—the sand-colored beard, the flowing earlocks, the dark suit, the caftan, the open-necked tieless shirt, the dark hat he wore on weekdays and the fur-trimmed cap he wore on Shabbat and festivals. He had glowed with his new freedom. And the glow had not dimmed even after he had settled down to the grinding routine of graduate work. He was doing very well in his studies, and his phenomenal memory was the subject of much conversation in the psychology department at Columbia. He was finding it somewhat difficult to make friends. The nonobservant Jewish students in the department were embarrassed by his skullcapped presence; the two other Orthodox Jewish students in the department were easier for him to talk to but not interesting enough for him to want their friendship; and the non-Jewish students treated him as some kind of holy man, an Alyosha Karamazov thrown suddenly into their midst, a Jew with the mind of an Einstein and the soul of a Schweitzer, someone to talk to perhaps about a sticky experiment, someone to use as a resource person when they needed a reference, but not someone to invite over to an apartment for a beer and idle talk, or to sit with in a corner cafeteria, or to talk to about the girls they went with, or to involve in a conversation about Senator Joseph McCarthy or Korea or the cold war. But Danny did not really care about his nonexistent social life. As a matter of fact, he would not have gone anywhere to eat even if he had been asked, for he was holding rigidly to the laws of kashruth and he ate only those foods he prepared by himself in his apartment. And he was not interested in idle talk, had never been interested in conversation that served merely to help time pass, was awkward and inept at it, and was not concerned at all about Senator McCarthy's anti-Communist crusade or the Korean War or the diplomatic maneuverings of Russia and the United States. He was interested only in his studies.

The apartment in which he lived that year was a dingy one-room affair on the top floor of an old three-story red-brick house on a side street off Riverside Drive. The floor was covered with a cracked and lumpy piece of linoleum. There was a sofa bed against a peeling wall and a tiny kitchen-stove-sink-refrigerator arrangement in a part of the room that had once been a walk-in closet. Danny had never been particularly neat in his personal habits and the room he now lived in reflected that lack of neatness. It was a wild disarray of books, papers, unwashed dishes, and dirty clothes. Books were strewn everywhere, on the unmade sofa bed, on the small table where he ate, on the floor near the bed, on the worn and scarred wooden desk near the single window that looked out onto a fire escape and an alleyway. The small bookcase that stood against the wall opposite the desk was jammed with books and monographs; they spilled out of the bookcase onto the floor, and precarious Pisas of books were piled high against the wall on both sides of the bookcase. A dim light illumined the room from the overhead fixture and cast bleak and gloomy shadows everywhere.

I had told him on a previous visit that it was a miserable apartment. He had told me he couldn't afford anything else; he was spending most of his money on books. All he needed was a place to eat, sleep, and study. What else did he need? Now he was sitting on the old wooden chair near the desk and I was on the unmade sofa bed against the peeling wall. Stale air pervaded the room like a foul mist. The window was closed. The shade was up. The dark night pressed against the window, adding to the dinginess of the room. I got up and opened the window and pulled down the shade. It billowed faintly in the breeze, scraping against the sill. I went back to the bed and sat down and looked at him. He was pale and gaunt, and the lines of his sculptured face jutted sharply and his sand-colored hair was uncombed and his eyes were dark with fatigue behind his black horn-rimmed glasses.

I became a little angry that night at the way he was living. I told him the least he could do was keep the place clean. I told him I had thought that one of the things he had wanted to do with his new freedom was abandon his old Eastern European small-town living habits. Open the window, I said. Let in some air. Wash the dishes. Make the bed. Arrange the books neatly. Get the laundry done. What kind of freedom was this? And what about his life outside the apartment? He was free. But what was he doing with his freedom? Did he go to the opera? Did he see a ballet? Did he take in any of the good movies?

He shrugged. He was too busy with his schoolwork, he said. He went to the movies occasionally. He had seen *Symphonie Pastorale* a few months ago. It was a beautiful movie. He had seen *Aïda* at the City Center and had liked it very much. He didn't care for ballet. But there was too much schoolwork. He didn't have time.

"You need a girl," I told him. "Why don't you find yourself a girl and go out and enjoy yourself?"

He fidgeted uncomfortably on the chair.

There seemed little I could do to get him to remake his life. He was obsessed by his hunger to attain perfection in the profession for which he had broken with the tzaddikate. So I stopped badgering him about his personal habits and we talked for a while about my father's book and about my own year at Hirsch, and we got onto the subject of the books I was reading that had nothing to do with my schoolwork and I asked him if he had ever heard of Abraham Gordon. Sure he had heard of Abraham Gordon, he said. Who hadn't heard of Abraham Gordon? I had just finished reading all of his books, I said. He sat up very straight on the chair and gave me a strange look. He didn't say anything. I had done some research on Abraham Gordon, I said, and was curious to find out more about him.

"Merely curious," I said.

"Of course," he said, giving me that strange look.

I told him that some Brooklyn College acquaintances had recently informed me that Abraham Gordon had a niece who was a junior at Brooklyn College and was majoring in English literature. I had decided that I wanted to meet her and had managed to obtain an invitation to a party she was going to be at. The party was in two weeks.

"It's amazing what you can turn up sometimes with some hard research," I said.

"Yes it is," Danny said.

"What are you looking at me like that for?"

"Why did you start reading Abraham Gordon's books?"

"I was curious."

"Only curious?"

"He's a breath of fresh air."

"Why do you want to meet his niece?"

"Why not?"

"More research?"

"Something like that."

"Don't let Rav Kalman catch you doing research into Abraham Gordon."

"Don't worry."

"Do you want some more coffee?"

"Not yet."

"How is Rav Kalman?"

"A beauty. An absolute beauty. Yesterday it was the graduate school. A twenty-minute tirade against the graduate school. It teaches goyische subjects and should be abolished. Twenty minutes. I timed it."

"They won't abolish the graduate school because of Rav Kalman."

"I'm a little tired of Rav Kalman."

"You're tired of Rav Kalman, so you're reading Abraham Gordon."

"That's right. I need the fresh air."

"You'll freeze to death in Abraham Gordon's fresh air."

"I'm choking to death with Rav Kalman. Listen, let's not talk any more about Rav Kalman. It depresses me. Let's talk about anything but Rav Kalman. Let's talk about politics. No, you're not interested in politics. Let's talk about the movies. Have you seen any good movies lately?"

Danny said nothing.

"All right, let's talk about baseball. You think the Dodgers can take the pennant this year?"

He looked at me. "We talked enough about baseball years ago," he said.

We had played a rather frenzied game of baseball years

back, he as first baseman for a team of Hasidic yeshiva students, me as second baseman and pitcher for my own yeshiva team—and his line drive to my head had put me into a hospital for five days and had almost cost me my left eye. That was how we had met. We were fifteen years old then.

"I should have ducked," I said. He had said that to me in the hospital.

He laughed softly.

"But I'm glad I didn't," I said. "Now I'll have that other cup of coffee, if you can plow your way through all that stuff near the sink. And then I'm going home. I need my sleep. I need to be fresh and alert for Rav Kalman. I need to be strong and fresh and alert so I can learn about all the dangers confronting Yiddishkeit. I take cream and two sugars."

"I remember what you take," Danny said quietly.

Two weeks later I met Rachel Gordon. There was a radiance about her, a luminous quality in her face and in the self-assured, poised way she carried herself. We went out together often, and sometimes she talked about Abraham Gordon and at other times I talked about Danny. We liked each other and thought the liking might come to mean something in time.

From Rachel I learned that Abraham Gordon traveled a great deal, lecturing to students in colleges and universities throughout the country, played the violin, had turned down an invitation to teach logic at Harvard in order to enter the Zechariah Frankel Seminary as a rabbinical student, admired John Dewey and William James and the Vienna Circle logical positivists, found existentialism obscure, liked Hemingway as a writer and detested him as a person, and, before his heart attack at the age of forty-two, had been a wicked handball player. He had completely recovered from the heart attack, but he no longer played handball.

Rachel and I had never really talked about her uncle's son, Michael, before the night of the carnival. She would respond to the questions I put to her about her uncle, but never volunteered any information on her own. And I had never been interested enough in Michael to want to ask about him.

Now I was very interested in Michael. They were having some kind of problem with him; that much was clear enough. I had told Rachel a great deal about Danny and the years we had been together: talking about him helped ease the ache of being without him. I realized now that she had been passing on all that information to her parents and her uncle. Now they wanted to meet Danny. They apparently wanted to talk to Danny about their problems with Michael.

So the coming of Rav Kalman to Hirsch University had led me to the books of Abraham Gordon. And the books of Abraham Gordon had led me to Rachel and Michael. And because of Rachel and Michael, the Gordons wanted to meet Danny Saunders.

I sat on the screened-in porch of the cottage and looked at the sunlight on the maple. It's strange how many different shades of green there are, I thought. I sat there, looking at the maple and waiting for Abraham Gordon.

Four

He came promptly at ten o'clock.

I heard the DeSoto pull up in front of the cottage and I had the front door open before he was halfway up the walk. He came quickly, a very tall, heavy-set man, broad-shouldered, thick-chested. His face was large and round and somewhat fleshy, not at all a good-looking face, with thick lips and a wide nose and thick dark eyebrows and balding dark hair. He wore dark trousers, a short-sleeved white shirt open at the neck, and brown loafers. His gray eyes fixed on me and then his face broke into a broad smile and he came up the short flight of stairs two at a time and shook my hand.

"The sailor," he said. "Horatio Hornblower himself. It is good to meet you, Reuven. Where is your father? Inside? Is he still working on that book? What a tan you've got! You don't get that kind of tan from studying Talmud."

His handshake was warm and strong and his voice was deep and cheerful, and I felt myself a little overwhelmed by his immediate friendliness. The apprehension I had been feeling during the past hour of waiting was complete-ly gone by the time I brought him out to the back porch to my father.

They greeted each other as friends. My father had on his small black skullcap—he always wore his skullcap when he studied sacred texts or worked on the book—and I saw Abraham Gordon immediately pull a skullcap out

of a pocket of his trousers and put it on his balding head.
I brought a chair over to the wooden table and Abraham
Gordon sat down.

"You've lost weight, David," he said affectionately to
my father.

"Yes, but I do not have a cold for a change. How are
you, Abraham?"

"Exhausted. Europe was fine, Israel was an experience,
and I'm exhausted."

"How is Kaufmann?"

"Lonely. But he'll only admit it at the end of a three-
hour walk. He asked to be remembered to you. They all
asked to be remembered to you. And they all asked about
your book."

"With God's help, the book will be published in January. Did you see Auerbach?"

"I saw everyone. They wish they were back on Scopus
but they have settled into Terra Sancta. They enjoy the
irony. The Hebrew University in the midst of crosses. The
conference in Europe accomplished a great deal. But
France exhausted me, and Naples and Rome finished me
off completely. In Israel I lived with my extra soul"—he
used the Hebrew expression "neshamah yetairah." "The
flight back was terrible but I redeemed it by writing seven
pages. David, I cannot get over your son. Bialik could
never have written 'Hamatmid' if he had seen your son."

My father smiled. "Reuven is of the enlightened variety
of yeshiva students."

"Such a category exists? I will have to revise my books.
David, listen, I must tell you of some of the things I found
in the Vatican Library. There is a gold mine in that
library. I was half an hour on the phone with Spiegel this
morning about what I saw in that library."

They spent the next forty minutes talking about rare
medieval manuscripts and how sometimes you found one
page of a manuscript in the Vatican Library and another
page in the Bodleian and a third page in the Leningrad
Library. They talked about scholars in Israel and America. Scholem was working on another book; Kaufmann had

an article coming out soon and was completing another
volume. One man was finishing an important work on
Job; another was still at work on his history of the Jews in
Spain; a third would soon be publishing a definitive work
on the Genizah fragments; a fourth was contemplating a
new translation into English of Maimonides's *Guide to the
Perplexed*; a fifth was doing a book on Koheleth that
would prove that the original had been in Aramaic and
not in Hebrew; a sixth was still at work on a critical
edition of the *Tosefta;* a seventh, a brilliant young man at
the Hebrew University, was thinking of exploring the
relationships that had existed between Jews and non-Jews
during the early, pre-Crusade period in Europe. They
talked on and on, and then my father's mood changed
abruptly and his eyes misted with sadness. How were
things in Israel? he asked quietly. Was the economic
situation very bad? Were the border incursions as serious
as the newspapers reported them to be? Things were bad,
Abraham Gordon said bluntly. There was no point in
deluding ourselves. The border incursions were bad. The
economy was bad. The immigrant camps were bad. But
he was an optimist, a hopeless optimist. They would solve
their problems. There had been worse problems. Every
young country had problems. Did my father know what
kind of problems America had when she was a young
country? Did my father know about the quarrels between
the states after the Revolutionary War? Did my father
know about the Whiskey Rebellion? Yes, my father knew.

I went into the kitchen and brought out tea for my
father and coffee for myself and Abraham Gordon, and I
sat there, listening to them talk. A warm breeze blew
gently across the lawn, stirring the leaves of the maple. I
sat there and listened and after a long time Abraham
Gordon finished his coffee and glanced at me briefly over
the rim of his cup. The cup clinked softly as he replaced it
on its dish on top of the wooden table.

"Well," he said, with a faint heaviness in his deep
voice. "Now I must talk with the sailor. From my friend,
the scholar, to his son, the sailor. Reuven, tell me about

the carnival. I know all about it but I want to hear it again from you. Do you mind, David? Thank you. From scholarship to carnivals is a jump, but I want to hear about this carnival."

I told him. He listened soberly, his thumb and forefinger rubbing the lobe of his ear, a huge man, dwarfing the chair he sat in. Then I was done. It had not taken very long.

"My niece and her county fairs," he muttered.

"The advertising fooled us. It wasn't her fault."

"You're sure he cheated you."

"Absolutely."

"Tell me again about Michael after he lost his temper."

I told him. He nodded heavily.

"I'm grateful to you for stopping him."

"I couldn't let him throw it."

"He blanked out, you say."

"Yes."

"You talked to him and he didn't respond?"

"I think Rachel talked to him."

"And you're absolutely sure you were cheated."

"Yes. Michael saw it too. You can ask Michael."

"Michael won't talk about the carnival. I can get nothing out of Michael. He acts as if it never happened. He seems to have blocked it out entirely."

"No, he remembers the carnival. He doesn't remember what happened after he lost his temper. But he remembers everything else."

He looked at me sharply. "How do you know?"

"He told me."

"When?"

"Monday. When I took him sailing. He talked about it."

"What else did he talk about?"

I told him.

"Michael told you all that?"

"Yes."

"While you were sailing?"

"Yes. We tied up in a cove and we talked."

"Giordano Bruno . . . He read about him in an astronomy book this past winter. So, you tied up in a cove and talked." He shook his head. "A sailor, a yeshiva boy, and a magician. David, you have a treasure here. Reuven, Michael does not like to talk about himself. Michael has been to three therapists in the past fourteen months and each of them gave up on him after a few weeks."

My father's eyes grew very wide.

"Michael has been in therapy?" I heard myself say.

"Has been. Yes. Has been. Three times. Michael resists therapy. Do you know what resisting therapy means?"

"Vaguely."

"Michael is a very sick young man. Any one of those therapists would give you a year's earnings to find out how you got him to talk. I cannot afford to give you a year's earnings. How did you get him to talk to you, Reuven?"

"I didn't do anything. I took him sailing."

"Why did you take him sailing?"

"He was very upset by the carnival. I wanted him to do something he would enjoy."

"He enjoyed it. I can report to you that he enjoyed it."

"Reuven has experience in getting others to like him," my father said quietly, giving me a sidelong glance.

But Abraham Gordon had not heard him. He tugged at his ear lobe and sat lost in thought. Then he said, "What time is Daniel Saunders coming up to see you tomorrow?"

"In the morning," I said.

"I would like you to do me a favor, Reuven. I want to make you a messenger for a righteous deed." He used the Talmudic term "shaliach mitzvah." "I would like you to ask Daniel Saunders to come over and see us. Would you do that?"

"Of course."

My father was surprised. "Excuse me, Abraham. You know of Daniel Saunders?"

"I know of Daniel Saunders from rumors, from friends, and from Rachel."

"He is—"

"I know who he is, David. I want to talk to him. I must

talk to him." He stopped tugging at his ear lobe and put his hand on the table and looked at me. "Tell him I want to talk to him. I would have called him anyway when we returned to the city. But since he'll be with you tomorrow we might as well talk to him here. There *will* be a slight problem getting Michael out of the house, but we'll manage that somehow. Reuven, you're a good sailor and a good Talmud student and a bit of a magician. Now be a persuader too and ask Daniel Saunders to come over and see us."

I told him I would talk to Danny.

"Fine," he said. He started to get to his feet, seemed to remember something, and sat back down again, heavily. He looked at me, his face suddenly taut. "You don't think there will be a problem getting him to come?"

"No. Why should there be a problem?"

He gazed at me intently for a moment, then nodded and rose ponderously to his feet. "I've got to get back. I promised to take Michael rowing before lunch. We have to discuss a telescope we're going to build. David, finish your book. It was a pleasure seeing you again. I'm only sorry I had to darken the pleasure with my private problems. Reuven, your father told me you like the questions I ask in my books. One day we'll have to sit down and talk about that. But now I have to go rowing." He shook hands with my father. "Walk me to the car, Reuven."

We came out of the cottage. He walked quickly. I had to make an effort to match his stride. The street was deep in shade. I could hear the trees moving in the gentle wind. The air was redolent with flowers and freshly cut grass.

We came up to the DeSoto.

"About the carnival," Abraham Gordon said. "I understand Michael owes you some money."

I looked up at him. I had to look up at him—he was a good five inches taller than I was. I told him Michael didn't owe me anything.

"The money you loaned him."

I told him again Michael didn't owe me anything.

He looked at me curiously. Then he smiled and

nodded. "Come over this afternoon if you have a chance. Bring a sailboat. Michael would like to go out with you again. And my wife wants to meet you."

I told him I would be over.

He removed the skullcap from his balding head, put it into a pocket, and climbed into the car. He looked at me through the window and gave me a nod and a smile. "Take care of your father," he said. "There aren't many people like him around any more." I watched the car go up the road and disappear around a curve, then I went back into the house and out to the porch. My father was seated at the wooden table, staring down at the galleys.

"Everyone has burdens," he murmured, shaking his head. "Who is without burdens?"

I said nothing.

"I must get back to work," my father said, speaking to himself. But he sat there, staring down at the galleys and doing nothing.

I called Michael after lunch. He was happy when I told him I was coming over to take him sailing again. There wasn't much of a wind, I said, but I would teach him how to control the mainsail and the tiller. That would make it a little more exciting. Were there any clouds? I hadn't looked out the window in the last few minutes to see if there were clouds. He laughed.

I rented a Sailfish and took it across the lake. There were clouds now. But there was the sun too, hot and bright on my face and in my eyes. I tied up to the dock and heard loud voices and thumping sounds from the direction of the house. I came off the dock and went up the steep slope of the shoreline and around the house to the back lawn. A net had been strung between two poles on a section of the lawn and there was a volleyball game going on, Joseph and Sarah Gordon on one side, Abraham Gordon and a woman I did not know—I assumed it was Ruth Gordon—on the other. Rachel was not around. Michael sat on a patio chair in the shade of the house, reading a book. He wore a bathing suit, a T shirt, and I saw he had tied his glasses around his head with a piece of string.

I stood there, watching them play. Abraham Gordon moved with remarkable speed for a man of his size; he was playing the back field and seemed to be everywhere at once, his long arms stretching for the ball, which he always sent to the woman who played in front of the net. He was dressed in shorts and tennis sneakers and was bare to the waist. His nakedness emphasized his hugeness. The woman on his side of the net wore white shorts and a white polo shirt and dark glasses. She was a striking woman, tall, slender, lithe, with short chestnut hair and beautifully proportioned features, and she moved about in front of the net with the agile grace of a natural athlete, twisting, turning, pivoting, spiking the ball over the net, carefully avoiding even those balls she could return by herself in order to let Abraham Gordon set them up for her. The two of them played together as a tight team, each seeming to anticipate instinctively the movements of the other, and Joseph and Sarah Gordon appeared to be not too much of a threat to them, though they were making them work hard for each point they scored.

Joseph Gordon saw me. He saw me as he was preparing himself to return a sharp serve heading his way from the arm of his brother, and he caught the ball instead and sang out, "The captain of the *S.S. Malter!*"

Abraham Gordon introduced me to his wife. She removed her sunglasses and I saw she had blue eyes, deep blue, Michael's eyes. She wore no make-up. She offered me her hand and greeted me in a deep contralto voice. "Michael speaks of you as though you were his brother," she said. "I'm very pleased."

I didn't know what to say to that, so I smiled and said nothing.

"I was wondering if you and your father were related to Henry Malter."

"No."

"Do you know who I mean?"

"The author of the critical edition of *Ta'anit*."

"You are not related."

"No."

"How strange. Malter is not a particularly common name. Was it shortened?"

"Yes. From Maltovsky."

"Your father is from Russia?"

"Yes."

"And he shortened his name?" Her manner was friendly but somewhat formal and distant.

"He lived with a cousin when he first came here. His cousin convinced him to shorten it."

"What is his cousin's name?"

"He's dead. We have no living relatives."

"I see."

"Reuven," Joseph Gordon said, "how about joining us for some volleyball?" He was standing next to Ruth Gordon, smiling and tossing the ball from hand to hand.

"Reuven has come to go sailing with Michael," Ruth Gordon said.

"I need help," Joseph Gordon said.

"Nothing will help you," Abraham Gordon said cheerfully. He wiped his brow with the back of his forearm. His body was covered with sweat.

" 'Let not him that girds on his armor boast as one who takes it off,' " Joseph Gordon quoted in Sephardic Hebrew from the First Book of Kings.

Abraham Gordon laughed.

"Where's Rachel?" I asked.

"Inside the house," Sarah Gordon said unhappily.

"Roaming through Ithaca," Joseph Gordon said. "I could have used her."

"I told you," Abraham Gordon said. "Nothing will help."

"She ought to be out in the sun on a day like this," Sarah Gordon said. "But she's inside the house."

Ruth Gordon gazed over at Michael, who was sitting in the shade of the patio overhang, absorbed in his book.

"Michael," she called.

Michael looked up immediately, startled.

"Reuven has come to take you sailing."

Michael looked at me and his pale face lighted up.

"You have made a sailor out of my son," Ruth Gordon said to me.

I saw Michael carefully insert a bookmark into place and put the book down on his chair. He came over to us, smiling.

"Hello," he said to me. "Did you bring a Sailfish again?"

"Yes."

Ruth Gordon was watching her son intently.

"Can we go out right away?" Michael asked.

I looked at Ruth and Abraham Gordon.

"Go ahead," said Abraham Gordon.

"Have a good time, dear," Ruth Gordon said to her son.

"Scram, you two," Abraham Gordon said. "I want to finish trouncing my brother on the field of battle."

"A ruthless warrior," Joseph Gordon said.

Abraham Gordon laughed and wiped his brow again with his forearm.

"No Geneva Conventions here," Joseph Gordon said.

Michael and I walked back across the lawn and the patio to the lake. Just before we started down the slope I turned and saw Ruth Gordon still standing on the lawn, watching us. She turned quickly and went toward the net.

We sailed for close to two hours and had a fine time. Michael was awkward for a while with the mainsail sheet and the tiller but the breeze was mild and we did not capsize and finally he caught on to it and we sailed smoothly. We did not go into any of the coves; we sailed, tacking back and forth in the warm breeze. I lay near the center board but the water was smooth and I did not have much to do. I closed my eyes and felt the gentle rolling of the Sailfish and the sun on my face. I felt myself drowsy and falling asleep and opened my eyes and looked up at

Michael. It seemed his own private sun shone out from behind his eyes. He looked at me and smiled, then looked up at the clouds. I saw him looking at the clouds and I closed my eyes and lay very still. I opened my eyes and saw him still looking at the clouds.

"What do you see?" I asked him.

"Clouds."

"Only clouds?"

"Clouds and things."

"What things?"

"Stars."

"Clouds and stars in the daytime?"

"I had a dream last Monday night. We were sailing and we sailed off the lake and into the sky and there were clouds and stars and I showed you the constellations. We sailed between the stars along the outlines of the constellations. It was a good dream."

"Do you have many dreams?"

"Yes. But I don't like to talk about them."

"Why?"

"I just don't."

"All right."

"Is a friend of yours coming up tomorrow for a visit?"

I looked at him.

"I heard them talking. They said a friend of yours would be coming over tomorrow."

"Yes."

"I'd like to meet him. But they want me to go to a movie or something. Why won't they let me meet him?"

"I don't know."

"There's something going on. I don't know what it is. But they're planning something."

I was quiet.

"That was a good dream," he said. "I really liked that dream."

We sailed smoothly and in silence and off in the distance was the faint line of the horizon and about one hundred yards to starboard were the trees of the shoreline,

the woods through which I walked from the cottage to
Rachel's house, and the lake glistened like satin in the
sunlight and Michael being ill seemed unreal. Later, tacking toward shore, I looked up and saw a figure in white on
the dock. We were very far away and I could not tell who
it was. It went quickly along the dock and up the stairway
and into the house.

Afterward, we all sat in the living room and there were
cold drinks and pleasant talk and much joking about the
volleyball game in which Rachel's parents had been
trounced, and Ruth Gordon smoked a cigarette and talked
about the museums they had seen in Europe—she talked
about art as if she might be able to take over one of her
sister-in-law's courses at Brooklyn College—and the in-
decent way the French had of ignoring you unless you
spoke French, and thank heaven they both spoke French,
and the poverty in the back alleys of Rome and the rooted
aristocratic loveliness—those were her words—of Oxford
and Cambridge. The living room was large, rambling,
with brightly colored Navajo rugs on the floor and a high
vaulted ceiling. Bookcases covered part of one wall and
Sarah Gordon's huge abstract paintings hung on the wall
opposite. The side of the room facing the lake was all glass,
sliding doors opening onto the porch. Sunlight streamed
through the wide expanse of glass, and the bright summer furniture and the rugs and the paintings gave depth
and brilliance to the room—and the talk gave it warmth.
They were a close family, and, of course, not awed,
as I was, by the fame and notoriety of Abraham Gordon.
They teased him good-naturedly about how he had misplaced the passports on the way out of France, had become airsick over the Alps, had let himself be fleeced
by a taxi driver in Naples. Yet there was a faint aura
of darkness about them too, a hint of strain to the
cheerfulness; a sense of foreboding seeped through the
occasional lapses in their talk. Michael sat quietly, listening and sipping at a Coke. Rachel came into the room
sometime between the misplaced passports and the airsick-

ness over the Alps. She had on her reading glasses and looked bleary-eyed. How was Leopold Bloom? I asked her. Unhappy, she said. He had lost his Stephen. He was a star in the constellation of Cassiopeia. But Molly Bloom— Molly Bloom was something else. Molly Bloom was recumbent and big with seed. And she, Rachel, would drink to that with a Coke because she was practically done with Ithaca. Ruth Gordon said that Rachel should be thankful she hadn't decided to do her paper on the Penelope section. Abraham Gordon laughed. Joseph Gordon grinned around the pipe he held between his teeth and said that was the best part of the book. Sarah Gordon gave him a sharp glance and nodded her head in the direction of Michael, who clearly hadn't the slightest notion of what they were talking about.

Later, Rachel walked with me down the dock to the Sailfish. She knew what my father and I had talked about with her uncle that morning. They all knew. They were grateful. What time did I think Danny would be able to come over tomorrow?

I told her I didn't know and would have to call her after my father and I talked to Danny. Then I told her that her aunt was one of the most beautiful women I had ever seen.

She nodded absently. She was still wearing her reading glasses and they gave her a schoolteacher look.

"What does she do?" I asked.

"My aunt? She takes care of my uncle and Michael."

"No, seriously."

"I meant it seriously. She edits my uncle's books. She edits them, types the final drafts, checks the galleys, goes over the footnotes, and sees to it that everything gets published correctly. In between she worries about Michael and about my uncle having another heart attack one day."

"He'll have another heart attack if he keeps playing volleyball like that."

"The volleyball is exercise. On doctor's orders. It was a mild heart attack anyway. Reuven, please call me as soon as you know when Danny will be over."

I promised I would. "Take off your glasses. Why do you wear your glasses when you're not reading?"

"I didn't even know I had them on."

"Molly Bloom big with seed can make you forget anything," I said.

She laughed.

I took the Sailfish back across the lake.

My father was on the porch. He sat at the wooden table, staring out at the sunlight on the lawn and the maple.

How were the galleys coming along? I asked him.

He did not look at me. The galleys were all right, he said. There were some errors with the Greek words, and he had had to revise some passages that seemed a little obscure now that he was reading them in print. Otherwise, the galleys were fine. He spoke quietly, his voice sounding hoarse. I could begin checking the footnotes and the variant readings as soon as we returned to the city, he said. He would call the librarian at the Zechariah Frankel Seminary. There would be no problem obtaining permission for me to use the rare manuscripts. He was silent a moment. His face was pale, unusually pale, even for him. "We did not even talk about the Dead Sea Scrolls," he murmured.

I was quiet.

"I meant to ask him about the Dead Sea Scrolls." He sat there, looking at the sunlight on the lawn and the maple.

Danny arrived the next day a little before lunch. He was tired. He looked haggard and he yawned repeatedly during lunch and said he hadn't slept most of the night because of that emergency and all he wanted now was a year of sleep. He had never been up to the cottage before and he gazed hungrily at the lawn and the maple. The maple looked inviting, he said. He could easily sleep a year in the shade of that maple. Maybe he would even go down to the lake later on, he said. But first he wanted to sleep. It had been a bad emergency with a schizophrenic boy. I had never seen him so tired. But after lunch my father and I took him out to the porch and the three of us talked for a while. Sure he would see Professor Gordon, Danny said. If we wanted him to see Professor Gordon ... He kept glancing at me. He was wide awake now.

I called Rachel. She would come over for Danny. It would be a while before she could get to the cottage. She would have to drive her mother and Michael to a movie in Peekskill first. They had found a good double feature for him. She would pick up Danny on the way back. She sounded a little frantic.

It was almost an hour before I heard the DeSoto. I opened the front door and saw Rachel getting out of the car. I called to her to stay where she was. She closed the car door and looked at me through the open side window. Danny and I went down the walk.

I introduced them. I saw Rachel glance at the small black skullcap on Danny's head and at his face. She seemed tense and weary. Danny slid into the front seat beside her. I watched them drive off.

He was gone more than three hours. I sat on the porch, trying to study Talmud. Then I tried reading *The New York Times*. Then I did some problems in symbolic logic. The sun paled behind thin, high clouds and the air grew cool. My father went inside for a sweater. He stared a while at the maple and the lawn before he returned to the galleys.

It had turned quite cool and my father had taken the galleys inside and was working at the kitchen table by the time I heard the DeSoto pull up in front of the cottage. I came down the walk and saw Danny and Rachel sitting in the front seat, talking. They looked at me as I came up to the car. Neither of them said anything.

Danny climbed out of the car. Rachel gave me a nod and a pale smile and drove off toward Peekskill.

"Well?" I said to Danny.

He said nothing. The lines of his face were tight. We came into the cottage.

"You were there a long time."

"There was a lot to talk about."

"Can you tell me about it?"

"Yes."

My father looked up from the galleys as we entered the kitchen. The three of us sat around the table. Outside the sky was bleak with clouds. A cold breeze blew across the lawn.

"Were you able to be of help?" my father asked gently.

"I think so."

"Are you permitted to talk about it?"

"They said I could tell you everything. But they don't want you to tell anyone else."

"Of course," my father said.

"What did you talk about for three hours?" I asked.

"Michael."

"Just Michael?"

"And the treatment center."

I stared at him. I saw my father stare at him.

"They wanted to know all about the treatment center," Danny said.

"What for?"

"They want to put Michael in."

"Into the treatment center?"

"Yes."

"My God," I said.

"Michael is that sick?" my father asked.

"Yes."

"I've been with him for weeks," I said. "I never saw him that sick."

"He's very sick. He breaks things. He burns books. He shattered his telescope a week before he came up here. He's a serious discipline problem in school. And he resists therapy. That's always an indication of something very deep-seated and serious. They've been told he might harm himself. They're very frightened. They thought the summer would help and he would change. They were deluding themselves, they realize that now. I'm going to talk to the administrator and my supervisor. There's a procedure everyone has to go through. But they're ready to start immediately."

"I never saw it." I felt my hands cold with icy sweat. "I never saw any of that in Michael."

"Yes you did," Danny said quietly. "But you didn't know what you were seeing."

He was moody and subdued all during supper. Yes, he would be in the same apartment next year, he said, in response to my father's question. It was a good apartment. They had promised to replace the worn linoleum and to give it a fresh coat of paint. He would be going to school and working three full days a week at the treatment center. I told him I hoped he would be opening his window. He smiled bleakly.

I asked him if he had ever read any of Abraham Gordon's books. Yes, he had read his books, he said. He couldn't think of any books he disagreed with more.

"Abraham Gordon is a great scholar," my father said.

Danny said he wasn't questioning Abraham Gordon's scholarship, only his theology.

"I understand how you feel, Danny," my father said. "But Abraham Gordon has achieved something that is remarkable. To develop a theology for those who can no longer believe literally in God and revelation and who still wish to remain observant and not abandon the tradition— that is a remarkable achievement."

Danny said he didn't have that kind of a problem.

He left shortly after supper. He had not rested at all. He looked tired to the point of exhaustion.

I sat at the kitchen table with my father. He was working on the galleys.

"Why did they pick that treatment center?" I said.

He looked up from the galleys.

"Why did they pick the treatment center where Danny is working?"

"They know of Danny."

"So what? Do you know how many good therapists there are in New York? What do they want with Danny?"

My father was silent a moment. "Reuven, did you ever mention to Rachel how Danny was raised?"

"Of course not."

"She knows nothing of the silence?"

"Absolutely nothing." From the time Danny was about six or seven until the end of his last year in college, Reb Saunders, Danny's father, had deliberately created a barrier of silence between himself and his son, except when they studied Talmud together. He was frightened of Danny's cold brilliance; he wanted to teach his son what it meant to suffer. Danny had suffered, all right. I did not understand what connection there could be between that and Michael, and I said so to my father.

He did not respond.

"This isn't a coincidence," I said. "You heard what Professor Gordon said. They were planning to talk to Danny anyway. What do they want with Danny?"

"I have no idea," my father said. He looked at me curiously for a moment, then went back to working on the galleys.

Rachel called me later that evening. They had had a good talk with Danny. Her aunt and uncle were deeply grateful. Did I know what a kind and warm and sympathetic friend I had?

How was Michael? I wanted to know.

Moody, she said. He knew something was going on that had to do with him, but he had no idea what it was. "We had an awful time getting him out of the house," she said. "He kept saying he wanted to meet Reuven's friend."

"When are they going to tell him?"

She didn't know, she said. But Michael and his parents were going back to the city tomorrow. Her uncle was impatient now to start the procedure for getting Michael admitted. Danny had really overwhelmed them a little with his warmth and the patient way he had answered their questions. Where had I found such a friend? she asked.

"On a baseball field."

I heard her laugh softly into the phone. "You should have ducked," she said. I had told her about the baseball game. She was imitating Danny's faintly nasal voice. "Isn't that what he said? You should have ducked."

I told her she had a very good memory. "How come your mother took Michael?"

She had volunteered. There had been no one else to go.

"Why didn't you go?"

"I wanted to meet Danny," she said. Then she said, "My mother has an awful headache from that double feature."

" 'Messengers for good deeds are never injured,' " I said in Hebrew, quoting the Talmud.

"Only in storybooks," she said, and we said good night.

Abraham Gordon called early the next morning. My father spoke with him briefly, then gave me the phone. He had called to thank us again, he said. He and his wife were taking Michael home that morning. He understood I would be at the seminary library helping my father with the book. "Come up to my office and we'll talk," he said.

Ruth Gordon came on the phone. She wanted to thank me and my father, she said. She hoped we would have an opportunity to meet in the city. We had hardly talked yesterday, she said.

I heard Abraham Gordon calling for Michael.

"Hello," Michael said, his voice thin and a little breathless.

"Hello," I said.

"I didn't meet your friend yesterday. They didn't want me to meet him."

I did not say anything.

"They're out of the room," Michael said. "We can talk. Why didn't they want me to meet him?"

I asked him how he had liked the double feature.

The science-fiction movie had been great, he said. The other had been only so-so. "Why didn't they want me to meet him?" he said. "I wanted to meet him because he's your friend. I may never be able to meet him now."

I told him there would probably be another chance for him to meet Danny one day. I felt very cold telling him that, but I didn't know what else to say.

"Reuven?"

"Yes."

"I'm sorry I acted that way at the carnival. I was terrible. I was terrible afterwards too. I was even a little terrible the first time we went sailing. But I liked the sailing." He paused. "Will I see you in the city, Reuven?"

"Sure," I said.

"You can come over and I'll show you my new telescope. My father is going to help me build a new telescope." He paused again. "They're planning something. I can tell they're planning something. We weren't supposed to go home today." He sounded a little panicky.

"I'll see you in the city, Michael."

"I don't know what they're planning. I wish they would tell me what they're planning."

Rachel called me about half an hour later. Michael had gone home with his parents. Her father was driving them home. Could I come over in the afternoon and keep her company? She was not feeling too well, she said.

We spent the afternoon together. The next day my father finished checking the galleys. For the first time that summer he went down to the beach and spent an afternoon in the sun.

On the Sunday before Labor Day my father and I went over to Rachel's house. The five of us were together on the patio most of the afternoon. Sarah Gordon had set up her easel on a corner of the patio and was filling a large canvas with a blinding mixture of colors. She wore a pair of old shorts and a paint-encrusted blouse, and she daubed energetically at the canvas, the palette in one hand, a brush in the other. My father and Joseph Gordon talked gloomily about Senator McCarthy. Rachel and I watched Sarah flinging colors onto the canvas. It was good to be painting again, she said. She hadn't painted all summer. She hadn't quite been herself all summer. It was very good to be able to paint again. Later, there was a barbecue. Joseph Gordon stood away from the smoke pouring from the white coals, his pipe between his teeth, tending zealously to the steaks and all the while continuing to talk with my father. It was a very friendly day. We did not once mention Michael.

That night Rachel and I swam together off the dock. It was a warm night and the sky was black and jeweled with stars. We swam in the bright light of the outdoor spots that illumined the stairway and the dock and a hundred yards of water. The water too was warm and we swam for a long time and later we sat on the dock and let the night dry us off and there were the pulsing sounds of frogs and crickets and the vaulting darkness overhead and the sense of the summer ending.

"Is Danny really very religious?" I heard Rachel ask.

"Yes."

"Does he wear a skullcap in the treatment center too?"

"I've never asked him."

"I don't know anything about Hasidism," she said.

We were silent awhile. The lake lapped gently against the shore.

"Reuven," Rachel said quietly.

"Yes."

"What have we learned about ourselves this summer?"

"That we're good friends."

"Yes," she murmured.

"Very good friends."

"Yes."

"And that Molly Bloom is big with seed."

She laughed and softly, very softly, kissed my cheek.

The next afternoon Rachel and her parents closed up the house and went home. My father and I spent the evening packing our bags. By noon the next day we were back in the city.

Williamsburg was stifling, narcotized by the heat. Our first-floor brownstone apartment felt drained of air. I went quickly through the rooms, opening windows. The apartment seemed suddenly strangely small.

Manya, our Russian housekeeper, returned the next morning. She gave me a hug that left my ribs aching and kept telling me in broken English how wonderful I looked, I had gotten so tan; but why was my father so pale, why hadn't he been out in the sun more? Her graying hair was combed straight back from her forehead and braided into a large bun on the top of her head. She talked excitedly with my father in Russian for a few minutes. Then she put on her apron. I could hear the sounds of her man-sized shoes as she moved about, cleaning the apartment.

The heat continued. Williamsburg baked and broiled in it; the asphalt-paved streets softened in it; the sycamores on my block drooped in it; the Hasidim walked in the shade alongside the houses and stores of Lee Avenue in vain attempts to avoid it.

That Friday morning I traveled to the Zechariah Frankel Seminary and began to work on my father's galleys. Ten days later, on a Monday, I returned to school.

I called Rachel almost every day during September. There was a great deal of trouble convincing Michael to enter the residential treatment center, more trouble than anyone had anticipated. His parents went through all the preliminary interviews and were told by the staff people at the center that Michael ought to be admitted. An interview was set up for Michael with the chief of clinical services for the fourth Monday in September. On the afternoon of the Shabbat before the interview his parents told him what they were planning. He was terrified. He became hysterical. He would not go. He screamed that he would not go. They called the chief of clinical services and he talked to Michael over the phone.

Michael went for the interview. He was calm, polite, responsive. Once back in the house, however, he became hysterical again. He would not go. He wasn't crazy, he screamed. He would not go to a place where people were crazy. What were they trying to do to him? He would never go to a place like that. Abraham Gordon called the chief of clinical services. They talked a long time over the phone. Then Abraham Gordon told his son that an interview would be set up between him and Danny Saunders, Reuven's friend. Yes, Reuven's friend worked there. Would Michael see Reuven's friend?

Michael and Danny spent almost two hours alone on a morning in the first week of October. In the second week of October, two days after Yom Kippur, Michael entered the residential treatment center.

BOOK TWO

—*And who do you think is the greatest poet?*
asked Boland, nudging his neighbor.

—*Byron, of course, answered Stephen. . . .*

—*You don't care whether he was a heretic*
or not? said Nash.

—*What do you know about it? shouted Stephen. . . .*

—*Here, catch hold of this heretic, Heron*
called out.

In a moment Stephen was a prisoner.

JAMES   JOYCE

Five

Then there were the twilight weeks, a length of gray time between October and December when the weave formed in the summer seemed to come apart and I had little contact with Rachel and none at all with Michael. The patterns of our lives were being spun out in different worlds, and as the sycamores turned and the air grew cold the summer became a distant dream, and I could recall it sharply only in the very early mornings as I lay in my bed, no longer asleep but not yet fully awake—the carnival, the old man, Michael's rage, the Sailfish, the cove, the clouds, the long days with Rachel, and the brief hours with Abraham Gordon. At odd moments of the day—in the classroom as Rav Kalman explained a passage of Talmud, in the manuscript room of the Zechariah Frankel Library as I worked on my father's galleys, on a bus, in a store on Lee Avenue—a disconnected piece of the summer would float slowly toward me and expand into dim memory, and I would hear Danny telling me he wanted to sleep for a year under the maple or Michael asking me what his parents were planning. But the strange conjunction of events that had begun with the carnival appeared disentangled now, and the summer faded together with the leaves of the sycamores.

I saw Danny on the third Shabbat in October. He was doing very well in school and working very hard at the treatment center. But he would say nothing to me about Michael, except that he was as well as could be expected.

No, it was not a good idea for me to visit him yet. His symptoms were volatile; the setting was open—so Danny's supervisor felt there should be no visitors outside the immediate family. Danny himself thought there would be no harm in my visiting Michael. But Danny was only a student. They would trust his judgment only just so far. I could not see Michael.

I was not certain I understood what he meant about Michael's symptoms being volatile, and I did not ask him to explain it. He would have explained it himself had he wanted to. But I could tell easily enough from the brooding look in his eyes and the set of his face that he was concerned about Michael.

I asked him if he was opening his window these days. He smiled. Yes, he said. He was opening the window now. Bravo, I said. We would make a Western gentleman out of him yet. He smiled again and said nothing.

I dated Rachel once that fall, in the last week of October, on a cold and windy Saturday night. She had let her hair grow and it lay on her shoulders, a silken flow of auburn. She wore a red dress and a white coat with a fur trim, and she looked lovely. I took her to see *The Moon Is Blue* at the Henry Miller Theatre in Manhattan, and both of us enjoyed it. Afterward, over ice cream in a crowded cafeteria on a side street off Broadway, we talked about the summer, about her parents, her uncle, a fight over loyalty oaths that was brewing in her school, her paper on Joyce, for which she had received an A; it seemed we talked about everything—except Michael. He was doing as well as could be expected, she said, echoing Danny. And that was all she would say about Michael. Yes, she had seen Danny a few times at the treatment center during the past weeks. Was Minkin's book on Hasidism any good? she asked. She wanted to find out about Hasidism.

"What for?" I asked.

Was Minkin's book any good? she asked again.

I told her it was a good book and I suggested other books on Hasidism. "You may as well get a rounded education if you're really curious. The section in Graetz's history will curl your hair."

Had I ever heard of the Kotzker Rebbe? she asked me.

"Who?"

"The Kotzker Rebbe."

I had never heard of him.

She picked moodily at her plate of ice cream.

"Who was the Kotzker Rebbe?" I asked.

A Hasidic rebbe of the last century, she said. Danny had once alluded to him. But she knew nothing about him, had also never heard of him, knew nothing at all about Hasidism.

"Why didn't you ask Danny?"

There had been no time to ask Danny. She was too embarrassed to ask Danny. Her words sounded lame.

"Ask your uncle."

She didn't want to ask her uncle.

"Why not?"

She just didn't want to, that's all. A crimson flush spread slowly across her face. She avoided looking at me. But I understood, and the understanding was edged with an emotion I had no right to feel but felt anyway. I told her she would probably find the Kotzker Rebbe mentioned in one of the books I had recommended to her. She did not mention Danny again that night.

A few days later I remembered her question and I asked my father if he knew who the Kotzker Rebbe had been. It was a Tuesday night and we were having supper at the time in the kitchen. Manya was standing guard over the stove and throwing glances at the table to make certain I was eating. My father seemed a little surprised at the question.

"Why are you asking?"

I told him.

"In what connection did Danny mention the Kotzker?"

"She didn't say."

He seemed puzzled. The Kotzker had been a Hasidic rebbe during the last century in the Eastern European town of Kotzk near Lublin, my father said after a moment. He was a very strange and erratic personality. He was always involved in quarrels and controversies with other Hasidic sects and sometimes with his own followers. For the last twenty years of his life he had closed himself in his room and refused to come out.

"Twenty years?"

My father nodded.

"Why?"

No one knew, my father said. There were many theories, but no one really knew. "What is Danny's interest in the Kotzker?"

I told him I didn't know and would ask him when I saw him again. But I did not see Danny for quite a while, and when I did see him next I had completely forgotten about the Kotzker Rebbe.

My days at school had settled into their normal routine: Talmud in the mornings and the early afternoons with Rav Kalman; philosophy courses in the graduate school on some late afternoons and evenings. I suffered patiently through Rav Kalman's periodic tirades during the early part of the fall and by November found them repetitious and dull. He was a great Talmudist, but I had nothing to do with him outside the classroom. I wanted no personal relationship with Rav Kalman.

The last batch of galleys for my father's book came at the end of September. I worked on them steadily in the rare-manuscript room of the Zechariah Frankel Library. My father sent them back in the third week of October. The book was done. My father roamed around the house for a week, looking like a man who was searching for something he had lost. Then, slowly, he returned to his Zionist activities. The book was due to be published in the second week of January, but advance copies would be ready for mailing to various scholarly journals by the middle of December. My father waited for the book as he had once waited for the news of the end of the Second World War and for the Declaration of Independence of the State of Israel.

One afternoon in October I met Professor Abraham

Gordon in the manuscript room of the Zechariah Frankel Library. He was seated at one of the small tables, peering through a magnifying glass at a manuscript written in Arabic. A black skullcap sat on top of his balding head. I came over to him, and he was glad to see me. He put down the glass and shook my hand and waved me into a chair. How was my father and was the book finished and why hadn't I come to talk to him? I asked him about Michael. Michael was doing as well as could be expected, he said, repeating the words that became the liturgical response to every question I asked about Michael that fall. We talked softly so as not to disturb the others around us. Had I seen the latest attack against him in the Orthodox press? he asked cheerfully, and named an Orthodox weekly published in Brooklyn. I told him I hardly ever read the Orthodox press. He smiled. The writer had called him a pagan. He laughed, and a bearded gentleman sitting at a nearby table threw him an annoyed look. "They are running out of names to call me," he said in a whisper. He was trying to sound cheerful, but he looked worn. His round, heavy face seemed to have taken on additional lines. "Give my warmest regards to your father," he said. I went home, wondering why I had once been so eager to meet him. Rav Kalman really was not too difficult to endure after all.

There seemed nothing unusual about that fall, and yet everything about it was strange, faintly distorted and askew, as if the summer had somehow affected the delicate mechanism of balance inside my ears. The High Holidays came and Hasidim choked the Williamsburg streets and blackened them with their dark caftans and dark suits and dark fur-trimmed hats. The Festival of Succoth came and a jungle of palm fronds and citrons moved about the streets. Simchat Torah came and there was dancing and singing into the night and the streets swarmed with gyrating Hasidim embracing the Torah scrolls and singing their joy to the dark sky. I had seen it all before, there should have been nothing strange about it now. And yet it all seemed strange, and I did not know why. I told myself it was because we were in a time of waiting: for my father's book, for news about Michael, for my ordination. But I did not really know why. Then there was another long Indian summer, and finally the leaves began to fall.

All during those last weeks of August it had seemed as if the separate lines of our lives were being manipulated somehow, purposefully and carefully brought together by some master weaver. Now it seemed the weaver had wearied of his game. The lines hung free. So the summer turned slowly into the mist and smoke of autumn.

Six

The twilight weeks came to an abrupt end in early December with a classroom conversation and a phone call.

December was cold, but without the snow and the sleet that often invade New York before the technical coming of winter. The leaves were gone from the sycamores but there was bright sunlight and clear skies and I enjoyed the bus rides to school in the early mornings through the waking streets.

The school stood on Bedford Avenue a few blocks from Eastern Parkway. The rabbinical and college departments were housed in a whitestone building that fronted directly onto Bedford Avenue. Alongside were the half-dozen brownstones that comprised the various graduate departments. It was a busy, asphalt-paved street, noisy with traffic and crowded with shoppers who frequented the many stores directly across the street from the school. Even with the windows closed the sounds of the street came into the classrooms: the roar of accelerating buses, the loud hum of wheels, the blare of automobile horns, and occasionally a human voice or the barking of a dog.

The whitestone building had six stories. For four years I had climbed up and down the stairs of that building to get to my various college classes. Now almost everything I needed was on the street floor. To the left of the large marble lobby beyond the stone stairs and the metal double door of the school was a long, narrow, tiled corridor. Along the right side of this corridor were the doors that led to the school synagogue, which stood parallel to the corridor, with the Ark against the far right wall and fixed pews taking up half the length of the huge floor. The rest of the synagogue was filled with chairs and long tables. From nine to twelve every morning—except Friday and Shabbat when we had no classes, and Sunday when we had a different schedule—I sat at one of those tables with some of my classmates and prepared for my Talmud class, or shiur, as these classes are called. At noon I went down one flight of stairs and had lunch in the school cafeteria. Then, from one to three in the afternoon, I attended the shiur given by Rav Kalman—in the classroom directly across the corridor from the synagogue. On Tuesday and Thursday afternoons I left the shiur at three o'clock and took a Bedford Avenue bus to a nearby synagogue where I taught Hebrew school. On Monday and Wednesday I came out of the whitestone building and went into the adjoining three-story brownstone for my graduate philosophy classes. It was a fine arrangement.

During my last year in college I had attended the shiur given by Rav Gershenson. He was a kind, gentle person in his late sixties, with a long, pointed gray beard, brown eyes, and a soft, often barely audible voice. He was the greatest Orthodox scholar of Talmud in the United States. He was also a magnificent teacher, and often I would sit in awe, watching the thrusting gyrations of his hands as they danced through the air, thumbs extended and carving invisible circles of emphasis for the explanations with which he would untangle a difficult inyan, or Talmudic discussion. I did not know anyone who had ever been in his class who did not speak of him with respect and love.

Then Rav Jacob Kalman entered the school and was given the *Chullin* shiur. The Talmud tractate *Chullin* deals with the laws of ritual slaughter and with the dietary laws. A thorough knowledge of this tractate is one of the requirements for Orthodox ordination. I entered Rav Kalman's shiur.

No one seemed to know anything about Rav Kalman beyond the facts that he had been a teacher in one of the

great yeshivoth in Vilna before the Second World War
and had spent two years in a German concentration camp
in northern Poland. But during the first few months after
his arrival at Hirsch the corridors and the cafeteria buzzed
with all kinds of rumors about him: his wife and three
daughters had been shot by Storm Troopers in front of his
eyes in a wood outside of Warsaw; he had escaped from a
concentration camp, been caught, and escaped again; he
had crossed the Polish frontier into Russia and fought with
Russian partisans for a year. One rumor had it that he had
organized a group of Orthodox Jewish partisans that spe-
cialized in blowing up the tracks of German trains carrying Jews to the concentration camps. Another rumor had
it that he had been concealed in a bunker for more than a
year by a Polish farm family, had been discovered, had
been forced to watch the execution of the family, and had
somehow escaped again. He was said to have made his
way across northern Russia into Siberia and from there to
Shanghai, where he had waited out the war under the eyes
of the Japanese, who were not possessed of Hitler's feelings toward Jews and who left the few Jews under their
rule alone. According to this version of the life of Rav
Kalman, he was brought to America by the administration
of Hirsch University and was promptly invited to teach in
the rabbinical department.

There were seventeen students in my class. The room in
which we attended Rav Kalman's shiur was large, with
light-green walls, a high white ceiling, and bright fluorescent lights. Almost the entire wall opposite the door was
comprised of tall, wide windows that faced Bedford Avenue. On clear days the sun streamed through those windows—but it made little difference, for the room was
always pervaded by the peculiar darkness that Rav Kalman brought with him whenever he came through the
door. He seemed to radiate darkness. He was short but
stockily built. He had a full black beard and dark eyes
and thick black hair. His face was quite pale and con-
trasted sharply with the blackness of his beard. He wore a
long black coatlike jacket that reached to just above the

knees, a starched white shirt, a black tie, sharply pressed black trousers, black shoes, and a tall, shiny black skull-cap.

He was an angry, impatient, sarcastic teacher. I had had angry teachers before, but their anger had always been accompanied by a redeeming humor. There was nothing humorous about Rav Kalman. He rarely sat still behind his desk. He paced. I would watch him pace back and forth along the narrow corridor of space between his desk and the blackboard, going to the windows, turning, going to the opposite wall near the door, turning, going back to the windows. Sometimes he would stop at the windows and incline his head and close his eyes for a moment, as if he were listening to an invisible voice—and I would see him nod his head. Then he would turn and continue his pacing. He smoked incessantly, waiting until the cigarettes were almost ashes in his fingers before dropping them into the ashtray on his desk. His voice was loud and high-pitched; often at the end of a shiur I had the feeling that a sudden silence had descended upon the school. His classes left me drained, nerveless, tense.

During our first week with him the year before, we had quickly realized that a student's request for further clarification of a passage, or the normal barrage of questions with which we had always confronted our Talmud teachers in the past, was now laden with danger. Two or three days after I had first entered his class, I asked him about a passage we were studying that seemed to me to be clearly contradicted by another passage I had suddenly remembered from a different tractate. He stopped pacing and fixed his dark eyes on me and tugged at his beard. He did not simply stroke his beard; he took strands of hair between the thumb and forefinger of his right hand, and tugged. "A contradiction," he muttered. "Malter has found a contradiction." I tensed in my seat. "Tell me, Malter, have you studied the"—he named an obscure late-medieval commentary no one in the class ever paid attention to—"on the inyan? You have not? If you would have studied that commentary, you would not find your contradiction. Come better prepared, Malter. You will find fewer contradictions." He did not answer my question. My father solved the problem for me that night by a simple emendation of the text in the other tractate. But I would not dare display that method to Rav Kalman. Textual emendation of Talmudic passages as practiced by those who studied Talmud in the modern, scientific manner was unheard of in my school.

We had no way of knowing how Rav Kalman might react to any of our questions, and I had no desire to become the target of his sarcasm. So I stopped asking questions. I read without errors whenever I was called on, answered all his questions correctly, and contributed nothing on my own to the class. A Talmud class in which a student is fearful of asking questions can become a suffocating experience. I suffocated.

His tirades were frightening. He talked about Hollywood as the symbol of American values; he ranted against a new instrument of horror called television; there was little about America he seemed to like. On occasion his tirades were based upon events occurring in the school. Students and teachers were attacked by name. A projected college course in Greek mythology was canceled because he labeled it paganism. A student was almost expelled because he caught him outside the school without a hat. The annual college senior show, to which girls had always been invited, was called off because he waged a vitriolic campaign against girls sitting together with boys in the yeshiva auditorium. The whole year was like that.

In somewhat cynical fashion we referred to those tirades as musar messages. "Musar" is the Hebrew term for ethics or a lecture exhorting one to ethical living. There had been a great musar movement among Jews in Eastern Europe, particularly in Lithuania, during the latter part of the last century and in the decades before the Second World War. Much about that movement had been quite ennobling. But there was nothing ennobling about Rav Kalman's musar messages. They were delivered with sarcasm and anger, and one is rarely ennobled by such exhortations.

It had taken a considerable effort on my part over the past months of autumn to grow accustomed to his tirades. But I had finally succeeded. At the onset of a tirade I would slump down in my seat. I sat in the last row of the class but I could not look away from him because he would notice that almost immediately. So I would look straight at him, moving my head to keep him in view as he paced back and forth—and not listen to his words. I would do a logic problem in my head; one part of me would be seeing to it that I kept looking directly at him; the other part would be doing a logic problem, or thinking of Michael and Danny and Rachel, or conjuring up images of the huge presses that were running off my father's book. There was a numbing sameness to those tirades, and by the end of November I discovered I could turn them off with ease and still convey the impression that I was listening. Then on the Monday morning of the first week of December he began to talk about something he had never mentioned before in class, and I found myself listening once again to his words.

We were studying the ninth chapter of *Chullin,* which deals with various kinds of uncleanness that can result from contact with reptiles and dead animals. One of the students was reading the text and explaining as he went along. The class was absolutely silent, except for the lone voice of the student. Rav Kalman paced back and forth behind his desk, smoking. He had called on the student to read at the beginning of the class, and then had not said a word. The student had been reading and explaining for almost a quarter of an hour. Rav Kalman remained silent. He stopped at the window for a while and peered out at the street. He closed his eyes and inclined his head and seemed to be listening to something. Then he resumed his pacing. I kept my eyes on the text—all of us kept our eyes on the text when someone was reading—but I could hear him pacing back and forth. Then the pacing suddenly stopped. I glanced up. He was standing behind his desk.

Others were looking at him now too. I could feel the class go tense. The student who had been reading became silent. Another musar message, I told myself, and started to set up a logic problem in my head. I slumped down in my seat.

"Read," Rav Kalman said. "Who told you to stop? Continue reading. Explain again the words of Rabbi Yehuda ... Yes. Go on. Go on. What does Tosefos say about the comment of Rashi? ... Yes. Continue reading."

I sat up in my seat and looked down at the text. The student went on reading and explaining. Outside, Bedford Avenue was bathed in sunlight and thick with traffic. Inside, the room was filled with its normal atmosphere of oppressive tension.

Rav Kalman stood silently behind his desk, smoking a cigarette. Abruptly, without warning, he broke into the words of the student who was reading. The student stopped immediately.

"If the body is made unclean by contact with the smallest of things that is unclean," Rav Kalman said in Yiddish, "how much more so is it made unclean by contact with bigger things which are unclean."

I started to work on my logic problem.

He did not pace. He stood stiffly behind his desk.

"In America, everything is called Yiddishkeit," Rav Kalman said. "A Jew travels to synagogue on Shabbos in his car, that is called Yiddishkeit. A Jew eats ham but gives money to philanthropy, that is called Yiddishkeit. A Jew prays three times a year but is a member of a synagogue, that is called Yiddishkeit. Judaism"—he pronounced the word in English, contemptuously: Joodaheeism—"everything in America calls itself Judaism."

He put his cigarette into the ashtray and looked at me across the room. "Are you listening, Malter?"

I nodded, without losing the thread of the logic problem. Outside, a car horn blared noisily, the sound strangely loud in the stillness of the room.

Rav Kalman took a pack of cigarettes from a pocket of his long jacket and put a cigarette between his lips. He lit it, placed the match carefully in the ashtray, and blew smoke from his nostrils. He took the cigarette from his lips and looked at me intently.

"In America there are schools that teach Judaism," he said, talking to the class and looking at me. "The students do not wear skullcaps and the teachers do not believe in Torah from heaven, and they teach Judaism." His voice was low but edged with contempt. "Judaism," he said. "Everything in America is Judaism."

I dropped the logic problem and sat up straight in my chair.

He was still looking at me. "What would you say of such a school, Malter?"

I stared at him and said nothing.

"How would you describe such a school, Malter? Is there a word for such a school?"

I saw some of my classmates glancing at me. This was the first time Rav Kalman had ever turned one of his tirades into a question-and-answer affair. I sat very rigidly in my seat, and said nothing.

"Unclean," he said, his voice suddenly angry. "Unclean. Such a school is unclean. And whoever has contact with it becomes unclean himself." Then he began pacing back and forth behind the desk and talking, not looking at us any more, but still talking. "Such a school is a falsehood. It is worse than a falsehood. It is a desecration of the Name of God. Do you hear? A desecration of the Name of God. It is a perversion. Where is the holiness in such a school? The Bible they change whenever they do not understand what they read. The Gemora"—he used the traditional synonym for the Talmud, though the Gemora, or Gemara, as I pronounced it, is actually only one part of the Talmud—"the Gemora they change. Whatever they do not like, they change. Where is the holiness in such a school?" He went on like that for a few more minutes. Then he carefully put out his cigarette in the ashtray and stood behind the desk. "Such a school is unclean. And whoever sets foot in it becomes unclean.

Remember what I tell you. Now read further. Who was reading? Goldberg. Read. Read."

Two seats in front of me, the student who had been reading earlier began to read again. I looked at my hands on top of the open Talmud. They were trembling.

I did not hear a single word of what went on during the rest of that class session. I sat there in a frightened daze, wondering whether Rav Kalman's words had been deliberately directed at me or had simply been an accident of timing that had somehow managed to coincide closely with the weeks I had spent at the Zechariah Frankel Seminary working on my father's book. But the way he had looked at me . . . I did not think it was a coincidence.

I found out soon enough. Chairs scraped noisily and I came out of my daze. The room began to empty quickly. Hardly anyone ever stayed around to talk with Rav Kalman after a shiur. I started for the door. I wanted to get out of there. I heard someone call my name. I thought it was one of the students and I ignored him. I was almost at the door when someone tugged at the sleeve of my jacket. Rav Kalman wanted to talk to me, a classmate said, giving me a wide-eyed look. I turned and went back into the room.

Rav Kalman was standing behind his desk, smoking another cigarette and gazing at me. I came over to him. Standing close to him, I could see the dark circles beneath his eyes and the long diagonal line of a white scar on his right cheek. He smelled strongly of tobacco. He took the cigarette from his mouth, placed it in the ashtray, and gazed at me intently. He tugged at his beard.

"Malter, you understood what I said concerning schools for Judaism?" he asked in Yiddish.

I told him I had understood. I spoke in English. We were able to use either English or Yiddish in class. My Yiddish was very poor. I used English.

"You know which school I meant?"

"No," I said.

"You do not know?" He looked at me intently. His

eyes narrowed. He swayed back and forth on his legs.
"Malter, tell me. You know Gordon?"

"Which Gordon?" I heard myself ask.

"Which Gordon," he repeated with a faintly mocking
smile. "Which Gordon."

"I know a lot of Gordons," I said.

"Yes? Very nice. I mean the Gordon of the Zechariah
Frankel Seminary. You know that Gordon?"

"Abraham Gordon? Yes."

"You know him well?"

"I know him."

"How is it that you know him?"

"I know him," I said again.

"Yes. You know him. That much is now clear. Malter,
tell me. You know Gordon has been put into cherem?"
"Cherem" is the Hebrew term for excommunication.

I felt my fingers tighten on the Talmud I held in my
hand. Yes, I knew about that, I said.

"You know that. You tell me you know that. Now I
must ask you, is it true that you were with Gordon in the
Zechariah Frankel Library last month?"

I stared at him and heard myself tell him that I didn't
know anyone who took that excommunication seriously.

"You do not know anyone who takes it seriously. You
do not—" He broke off. "Tell me, Malter, you think
placing someone in cherem is a light thing? Have you read
the books of Gordon?"

I lied. I told him I had never read any of Abraham
Gordon's books.

"Gordon destroys Yiddishkeit with his books. The
cherem is not a light thing. Such a man is a danger." He
paused for a moment. He had to tilt his head backward a
little to look up at me. His eyes were dark. The collar of
his shirt was white and starched. His tie was carefully
knotted. He was still tugging at his beard, and I noticed
for the first time that the third and fourth fingers of his
right hand were faintly misshapen, as if they had been
broken at one time and poorly reset.

"Tell me," he was saying. Danny's father talks that

way, I thought. Rav Gershenson talks that way. They all talk that way. Tell me. Tell me. "Tell me, Malter. What were you doing all those weeks in the Zechariah Frankel Seminary?"

I wondered where he was getting all his information about me. But it did not really matter. Anyone could have seen me going in and out of there. The Zechariah Frankel Seminary was less than a half hour's walk from Hirsch. Rav Kalman might even have seen me himself. It made no difference how he knew. As far as I was concerned, it even made no difference that he knew. I had not intended to conceal my going to that library.

I told him I had been doing some work for my father.

"What work?" he asked.

I told him I had been checking the footnotes and the variant readings in the galleys to my father's book to save him time and spare him the physical effort of having to go back and forth to that library. He was very tired after more than a year of work on the book, I said. He was not a well man, I said.

I had used the term variant readings. I saw his eyes open wide at that. "Your father has written a book?" he asked.

"Yes."

"I know of your father. Tell me, the book, your father's book, what is it about? It is a book on the Gemora?"

I told him it contained many of the scholarly articles my father had published over the years, as well as a lengthy introduction on the nature of the Talmud. The introduction had been written especially for the book, I said, a little proudly. I omitted mentioning that the introduction also contained a long section on the methodology of Talmudic text criticism.

He was silent for a moment. He tugged at his beard. Then he lit another cigarette.

"It is forbidden to punish without first giving a warning," he said, his voice abruptly cold. "So I give you a warning. That school is unclean. You are not to set foot in that school."

I stared at him, not quite believing what I had heard. I told him I had seen dozens of Orthodox Jews in that library, studying, doing research, writing.

He became angry then. "Orthodox! Everything is Orthodox! What kind of Orthodox? There is one Yiddishkeit. I know nothing about Orthodox. The school is unclean and its books are unclean. My students will not go into that school."

I said nothing. My face was suddenly hot. I felt the slow mounting of anger.

"Malter, you understand that a student does not receive smicha from me simply because he knows Gemora. You understand that."

I did not say anything.

"You understand, Malter? I do not give smicha only for Gemora."

I nodded or did something to indicate acknowledgment of his words.

There was a brief silence.

"When does your father's book come out?" he asked quietly.

I told him.

He dismissed me with an abrupt wave of his hand and a curt nod of his head.

I went through the corridor and the marble lobby and out into the street. The afternoon air was cold and sharp. I stood there for a moment, breathing deeply. Then I realized I had forgotten my coat in the synagogue. I went back inside.

Irving Goldberg sat in a chair near the coat racks that stood against the wall opposite the Ark. He had obviously been waiting for me. He was short, round-faced, chubby, very solemn, and very good at Talmud. We studied together every morning to prepare for Rav Kalman's shiur. He had read for today's shiur.

He got to his feet. He was wearing his coat and hat. I put on my coat. He watched me solemnly. I told him he had done a good job in the shiur.

He shrugged. "What did he want?"

"A private musar message."

"How private?"

I did not respond.

"Are you in trouble, Reuven?"

"I don't know."

He looked uncomfortable. He stood there in his heavy coat, looking short and round and uncomfortable.

"Reuven," he said.

I looked at him.

He glanced around quickly. We were alone in our part of the synagogue. "Are you thinking of applying to the Frankel Seminary?"

That did it for me. "No, I'm not thinking of applying to the Frankel Seminary," I almost shouted. "What's going on around here? What've we got, our own version of the Spanish Inquisition?"

He stared, frightened. "For God's sake, not so loud. Are you crazy?"

"I'm going," I said.

"There are rumors that you're planning to apply to that seminary," he said somewhat plaintively. "Don't get angry at me, Reuven."

"What rumors? Where have there been rumors? I haven't heard any rumors."

"There have been rumors for the past three weeks."

"I haven't heard a thing."

"No one hears rumors about himself. People saw you going in and out of that place. They thought—"

"I was checking the galleys of my father's book," I said.

"Oh," he said. "Oh."

"Yes. Oh."

"God," he said. "You could kill a person with rumors."

"I'm going. I've got a logic class in fifteen minutes."

"I'll walk out with you." We went out of the synagogue. "You were only working on your father's book," he said, shaking his head.

We passed Rav Gershenson's classroom, which adjoined ours. It was a quarter after three, fifteen minutes past the end of the class hour. I peered through the small square window set in the door. Rav Gershenson was still there, standing behind his desk surrounded by more than half a dozen of his students.

We came outside. The metal door slammed shut behind me. I went quickly down the stone steps to the sidewalk. The street was crowded with people and traffic. But it felt good to be outside.

Irving Goldberg stuffed his hands into the pockets of his coat. The coat lay tight around his heavyset round frame. He smiled solemnly.

"You'd really stand this place on its head if you ever went to that seminary," he said.

"Very funny," I muttered. I was in no mood for his gloomy humor.

"Star Talmud student at Hirsch goes to Frankel," Irving Goldberg was saying. "That would be like what's his name—your friend—Danny Saunders—that would almost be like Danny Saunders going to that seminary." He looked at me. "Were you really there only for your father's book?" he asked seriously.

"No, I was there to take lessons in conversion to Catholicism. For God's sake. How can something as small as this get blown up that way?"

"Lashon hara," he said. "Gossip, gossip, gossip. Rumors. Tongues. 'Life and death are in the power of the tongue,'" he quoted in Hebrew.

"I'll see you tomorrow morning," I said. Then I said, "Why didn't you tell me earlier about the rumors?"

He smiled soberly. "I was afraid they might be true."

"I'll see you tomorrow," I said, and went off to my logic class.

Late that night I sat at my desk at home and worked automatically and without effort at a series of complicated problems in symbolic logic. I had turned down the covers of my bed and turned off the ceiling light. But I knew I would be unable to sleep, and so I sat at my desk in my pajamas with only the desk lamp on and filled pieces of paper with the conventional notations that form the language of logic. I must have sat there for hours; the top of the desk became heaped with paper. There was comfort and satisfaction in the effortless manipulation of neutral symbols, and I worked at it steadily. The only sound in the room was the faint scratching of my pencil on the sheets of paper.

It was after two in the morning when my father knocked quietly on my door.

He stood in the doorway, wearing his dark-blue robe over his pajamas, his gray hair uncombed. "I saw your light, Reuven," he said softly. "It is late."

I looked at him and did not say anything.

"You are doing assignments for class?"

I told him I wasn't doing assignments. I couldn't sleep, I said.

He came into the room and closed the door. "You were so quiet tonight," he said. "Even Manya commented to me on how quiet you were tonight."

I put down the pencil. He came over to the bed and sat down, drawing the robe over his thin knees. He looked tired and frail and I felt something turn over inside me as I gazed at him, and I looked away. Quantifiers stared up at me from the piece of paper on my desk.

I heard him sigh. "Little children little troubles, big children big troubles," he murmured in Yiddish. "When my big Reuven is so quiet, there are big troubles. Can I be of help to you, Reuven?"

I told him it wasn't anything I couldn't handle by myself.

He regarded me in silence for a moment through his steel-rimmed spectacles, his eyes heavy with fatigue. "I did not mean to pry, Reuven," he said quietly. "I want only to help if I can."

"You're not prying, abba. Since when do you pry?"

"With a grown son a father never knows when he is prying. Can I be of help to you, Reuven?" he asked again.

I had not wanted to tell him. I had not wanted him to know it had come about as a result of the weeks I had spent working on his book. Now I found I needed to tell him. I spoke with as much calm as I could bring to my words.

He blinked wearily. He sighed. He rubbed a hand over the gray stubble of beard on his cheeks and shook his head.

"I was right," he said quietly. "It is a big problem."

"He's a detestable human being."

"Detestable? From a single conversation you conclude that a person is detestable?"

"I'm in his class, abba."

"And you know enough about him to call him detestable? I am surprised at you, Reuven."

"I know enough about him to know that I can't stand him as a teacher. He's poisoned everything at Hirsch for me." They're poison, Michael had said. They'll poison all of us with their crazy ideas. I felt cold and stared down at the sheets of paper on my desk. The symbols stared back up at me, silent.

"I understand how you feel, Reuven. I understand what it means to have such a teacher." He spoke very quietly, his eyes narrow with sudden remembering. He was quiet a long time. Then he said, speaking more to himself than to me, "A teacher can change a person's life. A good teacher or a bad teacher. Each can change a person's life." He was silent again. Then he said, very softly, "But only if the person is ready to be changed. A teacher rarely causes such a change, Reuven. I am not saying it is impossible. Do not misunderstand me. I am saying it is rare. More often he can only occasion such a change. You understand what I am saying." He smiled faintly. "You are a student of philosophy and logic. I am certain you understand."

I was quiet.

"Yes," he said. "I am certain you understand." He paused. "Reuven, was Rav Kalman angry when he spoke to you?"

"He's always angry."

"I have been reading some of his articles. He also writes

in anger. He attacked Abraham Gordon recently in an article. It was unpleasant to read. His choice of language was unpleasant. But he understands Abraham Gordon's thinking."

"He wants me to obey the cherem."

"What cherem?"

"Against Professor Gordon."

"You did not tell me you talked about Abraham Gordon."

"He said I was seen with Professor Gordon in the library. He wants me to obey the cherem."

"The cherem is nonsense."

"He wants me to obey it."

My father was quiet. "It is a bigger problem than I realized," he said after a moment. "What energies we waste fighting one another." He got slowly to his feet. "I am very tired, Reuven. I will not send you any more to the Frankel Library. The book is done. There is no need for you to go there any more. Unless you want to go for yourself. I do not know what to tell you about Abraham Gordon. I cannot think now. I am too tired." He looked at me wearily. "Reuven, you want smicha from the Hirsch Yeshiva?"

"Yes," I said.

"And Rav Kalman's approval is mandatory in order for you to obtain smicha?"

"Yes."

"You are no longer curious about the philosophy of Abraham Gordon?"

"I'm curious about Michael." Curious is not the word I wanted, I thought.

He sighed heavily. "I wish I knew what to tell you. I must go back to sleep. We will talk about it again another time. I do not know what to tell you now. Go to sleep yourself, Reuven. It is almost three o'clock. You will not be able to think in the morning."

He went slowly from the room. I heard the soft shuffling of his slippers as he moved through the hall. Then I heard nothing.

I sat at my desk and stared at the pieces of paper. I sat at my desk and the symbols stared back up at me, silent, inviting. I snapped off the lamp and went to bed and was awake a long time. The night wind blew against the window. In the apartment overhead a baby cried, then was silent. I fell asleep. There was the wind and the sun and the heaving waters of the lake and Michael and I on the Sailfish and Michael was shouting at me and I could not make out the words but I knew he was angry. I woke. I lay awake, thinking of Michael. Then I slid slowly into exhausted sleep.

The next day at the beginning of the shiur, Rav Kalman called on me to read. I was dull-headed with lack of sleep. Part of the time I did not even know what I was saying. Rav Kalman listened, asked questions, paced back and forth, smoked, tugged at his beard, asked more questions, and looked startled when I automatically and sleepily altered a word in the text that I instinctively sensed was wrong. He rushed to his desk, peered down at his Talmud, straightened, stared at me for a moment, then resumed his pacing. I realized then what I had done and glanced at the margin. The variant reading was listed; it had been inserted by a medieval scholar, which meant that it was an authorized reading. I took a deep breath. All of this had taken a second or two. But I was wide awake for the rest of the class session, reading slowly, explaining carefully. Rav Kalman paced and smoked. We had a brief skirmish over a passage in one of the major medieval commentaries. But I backed off quickly and went on reading. Rav Kalman said nothing to me when the class ended.

Two days later, he called on me again. I read. He paced and smoked and asked questions. Again, he said nothing to me when the class ended.

About half a dozen of my classmates followed me over to the coat racks inside the synagogue.

"He's picking on you," Irving Goldberg said mournfully. "Why is he picking on you?"

"Why don't you ask him?" I said.

"You're the best Gemora head in the class," another student said. "He always picks on those he loves."

"This isn't something to joke about," Irving Goldberg said.

I put on my coat. They crowded around me, waiting.

"All right," I said. "You want a public announcement. Here's a public announcement. I have not applied to the Frankel Seminary."

There were embarrassed smiles.

"They didn't believe me," Irving Goldberg said somberly.

"An unreliable witness," a student said in Hebrew, using the Talmudic term.

"You were really only working on your father's book?" another classmate said.

I looked at them. They stared back at me. The overhead fluorescents were reflected in their glasses; their faces seemed pale.

"You are all practicing to become future Rav Kalmans," I said.

There were more embarrassed smiles.

"He's got the whole school infected," I said.

"Not the whole school," someone said.

"Don't talk like that, Reuven," someone else said. "He's our Rav."

"I'm tired," I said. "I haven't slept much this week. And I've got to go teach. I'll see you all for the next musar message."

I left them there, bought an afternoon paper in a candy store across the street, and caught a bus. Inside the bus I read the paper, dozed for a few minutes, then woke and looked out the window at the streets. Dense clouds covered the sky. I sat there and stared out the window at the gray streets and did not look at the clouds.

I was tense and weary to the point of near exhaustion by the time Shabbat came that week. I almost fell asleep at the Shabbat meal on Friday night. I went to bed immediately after my father and I chanted the Grace and I tossed all night with ugly dreams but they slid steeply out of me and evaporated when I woke in the morning. I found myself heavy-lidded and nodding into sleep during the services, and later, after the meal, I went back to bed and slept and there were more dreams, and I woke late in the afternoon and felt my pillow cold with sweat, but I could remember nothing. My father and I said very little to one another all through that Shabbat.

Because Sunday Talmud classes at Hirsch ended at one in the afternoon, the period of preparation ran from nine to a few minutes before eleven, and the shiur ran from eleven to one. The next morning Rav Kalman called on me again. I saw my classmates exchange grim looks. I began to read. He let me read and explain for a long time. All the while he paced back and forth, smoking. Then he stopped me on a passage I had struggled with during the period of preparation and still did not clearly understand.

I started to give him one of the commentaries on the passage. He stopped me again.

"I did not ask you for the Maharsha, Malter. What do the words mean? Explain the words. Can you explain the words?"

I tried to put the words together as best I could; they did not hang together properly; there was clearly something wrong with the text.

"Explain it again, Malter," Rav Kalman said. "Make it clearer. It is not yet clear."

I explained it again. Then I was silent. He stood stiffly behind the desk. "You cannot explain it better? No. I see you cannot. Can anyone explain it better?"

His question was answered with a stonelike silence.

He put his cigarette into the ashtray. "American students," I heard him mutter to himself. Then he launched into a loud and lengthy explanation of the passage. It was clever; it was very clever. But it took no account of some of the grammatical difficulties in the text.

"You understand now, Malter?"

I hesitated.

"You understand?"

I nodded.

"Yes? Good. Now tell us what the Maharsha says." And he paced back and forth as I went wearily through the explanation offered by the commentary.

At supper that night I mentioned the passage to my father.

"What do you think it means, Reuven?"

I told him I thought the text was wrong.

"And how would you correct it?"

I emended three of the words and rearranged a segment of the passage.

His eyes shone and he smiled proudly. "Very good, Reuven. Very good. The passage has been written on extensively." And he cited some articles in scholarly journals in which the passage had been discussed at great length. Two of the articles, he said, had emended the text in precisely the way I had suggested. And my father agreed that this probably had once been the correct text.

At that point Manya, who had been standing patiently by the stove listening to us talk, told us in her broken English to eat, the food was getting cold. We ate.

After supper, my father went into his study to grade examination papers and I sat in my room at my desk and worked on a paper I was doing for a symbolic logic course. It was a complicated paper on epistemological assumptions and primitives in logistical systems, and I was enjoying it thoroughly. When the phone rang I looked at my watch and was surprised to discover it was almost eleven o'clock. The sound of the phone echoed shrilly in the hall of the apartment. I went out of my room, wondering who would be calling so late at night, and lifted the receiver.

"Reuven?" a voice said very faintly.

"Yes."

"Reuven Malter?"

"Yes."

"Hello, Reuven."

"Hello. I can barely hear you. Who is this?"

"Is this Reuven Malter?"

"Yes. I can't hear you. We must have a bad connection."

"No. The connection is all right. I can't talk loud. This is Michael. I'm not allowed to phone without permission."

"Michael," I heard myself say, and sank slowly into the chair next to the phone stand. I felt cold with shock.

"Do you remember me, Reuven?"

"Of course I remember you."

"Are you all right?"

"I'm surprised. I didn't expect—should you be calling if it's not allowed?"

"I need to talk to you, Reuven. I hate to be sneaky, but I need to talk to you. Can I talk to you, Reuven?"

"Sure you can talk to me."

"You have to promise you won't tell anyone. I don't want anyone to know I broke the rules. Will you promise?"

I did not say anything. I found I was pressing the phone hard against my ear in order to hear him better. The cartilage of my ear ached. I moved the phone away slightly.

"Reuven?" I heard him say. "Reuven?"

"Yes."

"You have to promise."

"All right."

"I don't want anyone to think I'm breaking the rules. Some of the people here are very nice. I don't want them to feel hurt."

"You have my promise, Michael."

I heard a rustling, clicking sound in the phone. Then there was silence. But the connection did not seem dead.

"Michael," I said. "Michael." Then louder, "Michael."

The silence of the phone was terrifying. I felt the skin prickle on my arms and on the back of my neck.

Then I heard a frantic whisper. "Someone is coming. Wait. Don't hang up." Then, again, silence.

The door to my father's study opened slowly. My father

came into the hall. He stood in the hall, looking at me. The hand with which I was holding the receiver began to tremble.

"There is news about Michael?" my father asked softly. "I heard you mention Michael."

I put my other hand over the mouthpiece.

"Michael is on the phone," I said. "He's calling from the treatment center."

"Reuven?" I heard Michael say. "Are you still there?"

My father stared at me.

I took my hand away from the mouthpiece. "Yes."

"He's gone. Whoever it was is gone. He didn't come in." His straining, whispering voice sounded tremulous with relief. "I don't want them to catch me. Reuven, are you all right? Are you feeling all right?"

"Yes, I'm all right."

"Why don't you come to visit me? You've never once come to visit me."

I gripped the phone tightly and did not say anything. My father walked silently past the door to my room and stood between me and the framed pictures of Herzl, Bialik, and Chaim Weizmann that hung from the wall.

"Reuven," Michael said.

"I'm here, Michael."

"Don't you want to visit me, Reuven?"

"I asked if I could visit you. They said only your family was allowed to visit."

There was a momentary silence. "Who said you couldn't visit?" He was still whispering. But his voice had changed. It was hard, suspicious.

I did not know what to do. I did not know whether it would upset him more if I continued talking to him and answered his questions or if I told him I could not talk to him at all because he did not have permission to call me. I did not know how much I could tell him. I did not know whether I could tell him anything.

Michael's tight whisper came clearly through the phone. "Who said that, Reuven?"

I felt it impossible to tell him we could not continue

talking. So I told him Danny's supervisor had not wanted me to visit until the period of adjustment was over. I did not know whether I was saying the right thing or not. I did not know what else to tell him.

I thought I heard a soft laugh and the muttered words "period of adjustment." Then I heard him whisper, "He's a jerk. I can't stand him. Dr. Altman is a jerk. I'm driving him crazy. I thought I'd be talking to your friend. But they want me to talk to Dr. Altman. Reuven, listen. Do you want to visit me?"

"Yes," I heard myself say.

"I thought you didn't want to, so I didn't say anything. Now I'll tell them I want to see you. They'll let you come. Will you come, Reuven?"

"Sure."

"I'll be glad to see you. I hate this place. Remember the times we went sailing? I think of them a lot. I hate this place." The words were tumbling out of him in angry, rushing whispers. "Some of the kids I go to school with here are awful. We have school right here. I really want to see you, Reuven. I'm going to scream my head off. They'll let you come."

His voice was considerably louder than a whisper now. He sounded deeply agitated.

"Michael, take it easy," I said. "Calm down."

"Remember the roller coaster?" he said. "Remember the first time we went sailing?"

"Yes."

"Are you still seeing Rachel?" he asked abruptly.

I hesitated.

"Reuven?"

"No," I said. "But we're still friends."

"You're not seeing her?" The agitation was suddenly out of his voice. He sounded strangely relieved.

"No."

There was a pause.

"Reuven," he said. "Listen. I want you to bring something when you come."

I did not say anything. My father stood very quietly, looking at me.

"Promise me you'll bring it," Michael said.

"Bring what?"

"There's a newspaper I want you to find and bring me. Promise me you'll bring it."

"What newspaper?"

He told me. I held the phone and said nothing.

"Reuven?"

"Let me think about it."

"Please."

"I want to think about it."

"It's only a newspaper, Reuven." His voice was suddenly angry. "For God—" His voice broke off. Then I heard a barely audible whisper. "Please visit me, Reuven. Good-bye."

There was a click. The line went dead.

I hung up the phone. The palms of my hands were icy with sweat. I looked at my father.

"I've got to talk to you," I said quietly.

He nodded and without a word walked quickly to his study. I followed. Michael's whispered voice echoed inside my head. *You have to promise you won't tell anyone. You have to promise.* My father went around the desk and sat down in his chair. The desk was large, with dark polished wood, deep drawers, and a green, leather-bordered blotter that covered almost its entire top. The blotter was piled high with papers. The room was dark, except for the goose-necked desk lamp, which cast a large, bright circle of light across the desk top and onto the gray-carpeted floor. My father sat behind the desk and regarded me intently. I told him about the conversation with Michael.

He was quiet a very long time after I was done talking. His eyes were dark and he seemed deeply troubled.

"That is the copy of the newspaper that contains Rav Kalman's article," he said.

"Which article?"

"The attack on Abraham Gordon."

I did not say anything.

"How did he find out about that article?" my father murmured. "It was published two weeks ago."

I told him I didn't know.

"I think you should call Danny," my father said. "You cannot undertake the responsibility of keeping this call a secret. You should call Danny."

"I promised Michael I—"

"You should call Danny. You must not conceal this from Danny. Michael is ill. You are not bound by a promise made under such a circumstance."

Michael's frantic whispering was still in my ears. It was as if I were still listening to him over the phone.

"Call Danny," my father said. "Immediately."

"It's after eleven o'clock, abba."

"I know what time it is, Reuven. Call Danny."

I got slowly to my feet.

"Tell him everything, Reuven. You must not conceal anything."

I went out into the hall and picked up the phone and dialed Danny's apartment. The phone rang a long time. There was no answer. I told my father Danny was not in. He said to try until I got him. I told him I could just as easily call Danny sometime tomorrow. No, I must call Danny tonight, he said. He seemed deeply disturbed and in no mood for any suggestion that the call be delayed. I went back into my room, worked on my logic paper for a few minutes, and called Danny again. I waited a long time before I hung up the phone.

Twenty minutes later, I called him again. There was no answer. I called him after my shower, waited a quarter of an hour, called him again, waited another quarter of an hour, and called him again. I wondered if he had decided to sleep over his father's house that night and go to Columbia in the morning. But he had always been in his apartment on Sunday nights. He's on another emergency, I thought.

I decided to call the treatment center. It was listed in the Brooklyn phone book. I dialed quickly and got the night watchman. He didn't know anything about a Mr. Daniel Saunders. He would connect me with the staff member on night duty.

"Hello," a man's voice said.

I apologized for phoning so late at night and explained the reason for the call.

"No, there's no emergency here tonight. Are you a friend of Dan's?"

"Yes. My name is Reuven Malter. Do you have any idea where he might be?"

"No, I'm sorry. What did you say your name was?"

I told him.

"Well," he said. "Isn't that something? Do you know a boy named Michael Gordon?"

"Yes," I said.

"Isn't that something? I just found him wandering around the halls here and sent him off to bed. He told me you were coming to visit him soon. Isn't that something?"

"Yes," I said. "Thank you."

I hung up and sat there and stared at the phone. It seemed alive. I went into my room and worked on my logic paper. It was twenty minutes to one. My father came into my room and told me he was going to bed and that I should keep trying to reach Danny. At least until one o'clock, he said.

I called Danny's apartment again at ten minutes to one. The phone was picked up after the second ring.

"Yes?" It was Danny's nasal voice.

"Reuven," I said, feeling a flood of relief.

"What?"

"Reuven Malter."

"Reuven?" There was a pause. Then, "What's wrong?"

"Where have you been? I've been trying to get you for more than an hour."

"I just got back from—" He stopped. "I just walked in the door. What's wrong?" he said, his voice very tight.

"Michael called me tonight."

There was silence.

"Danny?"

"Yes," he said quietly. "I heard you. Michael called you tonight. Just a minute. Let me get my coat off." I heard the phone scrape against something. Then, "Go ahead. Michael called you tonight."

I told him about the phone call. He listened without interrupting me. Then he was quiet for a while.

"You did right to call me," he said.

"You can thank my father."

"We have to talk."

"Go ahead," I said.

"Not now. Not over the phone. I want to see you."

"When?"

"Tomorrow. Tomorrow night."

"Tomorrow night is fine."

"What time should I come over?"

I thought for a moment. "I'll come over to you. At eight. I want to see if you're really opening your window these days." Then I said, "How is Michael?"

"Michael is not good," Danny said quietly after a moment.

"I'll see you tomorrow night at eight o'clock," I said, and hung up the phone.

My father was standing by his bedroom door, wearing his pajamas. He nodded soberly when I told him what Danny had said, murmured good night, and went into his room.

The next day Rav Kalman called on me again. I read and explained, and he paced and listened. Occasionally he interrupted and asked me to clarify something I had said or a passage I had gone through too quickly. We fought for more than ten minutes over a difficult passage. I did not back off this time. Instead, I fought very hard, using passages from other tractates to buttress my argument and raising my voice to counter his words. I was talking loudly and excitedly and he let me go on unopposed for a moment and I saw him close his eyes and incline his head in my direction. He listened to me, his eyes closed. Then he opened his eyes and broke into my words. From now on I would sit in the front row, he said. I would sit between Schwartz and Steinberg in the front row, and I would not have to shout to make myself heard. He spoke without sarcasm, but I felt hot with anger and embarrassment.

I did not go directly to the coat racks after class. I went up to the third floor where there was a Judaica library which I rarely used; most of the books I needed for Talmud I could find in the synagogue bookcases; the others I either owned or borrowed from my father. It was a small library, the size of two classrooms, poorly lighted and musty with the odor of old bindings and yellowing pages. Its windows were rarely open, its walls needed paint, and its four reading tables were old and scarred. To my knowledge, it contained not a single work of modern, scientific Jewish scholarship.

The librarian was a short, wrinkled old man with a white beard, a dark skullcap, and nearsighted eyes behind thick glasses. I asked him if the library kept back copies of—and I named a newspaper. No, the library did not have that newspaper, he said. But he had his own copies of that newspaper around somewhere. Which issue did I want? I told him. He went to his desk in the corner of the library and looked through a mountainous disarray of books and papers. He found it and brought it over to me. He had meant to throw it out, he said. Yes, I could have it. I thanked him and stuffed it into a pocket. Then I went over to the catalogue. The file cards on Rav Kalman were almost an eighth of an inch thick. I flipped through them quickly. All of the books listed had been published before the war, some in Warsaw, most in Vilna. With only one exception, they dealt with matters of Jewish law. The exception was a book on ethics. I made out call slips for the work on ethics and three of the books on Jewish law which I selected at random. Fifteen minutes later I came out of the building with the four books in my hands. They were old, dusty books, with cracked bindings that crumbled at the edges. I was five minutes late for my logic class.

I had never been interested enough in Rav Kalman before to want to read any of his writings. Nor had he ever mentioned any of his writings to us in class. That night on the subway ride over to Danny's apartment I read his book on ethics.

✤✤✤✤✤✤✤✤✤✤✤✤✤✤✤✤✤✤✤✤✤✤✤✤

Seven

It was cold and dark and an icy wind blew along Broadway and up through the narrow side street where Danny lived, a fierce wind that came off the river, which I could not see for the darkness. The house was small, three stories, red brick, and old, very old. Five worn stone stairs, a badly fitting wooden front door, a tiny overheated foyer with mailboxes, buttons, and nameplates. I pressed the button over the name Saunders. There was a loud answering buzz. I pushed open the heavy inner door and started up the steep, carpeted, narrow staircase. The door closed with a loud click. It was a little before eight o'clock. Someone inside the house was frying bacon. The staircase was poorly lighted; the carpet was worn. It was a long climb up to the third floor.

Danny was waiting for me in his doorway. He had on a dark woolen sweater and dark trousers. There was a skullcap on his head. His face was pale and he blinked at me wearily from behind his black shell-rimmed glasses.

I took off my coat and hat. Danny put them into a closet. I put on my skullcap.

"Well," I said. "How are you?"

"I'm all right."

"What have you got that I can thaw out with?"

"Coffee."

"Kosher coffee?"

He smiled.

"It's good to see you," I said.

"Yes," he said quietly.

"The place is different. You've entered the twentieth century."

He did not say anything. He went over to his tiny kitchen and started preparing the coffee.

"I didn't know you liked abstract art," I said.

"I'm learning." His back was to me. He did not turn around.

"Very nice. New linoleum. Fresh paint. Very neat. And clean. It's a nice apartment when you keep it clean. And the window is open. Very nice. How did you like *Barefoot in Athens?*" I asked, looking at the handbill near the typewriter on the desk.

He turned then and followed my eyes to the handbill. "I liked it," he said, very quietly.

"I take cream and two sugars," I said.

He looked at me, then turned slowly away. I heard gas jets come to life with a tiny puff of sound.

I went over to the bookcase. It was the old bookcase I had seen in the apartment in the spring. Alongside it stood a new four-drawer gray filing cabinet. On the other side of the filing cabinet was a new bookcase. There were no books on the floor. The bookcases were filled with technical books and journals, all of them neatly arranged on the shelves. The new bookcase contained an entire set of the Talmud.

"It's about Socrates, isn't it? *Barefoot in Athens.*" I had gone over to his desk, which was covered with papers and books, and was looking at the handbill again.

"Yes," I heard Danny say as if from a very long distance away.

"Which Byrd is this? Admiral Byrd?" A book on his desk had caught my eye.

I thought I saw his shoulders stiffen. He spooned sugar into the cups. "Yes. Admiral Byrd."

"The explorer?" The book was titled *Alone.*

"Yes," he said.

I picked up the book, then noticed the titles of the two books on which it had been placed. One was *A Philoso-*

phy of Solitude by John Cooper Powys; the other was a fat little book of the sort published in the last century. It was called *Solitude*. The author's name was given as Zimmerman.

I put the Byrd book back down on the desk and stood there, trying to recall something. After a moment I gave up and crossed over to the sofa bed and sat down. It was soft and comfortable. I leaned back against the wall and looked at Danny, who was still standing in front of the sink, his back to me.

"How are you, Danny? How are you really?"

"Tired."

"You're always tired. Whenever I see you you're tired."

"It's the occupational disease of graduate school."

"How is your father?"

"My father is all right."

"How is Rachel?"

"Rachel is—fine."

"The water is boiling."

He turned off the flames, filled the cups, brought me one, and took the other with him over to the desk. He sat down on the chair in front of the desk and did not look at me.

"It's all right," I said quietly.

He looked at me then and blinked his eyes.

"It's all right," I said again.

"No. It's not all right."

"There was nothing there. We were good friends. We still are friends, I think. But there was nothing there, Danny."

"It's wrong. There isn't a thing that's right about it."

I sipped at my coffee. It was very hot.

"How does a Hasid go out on a date with a girl?" I asked.

Danny said nothing.

"We never talked about that."

He looked away. "There are some things you don't talk about."

"There's nothing people don't talk about these days."

"There are some things I don't talk about."

"Danny."

He looked at me.

"How long is it now?"

"Since November."

"Is it really serious?"

"Yes."

"Very serious?"

"Yes."

"On both sides?"

"More on her side than mine."

"Because she's a Gordon?"

"I don't give a damn about her being a Gordon."

"Your father will give a damn."

"I'm not worried about my father. I'm worried about Michael."

"Are you working with Michael? I thought someone called Altman is working with Michael."

"They're changing it. They're going to try something else. It's all wrong."

"You mean it's wrong professionally. Is that what you mean?"

"Yes."

I drank some more coffee. It was not so hot now as before.

"You have no idea what a mess this can become."

"No," I said. "I have no idea about that at all."

He drank some coffee and put the cup down on the desk next to the typewriter. The desk lamp shone on his face, bathing it in light and shadows. I saw him blink his eyes.

"You're making better coffee these days," I said.

"I'm learning."

"You're learning about a lot of things."

"Yes," he said.

"It's called motivation. That's what it's called, isn't it?"

He looked at me and blinked his eyes.

"You'll be a twentieth-century man before you know it."

"You are angry."

"No," I said. "I have no right to be angry. I'm not even surprised. There was nothing there."

"All right."

"Tell me about Michael."

He picked up his cup, sipped some coffee, and put it back down on the desk. "Michael is very sick," he said.

"Thanks. Now tell me something about Michael I don't already know."

"You're angry," he said. "I can't talk to you when you're angry."

I said nothing. I finished the coffee and put the cup down on the floor and leaned back against the wall. The window shade fluttered softly and scraped against the sill. A faint hissing sound came from the radiator near the desk.

"Tell me about Michael," I said quietly. "Will I be able to visit him?"

"Yes. I can arrange that now."

"He told me he's driving Altman crazy. He bragged about it."

"He's not driving him crazy. Professor Altman doesn't get driven crazy by his patients. He's a great therapist. But Michael isn't cooperating."

"What does he do?"

"He doesn't do anything. He comes into a therapy session and just sits there. Or he spouts dreams and fantasies that are absolute lies. He won't cooperate at all."

"Are you taking over the therapy?"

"Under very close supervision."

"Isn't that unusual?"

"Yes."

"They have recognized your genius."

"They're willing to try almost anything now. It's very serious with Michael."

"Because he's resisting therapy?"

"There have been fist fights. Between Michael and some of the other boys. He hates to be called only by his last name. Some of the boys have latched on to that. He hates to be called Gordon."

"Fist fights," I said. I could not imagine Michael in a fist fight.

"He kicked a boy in the groin. During a lunch hour. He pushed him out of the chair and kicked him."

"God," I said.

"He has sex fantasies about Rachel."

I stared.

"Those are the only fantasies he's told us about that we think are real."

"God," I said again. "Rachel."

"His father gave him a small Tanach." "Tanach" is the acronym for the Hebrew Bible. "He got hold of some matches a few days ago and burned it in the bathroom. One of the child-care people smelled the smoke. It was completely burned. Ashes."

I stared at him and did not say anything.

"Three days ago, Shabbos afternoon, he disappeared from the grounds. A child-care worker found him four blocks away, shouting obscenities at people coming out of a funeral parlor. You know what that does to the treatment center in terms of its relationship to the community? They're uneasy with us around to begin with. He's a very sick boy, your Michael. And we haven't the least notion of what it is that's bothering him."

"He doesn't like very Orthodox Jews. I know that bothers him."

"That's not what is really bothering him."

"The symptom, not the disease."

"Very good," he said. "Go to the head of the class."

"I remember something at least from your days with Freud."

"Those were different days," he said.

"Why different?"

"It's always easier to learn something than to use what you've learned."

I did not say anything.

"You're alone when you're learning. But you always use it on other people. It's different when there are other people involved."

I was quiet.

"You don't want to make mistakes with people. Sometimes when you make a mistake you lose a human soul." He used the Hebrew word "neshamah" for the soul, giving it his Ashkenazic pronunciation, "neshomeh," and accenting the "sho."

I did not say anything for a long time. The noise of the radiator seemed suddenly very loud. I felt the wall cold against the back of my neck and moved forward slightly on the sofa bed. Danny finished his coffee.

"What if you can't get through to him?" I asked.

He shrugged and said nothing.

"How much time do you have?"

"A month. Two months. It depends on whether there's any kind of progress."

"What if there's no progress?"

He did not say anything.

"What if there's no progress, Danny?"

He glanced down at his desk and said nothing.

"Will he have to be institutionalized?" I said.

He did not say anything.

"My God," I said. "My God."

We were silent. The shade scraped against the sill. Danny sat staring down at his desk.

"I could use another cup of coffee," I said.

Danny got to his feet and brought the cup over to the sink.

"Is it really all right for me to see him?"

"Yes."

"Do his parents know you'll be working with him?"

"Of course they know."

"The son of Reb Saunders working with the son of Abraham Gordon."

He came back with the coffee and went over to the desk and sat down. "I'm working with a human being," he said.

"Should I let him see that article by Rav Kalman? He wants me to bring it."

"Yes."

"It's a disgusting article."

"I read it."

"It's disgusting."

"The language is in bad taste."

"It's disgusting," I said.

"All right."

"You really want me to show it to him?"

"Yes."

I drank some coffee. "All because of a stupid carnival."

He looked at me. "Michael was sick long before that carnival. Crooks at carnivals don't make people sick. You have to be sick already to be affected that way."

"We had a beautiful time on that lake. He likes to read clouds. Did I tell you about that? He reads clouds."

"You told me."

I finished the coffee. "The summer seems very far away."

He was quiet.

"It is far away," I said. I put the empty coffee cup on the floor and leaned back against the wall and closed my eyes. I found I could not stop thinking about Michael. I heard the sounds of traffic and the vibrating hum of an aircraft. There was the lake again and Michael's thin body near the center board of the Sailfish and the gusting wind and clouds scudding smoothly across the blue sky. I sat there and thought about Michael. I could not stop thinking about Michael. Danny was talking to me. I opened my eyes and saw him talking to me but I could not hear the words. There was the wind on the lake moving against the Sailfish and Danny talking to me. I listened to him talking to me. He was asking about Rav Kalman. I told him about Rav Kalman. The back of my neck was against the wall. I felt the wall vibrating as the aircraft passed overhead. I told him about Rav Kalman, and saw Michael standing up in the roller coaster, his face to the wind, and pulling up on the center board of the Sailfish, the muscles bulging in his long thin arms, and it seemed the sofa bed moved in the wind.

"Nota Finkel?" Danny said. "Are you sure?"

"He was head of the Slobodka Yeshiva. He died in 1928."

"I've heard of Nota Finkel. He was a musar teacher Nathan Zvi Hirsch Finkel. Yes. He was a great anav."

"Anav" is the Hebrew word for a person of extreme modesty and gentleness.

"He was a great Talmudist and a great musar teacher and a great anav. He was all of these things. There was a rebellion. Have you heard about the rebellion?"

"What rebellion? Against Finkel?"

"In 1905. A rebellion of the students in the Slobodka Yeshiva. He mentions it in the introduction to the book. They wanted more freedom. They wanted the right to read secular books and periodicals and newspapers. They wanted secular studies introduced into the school. A rebellion in a yeshiva. The Slobodka Yeshiva no less."

"I didn't know anything about that."

"It's in the book. You know what happened to the great and gentle teacher of musar? He stopped being gentle. He excommunicated some of the students and made sure no one in town would sell them food or clothes or rent them a place to live. He talked other students into coming over on his side. The ones who wouldn't quit he had thrown out of town. End of rebellion."

"Rav Kalman couldn't have been in that rebellion. You said he's in his early forties."

"I didn't say he was in it. I said he writes about it. He explains and justifies Finkel's actions. It was for the sake of Torah, he says. It was in order to preserve Torah. I've got another Nota Finkel on my hands. Without the gentleness. A permanently ungentle Nota Finkel."

There was the cove and the smooth shallow water with the tall trees of the shoreline breaking the force of the wind and Michael lying on his back reading the clouds. There was the cove and the birds high overhead and the clouds white against the deep blue of the sky and the whisper of the wind through the trees, a loud whisper that was a roller coaster roar, and the sensation of dropping into the night.

"We are at war, friend. Didn't you know we are at war?"

Danny said nothing.

"The enemy surrounds us. The evil forces of secularism are everywhere. Look under the bed before you say the Kriat Shma at night. Look under the bed before you pray the Shacharit Service in the morning. And while you're at it check the books on your desk and look in your typewriter and close the window because they come in with the wind. Did you know they come in with the wind?"

"All right," Danny said quietly.

"The hell it's all right. We become like dead branches and last year's leaves and what the hell good are we for ourselves and the world in a mental ghetto. The hell it's all right."

Danny said nothing. There was a tense silence.

"I'll survive," I said.

He was quiet.

"If I can have another cup of coffee."

He smiled then and got slowly to his feet.

"One derives great moral strength from a cup of coffee," I said.

"Kosher coffee," Danny said.

"Yes, of course. Kosher coffee. Of course."

We talked over the third cup of coffee, about ourselves, about the past, and there was silence and more talk and silence again and more talk. That was the best cup of all, that third cup of coffee. It took us a very long time to drink it.

Then I was putting on my coat and hat and we were standing at the door.

"Are those books some kind of project?"

"Which books?"

"The Byrd and the Zimmerman and the other one. I don't remember the author's name. Powys, I think."

"Yes," he murmured. "A project."

"For class?"

"Something like that."

"For a moment there I thought you were planning to practice solitude."

He gave me a queer look.

"You won't have much solitude if you and Rachel are really serious."

He did not say anything.

"You'll call me about the visit."

"Yes."

"It was good to talk to you again, Danny."

We shook hands. I went down the narrow staircase and into the street. The air was bitter cold and the wind blew stiffly from the river. I went up the street to the subway. I sat in the subway and felt Rav Kalman's book in the pocket of my coat and took it out and began to reread the introduction. In the middle of the introduction I remembered Rachel telling me about Danny's allusion to the Kotzker Rebbe. It was the Kotzker Rebbe and his twenty years of solitude I had been trying to remember when I had seen the books in Danny's apartment. I sat there, staring down at Rav Kalman's book and no longer seeing the words. It was after eleven o'clock. There were six people in the subway car. The man sitting opposite me was drunk. It seemed a long ride home.

Eight

The next day Rav Kalman called on me again. I read a long and fairly uncomplicated passage and he let me go on without interruption. I took a little too much time explaining one of the medieval commentaries and he told me to read on, the commentary was simple. I read on and continued explaining. At one point he stood near the window, his head inclined toward me, listening. We came to a difficult passage and I explained it. He stopped me. "Explain it again, Malter." I explained it again. "Say again what the words mean, Malter." I said it again. "That is how you explain it?" I told him that was how most of the commentaries explained it. He paced back and forth. "Read on, Malter." I was in a nervous sweat by the time the shiur came to an end and got pitying glances from my classmates as we came out of the room.

He did not call on me the following day. He called on someone else.

I sat directly in front of his dark-wood desk and listened to the rain on the windows and the traffic on the wet asphalt street outside and the tense voice of the student who was reading. The student sat three seats away to my right, thin-shouldered, pale faced, bent over his open Talmud, his voice faintly quavering. He had been reading for the past twenty minutes. A moment after he had begun to read it had become painfully obvious that he had come into the shiur unprepared.

I had expected Rav Kalman to call on me again. He

entered the class promptly at one o'clock, walking very quickly, short, intense, immaculately dressed as always, starched white shirt, dark tie carefully knotted, trousers pressed. He had arranged his books on the desk, one piled neatly on top of the other, and had opened his Talmud and lit a cigarette, and had stood behind the desk, smoking, surveying the class intently, and tugging at his long dark beard. We all knew that the thing to do then was stare back at him whenever his eyes met yours because if you looked away it meant you had something to hide, you were unprepared, and you would be called on to read. I had felt his dark eyes on my face a long time and had not looked away. The student three seats to my right had looked away immediately. Now he was reading.

Rav Kalman smoked and paced and hurled questions. It had been an ugly twenty minutes so far.

"Also what?" Rav Kalman asked. "What does 'also' mean?"

The student struggled for an answer.

Rav Kalman moved in front of him. His voice was thick with sarcasm. "That is what it means? How can that be what it means? Say again, Greenfield, what does 'also' mean?"

Abe Greenfield finally managed to blurt out the answer. He was a fairly good Talmud student but it was obvious he was seeing the text for the first time. His face was pale and his eyes were frightened and filled with shame. He kept his eyes on the text and continued to read.

A moment later, Rav Kalman stopped him again. "Included with what?" he asked sharply. "What is Resh Lakish saying?"

Abe Greenfield stared down at his Talmud.

"Included with what?" Rav Kalman persisted.

I could see Abe Greenfield frantically scanning the commentary of Rashi.

"*Now* you study Rashi?" Rav Kalman said. "*Now*? In class you study Rashi?"

Abe Greenfield stared down at his Talmud.

"Did you prepare the Gemora, Greenfield?"

Abe Greenfield shook his head. He sat there, drenched in misery, and stared down at the Talmud and shook his head.

"Nu, at least you are not prepared. If you had prepared and did not know I would wonder what you are doing in my class." He paused. "Tell me, Greenfield, why are you not prepared?"

He had not had time to prepare, Abe Greenfield said in a very small voice.

I looked at him. Everyone looked at him.

Rav Kalman tugged at his beard. "You did not have time? What do you mean, you did not have time?"

Abe Greenfield stared down at his open Talmud and said nothing. I looked at him pityingly. He had said the one thing we all knew never to say to Rav Kalman, or to any Talmud teacher, for that matter.

"There is sickness in your family?" Rav Kalman was saying. "You were not well?"

"No."

"What do you mean, you did not have time?"

There was a math exam in his graduate-school class that afternoon, Abe Greenfield said. A very important exam. He had needed all his time to study for it. He spoke in English in a low, tremulous voice.

Rav Kalman slowly put out his cigarette in the ashtray on the desk. He brushed tiny specks of ashes from the top of his Talmud. He gazed at Abe Greenfield. "You have a mathematics examination," he said, his voice very cold. "You came unprepared to the shiur because of a mathematics examination?"

"It's a final," Abe Greenfield said. He was looking at Rav Kalman now. His face was pale but his lips had drawn tight. I looked around quickly. Everyone was staring at him. Abe Greenfield was the quietest student in the class. He had sat in that same seat for almost a year and a half now and had not said a word, except when called on to read. He was something of a genius at math. He had received a fellowship to the Massachusetts Institute of Technology but had decided to do his graduate work at

Hirsch and go on for smicha at the same time. He had wide glasses and large eyes and a somewhat pimply face. He was shy, withdrawn. He came and went in silence. He never spoke unless spoken to first, and then he responded haltingly, with a fixed smile on his thin lips and without gazing directly at the person to whom he spoke. Now he was staring at Rav Kalman. "This is the first time I'm unprepared," he said.

"The first time?" Rav Kalman said.

"Yes."

"I could understand if you were sick."

"I wasn't sick."

"For mathematics you take time from the study of Torah?"

Abe Greenfield said nothing. He scratched at the side of his face and sat there, staring back at Rav Kalman and saying nothing.

"How does one do such a thing?"

Abe Greenfield said nothing.

"How does one dare do such a thing?"

I saw Abe Greenfield sit up very straight in his seat then. His eyes seemed to bulge slightly behind his glasses. Still he said nothing.

"You made a choice, yes?" Rav Kalman said coldly. "You had for yourself a choice between the Gemora and mathematics, and you chose mathematics. Yes? You understand what it is to make a choice, Greenfield? A choice tells the world what is most important to a human being. When a man has a choice to make he chooses what is most important to him, and that choice tells the world what kind of a man he is. You understand me, Greenfield?"

Greenfield said nothing. I watched his hands. They were clenching and unclenching on top of the Talmud. There was a fixed, empty smile on his face now.

"So, Greenfield, you have told us what is most important to you. Between Gemora and mathematics, you chose mathematics."

Abe Greenfield said nothing. The room was deathly still.

"It is important to choose," Rav Kalman was saying.

"A man must be forced to choose. It is only when you are forced to choose that you know what is important to you. It is very clear, Greenfield, that the Gemora is not as important to you as mathematics."

Abe Greenfield scratched at a pimple on his face. "It's a final exam," he said. "It's the only time I've ever come unprepared." His face was tight but his voice came out whining.

"You made a choice," Rav Kalman said. "Yes? You made a choice."

Abe Greenfield squirmed on his seat.

Rav Kalman came right up to Abe Greenfield's desk and peered down at him. I wished he would leave him alone. He had made his point. Why couldn't he leave him alone now? Leave him alone, I thought. Can't you see how miserable he feels?

"Tell me something, Greenfield. You are trying to get a doctorate in mathematics?" He pronounced it "duk-tu-rot," with a hard "r." And he said it derisively.

"I'm trying," Abe Greenfield said in a tremulous voice.

"And how much time does it take to get a dukturot?"

"Years."

"Years. It takes years. And in all those years, how much time do you take from the study of Torah?"

Abe Greenfield said nothing.

Leave him alone, I thought. For God's sake, leave him alone. Of all the people to pick on.

"How much time do you take, Greenfield?"

Still Abe Greenfield said nothing. But a flush was rising on his face.

"You have no tongue? What happened to your tongue?"

There was a cruel relentlessness to him, and I found myself beginning to be angry. Choices. He had written about forcing people to make choices. I had read that in his book on ethics two nights ago during the subway ride over to Danny: "A man must sometimes be forced to make choices, for it is only by his choices that we know what a man truly is."

"How much time do you take, Greenfield?"

"What do you want from me?" Abe Greenfield said quietly.

"What do I want from you?"

"I studied for a math exam. Why is that so terrible?"

"You have made a choice."

"I don't know what you're talking about. I made a choice. *Once* I didn't come prepared. *Once.* In a year and a half, I didn't come prepared *once.*" His voice was rising. "What do you want from me? You're shaming me in public. You're shaming me in front of the whole class. What do you want from me?"

Rav Kalman gazed down at Abe Greenfield. He seemed surprised.

"It's wrong to shame someone in front of others. Why do you shame me like this?" His voice was quite high now, not loud, but high, straining. "You're making an example of me. You're using me. I'm not a child. We're not children. This isn't a European ghetto. You can't use me like that. You should apologize. You committed the sin of shaming me in public. You should at least apologize."

Rav Kalman stared at him.

"Apologize," Abe Greenfield said.

"Enough!" Rav Kalman shouted. "This is how you talk to your teacher?"

"You won't apologize?"

"Enough!"

"You won't apologize?"

Rav Kalman stared at him out of dark, narrow eyes and seemed unable to respond. His face was quite pale around the black beard. He put a finger to the knot of his tie, then went quickly to his desk and lit a cigarette. He held the cigarette in his fingers. His hands were shaking.

"You won't apologize?" Abe Greenfield said, his voice still rising. His eyes were wide and he was sitting on his seat, staring straight at Rav Kalman. Then he got slowly to his feet.

"Stop picking on me," he said, his voice suddenly very low.

Rav Kalman stared at him. There was a stir from the class.

"Stop picking on people," Abe Greenfield said, standing there among the front row of seats and looking fixedly at Rav Kalman. "Stop picking on people," he repeated.

"What does he say?" Rav Kalman asked, looking at the class. He did not understand the English expression to pick on someone.

"Pick on someone else. Pick on the goyim," Abe Greenfield said. He looked as though he no longer knew what he was saying.

"Respect," someone said loudly behind me in Yiddish.

"Sit down," someone else said.

"Leave us alone," Abe Greenfield said. "Scream at the goyim."

"How do you talk this way?" Rav Kalman said, trembling.

"How do you talk this way? How do you talk this way?" Abe Greenfield was imitating Rav Kalman in Yiddish. Then he went back to English. "I should have gone to the Massachusetts Institute of Technology. But my father wanted me to get smicha."

There was an angry murmur from the class.

"Sit down, Greenfield," Rav Kalman said. His voice shook. He seemed a little frightened. He touched the knot of his tie again and put the cigarette out in the ashtray with quick, nervous jabs. There were ashes on the desk. He ignored them. He seemed not to know what to do with Abe Greenfield.

"Sit down," someone in the class said again.

But he stood there, tense and taut and a little wild-looking. "You wasted ten minutes just now. You wasted hours all this year and last year. *That's* taking time from the study of Torah."

There was a loud stirring from the class. The student sitting to the right of Abe Greenfield tugged at his sleeve to get him to sit down. He shook off his hand.

"Shah!" Rav Kalman shouted at the class. He turned to Abe Greenfield. "Sit down," he said quietly. His voice was strangely soft. "Sit down," he said again. "I did not mean to upset you."

Abe Greenfield stared at him. I saw him blink his eyes. He seemed to come suddenly awake. He looked quickly around the room and became aware that he was the only one standing. He stared at the eyes that were staring at him. A look of enormous astonishment came over his thin face. Slowly, he sank into his seat and looked down at his open Talmud. I could see his hands trembling. Then, with an abrupt movement of his right hand, he closed his Talmud. He got to his feet and picked up the Talmud. His eyes were wet. He went through the room, stiffly and with dignity. The door closed quietly behind him.

There was a long moment of frozen silence. The rain fell loudly against the windows. Bedford Avenue looked drained of color, its asphalt glistening darkly in the heavy rain.

Rav Kalman pointed a finger at me. "Malter, go outside and see if he is all right."

I got quickly to my feet and walked between the chairs to the door.

"Malter."

I turned.

"Bring him back inside if he is all right. Tell him I asked that he come inside."

I went out into the corridor. He was not there. I went quickly through the marble entrance hall and pushed open the metal front doors and put my head outside. I felt the cold rain on my face. He was not anywhere in sight. I went back along the corridor and into the synagogue. I found him in the synagogue at one of the long tables near the coat racks. The synagogue was empty. Everyone was in class. We were the only ones there. He sat at the table and stared at the wall beyond the coat racks. He held his head in his hands and stared at the wall. I sat down next to him.

"How do you feel?"

He looked at me.

"Are you all right?"

He looked at me and did not seem to see me.

"Rav Kalman sent me to find out if you were all right."

He blinked. His pimply face was sallow. He looked a pathetic figure and seemed on the verge of tears.

"What did I do?" he said. "I just killed myself."

"Don't be silly."

"I didn't know what I was saying. My God, what did I do? My father will have a heart attack when he finds out."

"He doesn't have to find out."

"The whole world will know. How can he not find out? What did I do? It was like a dybbuk suddenly got into me. What did I do?" He was a graduate student in mathematics and he was talking about a dybbuk.

"Do you want some water?"

"Why did I do that? I don't understand why I did that. Something broke inside me. I could feel it break. It was a dybbuk. A dybbuk came inside me."

"You lost your temper."

"I just killed myself. How can I go home? My God, what happened to me?"

"Nothing happened to you. You lost your temper. Calm down. You'll be a wreck for your math exam if you don't calm down."

He looked at me.

"The math exam," I said. "You don't want to mess up your math exam."

"That's right," he muttered. "You're right."

"Okay," I said.

He took out his handkerchief, wiped his eyes and blew his nose, and put the handkerchief away.

"You feel better now?"

"Yeah."

"Then let's go back in."

He looked at me, startled.

"Rav Kalman asked me to bring you back inside."

"Are you crazy? I can't go back in there."

"Yes you can," I said.

"I can't go in there. What can I say to him?"

"You'll apologize after the shiur."

"Leave me alone. I can't go."

"Come on," I said. I took his arm.

"Leave me alone."

"All right," I said. "Are you through with Hirsch? Finished? All through? Because you lost your temper once? Because if you don't go back in you *are* through."

He stared at me miserably.

"Come on," I said.

"He'll cripple me if I go back in there."

"He'll cripple you if you don't."

He got slowly to his feet.

"You'll sit and you'll listen and you'll tell your dybbuk to stay the hell away. All right?"

He stared at me and did not say anything.

"Come on," I said quietly.

He walked alongside me, carrying his Talmud. We came together into the class. I saw heads turn. Rav Kalman was explaining a passage. He did not look at us. Abe Greenfield slid into his seat and opened his Talmud. Rav Kalman went on explaining. I took my seat. Everyone's eyes went back to Rav Kalman. He did not once look at Abe Greenfield. Someone else was reading now, a student in the back row. He read and answered questions. I forced myself back into the passages of Talmud. I sat there and listened and remembered Rav Kalman talking about choices and fought to keep my mind on the Talmud. A quarter of an hour before the end of the shiur he called on me to read a difficult three-line passage. He was asking me for the third time to explain the words when the bell rang. He dismissed us. Abe Greenfield remained behind as the class quickly emptied.

Half a dozen of us waited near the coat rack for almost twenty minutes until he came back into the synagogue. There was a grim look on his face.

"Well, he didn't cripple you," I said.

He reached for his coat.

"What happened?" someone asked.

"I apologized."

"For twenty minutes?"

"He gave me a musar message."

"Are you still in the class?" someone else asked.

He nodded gloomily.

"What did you do that for? You were crazy to do that."

Abe Greenfield put on his coat and hat. "I got a math exam," he said. "I got to go."

"What did you do that for? Why didn't you say you were sick?"

"I don't lie," Abe Greenfield said with dignity.

"What was the musar message?" I asked.

"Respect for teachers. And to make choices for Torah."

"That's all?"

"Yeah. He was very nice about it."

"*Nice?*" someone said. "*Nice?*"

"I got to go," Abe Greenfield said.

We watched him walk from the synagogue.

"What a jerk," the one next to me said. He used the uncomplimentary Yiddish word.

"Don't talk like that," Irving Goldberg said. He had been standing there all the time, silent and solemn.

"He's a jerk."

"That's dirty talk," Irving Goldberg said, using the Talmudic term "nibul peh."

"He's still a jerk."

"Rav Kalman was nice," someone else said. "Did you hear, Reuven? Rav Kalman was nice."

"I heard."

"He wasn't thrown out of the class, so Rav Kalman was nice."

"Maybe the Messiah has come," another student said. "Maybe we ought to look out the window. Does it say anywhere the Messiah will come when it rains?"

I was suddenly weary of their talk. I put on my coat and hat. I wanted to get away from there. I wanted to sit in my logic class and forget Rav Kalman. I went quickly from the synagogue. Passing Rav Gershenson's classroom,

I glanced through the small window in the door. He was sitting behind his desk and as usual about half a dozen students were standing intimately around him. I could hear his gentle voice through the door.

Outside I felt the cold winter rain on my face and raised the collar of my coat. The asphalt street was black and glistening. There were puddles on the sidewalk. A bus went by close to the curb and sprayed water onto my shoes. I turned into the adjoining brownstone and started up the stairs to my logic class. I was ten minutes late.

I sat near the window and listened to the rain and stared at the blackboard, which was being rapidly covered with symbols by my logic professor, a tall, dignified-looking man in his forties. He had a brown mustache and wore a tweed suit, and he spoke softly as he wrote on the board. I listened to him talk and copied symbols into my notebook and thought of Rav Kalman. I was sick of Rav Kalman, sick of being picked on, sick of watching him pick on others, sick of the oppressive Eastern European ghetto atmosphere of his class, sick of his fanatic zeal for Torah. I had about four months left until the smicha examinations. That was a long time. I would control myself and be very careful. I would take the examinations and be done with him. But I would have to be very careful in class. I sat there and thought a while longer of Rav Kalman, and then began to forget Rav Kalman because an interesting problem in logic was being put on the blackboard, and soon I had forgotten completely about Rav Kalman and was lost in the convolutions of set theory.

There was a message for me on the telephone stand in the hall when I got home that evening. Danny had called a few minutes earlier and wanted me to call him back at the apartment. The message was in my father's handwriting. I could hear his typewriter going in the study. He had begun working on another article. I put away my hat and coat and dialed Danny's number. The phone was picked up after the first ring. Danny had arranged for me to visit

Michael next Sunday at three o'clock. Was that okay? It was okay, I said.

"How is he?" I asked.

"You'll see for yourself."

"Are you working with him?"

"Yes."

"Well?"

"I don't know."

"What do you mean, you don't know?"

"I've only had him once."

"How was it?"

"He talked about you the whole hour."

"Are you seeing him again?"

"Tomorrow."

"Will you be there on Sunday?"

"No. Look, I've got to run. I've got a seminar in half an hour."

I hung up the phone and stood there a long time, staring down at it. Manya called us in to supper. I washed my hands and sat down at the kitchen table. My father was lost in thought, his mind on the article he was writing. I was not hungry. But I ate. With Manya inside that kitchen I always ate, whether I was hungry or not.

The next day Rav Kalman came into the classroom, arranged his books neatly on the desk, lit a cigarette, peered intently at our faces, and called on Abe Greenfield. There was a jubilant quality in Abe Greenfield's voice. He had expected to be called on and had come superbly prepared. He read excitedly for three quarters of an hour, showing off what he knew, and Rav Kalman paced and smoked and did not interrupt. Then he came up to Abe Greenfield's desk and stopped him.

"Very good, Greenfield. You came prepared and you know the Gemora. Very good."

Abe Greenfield's face shone with joy.

"Tell me, Greenfield. How did you do in your mathematics examination?"

Abe Greenfield's face darkened a little. "Okay," he said, guardedly.

Rav Kalman tugged at his beard and nodded. "In Europe I had a student who was a great mathematician. But he never came to class unprepared. In America students come unprepared because of mathematics. He died in Maidanek. The student. They killed all my students in Maidanek. But he was the best." He stood stiffly in front of Abe Greenfield's desk and looked out at the class. "I do not expect that American students will be like my students in Europe. But I expect that everyone will come to the shiur prepared. If there is a choice, I expect everyone to choose the Gemora. I received my smicha from one of the greatest scholars and saints in Europe. It is not only my name I will place on your smicha. My name carries the name of my teacher, Rav Zvi Hirsch Finkel, of blessed memory, and the name of his teacher—all through the generations of great teachers who handed down the smicha. Do you understand? If you must make a choice, make it for Torah. I cannot give you my smicha otherwise. I have a responsibility." He looked at Abe Greenfield. "You were angry at me yesterday, Greenfield. I made you angry, yes? You lost your temper at me and I accepted your apology. Now I must apologize for shaming you before the class. A teacher has a right to be angry at a student if he does not come prepared. Your mathematics professor would also be angry at you if you came unprepared. But I went too far with you, Greenfield. I apologize."

The class sat very still. I saw dust motes dancing in the rays of sunlight that came through the windows. Abe Greenfield's mouth had dropped open. A lot of mouths had dropped open.

"I did not want you to be so angry, Greenfield. I wanted you to understand what it means to make a choice for Torah. You understand now, yes? All right. Enough. We have spent enough time away from the study of Torah." He looked at me. "Are you prepared, Malter?"

I nodded.

"Yes. You are always prepared. You study philosophy but you are always prepared." He looked straight at me. "Schwartz, read the Gemora."

Stanley Schwartz, the tall heavy-set student who sat to my left, looked startled for a moment. Then he bent over his Talmud and commenced reading.

Half an hour later, Rav Kalman called on me to read. It was another difficult passage and I gave him all the major commentaries on it and sat there, listening to him ask me for the fourth time to explain the words again.

I took a deep breath and told him I couldn't explain it any better than the commentaries and that I didn't understand what was being gained by going over and over the same passage. I said it quietly and respectfully, though my voice quavered a little as the words came out.

Rav Kalman gave me a sharp look and for a long moment said nothing. Then he said, "You cannot explain the words?"

"I explained the words."

"You cannot explain the words better?"

I told him I didn't understand what he meant. Did he want me to explain them better than the Maharam and the Maharsha? I asked. Was he saying that the explanations given by the Maharam and the Maharsha were wrong? I spoke very respectfully. What did he mean by better? I asked. How could I explain them better than the commentaries?

He seemed a little startled by my words. He stood in silence for a moment, his face dark. Then he blinked his eyes and cleared his throat. "Go on, Malter," he said in a low voice. "Continue to read."

He had not answered my question.

I had no classes the next day, Friday, and I spent the morning and early afternoon at home working on a paper for one of my philosophy courses. A bulky package arrived in the mail from my father's publisher. It was addressed to my father and I would not open it. My father came back from his teaching shortly before two o'clock.

His hands trembled as he tore open the package. It contained ten copies of his book.

They lay on the desk in his study, covered with pale-blue dust jackets, and we looked down at them, and my father picked up one and held it in his hands and opened it and peered at the title page and riffled the pages and closed it and put it back down on the desk. His eyes were moist and his face shone and he stared down at the books and shook his head in disbelief. "So much work," he murmured. "So much work in those pages." Then he picked up a copy and turned pages quickly and read and nodded. "Yes, they made the correction," he said, smiling. "You caught it just in time, Reuven. They were able to correct it." He put the book down and sat behind his desk. "A book," he murmured. "It is only a book. But what it means to write a book."

I took a copy into my room and lay down on my bed and opened it. I held it close to my face and smelled the ink. I have always loved the smell of ink in a new book. I hoped I hadn't overlooked any errors while checking the galleys. I began to read. I was halfway through the fourth page when the phone rang.

It was Danny. He was calling to remind me of my visit to Michael on Sunday.

"Where are you?" I asked.

"Home." Home meant five blocks away in his parents' brownstone. "You want to come over tomorrow?" he asked after a moment.

I told him I planned to spend Shabbat reading my father's book which had just arrived in the mail.

He sounded very happy to hear that and asked me to send him a copy. I said I would bring a copy over during the week and leave it with his father.

"Bring it over next Friday afternoon," he said. "My father won't enjoy having to receive a book filled with scientific criticism."

"How is Michael?" I asked.

"So-so," he said. "He talked about you again the whole

second hour. You never told me you were that good at sailing."

"Does that mean he's not resisting therapy any more? I mean the fact that he's talking so much about me."

"I don't know what it means yet."

"How's Rachel?" I asked.

"I'm seeing her tomorrow night."

I did not say anything.

"Have a good Shabbos," Danny said.

"Shabbat shalom," I said.

Later, my father and I went to the small synagogue on Lee Avenue where we prayed the service that welcomes the Shabbat. It was dark when we returned home and a winter wind blew through the naked sycamores on our street. After dinner I took a copy of my father's book into the living room and sat by the light we kept burning all through Shabbat, and read. I read until late that night and all of Shabbat afternoon. I read very carefully, on a nervous hunt for errors that might have slipped by us but at the same time reading in order to study again what my father had written. I found no errors and more than half a dozen places where my father's words took on meanings I had not seen in them before. I marveled at his scholarship. I never ceased being amazed at his scholarship. It was a beautiful book, and I told him so as we sat down to supper.

His eyes shone behind their steel-rimmed spectacles.

"I couldn't find any mistakes," I said.

He had found one typographical error, he said. But it was insignificant and did not affect the meaning of his words.

"It's a beautiful book, abba," I said again. "Especially the introduction."

"We will see what others have to say," he murmured.

"You're not worried about critics?"

"A writer always worries about critics," he said. He looked up at the clock on the shelf over the refrigerator. "It is almost time for Ma'ariv. You are going out tonight, Reuven?"

"Yes."

"I have a Zionist meeting I must attend. You will be home late?"

"No. I want to be wide awake tomorrow."

"You will see Rachel there too?"

"I don't know. We have to ask Danny about Rachel."

He looked at me.

"That's right," I said.

"Danny and Rachel?" he asked, his eyes very wide.

"Danny Saunders and Rachel Gordon. Saunders and Gordon. Sodium and water. I don't know which is the sodium and which is the water. But it's sodium and water, all right."

"Danny and Rachel," he said again.

"Let's finish up and make Havdalah," I said.

Nine

A block away from the Hirsch Yeshiva, across the street, stood a Catholic church. At precisely eleven o'clock every Sunday morning the bells of that church would toll. They tolled every hour on the hour every Sunday morning, and we assumed they were tolling to announce the Mass. But we especially noted the eleven-o'clock tolling because it was then that Rav Kalman entered the class. He always came into the class together with the tolling of the bells.

That Sunday morning the bells tolled and the door opened and Rav Kalman entered the classroom, carrying his Talmud and the books of commentaries under his arms. The Talmud and the other volumes had old, worn brown or black bindings, and so the book with the blue dust jacket was easy to see. I watched him put the Talmud on the desk, then place the books of the commentaries neatly one on top of the other to the right of the Talmud, face down on the desk. He opened the Talmud, turned to the page we were on, and stood there, surveying the class. I sat in my seat, frozen, staring at my father's book.

He lit a cigarette and called on a student to read. Outside, Bedford Avenue was silent, deserted, its black surface glistening in the bright winter sunlight. I saw Rav Kalman glance at me. I looked down at my Talmud and tried to concentrate on the words. Rav Kalman stood behind his desk, smoking and listening to the student. Half an hour before the end of the shiur he sat down and put his hands against the sides of his face, elbows on the

174

desk, and sat very still. He said almost nothing during that entire two-hour period.

A minute before the end of the period, he looked up and told the student to stop reading. Then he said quietly to me, "I want to speak with you, Malter," and he dismissed the class.

I remained in my seat and he remained behind his desk and the students went quickly out and we were alone.

He closed his Talmud and I closed mine. He sat behind his desk, smoking and looking down at his closed Talmud. Sunlight came through the windows onto his tall black skullcap and pale features and dark beard and dark clothes and starched white shirt. The almost milk-white fingers of his right hand drummed soundlessly on the Talmud, the two misshapen fingers moving up and down together as if operated by a single set of muscles and tendons. His eyes were dark and narrow.

"I do not know what to do with you, Malter," he said. He was silent a moment. "I have never experienced such a problem." He was silent again. Then he said, "Tell me, Malter. This is the book you were working on in the Zechariah Frankel Seminary?"

I heard myself say, "Yes."

"Tell me again what you did for the book."

I told him I had checked my father's footnotes and had gone over the many variant readings he had cited in the book to make certain the quotations were accurate.

"You are familiar with all the manuscripts your father brings in the book?"

"Yes."

"And you are familiar with all the works by other scholars your father quotes?"

"Yes."

"You have studied these works?"

"I know about them. I haven't studied them carefully."

"You study Gemora with your father?"

"Yes."

"And the Gemora you prepare for the shiur, you also study that Gemora with your father?"

"No. I prepare by myself."

"But sometimes when there is a problem with the Gemora you discuss it with your father, yes?"

"Yes."

"And sometimes he solves the problem by changing the words?"

"Sometimes."

"You know this method of studying Gemora?"

"Yes."

"Tell me, Malter, why do you never use this method in my shiur?"

I stared at him.

"Because Gemora is not studied this way in a yeshiva? That is the reason?"

"Yes."

He nodded slowly and was silent a moment, his fingers drumming soundlessly on the Talmud. "I have read your father's book, Malter. I discovered I knew enough English to be able to read it. It was easier for me to read than the works of Gordon. But I did not understand the Greek words your father uses. Tell me, Malter, you understand Greek?"

"A little," I said.

"You understand the Greek in your father's book?"

"Yes."

"Then I will ask you to explain some things to me. There are explanations based upon Greek words, and I would like to understand what your father is saying. Come, bring a chair over here, Malter, and sit beside me. You will teach me what your father is saying."

I moved a chair next to him behind the desk and sat down. I felt the blood beating in my head but I sat very quietly and watched him open my father's book to one of the very technical scholarly essays that dealt with a passage of Talmud that contained a number of Greek words written in Hebrew letters.

"That is a very difficult inyan, Malter. I have never clearly understood that inyan. Your father writes at the end of this chapter that the inyan is very clear to him.

Explain it to me, Malter. How does your father make clear the inyan?"

The article only cited the difficult passage. But I knew by heart the entire Talmudic discussion in which that passage was located. I reviewed the discussion that led up to the passage. He listened intently. I reviewed some of the remarks of the commentaries on various points in the discussion. Then I read the passage with the Greek words and showed him how the commentaries had struggled with it because they had not known Greek. They had simply not known what to do with the words. Then I explained the meaning of the Greek words and showed him how simple the passage was once the Greek was understood.

He stared down at the book in silence, his fingers tapping soundlessly on the Talmud, the two misshapen fingers moving together up and down.

"You are saying to me that your father understands the Gemora better than the Rishonim?" "Rishonim" is the Hebrew term for the earliest and greatest of the medieval commentators on the Talmud.

I hesitated for a moment. "He understands it differently," I said.

He gazed at me narrowly. "If an understanding of the passage is based on a knowledge of Greek and if the Rishonim did not know Greek, then your father understands the Gemora better than the Rishonim."

I did not respond to that. In a yeshiva you never said that a contemporary scholar could understand Talmud better than the Rishonim.

There was an uncomfortable silence. I looked away from him and down at his fingers drumming soundlessly on the Talmud.

"Let me ask you something else, Malter. In this chapter your father explains an inyan by changing the words of the Gemora. Explain to me why it is necessary to change the words in order to understand the inyan."

It was a fairly simple passage and it seemed quite clear to me that an easily identifiable scribal error had been made at one point by someone who had been copying the text. I explained it to him.

"How can you change the words of the Gemora? Just like that you change the words of the Gemora? By what authority does your father change words?"

"A lot of the commentaries changed words. The Vilna Gaon was always changing words he thought were wrong." Rabbi Elijah of Vilna, who is known as the Vilna Gaon, was the greatest Talmudist of the eighteenth century. "There's nothing new about changing words in the Talmud," I said.

Rav Kalman raised his eyebrows. "The Vilna Gaon? You are comparing your father to the Vilna Gaon?"

I had expected that question. No one in the present could possibly be compared in depth of learning to the great ones of the past. So the works of the commentators of the past had to be accepted as valid for the present; and the liberties these commentators had taken with the text could not be practiced today because no one equaled them in knowledge. You could never say that a great contemporary Bible scholar had a better knowledge of the Bible than, say, Rashi, who was one of the greatest medieval commentators on the Bible; nor could you say that a modern scholar of the Talmud knew more than the accepted classical commentators on the Talmud. I knew that attitude, and so I said nothing to Rav Kalman's remark.

We spent the next few minutes going over some additional passages in my father's book. I was beginning to feel quite uncomfortable. This was the first time I had ever used this method of study at Hirsch, and it felt strange and awkward, and I kept glancing at the door and worrying about someone suddenly coming into the room and seeing us studying my father's book.

We sat there almost an hour. Then Rav Kalman closed the book face down on the desk. He stroked his beard and gazed at me intently, then lit a cigarette and dropped the match carefully into the ashtray.

"I see you know this method very well, Malter. Your father has taught you well." He inhaled deeply on the cigarette. Smoke curled from his mouth and nostrils as he spoke. "I also see you enjoy this method of study. That is very clear to me. Tell me, Malter, do you believe the written Torah is from heaven?" He was asking me if I believed the Pentateuch had been revealed by God to Moses at Sinai.

I hesitated a moment. Then I said, "Yes."

He had noticed my hesitation. I saw by the sudden stiffening of his shoulders that he had noticed it. "You believe that every word in the Torah was revealed by God blessed by He to Moses at Sinai?"

"I believe the Torah was revealed," I said carefully. My own understanding of the revelation was based on enough sources within the tradition for me to be able to answer that question affirmatively even though I knew mine could not be the same kind of understanding as Rav Kalman's.

"Do you believe the oral Torah was also given to Moses at Sinai?" He was asking me whether I believed the various discussions of the Talmud had also been revealed by God to Moses at Sinai. He was putting me through a theological loyalty test.

"No," I said.

"No? Then what is the Gemora?"

"It was created by great men who based their traditions and arguments on the Chumash." "Chumash" is the Hebrew word for the Pentateuch.

"You believe this?"

"Yes."

"That is why you use this method?"

"Yes."

"And your father believes this too?"

"Yes."

"Tell me, Malter, your father is an observer of the Commandments?"

"Yes," I said emphatically.

He nodded. "So have I heard," he said. He stroked his beard and shook his head. "I am afraid I really do not know what to do with you, Malter." He shook his head again. "I have never had such a problem. Tell me, Malter, do you know who you are? Who are you?"

I looked at him in bewilderment.

"The holy Rav Yisroel Salanter used to say, 'Know yourself.' " He was talking about the nineteenth-century European rabbi who was the founder of the musar movement. "A person must know who he is. A person must understand himself, improve himself, learn his weaknesses in order to overcome them. It is hard for a person to understand his own weaknesses. I know. Do you know yourself, Malter? Where do you stand? Do you stand with true Yiddishkeit, or do you stand perhaps a little bit on the path of Gordon? Where do you stand, Malter?"

I did not say anything.

"I must know where you stand before I can give you smicha. Can you tell me?"

I was quiet.

"You cannot tell me anything?"

Still I was quiet.

"Know yourself, Malter. A man who does not know himself is lost. I know this. From bitter experience I know this. You do not have to tell me now, Malter. But you will have to tell me before I give you smicha. I will not give you smicha unless I have an answer from you. The Hasidim are not the only ones who guard the spark. I too have an obligation." It was a moment before I understood the significance of that remark. "I cannot give smicha to someone who does not stand with true Yiddishkeit, no matter how great a Gemora student he is. Do you understand me?"

I nodded.

"I would like to give you smicha, Malter. But I will not give it to you before I know where you stand." He stared darkly at my father's book and was quiet for a moment. "Your father is a great scholar. It is a pity he uses such a method. He endangers Yiddishkeit with his method." He looked at me sadly. "We will talk again another time, Malter. Do you have any questions you wish to ask me?"

I shook my head.

"No questions. All right. You may go now."

I got to my feet, picked up my Talmud, and started from the room. My legs were trembling.

"Malter."

I turned to look at him. He was seated behind the desk. He seemed strangely small and a little forlorn.

"Speak to me anytime you wish," he said stiffly. "I am not so difficult to speak to as it sometimes appears."

I nodded and left him at his desk and closed the door softly behind me and leaned heavily against it to steady my legs. The corridor was deserted. The building seemed empty. It was a moment before I remembered my visit with Michael. I looked at my wristwatch. It was a little after two o'clock. I got my coat and hat and came out of the building into the bright sunlight. The sky was a deep, clear, cloudless blue.

I got to the station just as a train was pulling out and had to wait more than ten minutes for the next train because of the Sunday subway schedule. I sat in the train and barely knew where I was and felt dazed and shaken and did not know what I would do. I wanted to talk to my father. The train roared along its tracks. I thought of Rav Kalman. Know yourself. I thought of Rav Kalman and listened to the clacking of the wheels. The car hurtled around curves and I braced my feet and felt my body swaying. Know yourself. He was forcing me into a choice and I did not know what I could do. The train stopped at a station, then pulled out again, picking up speed swiftly. I closed my eyes and listened to the wheels and felt my body swaying with the motions of the car. We went around a curve and there was a sudden fierce crescendo of screeching wheels and I thought I heard distant screams and shouts from the other passengers and a wild laugh and I opened my eyes and they were all in their seats and I did not close my eyes again the rest of that trip.

It was ten after three when the train pulled into my station. I got off quickly and ran through the station and up the stairs into the street. There was a wind now and it was cold and I pulled up the collar of my coat and walked very quickly through a quiet residential area with wide front lawns and expensive homes and old trees along the sidewalks and children on bicycles in the streets, and then crossed to a block where a low stone fence ran around an old rambling graystone house set deep on a huge rolling lawn studded with trees and flower beds and laced with tiny gravel paths. There were cars parked all along the side of the street adjacent to the open front gate. Set into the low stone fence to the right of the gate was a small metal plaque that had carved into it the words THE ROBERT H. SELBY RESIDENTIAL TREATMENT CENTER FOR CHILDREN. A gray-uniformed guard stood by the front gate but he barely glanced at me as I went in. There were benches along the paths on the lawn and on some of those benches I saw couples sitting with children who looked to be in their young teens. I went quickly up one of the paths toward the house. I saw children strolling among the trees with adults. I did not see any other uniformed guards.

The house was quite large, with wide stone front steps topped by an overhang supported by huge white-painted colonnades. It had three stories, a gabled roof, tall windows trimmed in white, a huge wooden double door in front with large brass hinges and knobs. It seemed a lovely old house, obviously very well kept up, and there were shrubs all around it and more flower beds and tall trees behind it, and people kept going in and coming out of it, and it did not look at all like a place for the sick.

I went up the wide stone stairs and through the wooden front door and found myself in a large carpeted foyer with paintings of New England winter scenes on the walls. Near the end of the foyer, and against the right wall, was a small desk behind which sat a man in his middle twenties wearing a dark suit and dark horn-rimmed glasses. He glanced at me as I made my way through the foyer and asked very politely if he could be of any help. I told him I had come to visit Michael Gordon and gave him my name. He consulted some cards on his desk and smiled.

"Michael is waiting for you right inside. Have a pleasant visit."

The foyer led directly into a huge living room with a beamed ceiling and a dark-green carpet and couches and easy chairs and pale-green drapes on the windows and more New England winter landscapes on the walls, which were paneled with oak. Set into the wall to the left of the entrance was a huge stone fireplace with a protruding mantelpiece. On top of the mantelpiece was a large model of a schooner, its sails white, its hull and masts a deep reddish brown. At the far end of the room was a wide wooden staircase carpeted in green and winding upward to the floor above. The banister of the staircase was built of intricately carved oak. There were adults and young teen-age boys sitting around on the couches and easy chairs, talking in quiet voices. They seemed relaxed and quite at ease. I removed my hat and coat and held them in my hands.

I stood just inside the entrance to the living room and scanned the room, searching for Michael. I saw a boy seated in an easy chair across the room near one of the windows reading a magazine. I looked around the room but could not find Michael. It was twenty-five minutes past three. He had waited for me and gone. I wondered where he might be and was about to turn back to the desk in the foyer when I heard someone behind me say, "You're here to visit Michael Gordon?"

It was the man who had been at the desk. He came alongside me and regarded me curiously.

I told him I didn't see Michael anywhere in the room.

"He's right there near the window." He pointed to the boy with the magazine. I stared and felt my heart turn over. I had not recognized him. His hair was cut and he had lost at least ten pounds and I had not seen him in about four months and now I had not recognized him.

"Thank you," I said, and went quickly through the room and up to Michael. He did not see me come over. He sat leafing through the magazine, his long face very pale, his glasses down along the bridge of his straight nose, all of him looking gaunt and dejected and lonely. The laces of his black shoes were untied. He sat hunched over the magazine, his thin body curved over it, and he turned pages mechanically and seemed not to be reading at all.

I stood behind the chair.

"Michael," I said softly.

He looked up immediately.

"Hello," I said.

He jumped to his feet and the magazine fell to the floor and his face broke into a radiant smile.

"I thought you forgot. I thought you weren't—" He stopped and smiled and laughed and seemed not to know what to do with his joy.

"I'm sorry to be late. It's good to see you, Michael." I offered him my hand. He seemed a little embarrassed to be shaking hands in an adult way. I looked around. Some of the people were gazing at us curiously. I saw one of the young teen-agers, a dark-haired, sullen-faced boy, turn to the man sitting next to him and nod toward Michael and say something softly. The man looked at Michael, then looked away.

"Let's sit down somewhere," I said. "Over there on the couch. How are you, Michael? You've lost weight. How are you feeling? What's wrong?"

"I don't want to talk to you here."

"Where do you want to go?"

"Let's go to my room. We'll be alone there."

"Is it all right?"

"Sure. We can go anywhere we want. We just can't go off the grounds."

I followed him through the living room to the staircase. He walked quickly. His clothes were too large on him. His jacket hung loose at the shoulders. He stopped at the foot of the stairs and pointed to the corridor that led off to the right. It was brightly lit and carpeted in dark green and lined with offices.

"Your friend has his office here," Michael said. "The third office on the left. That's where we meet."

"Where do the big doors lead?"

"That's a recreation room. Then there's a dining room

on the other side of the stairs. They serve kosher food if you want. They make it up special for me."

"Where do you go to school?"

"There's a separate building out back. You know what they call this house? A cottage. There's a married couple that live here and take care of us. They're supposed to be like our parents. Then there are four men who come in every day, but they don't live here. A cottage. That's very funny."

"It looks like a beautiful house."

"You think so?"

"Yes."

"I hate it. Let's go upstairs."

I followed him up the winding carpeted stairway. We went through a double door and down a wide corridor. He stopped in front of a door.

"The person on night duty stays here. There's a phone inside. That's where I called you from. Come on. We'll go to my room. Did you bring that article by Rav Kalman?"

"Yes."

"My room's two doors away."

"Do you live in it alone?"

"Yes."

"Well, that's very nice."

"I hate living alone," he said.

His door was unlocked. It was a small room but very clean and neat, with white-painted walls and a rug on the floor and a bed against a wall and a chest of drawers and a bookcase across from the bed. There was a deep closet, and prints of New England landscapes on the walls. A single tall window divided the wall opposite the door. The window was covered by a heavy iron screen. To the right of the window stood a long, black, gleaming telescope mounted on a tripod. Near the door was a desk and a chair. In a corner of the room was a second chair. The room was quite warm and smelled vaguely of disinfectant.

Michael sat on the bed and I brought over the corner chair and sat next to him.

"Well, how are you? Tell me really how you are."

"I don't know," he said quietly, not looking at me.

"How have your talks been with my friend?"

"Let me see that article," he said, turning to me abruptly.

"Don't you want to tell me about yourself first?"

"No."

"I'd like you to."

"I want to see that article."

"All right." I took it out of my jacket pocket and handed it to him. He snatched it from my hand and read it hungrily. I could see his eyes racing across the printed lines. His pale face was without expression. He gave it back to me and lay down on the bed and put the palms of his hands under his head and stared up at the ceiling.

"You see what I mean now?" he said softly. "You see how vicious he is."

I did not say anything.

"Why don't they leave us alone? What do they want from us?"

"How did you know about the article?"

"My aunt and uncle were talking about it outside the door on a visit. He told her not to mention it to me."

"It's very warm in here, Michael. Can we open the window?"

"I have to call someone in to do that. They lock the screen from the inside. I can't open it myself."

I stared at the screen and saw the lock. I had not noticed it before.

"Do you want to go for a walk?" Michael said. "We could go for a walk and I could show you the grounds."

"If you want to."

"I hate this room anyway. Let's go for a walk."

I put on my coat and hat and he put on a knee-length dark-blue winter jacket and we went downstairs and out of the building. It was cold outside and there was a wind. The sun was pale on the tall winter trees. We walked along a narrow path between the trees. There were dead leaves on the ground. The hedges were trimmed and there were shallow grooves on the sides of the paths between the gravel and the year-round grass. We passed a one-story gray-brick building with large plate-glass windows, and I could see dark-green blackboards and beige walls and new desk chairs. Michael said nothing as we went by. He walked slightly stooped over, his eyes gazing at the ground near his feet. There were not many people outside now. I listened to the wind in the branches of the trees. We walked in silence and came to a small round structure set in among the trees, a lovely pagoda-like structure without walls and with a white circular bench attached to the carved red beams that supported its sharply slanting Oriental-style red roof. Michael stopped and looked at it and I saw his eyes become moist and dreamy, and he pushed his glasses up along the bridge of his nose, then stood very still, his hands deep inside the pockets of his coat.

"It's very pretty," I said.

"It's beautiful," he murmured. "It's my house."

I did not look at him. "Do you live in it?" I asked.

"Not yet. But it's my house. I'm going to live in it one day soon."

"Are you going to live in it alone?"

"No. I hate being alone. I only like being alone when I'm outside."

"Who is going to live in it with you?"

"Rachel."

I kept my eyes on the pagoda and did not look at him.

"We're going to live in it and I'm going to take care of her." His voice had a distant dreamy sound to it. "She took care of me all those years and I'm going to take care of her."

"When did she take care of you?"

"She was very nice when she took care of me. She really worries about me. And I'm going to worry about her and take care of her. You can visit us sometimes if you want, Reuven. Yes, I'd like that. You can visit us if you want. Maybe Rachel will even stay with your children one day when you're married and you go away on a trip. I used to love to have Rachel stay with me when my parents were traveling to lectures or conferences."

"Does your mother always travel with your father?"

"Yes. Ever since his heart attack."

"And your father does a lot of traveling?"

"He lectures to Jewish students in universities. He comes home very tired and very sad. He's afraid religion is going to die. Yes, I'd like you to visit us, Reuven. That would be very nice. Would you promise to visit us?"

"Sure," I said, still not looking at him.

"I could set up my telescope right there in that clearing and I could show you the constellations. I never showed you the constellations, did I, Reuven. But I dream a lot that we go sailing right off the lake and into the sky and I show you the stars. But those are only dreams. How long has it been since we went sailing, Reuven?"

"About four months."

"Four months? Has it been four months?" He was silent a moment. I could hear the winter wind in the trees. It was very cold now and the sky was pale with the oncoming evening. I saw Michael bend down and pick up a dead leaf and hold it in his hand. It was a sycamore leaf, brown and brittle and papery with death, and he held it in his left hand and with the thumb and forefinger of his right hand he tore a piece of it away and ground it to dust between his fingers. He looked at me.

"Why did they put me in here?" he asked quietly. "What do they want me to do?"

I did not say anything. He tore away another piece of the leaf.

"I don't understand what I'm supposed to do."

"People are trying to help you, Michael."

"But what am I supposed to do?"

"Why don't you talk to Danny—to Mr. Saunders about it."

"Mr. Saunders. He's nice. I like him. Does he always wear a skullcap? He's very religious. I think he's more religious than you are. But he's honest and I like him."

"Then talk to him, Michael."

"About what? What do they want me to talk about?"

"Aren't there things that are bothering you?"

"I can't talk about that."

"Why not?"

"I can't."

"But why not, Michael?"

"I don't know. I can't." He tore off another piece of the leaf and shredded it between his fingers. "Listen, Reuven. I want to go home. Can't you tell them to let me go home?"

"I can't do anything like that, Michael."

"How do I get out of here? Am I supposed to be here all my life?"

"Talk to Mr. Saunders about it."

"You won't help me?"

"I think we had better go back. It's getting dark."

"Okay," he said quietly. He closed the palm of his left hand over the remaining portion of the leaf and crushed it and let it fall slowly to the ground. He looked at the pagoda. "I don't think I'm going to invite you to visit us. I don't think I'd want that at all."

He walked off. I followed behind him. A few feet before the wide stone staircase in front of the house, he stopped abruptly and turned to me.

"Did you read that article?"

"Rav Kalman's?"

"Did you read it?"

"Of course."

"Why does he say those things about my father?"

"He disagrees with him, Michael."

"But why does he have to say those things about him? My father is killing himself for religion. Why does he say those things?"

"That's the way Rav Kalman expresses himself, Michael. You shouldn't take it so seriously."

"But they're all like that, Reuven. Why are they all like that?"

I did not say anything.

"I don't understand it. I don't understand any of it."

He started up the stone stairway. I walked alongside him. We were almost to the wooden double door at the head of the stairs when it was opened from inside and Ruth and Abraham Gordon came quickly out. Michael saw them and ran up the few remaining steps and I saw Abraham Gordon, hatless, his coat collar raised—I saw Abraham Gordon spread his arms wide and then close his arms around his son in a tight embrace. They embraced a long time and Abraham Gordon kissed his son on the forehead and then Michael embraced his mother and kissed her and I could see they were all fighting back their tears. Abraham Gordon put his arm around Michael's shoulders and turned his head to me and nodded toward the door, and I followed them through the door and the foyer and into the living room. We sat on a couch near one of the windows. The living room was almost empty. I sat very still and listened to Michael and his parents talk. Did he need anything? his mother asked him gently. She looked very beautiful in a dark-blue woolen suit and a small white hat over her chestnut hair. But she seemed fatigued and there were dark circles under her eyes. No, he did not need anything, Michael replied. Why wasn't he eating? she asked. Michael stared down at the carpeted floor and was silent. Had he read the Hebrew books they brought him last time? his father asked. Not yet, Michael said. Did he want any more books on astronomy? Yes. Was he able to use his telescope? Sometimes. The talk moved on to the activities of relatives and friends. They talked quietly together, intimate family talk, and finally Ruth Gordon turned to me and asked how the visit had been, and before I could respond Michael said, "It was a wonderful visit. Reuven promised to come next Sunday too. Didn't you, Reuven?"

I had made no such promise. But I nodded.

"I'm so very pleased you had a good visit," Ruth Gordon said.

"When can I go home?" Michael asked suddenly.

Abraham and Ruth Gordon looked at each other uncomfortably.

"Not for a while yet," Abraham Gordon said quietly.

Michael did not ask them again. They talked a while longer about some of the trips Abraham Gordon was making to universities and the book he was writing and how Mother was up very late every night editing the manuscript and how much they missed him. They loved him very much and concealed none of their feelings from him and at one point there were tears in all their eyes and Ruth Gordon cried silently and Abraham Gordon put his arm around her shoulders and Michael looked at his mother and I saw tears flowing down his cheeks.

Then we were putting on our coats and Michael came with us to the door. We stood inside the foyer. Michael embraced his parents. I shook his hand.

"Will you come next week, Reuven?" he asked eagerly.

"Sure."

"Maybe you can stay late and we can look at the stars through my telescope."

"I can't next week, Michael. It's the first night of Hanukkah. I'll want to be home with my father."

"That's right," Abraham Gordon said. "We'll light the candles in your room, Michael."

"They won't let you. You can't have any kind of matches or fires in the rooms."

Abraham Gordon stared at him. Ruth Gordon looked down at the floor.

"We'll arrange something, son. We'll stay until the candles go out."

"Reuven, will you have dinner with us sometime during Hanukkah?" Ruth Gordon asked.

I looked at her.

"We would so like to have you. A week from tomorrow night."

I saw Michael looking at me.

"We've hardly even talked," she said. "Do have dinner with us next Monday night."

Michael was looking at me intently, his blue eyes narrow. I did not know what to say.

"Reuven is a busy young man," Abraham Gordon said.

I felt Michael's eyes on my face. It was quite warm in the foyer and I was sweating inside my coat.

I told them I would be very happy to accept their invitation.

Michael's face broke into a delighted smile and I saw his eyes shining. He looked suddenly a different person. His parents saw it too. I was not certain I understood why, but there was the same light in his eyes now I had seen during the times we had gone sailing—that private blinding sun shining out again from behind his eyes. And he was still looking like that when his parents and I went out the door.

We came silently down the stone stairs and walked through the grounds to the street. The sky was very pale now with the last remnants of the day's light.

"I owe you a great deal, Reuven," Abraham Gordon said quietly.

I told him he didn't owe me anything.

"Everything gets balanced out sooner or later," he said. "One day I'll be able to repay you."

I was quiet. His round, fleshy face was red with cold. He had his hands in his pockets and the coat collar up around his neck.

"How well do you know Daniel Saunders?" he asked softly.

I told him I knew him very well.

"Are you still very close?"

"Yes. I don't get to see him too often though."

"He's incredibly brilliant. Tell me something. Why did he rebel against taking his father's position?"

"He wanted to study psychology."

"Why?"

"He liked it."

"He is still very much a Hasid, isn't he? Except for the beard and the clothes."

"Yes."

"But he seems an enlightened Hasid, almost a Lubavitcher."

"I suppose so."

"I have great regard for the Lubavitcher Hasidim. They're not afraid of the twentieth century."

"I suppose he thinks a lot like the Lubavitcher Hasidim."

"He might not have rebelled were his father a Lubavitcher."

"I don't know. I think he would have rebelled anyway."

"Yes?"

"His mind forced him to rebel."

"His mind."

"He felt trapped."

"His mind felt trapped?"

"Yes."

"That's interesting. I have the impression it was his soul that felt trapped."

I looked at him.

"It's his soul that interests me, not his mind." He smiled sadly. "Does that sound strange coming from Abraham Gordon?"

"Abe, we can talk on Monday night," Ruth Gordon broke in quietly. "There's the meeting we must get to."

"That's right. Also, I'm freezing. I should have listened to you and put on my long underwear. I don't listen to her enough, Reuven. Good night."

I watched them walk up the street, two very tall people, walking quickly and close together, their dark coats looking fused in the disappearing twilight.

I got home after six o'clock. My father was eating supper. I washed my hands and sat down at the kitchen table and received one of Manya's stern frowns, my reward for coming late. The frowns got darker and more frequent as I ate and told my father all that had happened that day. Manya had definite ideas about how her meals were to be eaten. They excluded excessive conversation. It was bad for the stomach and it let the food get cold.

I ate and talked and my father ate and listened and Manya stood in front of the stove and frowned.

"I thought it would come to that, Reuven," my father said quietly after a brief silence. "I am not surprised. The influence of those who came after the war is felt everywhere. I am only surprised it did not happen sooner. Reuven, you will have dinner with the Gordons?"

"Yes. I couldn't say no. You had to have seen Michael's face."

He was silent.

"What do I do?"

"What do you do? I do not know what to tell you. You must make your own choice. You are a man, not a child, and a man must make his own choice." He seemed strangely tense and resigned. "I cannot help you, Reuven."

"I want smicha. But I'm not going to lie to get it."

"They are so rigid," he said in a sudden angry voice. "Why do they not see that this rigidity turns away our greatest minds?" His face was gray. "Our greatest young minds," he said. "We lose the best we have."

Manya turned to look at him. I saw him put his hand over his chest.

"Are you all right, abba?"

Manya said something to him in Russian. He responded in Russian. She went quickly from the kitchen.

"What's the matter?" I said. "What's wrong?"

He closed his eyes and sat in the chair and did not answer. Manya returned with a bottle of pills, babbling excitedly in Russian. He swallowed a pill and some water. He sat quietly for a moment, his eyes closed. Then he took a deep breath and opened his eyes.

"Nothing," he said. "A spasm. I am fine."

I sat there and stared at him. Manya said something in Russian to both of us. My father smiled again and picked up his fork.

"No more talking," he said. "Until we are done eating. Very strict orders."

"Are you all right now?"

"Yes."

"Should I call Dr. Grossman?"

"No. If we called Dr. Grossman every time I had a spasm we would be paupers. Eat your food, Reuven. We will talk after the meal."

But he was very tired by the time the meal was over, and he went immediately to bed.

I sat at my desk in my room and studied Talmud. Then I worked on some logic problems. Then I thought I would call Danny and I dialed his number but there was no answer. I went back to my desk and studied some more Talmud and did some more logic problems. At about nine thirty I went into my father's room and saw he was asleep. I left a note on the kitchen table in case he should waken and put on my hat and coat and went out of the apartment. I needed to walk. I walked for over an hour along Lee Avenue, past the shops of the Hasidim, some of which were still open. It was dark and cold and an icy wind blew along the street and sent the black city dust swirling across the sidewalks and there were many Hasidim on the street and I listened to their Hungarian Yiddish and they seemed strange to me, so far apart from me, though they were my own people and we shared the same distant origins and studied the same Torah. I walked past the synagogue where my father and I prayed and on past the block where Danny's father lived and thought how these remnants of the concentration camps had changed the face of things. They were the remnants, the zealous guardians of the spark. And now everything traditional was being drawn toward that zealousness. They had changed everything merely by surviving and crossing an ocean. They had brought that spark to the broken streets of Williamsburg, and men like Rav Kalman who were not Hasidim felt swayed by their presence and believed themselves to be equally zealous guardians of the spark, and no one at Hirsch would fight them because the spark was precious, it was all that was left after the blood and the slaughter, and you dimmed it when you fought its defenders. It had been merely a matter of time for me. I had not really seen it until now, but it had only been a matter of time until it all caught up to me. Now it had caught up because I had been seen in the Zechariah Frankel Seminary working on my father's book and I was in the middle and my father could not help me and I walked the Williamsburg streets in the cold and the wind and did not know what to do.

Ten

He did not call on me to read but he asked me to remain behind after class. He had my father's book with him and when we were alone he motioned me alongside him and I pulled over a chair and we sat together behind the desk. He moved the Talmud aside and opened the book.

"Tell me what this means, Malter. I do not understand the difficulty your father sees in this passage."

I explained it to him. He stroked his beard and listened and then looked down a long time at the book.

"Yes," he murmured. "I understand. But it is not necessary to change the words in order to obtain that meaning from the Gemora."

I told him the words as they stood could not possibly have that meaning. There was a problem with the Aramaic grammar, I said.

"Explain the problem, Malter."

It was a very technical problem and I tried to make it as simple as possible.

"I understand," he said. "I understand. For grammar you change the words."

I decided not to respond to that and glanced at my wristwatch.

"You are in a hurry?" he asked.

I told him I had a logic exam in five minutes.

"Ah," he said. "A logic examination. But you came prepared today, yes?"

"Yes."

197

"Go take your logic examination, Malter."

I left him behind his desk and raced up to my logic class and did quite well in the exam.

The next day he asked me again to remain behind after class. We sat together at the desk and there was sunlight on the dark wood and on the pages of my father's book. We argued back and forth a very long time over an impossibly complicated passage of Talmud and I found myself quoting from half a dozen different tractates in support of the explanation my father had given the passage, and to my surprise one of the tractates I quoted from was not listed in the footnotes to the book. I would have to tell my father about that, I thought. Rav Kalman listened and argued and began scratching at the scar on his cheek with the two misshapen fingers of his right hand. After a while I found myself looking at those fingers, watching them move together across his cheek, and he noticed me and quickly put his hand on his lap. A moment later he dismissed me. I turned at the door. He sat behind the desk, his head in his hands, staring down at my father's book. I thought I heard him sigh.

I told my father about the passage when I got home that evening. We were in his study. He looked at the footnotes, then checked the passage in the Talmud.

"You are right, Reuven. I did not remember the passage. I will have to correct the footnote if there is another printing. How did you come to think of the passage?"

I told him about my after-class sessions with Rav Kalman.

"You have been going over the book with Rav Kalman?" He looked astonished.

"I told you he asked me about some passages on Sunday."

"But every day? He has asked you about it every day?"

"What's wrong with that?"

He stared down at the book and said nothing.

"What's going on?" I said.

He said nothing.

"Something's going on. What's happening?"

I heard Manya calling us in to supper.

"Rav Kalman has been asked to write an article about the book," my father said.

I stared at him. "How do you know?"

"From a colleague in my yeshiva."

"Why are you so upset?"

"It will be an attack against the book."

"How do you know that? From your colleague?"

"Yes."

I heard Manya calling us again.

"We should go in to eat, Reuven."

"Why would he want to attack the book? They never attack works of technical scholarship."

"The introduction. Anyone can read and understand the introduction."

Manya called us a third time.

"Let us go in, Reuven. And let us not talk about this during the meal. We will talk afterwards."

But shortly before the end of the meal he remembered he had a meeting that night with some of his colleagues. He did not return until after eleven o'clock. His face was gray and he seemed exhausted. We sat together at the kitchen table. He drank tea and I had some milk and cookies. He was silent and withdrawn. I heard the soft electric throb of the refrigerator and the ticking of the kitchen clock. Then I heard him sigh and say quietly, "At least it is for Torah. We are fighting for Torah. It is not this horrible insanity with Senator McCarthy. There is some consolation."

I drank from my glass and looked at him and did not say anything.

He shook his head. "It is strange how ideas can float about and be ignored until they are put into a book. A book can be a weapon, Reuven. But I did not intend my book to be a weapon. I simply intended it to be—a book." He was silent a moment. Then he shook his head again. "I expected it. But what could I do? I could not stop writing. I cannot stop writing because some people do not like what I say."

"Rav Kalman?"

He looked at me and blinked his eyes wearily. "Yes," he said. "Rav Kalman. And others."

"Which others?"

"There will be others," he said sadly. "Rav Kalman has great influence. There will certainly be others."

"Two years," I said. "Why couldn't he have missed us by two years?"

"What are you saying, Reuven?"

"Why couldn't he have come to America two years later?"

"You would like him to have suffered two more years somewhere in China merely to have avoided causing us a problem? That is a terrible thing to say, Reuven."

I finished my milk and said nothing.

"Besides, there would have been someone else. The times are different. The climate is different. Everything is different. There would have been another Rav Kalman."

"Not for my *Chullin* teacher."

"Perhaps. But it is childish to think of what might have been."

"You said China. Was he really in China?"

"Yes."

"How do you know?"

"I have discovered a great deal about Rav Kalman."

"From your colleague?"

He smiled faintly and nodded. "He is a great Talmud scholar and a fierce follower of the musar movement. He might have become another Rav Israel Salanter or Rav Nathan Finkel had Hitler not destroyed European Jewry. He is one of the great men in Orthodoxy today. That is why your yeshiva brought him over. They wanted to bring him over sooner, but he had established a yeshiva in Shanghai and would not leave earlier. If his signature is on your smicha it will be a great smicha, Reuven. You will have a right to be very proud of the smicha."

"I'm not going to be proud of a smicha I have to lie for."

"No," he said soberly. "I do not expect that you will lie

in order to receive smicha. You will have to make a choice."

"What choice? There is no choice. I realized tonight while you were out that I have no choice at all. He's not asking me to make a choice. He's telling me to take a stand. I'm either with him or against him. All or nothing. I'm disgusted with the whole business. I don't want smicha if the price I have to pay for it is to stop thinking. He can keep his smicha."

"You will not receive smicha? What will you do, Reuven?"

"I don't know. Maybe I'll sit out the *Chullin* class until June, and then take a doctorate in philosophy. You always wanted me to teach in a university. Maybe I'll teach in a university. I don't know."

"You have to make a decision now, Reuven?"

"No."

"Then wait. Wait until you will have to make it."

"I'll have to make it by March or April."

"Then wait until March or April."

"I'm sick of it," I said. "I've had it up to here now with Rav Kalman. I'm not going to change the way I study Talmud just because Rav Kalman has his head buried in a ghetto."

"Do not talk that way, Reuven. It is disrespectful."

"I'm sorry, abba. I'm angry."

"Yes. I can see that. You will be a lot angrier before this is over. It is when you are angry that you must watch how you talk."

"I'll bet he asks me tomorrow to explain more of the book to him."

"If he does," my father said, "I expect you to answer him with respect."

But I was wrong. Rav Kalman did not ask me to remain after class the next day. Nor did he call on me to read. And the same was true of the day after. I sat in the class and listened and from time to time I noticed him glancing at me, but he left me alone.

Early Friday afternoon I brought a copy of my father's

book over to Danny. It was a cold, bleak day. The streets teemed with caftan-garbed Hasidim rushing about in preparation for Shabbat. I turned up Danny's block, which was almost a precise duplicate of mine, but looked older, more worn, the brownstones unkempt, the stone banisters on the outside stairways chipped and smudged with dirt, and many of the front lawns paved over with cement. This block had always looked less neat and clean than mine, but mine had begun rapidly to resemble it in the past two years.

I came up the worn stone steps to Danny's house and went through the front double door and the small foyer into the hallway. At the right of the hallway was the door that led to Reb Saunders's synagogue. The door was open and I stopped for a moment and peered inside. Nothing about the synagogue had changed. It looked transplanted from another age, its individual stands, its old chairs and tables, its podium and Ark, the cushioned chair alongside the Ark where Reb Saunders sat, the separate screened-off section for women, the exposed light bulbs hanging from the ceiling, the walls that needed paint—so much of my life had once been tied to the things I had experienced inside that synagogue and all of it seemed strange to me now, quaint, almost exotic, as if it were a movie set or something I were watching an author describe in a historical novel. I turned away from the door and went to the foot of the stairs and called Danny's name. I heard my voice echo through the empty hallway and up the staircase and through the house. Then I heard footsteps and I looked up and I saw a beardless caftaned figure come to the head of the stairs, a young caftaned figure, a boy of about fifteen, with dark hair and a sculptured face and dark eyes, and I looked up at him and in the shadows of the stairway he looked to be Danny and I felt a shock go through me and I put a hand on the banister. But it was not Danny; it was his brother Levi. I leaned against the banister and felt my heart beating.

"Hello," Levi said in English. "Danny says to come up

to his room." He had a gentle voice and pale features and he smiled at me as I came toward him up the stairs.

"How are you, Levi?"

"Thank God. Thank God."

"Your mother?"

"Thank God, all right."

"Is your father upstairs too?"

"In his study. How are you, Reuven?"

"I've had better days and worse days."

"I can imagine," he said, changing to Yiddish. "Nu, have a good Shabbos."

"Shabbat shalom," I said. I was almost to the third floor when it occurred to me to ask myself what he had meant by "I can imagine."

Danny was in his room at the far end of the apartment hall on the third floor. The door was open. I poked my head inside and saw him seated at his desk over an open Talmud.

"Your Mitnaged friend is here with his heathen literature," I said.

He looked up and smiled, a little grimly I thought, and told me to come in.

I gave him my father's book. He thanked me for it and put it on his desk. Then he closed the Talmud he had been studying from and told me to sit down. I sat on the bed. There were bookcases against the walls and a worn rug on the floor. Outside in the back yard the naked branches of an ailanthus moved against the gray sky.

"Levi doesn't look too well," I said.

Danny said nothing.

"You've cleaned up the room."

He smiled. "How are you?" he asked.

"I'm not sure any more."

"You're having a bad time."

"How can you tell, doctor?"

"Rachel sends you her regards."

"How is Rachel?"

"Fine."

"How is the great doctor?"

"Tired."

"Michael has been talking all week about your visit."

"Is that good?"

"It would be better if he talked about himself."

"Shall I stop seeing him?"

"No. Are you going to the Gordons?"

"Yes."

"The cherem doesn't bother you?"

"Does it bother you?"

"No."

"It doesn't bother me either."

"It doesn't really apply to me."

"You mean pickuach nefesh."

"Yes."

In the Jewish tradition, a religious law must be violated if it is even vaguely suspected of endangering a human life. "Pickuach nefesh" is the technical legal term for saving a life.

"How is Michael?" I asked.

"I don't think Michael is going to talk. I can't get to him."

"It's been less than two weeks, Danny."

"I know how long it's been. But I can already feel it. He talks to me more than he's ever talked to anyone. But I can't get to him with talk. There's a thick shell around him and I can't get through it."

"A shell," I said.

"I can't get through."

"You want to get through to his spark of a soul? You sound like your father. I'm surrounded by you people."

He looked at me sadly.

"Between Rav Kalman in class and Hasidim on the streets I'm beginning to feel I could use some therapy myself."

"You don't need therapy."

"What do I need, doctor?"

"You don't need therapy."

"I need a vacation from Rav Kalman, that's what I need. You want to hear about his latest little game?"

"I know about it."

I looked at him.

"I read it."

"You read what?"

"It's in the paper."

"What's in the paper?"

He stared at me. "I thought—" He stopped. "You haven't seen it?"

"Seen what? What are you talking about?"

"Don't you get that paper Rav Kalman writes for?"

"No."

He reached up to a shelf over his desk, pushed some papers aside, and handed me the newspaper. It was a rather shabby weekly publication but it was reputed to have considerable influence upon those in positions of power in Orthodoxy. You could see it on the newsstands in Brooklyn, its masthead thick and black: *The Jewish Guardian*. It was of tabloid size, poorly printed and edited, its English often embarrassingly clumsy. Its readership comprised the very Orthodox, especially those who had come to America from the concentration camps. It had been in existence for about two years. I had read through one of its issues about a year ago and had found it smug, self-righteous, faintly hysterical, and generally dull. Then last week I had brought a copy to Michael, the copy containing the attack against his father. Now I was reading about my father.

Rav Kalman's article was set in two wide columns on page three, and was headlined: NEW BOOK A THREAT TO TORAH JUDAISM. Beneath the headline, in italics were these words: *This is the first of a two-part article on* THE MAKING OF THE TALMUD: STUDIES IN SOURCE CRITICISM by *David Malter. The author of these articles is the world-renowned Talmud scholar Rav Jacob Kalman, of the Samson Raphael Hirsch Yeshiva.*

I read the article very quickly. My face was hot and my hands were trembling and when I was done reading it I gave it back to Danny and he put it on his desk.

"He didn't waste any time," I said, feeling the anger and the shame deep inside me.

Danny said nothing.

"The advance copies just came out last week. He didn't even wait for the official publication date. He must have worked around the clock to write that."

Danny was quiet.

"At least he doesn't call my father a pagan."

"It's an honest article," Danny said.

I looked at him sharply.

"You have to admit it's honest. He knows what he's talking about. He studied the book. It's an honest difference of opinion."

"Sure he studied the book. You know who he studied it with?"

"Who?"

"Me."

He stared.

"That's right. Me. 'Explain this to me, Malter. I want to understand better what your father is saying.' Me. Sunday, Monday, Tuesday. After class. Me. What kind of person does that? He *used* me against my own father. I wonder who he used when he was reading Abraham Gordon's book. My God, I feel like I'm living in the Middle Ages. I need some fresh air." I got to my feet and went to the window. It was open. "Why is it so hot in here?" I sat down. "I feel like I'm suffocating."

"It isn't hot at all," Danny said quietly.

"It's hot. Don't tell me it isn't hot."

"All right."

"Can I take that paper with me? I'll want to show it to my father."

"Yes."

"It's stifling in here. I wish it were the summer. I wish I could get in some swimming. Maybe I'll go to one of those indoor pools in a Y and get in some swimming. I wish I could do some sailing. Have you ever gone sailing? No, of course you haven't. In a good wind a Sailfish goes like a motorboat. But you have to watch the center board. It gets warped and you have trouble with it in shallow water sometimes. You have to watch that center board, Danny."

"Take it easy," I heard Danny say as if from a distant part of the house.

I was quiet. I sat there quietly and took a deep breath. My head felt foggy. I took another deep breath. The fog was gone.

"I'm all right," I said, and got to my feet. "I had better get home."

"Please go in and see my father," Danny said. "He wants to talk to you."

"About what?"

"I don't know. Are you sure you're all right?"

"I'm fine. I'm—splendid."

I wished him Shabbat shalom and started down the hall to his father's study. I saw the newspaper in my hand and stuffed it quickly into a pocket. I was about to knock on the door to the study when I remembered something and turned and went quickly back to Danny's room. His door was closed. I opened it without knocking and came inside. He was at his desk, studying Talmud. He was bent low over the Talmud, swaying slowly back and forth, and the thumb and forefinger of his right hand caressed his cheek and played with an imaginary earlock. I stood just inside the room and watched him and felt the room swaying in rhythmic accompaniment to the motions of his body, the floor moving slowly back and forth, and I closed my eyes. The swaying ceased. I opened my eyes. Danny was looking at me.

"What is all this about the Kotzker Rebbe?" My voice sounded strangely loud. "What is this with Byrd and Zimmerman and the Kotzker Rebbe and solitude?" Easy, I thought. Why are you shouting? You don't have to shout.

Danny looked as if he had been struck a blow. A look of enormous astonishment spread across his face. He opened his mouth and closed it immediately. He sat there, staring at me, and seemed incapable of responding.

"Is that all it is? A project for class? Solitude?" Stop

shouting, I told myself again. It's none of your business anyway what it's all about ... The hell it's none of my business. But stop shouting. "Well?" I said. "Well?"

"How do you know about the Kotzker?" I heard him ask in a tight voice.

I told him.

"It's got to do with an idea I'm working on," Danny said very quietly.

"What idea?" My voice still sounded very loud.

Danny said nothing. But the lines of his face had hardened with annoyance.

"For class?" I said loudly. "A class project. Is that all it is? I know how your mind works. You don't suddenly start pouncing on a bunch of books dealing with one subject just out of curiosity. What are you doing? Is it for class?"

"No," he said.

"I know. It's none of my business. But what are you doing?"

He was silent.

"It has something to do with Michael. You're dreaming up something for Michael. What are you doing?"

"Take it easy, Reuven."

"What are you doing?"

"I don't want to talk about it."

"You don't want to talk about it. Just like that. You don't want to talk about it."

"I can't talk about it."

"I got you involved in this whole thing. Don't you owe it to me to tell me?"

"No. I can't talk about it to anyone yet."

"All right. Don't talk about it. All right. More silence. That's what I love about you Hasidim. You either don't talk at all or you talk too much. Sneaky Kalman and silent Saunders. Everything is falling apart. Don't you see it falling apart? Can't you hear it falling apart?"

"I hear you shouting," Danny said softly. "That's what I hear."

I stared at him. He was looking at me and blinking his eyes rapidly.

"Have fun," I said bitterly. "Enjoy your solitude. Give my love to the Kotzker and Admiral Byrd. Let me know when you're ready to talk about it."

I went out of the room and closed the door and went quickly down the hall and out of the apartment to the stairway. Halfway down the third-floor stairs I remembered that Reb Saunders wanted to see me. I went back up and knocked on the door to his study and heard him say in Yiddish, "Come in."

He was seated behind his desk over an old Hebrew book. The room was cluttered with books; it was always cluttered with books. I wished he would open a window. The musty odor of old books was suffocating. He shook my hand and waved me into a chair. He looked old and weary. He closed the book and moved it aside. He asked me how my father was feeling. Then he asked me how I was feeling. Then he told me he had read Rav Kalman's article about my father's book. He did not say whether he approved or disapproved of the article; he merely said he had read it. But his voice was thick with sadness as he talked. Then he was silent for a while and his hands trembled faintly on the desk. I noticed there was a slight tremor to his head now too. He sighed softly and began to play with an earlock, curling it around the bony forefinger of his right hand.

"A telephone is a mighty thing," he said softly in Yiddish. "A mighty thing. An invisible messenger."

I stared at him.

"A wire. Two instruments. And human beings who are far apart are suddenly close together. We have been given a world full of wonders by the Master of the Universe. People whose lives are separated come together because of a wire. Is it not a mighty thing, Reuven?"

I nodded and wondered what he was talking about and had a moment of black dread that he had become senile.

"Where I grew up in Europe it would take days sometimes to deliver an important message. Lives would be lost because there would be no way to call a doctor. I remember my father, of blessed memory, once fell on ice and hurt his hip and was in pain for a day and a half before someone could bring a doctor. Now a man can pick up a telephone. It is a wonder, a mighty wonder. We should thank the Master of the Universe every day for such a wonder."

I glanced at my wristwatch and squirmed on my seat and was quiet. I wanted to get home and talk about that article with my father. I wondered if that colleague of his in the yeshiva might have told him about the article. I wanted to be home when my father came in. But I did not move.

Reb Saunders seemed unaware of my discomfort. He went on talking. "The Master of the Universe has so created the world that everything that can be good can also be evil. It is mankind that makes a thing good or evil, Reuven, depending upon how we use the wonders we have been given. A telephone can also be a nuisance. But if it is used wisely, it is a mighty thing." He stopped playing with the earlock and put his hand on the desk. "My Daniel receives many telephone calls when he is here. Sometimes they are from his friends in school. Sometimes they are from the hospital where he works. It is not so big a house, Reuven, that telephone calls can be easily concealed. Tell me, Reuven, Daniel has a patient by the name of Michael Gordon?"

I was beyond surprise. I was too tired and drained to feel surprise. I simply sat there and looked at him.

"Nu, Reuven?"

I nodded.

"This is the son of Gordon, yes?"

"Yes." Why do they all call him by his last name like that? I thought. Why do they make it sound as if he were the only Gordon in the world?

"And who is Rachel Gordon? His daughter?"

"His niece."

"Ah," he said, nodding his head slowly and sounding a little relieved. "His niece. Rachel Gordon is his niece ...

Tell me, Reuven, the family of Rachel Gordon observes the Commandments?"

I was beginning to feel that I had no business answering questions about Rachel and her family. Let Danny answer them. Let Reb Saunders ask Danny. The days when he talked to Danny through me were over. Let him talk to Danny himself. I wanted nothing of that part of the past repeated.

I told him quietly that I thought he ought to talk about it with Danny.

He ignored me. "The family observes the Commandments?" he asked again, his voice somewhat sharper now.

"Yes."

"And the girl, is the girl also an observer of the Commandments?"

I told him respectfully that I did not feel comfortable talking about Rachel and that he ought to ask Danny.

He blinked his dark, deep-socketed eyes and nodded heavily. "I understand," he murmured. "You are remembering what was once between us and you do not want it again. But how can it be the same, Reuven? My Daniel is a man now, and men hesitate to talk to their fathers. A boy always wishes to be able to talk to his father. And a father waits for the boy to become a man so they can talk as men. And then the boy becomes a man and no longer needs the father. It is a strange thing. I worry myself about my Daniel. I worry that the girl he will find will not be an observer of the Commandments."

"She observes the Commandments."

"Yes?" His lined face lighted up.

"They all observe the Commandments. The whole family."

"Gordon observes the Commandments?"

"Yes."

"You know this by yourself?"

"Yes."

He seemed really surprised. "How do you know?"

"I know Abraham Gordon."

"You know Gordon?"

"I know them all."

"Daniel tells me nothing."

I was quiet.

"It may be he is afraid to upset me. The niece of Gordon . . ." He lapsed into brooding silence.

I told him I had to go home.

He nodded. Then he sighed and leaned forward against the desk. "I have been asked to write about your father's book," he said softly. "There will be trouble with that book. When a scholar as great as your father writes such a book it cannot be ignored." His voice was heavy with sadness. "Rav Kalman is an influential man. There will be trouble. But I will not write about it. I will say nothing. I owe your father—too much. You will tell your father this for me."

I felt myself nodding.

"There will be great trouble with that book. Rav Kalman has taken it upon himself to combat it. No one will stop him. But I will not help him. Please tell your father that, Reuven. Have a good Shabbos. It is always good to see you. Give my good wishes to your father." He spoke very quietly and seemed visibly fatigued. "Nu, at least she is an observer of the Commandments . . . But the niece of Gordon . . . Ah, what a world we live in . . ."

I came out of the room and stood near the door a moment. A melody floated thinly through the hall. It was a Hasidic melody, wordless, set to the syllables bim bam bim, and it moved through the hall from Danny's room. I stood there, listening to the melody. It seemed filled with quiet joy, its syllables, carried by Danny's faintly nasal voice, rising and falling to the gentle, lively notes of the tune. Bim bam bim. Bim bam bim. It followed me through the hall to the head of the third-floor stairway, soft, thin, barely audible now, but its happiness unmistakable, a thin thread of joy in the silence of the house. I stood at the head of the stairs and listened to it. Then I turned and went quickly back into the hall and up to Danny's door. I knocked. The melody ceased abruptly. I went inside.

Danny sat at his desk in front of the open Talmud and stared at me in surprise.

"The suffering son of a heathen writer is back," I said. "The silent one is surprised. Yes. I can see he is surprised. I bear a message from the king. A telephone is a mighty thing. It can also be a nuisance, but used wisely it is a mighty thing. Don't look at me like that. I do not as yet need your services. I am quoting the words of the king, the messenger of the Lord. Your father knows about you and Rachel. He asked me and I told him. I didn't want to tell him. But the king has a relentless way about him sometimes. So I told him. He heard you on the phone. He knows about Michael. The king knows all. Have a merry Shabbos. Give my—give my regards to Rachel and her parents. I am going home to my heathen father."

I closed the door and went quickly through the hall. I heard the door open behind me, but I was out of the apartment and going down the stairs. On the second floor I stopped and listened. The house was silent. I went downstairs and was passing the door to the synagogue when a dark figure came suddenly out of the shadows.

"Reuven."

It was Levi. He stood alongside the synagogue door, thin and wraithlike in the dimness of the hallway.

"It's late," I said. "I've got to go home."

"A minute," he said in Yiddish. "Only a minute."

"What do you want, Levi?"

"My brother," he said, looking a little uncomfortable. "He will be a great psychologist, yes?"

I looked at him.

"Yes, Reuven?" he asked softly, eagerly. "Tell me. Yes?"

He needed the assurance. He needed to know that the years the tzaddikate would eventually take from his frail life would be worthwhile.

"Yes," I heard myself say.

I saw him nod. "I am glad," he said quietly. "Have a good Shabbos, Reuven."

I came out of the house into the gray, cold winter and

walked home through streets that seemed choked with scurrying Hasidim on last-minute errands before the Shabbat.

My father was in his study. He had seen Rav Kalman's article. His colleague at the yeshiva had brought it to his attention.

"There is nothing anyone can do," he said. "Rav Kalman has a right to express his opinion."

"He used me."

My father said nothing. I told him what Reb Saunders had said. He nodded heavily.

"There will be other attacks, Reuven. But I am grateful to Reb Saunders for his silence."

"Why is he picking on your book? I don't understand it. There are so many other books he can attack."

"No," he said quietly. "Mine carries a certain authority. It is my reputation that he sees as a threat. He is a musarnik. He is defending the Torah."

"He's a sneak, that's what he is."

"Reuven—"

"He had me believing he really wanted to understand the book, and all he did was use me."

My father shook his head and made a waving motion with his hand. "I do not want to talk about it any more. It is time to prepare for Shabbat. But you will do me a favor and not speak disrespectfully of one of your teachers. Now we will have to hurry or we will be late for Kabbalat Shabbat."

But a few minutes later it began to rain very hard and we did not go to the synagogue but prayed at home and then had our Shabbat meal with the rain loud on the window of the kitchen and a feeling of gloom thick and oppressive all around us as we sang the Shabbat songs and chanted the Grace and sat around the table for a while, talking of Michael and Rachel and Danny and Rav Kalman and the way things had begun to change for me— and as the minutes went by I began to notice for the first time that week how tired my father really looked and to hear the strange quality of resignation in his voice, and it occurred to me that I had been so involved in my own problems with Rav Kalman that I had not thought to ask my father what had been happening to him on account of the book, what was going on in his own yeshiva. I asked him.

He gazed at me wearily and did not respond for a moment. "There are problems," he said.

"What's happening?"

"Some of the new people are—dissatisfied."

"But what's happening?"

"We will talk of it another time. But it is nothing to worry about."

"They can't do anything to you. You helped build that yeshiva. You've been there more than twenty years."

"Twenty-four years," he said softly.

"Can they do anything?"

"I do not think so."

"My God, it's like living in the time of Spinoza."

"Yes," my father murmured. "There is that feeling sometimes."

"Are those new people musarniks?"

"No. But they are all under the influence of Rav Kalman."

"Two years," I said. "Why couldn't he have come just two years later?"

My father grimaced but said nothing.

It rained all through the night and the next day and we prayed at home and had our meals and talked. In the early afternoon my father went into his room to rest and I stood by my window and watched the rain falling on the ailanthus in our back yard, the branches bare and black and dripping, rain splattering into the puddles on the earth, rain streaking the window, rain blowing against the house in the wind. I thought of the summer and the lake and the wind against the mainsail of the Sailfish and the waves high and white-crested and churning and Michael moving back and forth alongside the center board and Rachel and I swimming in the lake and the old man in the carnival and Joseph Gordon saying "No Geneva Conventions here" and Molly Bloom big with seed. It all seemed another world and another time and I turned away from the window and lay down on my bed and tried to read a book but could not and I closed my eyes and listened to the rain. It rained all day and into the night and it was still raining when my father and I finally went to bed.

Eleven

I sat at one of the long tables in the yeshiva synagogue the next morning trying to prepare for the class with Rav Kalman, and found myself unable to concentrate on the words. Irving Goldberg sat alongside me, looking round and solemn and gloomy. There were about one hundred students at the tables in the synagogue and the sing-song of their voices was loud. I could see them studying and glancing at me. It had not taken long for the news of Rav Kalman's article to get around. So I was the center of much attention that Sunday morning, and students kept coming over to talk to me about the attack against my father.

But there were those who did not come over to me but kept looking my way and talking among themselves and nodding and smiling, not without some glee, I noticed. And by the time the preparation period was over and we were all going to our classes, it was quite evident that the student body of the rabbinical department had polarized into two camps, one that agreed wholeheartedly with Rav Kalman's attack against my father because text criticism was a dangerous threat to the sanctity of the Talmud, and a second that felt Rav Kalman's article to be typical of his effort to make the yeshiva a throwback to the ghetto yeshivoth of Eastern Europe. There were loud arguments and they went on in the corridor and continued inside the classroom. I heard them all around me, but I stayed out of it. I was afraid of what I might say.

The church bells rang. The classroom grew silent. We gazed tensely at the door. Rav Kalman entered and came up to his desk. The bells ceased ringing. He arranged his books on the desk, lit a cigarette, and called on someone to read. I sat listening to the student read. Rav Kalman paced back and forth. He did not call on me. He barely looked at me. It is a strange experience to sit across a desk from a man who has attacked your own father in print and used you to help stage that attack. It was not difficult for me to hate him.

After class I had a quick lunch in the school cafeteria and took the subway. At five minutes to three that afternoon I was climbing the stone steps of the huge, mansion-like building of the residential treatment center.

Michael was waiting for me in the downstairs living room. He was sitting in an easy chair next to one of the draped windows, reading a newspaper. It was very cold outside and the living room was quite crowded. There was a hum of subdued conversation. A lavishly decorated Christmas tree stood in a corner and a large brass electric Hanukkah menorah was on the mantelpiece next to the schooner. I came quickly over to Michael and saw he was reading the Orthodox newspaper in which Rav Kalman had published his article about my father.

He looked up at me and blinked his eyes. "Hello," he said. "You're on time today."

"How are you, Michael?"

"Did you see this?" He indicated the newspaper.

I nodded. "Where did you get it?"

"Mr. Saunders gave it to me on Friday morning. We had a session on Friday morning." He sounded agitated. "Let's go for a walk," he said.

We came outside and went down the marble stairs.

"Are your parents coming today?" I asked

"Tonight. They're in Washington now for a conference on Jewish education. Let's go this way."

He led me into the trees. The wind blew the leaves across the ground. The sun was bright, but the wind felt knife-edged with cold and I put up the collar of my coat.

Michael walked bareheaded, one hand holding the newspaper, the other in his pocket. "It's nothing," I heard him say. "Compared to what they say about my father, this is nothing."

"It's enough," I said.

"How does it feel?"

We walked on a moment in silence. "Uncomfortable."

"That's all? You only feel uncomfortable?"

"Very uncomfortable."

"That's because it's nothing. When I read what they say about my father it makes me feel like a toilet."

I said nothing. We continued walking in silence.

"Why did Mr. Saunders give you that?" I asked.

"I don't know. He said I might want to read it." We were walking slowly through the trees and there was shade and the wind was loud in the swaying branches and cold against my face. "It doesn't feel good, does it? It feels very bad. It feels like you're a bug and they're stepping on you. Isn't that what it feels like?"

"It's not quite like that, Michael."

He looked at me, his face pale, his lips drawn tight, the glasses down along the bridge of his nose. "Don't you hate him?" he asked. "Don't you hate Rav Kalman?"

I did not say anything.

"Like a bug," he muttered. "That's what it feels like. There it is. There's my house."

We had come to the pagoda-like structure.

"Come on inside," he said. "Rachel's inside."

There was no one on the white-painted circular bench. I came up the two wooden steps. We sat down on the bench. Overhead the wind moaned around the sharply angled red roof. Michael put the newspaper in his pocket. He stared down moodily at the wooden floor, then looked at me.

"Why don't you get out of there?" he asked in a high, thin, agitated voice.

"Out of where?"

"Your school."

"Why should I get out of my school?"

"It's full of spiders and cobwebs and old men who cheat you."

I did not say anything.

"Evil old men."

"They're not evil. If they were evil it would be easy to get out of the school. They're very sincere."

"The people who burned Giordano Bruno were sincere."

I said nothing.

"Torquemada was sincere. You know about Torquemada?"

"Yes."

"He was sincere. The people who excommunicated Spinoza were sincere. The people who excommunicated my—" He stopped suddenly, his eyes blinking repeatedly. "Evil," he muttered through thin, curled lips. "Ugly and evil and sincere. So what? You don't know anything about it. Are you going over to my parents' tomorrow night?"

"Yes."

"I'm glad. I'm really glad. You're a friend. I never met an Orthodox person like you before."

"Mr. Saunders is Orthodox."

"He doesn't go to your school. Besides, he's going to be a psychologist, not one of your rabbis. He's not yeshiva Orthodox." He leaned forward intimately and pushed his glasses up along the bridge of his nose. "Listen. I was looking at the sky last night through my telescope. It was beautiful. I could see Sirius. I could even see its white dwarf star. I could see Procyon too, but I couldn't find its white dwarf." He was staring down at the floor and talking very rapidly in a high, tense monotone. I looked around quickly and could see no one. Michael went on talking. "Those red giants are something. They're the opposite of the white dwarfs. Some of them are a million times brighter than the sun. Did you know that? Did you?"

"No," I said very quietly.

"Epsilon Aurigae has a star that's a billion miles in diameter. What do you think of that?"

"That's big."

"A billion miles in diameter."

"I'm feeling a little cold, Michael. Should we go inside?"

"Once they thought the dark rift running along the Milky Way was a tunnel. They thought they could see extragalactic space through that tunnel. But it's not a tunnel. It's just cosmic dust. You can't see the stars behind it because it's so thick. It's like black clouds. You can't see some of the stars because of the black clouds. You didn't know that."

"No."

"I saw a lot of stars last night, but I don't want to talk about it any more."

I did not want to tell him he could not have seen any stars last night because it had rained. I said nothing.

"I'm cold too," he said. "Stay here for a minute. I'll be right back."

"Where are you going?"

"Inside for something. Wait for me here."

He was on his feet. I got up.

"Wait for me here."

"I'm freezing," I told him.

"I'll change it. Just wait for me. Will you wait?"

"All right."

"I'll change it if you wait. I'm tired of it anyway. Look at the way they painted it."

He ran out of the pagoda and into the trees and was gone.

I sat there and waited. It was very cold. I was a little frightened and wondered if I ought to get help. Why the devil had Danny given him the newspaper? I sat there, worrying about Michael. I looked at my watch. It was close to four. He had been gone more than five minutes. I sat there a while longer. It was bitter cold. I got to my feet and came out of the pagoda. Leaves eddied like waves in the wind. I felt my shoes on the leaves and the leaves skittering against my trousers like dried insects. Through the naked branches of the trees I saw winter birds circling overhead against the pale afternoon sky. I moved quickly through the trees toward the house and thought I saw someone in the distance and called Michael's name but got no response. I went up the front stairs two at a time and into the large foyer.

The man behind the desk looked at me curiously as I came over to him. He was the same one who had been there the week before. I asked him if he had by any chance seen Michael.

"Michael who?"

"Michael Gordon."

"He's outside somewhere. May I have your name please?"

"I'm Robert Malter. I was visiting with him."

"Oh yes. Michael just went outside a moment or two ago."

"He went back outside?"

He looked at me narrowly. "Is everything all right?"

"Yes, of course."

I went quickly out and down the stairs and into the trees toward the pagoda. I walked very quickly and finally I was running and there was the pagoda and Michael was on his knees on the wooden floor over a pile of leaves. He did not look up as I came behind him. He was on his knees over the leaves and I saw his hands move in a swift upward stroke and there was a sudden flare of light but the wind caught it and it was gone.

"What the devil are you doing?"

He did not look up.

"You stop that."

"Go away."

There was another movement of his hands, very close to the leaves this time, and now there was smoke and the sudden swift spreading of the flame and I pushed him aside and put a foot on the flame and heard him curse and felt his arms on my back and I was falling over the bench, my right leg scraping against it, my arms flailing outward for one of the roof support beams and missing. I landed on my face on the leaf-covered earth and heard Michael screaming and cursing behind me. I got to my feet and jumped the bench back into the pagoda and knocked the box of matches from Michael's hand. He screamed at me. His voice was loud and piercing against my ear. He screamed and I held him and he broke loose and scrambled for the matches, cursing and screaming. I grabbed for the matches and he kicked my leg but I had the matches in my hand now, a small box of wooden matches, and he was screaming in my ear and pleading with me to give them to him and I tried talking to him but he kept on screaming and suddenly there was someone else in the pagoda and I looked around and it was the uniformed guard who stood at the gate.

Michael froze. I stood very still, feeling the pain in my leg. The guard, a beefy heavy-set man in a gray uniform, was staring at the matches in my hand. He had his right hand in a tight grip on Michael's arm.

"What's going on?" he said.

Neither of us said anything. Michael was staring blankly at the floor of the pagoda. I could hear his heavy breathing.

"Give me those matches," the guard said.

I handed them to him. He slipped them into a pocket.

"You two better come inside."

Michael whimpered. "Look at the way they painted it," he said. His voice was flat and without emotion.

"Sure, kid," the guard said. "Come on."

He kept his arm on Michael. We went back into the trees and up the stairs into the house. Inside the foyer, the guard took his hand from Michael's arm and brought us over to the man at the desk. They spoke briefly. The guard put the matchbox on the desk.

"Thank you, Tom," the man said quietly, looking at me and Michael.

The guard put two fingers to the peak of his cap and went out the door. I glanced into the living room. There were not more than half a dozen people there now.

"Would you like to go to your room now, Michael?" the man said in a low voice.

Michael stood very still in front of the desk and looked at him and said nothing. His hair was wildly disheveled and the glasses were askew on his face.

"Michael," the man said.

Michael said nothing.

The man peered at him closely, picked up the phone, dialed, and turned his back to us. I looked down at my clothes. My coat was filthy and matted with leaves. My right leg throbbed. I heard the man talking softly into the phone. He put the phone down and turned.

"We'll wait here a moment. Are you all right?" he asked me.

"Yes."

"It will be just a moment."

I saw a woman come quickly down the inside stairway and go through the living room. She had on a white blouse and a dark skirt. She came over to us. She wore no make-up and had short black hair and looked to be in her late thirties. She smiled at Michael in a warm and friendly way and took his arm.

"Shall we go upstairs?" she said softly.

Michael went with her meekly. I saw them go up the stairs. He did not once turn around to look at me.

"Tell me what happened," the man said.

I told him.

"Would you like to get cleaned up?" he asked. "There's a men's room along the corridor to your right. Then I'll ask you to wait in the living room. Would you do that, please?"

I went through the living room and along the corridor, past the door to Danny's office, and into the men's room. I brushed the dirt and the leaves from my clothes, then collected the leaves and flushed them down a toilet. The men's room was tiled and very clean and there were fluorescent lights on the ceiling. I wet a paper towel and raised my right trouser leg and saw a three-inch scrape that had bled and dried and was now throbbing painfully. I decided to leave it alone and tossed the wet towel into the waste basket. When I was done, I stood in front of the mirror and leaned heavily on the sink and let the trembling take me and waited until it was gone. It took a long time for it to be gone. I washed my face and hands and went back outside and sat down on a sofa in the living room. The man behind the desk in the foyer was gone. The living room was empty. I heard voices from distant parts of the house. I looked at my watch. It was ten minutes of five. I pushed aside a corner of a drape and saw the dark night against the window. I looked around the room, then got up and walked behind the stairway and back along the corridor. I went to the foyer and picked up the phone on the desk. I heard a click, and a woman's voice said, "Yes?"

"May I have an outside line?"

"Press down 2179 on the phone." There was a pause. "Who is this?" she said.

I pressed down the button over the number 2179, and there was an immediate buzz. I dialed quickly. Manya answered. My father was not home yet, she said in her broken English. I told her I did not know when I would be home and that she was to tell my father I was with Michael and there was nothing to worry about. I hung up the phone and turned and saw the dark-suited man standing there looking at me. I had not heard him come back.

"Do you mind my using your phone?"

"No."

"I couldn't find a pay phone."

"We don't have any."

"How is Michael?"

"Very quiet. He had a slight nosebleed. But he is quiet now. We called the person who is treating him. He will be here soon. He asked that you wait for him. Can you do that?"

"Yes."

"Fine. Please make yourself comfortable inside. Can I get you a cup of coffee?"

"No, thanks."

I went back into the living room and sat on a sofa and waited. I found I was trembling again and took a deep breath and sat very still. My leg throbbed faintly. I leaned back and closed my eyes and after a while the trembling was gone but I remained seated with my eyes closed and kept hearing Michael screaming and there was the old man in the carnival again and Michael was screaming and I was grabbing for the dice cup. I opened my eyes. From somewhere deep inside the house came the voices of children. I looked at the large model of the schooner on the mantelpiece and thought I saw its sails moving in a wind. I fixed my eyes on the Hanukkah menorah. Tonight was the first night of Hanukkah. Tomorrow was Christmas Eve. I closed my eyes. A clock chimed the first eight notes of Big Ben. It was five thirty. I sat there with my eyes closed. A moment later someone spoke my name and I opened my eyes and it was Danny.

"Are you all right?" he wanted to know. He spoke softly and calmly. The dark-suited man stood alongside him.

He sat down next to me on the sofa. He had on his coat and hat. The hat was tilted back on his head, revealing the thick sand-colored hair. His eyes were blue and alert and very calm.

"Tell me exactly what happened," he said.

I told him.

"Can you stay for a while?" he asked.

"Yes."

"You ought to call your father and tell him you'll be late."

"I called him."

He looked at the dark-suited man, who had remained standing in front of us. "Is Mary still with Michael?"

"Yes."

"I'm going upstairs."

"Shall I call Altman?"

"I'll call Altman. First I want to talk to Michael." He turned to me. "Stay right here, Reuven. I may want you upstairs in a little while. Jack, come on up with me."

They went across the living room and up the winding wooden stairway. I waited. The clock chimed twelve notes

of Big Ben. It was an old grandfather clock and it stood
against the wall a few feet to the right of the fireplace. I
listened to it whir and chime. Then the room was silent,
except for the distant voices of children. Five minutes
after it chimed all sixteen notes of Big Ben I saw the
dark-suited man come down the stairs. He stopped at the
foot of the stairs and motioned to me. I came quickly over
to him.

"Do you know which is Michael's room?" he asked.

"Yes."

"Mr. Saunders asked that you go up there."

I went up the stairs two at a time. The second-floor
corridor was deserted. I wondered where everyone was
and then realized they were probably all eating supper. I
went along the corridor to Michael's room and tapped
softly on the door. I heard Danny tell me to come in. I
stepped inside and closed the door quietly behind me.

Michael lay in his bed. He was in pajamas and he lay
beneath the pale-blue cover, his head on the pillow and
his eyes closed. Danny sat on a chair alongside the bed.
He had removed his coat but was still wearing the hat,
tilted back on his head. There was a chair near the foot of
the bed. He waved me into it. I sat down and looked
closely at Michael. His face was gray and he seemed
asleep.

"Is he all right?" I whispered.

"You needn't whisper," Danny said in his normal
voice. "Michael isn't asleep. Are you asleep, Michael?"

Michael did not move.

"It's Reuven," Danny said. "Reuven is here."

I saw Michael's eyelids flutter. He opened his eyes and
looked at me.

"Hello," I said, managing a weak smile.

He did not say anything. He closed his eyes and lay
still.

"Why don't you tell Reuven what you told me?" Danny
said.

Michael said nothing.

"You won't tell him?"

Still Michael said nothing.

"All right," Danny said quietly. "I guess there's no reason for Reuven to stay."

Michael opened his eyes.

"Well," Danny said, smiling at him. "Are you back?"

"You tell him," Michael said. "I'm too tired."

"I think Reuven would rather hear it from you. Wouldn't you rather hear it from Michael?" Danny asked, looking at me.

"Sure," I said.

"Go ahead, Michael," Danny said quietly.

"I sneaked the matches from the kitchen. Nobody ever watches when they're cooking the meals. So I sneaked them out."

"It took awhile for Michael to get up the courage to admit that," Danny said to me. "Do you want to tell Reuven why it took awhile?"

"I was afraid you would be angry." He peered at me anxiously. "Are you angry?"

"Of course not."

"Michael," Danny said quietly. "Why did you need matches?"

"I needed them."

"I know that, Michael. Why did you feel you needed them?"

"To keep warm."

"Were you lighting the leaves to make you warm?"

"Me and Reuven."

"Was Reuven cold?"

"He said he was freezing."

"And you wanted him to be warm?"

"I'll do anything for Reuven."

"Were you cold too, Michael?"

"I was cold."

"Did you feel anything else besides the cold?"

"I was dirty."

"Why did you feel dirty?"

"I was."

"What part of you felt dirty, Michael?"

"All over. Especially my hands. I'm tired. I want to go to sleep."

"In a minute, Michael. Why do you think you felt dirty?"

"I was. I said I was."

"Were you really?"

"I was a toilet. That's what I was, a toilet."

Danny said nothing now. He was waiting. I could sense him waiting.

"I was a dirty toilet and they were flushing things down into me. I held it in my hands and read it and it was in my pocket and I didn't want Reuven to feel like a toilet also, so I wanted to burn it out."

"Burn what out?" Danny asked very softly.

"The paint was wrong. I would have burned it out and they would have rebuilt it and changed the paint. The schooner has the same paint but it's different because it sails. What do you want from me? Why don't you go away?"

"Would you like us to go away?"

"No. Don't leave me alone. I don't want you to leave me alone."

"We won't leave you alone, Michael. I promise. You like the schooner because it reminds you of sailing?"

"Yes."

"You like sailing?"

"I love it."

"Why do you think you love it?"

"Because I do."

"How do you feel when you're sailing?"

"Clean. Very clean. And free. And I like the clouds because they're never black. And you can't be dirty and a toilet in all that water. It's the most wonderful feeling in the world."

"What does the pagoda remind you of?" Danny asked.

Michael hesitated. "A house."

"Do you like the house?"

"Yes."

"What else does it remind you of?"

"Dirt."

"Why does it remind you of dirt?"

"Because it does."

"What else does it remind you of?"

"More dirt."

"Nothing else?"

"Dirt and dirt and dirt and dirt and dirt and—"

"All right, Michael," Danny said very calmly.

"—dirt."

Danny was quiet.

"I want to go to sleep now," Michael said, staring up at us from the bed.

"Would you like supper?"

"No."

"All right." Danny got to his feet. I stood up.

"Don't leave me alone," Michael said, his voice panicky. "I don't want you to leave me alone."

"I'll send Mary in to sit with you for a while," Danny said gently.

"Good night," I said.

Michael looked at me. His eyes were wet.

"I'm sorry," he said brokenly, "I'm sorry sorry sorry. I was terrible. It was a terrible visit. But you'll see my parents tomorrow. You won't let this keep you from seeing my parents."

"Of course not," I said.

"I'm sorry. I'm sorry. I only wanted to change the paint. I needed the paint to be different."

"Go to sleep, Michael," Danny said gently. "I'll send Mary right in."

He looked at me and nodded toward the door. We went out. I followed him to a door at the end of the corridor. He knocked softly and it was opened by the black-haired woman I had seen earlier.

"Give me a minute," Danny said to me, and went inside. He came out shortly and we went up the corridor to the stairway. As we started down the stairs, I turned and saw the woman go along the corridor and into Michael's room.

"Let's go into my office," Danny said. "I want to talk to you."

"The pagoda is red and white," I said. "The board in that gambling game at the carnival was red and white."

"I know about the board."

"Why did you give him the article about my father?"

"So he would have something to talk about when I saw him again."

"He had something to talk about, all right. It could have been a disaster."

"Nothing would have happened tonight if you hadn't come. He connected you with the article and himself with you, and that did it. I didn't think he would react that way." We were outside his office. He was putting a key into the door and giving me a grim look. "That's what I meant," he said. "You can't afford to make mistakes with human beings. Let me turn on the light. Come on in and sit down. We have a lot to talk about. But first call your father again and tell him you'll be here about half an hour longer."

I looked at him.

"I'm going to need your help," he said.

I dialed the phone. Manya answered. My father was at a meeting and had not yet come home. She sounded upset. This was very unusual for my father; he never missed supper; his doctor had ordered him to avoid an erratic eating schedule. I told her I was not sure when I would be home. That upset her even more. I hung up.

Danny was sitting in the wooden swivel chair behind his desk. The office was small but very clean and neat, with white walls and a beige tiled floor and a filing cabinet and bookcases. There was a single window covered with light-brown drapes. On the wall on either side of the window were color prints of New England winter scenes. An easy chair stood in a corner and there were two wooden chairs against a wall. Danny's desk was a small brown metal affair, with papers neatly piled on top of it. One of the piles consisted of monographs. He sat behind the desk, his hat tilted back on his head, and gazed at me calmly.

"Did Michael say anything at all before that he hadn't said to you earlier?"

I thought about that a moment. "No. Except the part about where he got the matches."

"What are black clouds?"

"Cosmic dust. He rambled about red giants and white dwarfs and cosmic dust when we were in the pagoda. He said he had been looking through his telescope last night."

"It poured last night."

"Yes."

"That telescope is very important to him. Freud would probably say it's a sex symbol. He's using it to assert his manhood."

"What do you say?"

"I think Freud is right. I also think the sky is the only thing Michael feels is safe. It's constant and far away and it never attacks you even when you're poking around in it. You can also be angry at the sky if you want to without worrying about hurting it or being hurt by it."

"Is Michael afraid of hurting someone?"

"I think that's what it's all about. He's terrified of his rage. He's so terrified he doesn't really know what he's angry at. You get through to him up to a point. He really trusts you. But you don't know what to do with it. Then he comes to me and repeats what he's told you because I'm your friend. But when it gets to something crucial he turns it off. That's called resisting therapy. He's terrified of going any further. So he instinctively blocks everything out and turns himself off. Or he simply lies and invents dreams and fantasies. He has incredible defenses."

"What does Rachel have to do with all of this?"

"His rage is all mixed up with sex fantasies about her. That's not too unusual for someone his age. But it complicates things."

"Does he know about you and Rachel?"

"No. I'm not sure he would want to talk to me again if he ever found out."

"What's going to happen? Is he just going to lie around here forever?"

"No. This place doesn't keep children for too long unless there's some indication of improvement."

"What's going to happen?"

"We've got to try something. We've got to take some kind of a gamble and break this impasse."

I stared at him. "What sort of a gamble?"

"I've spent a lot of time thinking about this." He was leaning against the back of his chair, speaking calmly and quietly. "I've talked it over with Altman. He's willing to go along if his parents approve. If I can convince you and you can convince them I think we'll be able to go ahead with this."

"Go ahead with what? What are you talking about?"

Danny was silent for a moment. He leaned forward against the desk, his face calm, his eyes very bright. "Let me ask you something," he said softly. "Do you remember when my father wouldn't let us talk to each other and your father was in the hospital recovering from his heart attack and you were all alone?"

"I remember," I said. "God, I remember."

"What did you want most then?"

I was quiet.

"Can you remember?"

"I wanted to smash your father."

Danny smiled. "What else?"

"I wanted to be able to talk to you."

"Yes," Danny said. "That's exactly how I felt. All those years of silence, I needed someone to talk to."

"And then I didn't duck."

"And then you didn't duck, and we became friends— and suddenly you weren't there any more. People are frightened of being alone. Most people, anyway. Zimmerman and Powys and others—those books that you saw— they talk about the beauty of solitude. But they enjoyed their solitude because they knew they could always come back to people. You don't enjoy it when you're really cut off. You hate it. Unless the solitude is a withdrawal as a

result of some kind of breakdown. That's what probably
happened in the case of the Kotzker Rebbe. You ought to
read up on him sometime. He was a lonely, bitter, angry
man. I think he really hated being a rebbe. He wanted
rational and spiritual perfection in everyone, and in himself too. It all tore him to pieces finally and he ended up
denying the existence of God and broke down and with-
drew. But I can't imagine that he enjoyed his years of
solitude. I can't imagine anyone not hating solitude, especially a solitude that is involuntary. Even Byrd hated it
finally. He thought he would enjoy it. But it ended up
terrifying him. A man begins to disintegrate when he's
completely alone. Strange things happen. You know what
happened with Byrd? He set up an advance weather station in the Antarctic in 1934 and manned it alone for four
and a half months. He was connected by radio to the
outside world, to Little America. He wanted to be alone.
He actually looked forward to the solitude. And at first it
was a beautiful experience and he even regretted having
the radio. Then it slowly became what he called the
'brain-cracking loneliness of solitary confinement.' Those
are his words. Let's see." Danny was silent a moment.
Then he began to quote from memory. " 'At home I
usually awaken instantly, in full possession of my facul-
ties. But that's not the case here. It takes me some minutes
to collect my wits; I seem to be groping in the cold
reaches of interstellar space, lost and bewildered.' Somewhere else he says, 'Now when I laugh, I laugh inside; for
I seem to have forgotten how to do it out loud.' He says
that the absence of conversation makes it difficult for him
to think in words. 'I talk to myself and listen to the words,
but they sound hollow and unfamiliar.' A few paragraphs
later, he writes that he's been trying to analyze the effect
of isolation on a man. I'll just give you a few of his
remarks. He says, 'The silence of this place is as real and
solid as sound. More real, in fact, than the occasional
creaks of the Barrier and the heavier concussions of snow
quakes.' Then he says something very important. 'Very
often my mood soars above it; but when this mood goes, I

find myself craving change—a look at trees, a rock, a handful of earth, the sound of foghorns, anything belonging to the world of movement and living things.' That's a very interesting observation. But Byrd was able to withstand the real disintegrating effects of isolation because he had records to keep and instruments to watch and because, as he put it, 'my defenses are perfected.' Things didn't go too well for him later on, but that's another story. The point is that Michael has tremendous defenses, and isolation has a way sometimes of penetrating those defenses and making you want to talk. I want Michael to talk. And I think this may be the only way to get him to do it."

I was staring at him in astonishment and fear. "You want to put Michael through this on the basis of a book by an explorer—on the basis of a single experience?"

He shook his head slowly. "No. There's some technical material that's been written about the effects of isolation. I have some of it here." He went through the pile of monographs on his desk, selected a few papers, and handed them to me. I glanced quickly at the titles: "Extreme Social Isolation of a Child," by K. Davis; "Final Note on a Case of Extreme Isolation," also by K. Davis; "Infant Development Under Conditions of Restricted Practice and of Minimal Social Stimulation," by W. Dennis.

"I have some other material at home," Danny said. "Some of it is in German."

"Has this kind of thing ever been done before with someone who's sick?"

"I can't find anything on it. Altman doesn't think there is anything."

"You mean it's never been done before?"

"I don't think so."

"You want to try an experiment with Michael that's never been done before?"

"Yes," he said very quietly. Then he said, "Don't look at me like that."

"How the hell do you want me to look at you? That's a

suffering boy you've got. How can you experiment with him when you don't really know what you're doing?"

"I know he's suffering," Danny said, the calmness abruptly gone from his voice. "You don't have to tell me he's suffering."

"I think it's a crazy idea. What do you do, lock him in a room, alone, without furniture, or even a clock, and just let him lie there by himself until he falls to pieces and begs to talk? Is that the idea?"

"It's a lot more technical and complicated than that. But that's the idea."

"I think it's crazy."

"Do you know what the alternative is?"

"What?"

"Michael will be institutionalized."

I stared at him and said nothing.

"Tonight was very serious. How long do you think the people here are going to let him roam around loose? He's dangerous, Reuven. He's dangerous to others and to himself."

"And you think this experiment will cure him?"

"No, it won't cure him. If it works it will get him to talk. He'll be able to go through the process of normal therapy. That's what might cure him, or at least enable him to live with his problems. The experiment will make him really sick, so sick that he'll want normal therapy."

"I don't know the first thing about any of this. How can I decide whether it makes sense or not?"

"I want you to trust me. Altman thinks it makes sense. I want you to trust me and to back me when I talk to the Gordons about it."

"What difference will it make what I say?"

"You have no idea how much your word counts with the Gordons."

"Let me think about it. Let me—I want to think about it."

"Think about it until tomorrow night."

"What's tomorrow night?"

"A family conference after your dinner with the Gordons. Rachel and I and her parents are coming over. I set it up when I found out you would be there. I want a decision."

"Do Michael's parents know about the experiment?"

"Yes. They also want to think about it."

"I don't know what—"

There was a knock on the door. Danny looked across the room. "Come in," he said, his voice suddenly calm again.

The door opened and Abraham and Ruth Gordon came inside and closed the door behind them. They had on their coats and looked frightened.

"We found Michael asleep," Abraham Gordon said. His round, fleshy features were gray. "The girl said to go down to your office."

"Did something happen?" Ruth Gordon asked. Her eyes were dark with fear.

"Yes," Danny said quietly.

"Something serious?"

"Please take off your coats and sit down." He sounded very calm and professional. "Reuven, think about it."

He was telling me he wanted me to leave. I got to my feet.

"Must you go?" Ruth Gordon asked quickly.

"Yes."

"We're expecting you tomorrow night."

I nodded.

"We came to light the Hanukkah menorah," Abraham Gordon said. He seemed tired and confused. "We came straight from the airport. I bought him a new menorah." He indicated the package in his hand.

"Please sit down," I heard Danny say, and closed the door softly behind me.

It was very late, and I took a cab home. Manya was gone. I found my father at the kitchen table, eating alone. He had decided to wait for me before lighting the Hanukkah candles. He looked haggard. There was some cold chicken in the refrigerator. I ate quickly, and we talked.

"When the alternative is possible disaster, a man must gamble," my father said, looking at me intently, his eyes bright and weary behind his spectacles. I had the impression he was talking as much about himself as about the Gordons.

Later, we went into the living room, and his thin voice chanted the blessings as he lit the candles on the Hanukkah menorah in the window—hours after they should have been lighted. We sang the songs together. Then we stood there for a long time, staring down at the two tiny flames that flickered against the enormous darkness of the night.

Twelve

I woke in the night and saw slivers of light framing my door and came quickly out of my room. The hall and kitchen lights were on. I found my father at the kitchen table. He sat very still, staring down at the table, and all he said was that he could not sleep and that I should go back to bed. I went back to bed and lay awake, and after a long while the lights were turned off and I heard him go to his room.

The phone rang at ten to eight the next morning. I had just finished praying the Morning Service. I put away my tefillin and answered it on the third ring. It was Ruth Gordon. Her husband was not feeling well. The dinner would have to be postponed. No, it was nothing serious. She would call me again.

My father looked as if he had not slept at all. He ate breakfast automatically and without appetite. His eyes were rimmed with dark circles and his face was pale. He had forgotten to comb his hair and grimaced with annoyance when I told him about it. He seemed reluctant to leave the house. When I asked him what was wrong he replied somewhat testily that nothing was wrong. He was still at the kitchen table when I left for school.

Rav Kalman ignored me completely that day and acted as if I weren't in the room. I found it increasingly difficult even to listen to his voice. I sat there most of the period, staring down at my Talmud and doing logic problems in my head.

I called Danny at his apartment that night. He told me there had been a staff meeting at the residential treatment center that afternoon. They were beginning to re-evaluate Michael's situation in the light of last night's episode. He did not think anything really serious would result; a re-evaluation of this sort was more or less routine. But it didn't help matters. Had I thought about what he had told me? Yes, I had thought about it, I said, and had talked it over with my father. I wanted to think about it some more, I said. And then I added that I still wasn't sure I understood why he felt that my support would count very much with the Gordons. What was the matter with Abraham Gordon? I asked. He had had some chest pains and the doctor had told him to rest for a few days, Danny said. We would probably all be getting together sometime next week.

My father went to sleep very early that night. He looked ashen. There was clearly something going on in his school that was causing him considerable anguish. But he would say nothing about it.

Rav Kalman continued to ignore me. I sat across from his desk on Tuesday and Wednesday of that week and he seemed hardly aware of my existence. But I noticed two changes in him that perplexed me. He had virtually stopped pacing back and forth behind his desk. He sat at the desk now or stood quietly behind it, smoking one cigarette after another. And much of the sarcasm was gone from his voice. He seemed quieter somehow; his voice was subdued; much of his usual relentlessness was gone from him. On Thursday I noticed him looking at me from time to time during the first hour of the class. Then, in a very quiet voice, he called on me to read. He let me read for half an hour without interruption. Then he called on someone else. After class, on our way over to the coat racks in the synagogue, Irving Goldberg asked me if I had noticed that there hadn't been any tirades from Rav Kalman ever since the incident with Abe Greenfield the other week. I hadn't noticed, I said, and added that it didn't really make any difference to me one way or the other about Rav Kalman's tirades.

Abraham Gordon called me at a few minutes past nine that night. Could I come over to his office at the seminary tomorrow? He had a class from ten to twelve and would like to see me at about twelve if I could make it. We could have lunch together in the seminary dining room and talk. There was something important he wanted to talk to me about. He had thought I would be able to come over to them for dinner sometime next week, but something had come up and they would be out of town all of next week. Would I come to the seminary? He wanted to talk to me about Michael. His voice sounded hoarse and urgent. Yes, I said. I would come.

The next morning I took a bus to Eastern Parkway, a wide street with two islands and eight lanes of traffic, and trees lining the sidewalks, and elegant private homes and well-kept, pre-war apartment houses. It was a cold, sunny morning, and I walked quickly to the five-story, gray-brick building of the Zechariah Frankel Seminary and up the stone steps and through the huge wooden front door into the lobby, where there were display cases of Jewish ceremonial objects and a collection of first editions of scholarly works by the faculty, arranged, title pages exposed, inside a glass-enclosed cabinet. Two students stood in front of the elevator door, arguing about a passage having to do with a cat in Martin Buber's *I and Thou*. They continued arguing as we rode up the elevator. One of them wore a skullcap; the other did not. They were still arguing as I got out on the fifth floor.

I walked down a silent corridor to Abraham Gordon's office and knocked on his door. I heard quick footsteps and the door was opened and Abraham Gordon shook my hand warmly and told me he was grateful I had come. The office was long and narrow and lined with floor-to-ceiling bookcases. A single window took up almost the entire wall opposite the door. There was a small wooden desk near the window and a long table perpendicular to the back of the desk. The desk and the table and the chairs and the bookcases took up most of the space of the office.

Abraham Gordon was quite visibly fatigued. His huge frame seemed somewhat bowed and his fleshy face sagged. He thought it would be best if we had lunch first and then came back to the office and talked. I agreed. We rode the elevator downstairs to the floor below the lobby. The dining room was brightly lighted and quite crowded. We went through a cafeteria-style line and then brought our trays over to a corner table. There was a small sink against a wall and a metal cup on a shelf alongside it. We washed our hands and pronounced the blessings and sat alone at the table and ate. Students kept coming in and out of the dining room. A loud hum of conversation filled the room. I heard a heated discussion about the relevance of traditional Jewish law to the modern world, another discussion about the way a professor had rearranged a chapter of Hosea earlier that morning, a third discussion about the advantages and disadvantages of small-town pulpits—all of it going on at the tables near us. I noticed some people eating without skullcaps and wondered whether they were students or outsiders. An elderly man came over to our table and he and Abraham Gordon talked briefly about a law committee meeting that was scheduled for next week. Abraham Gordon couldn't attend; he would be out of town next week. Then he introduced me to the man as Reuven Malter, David Malter's son. The man's face lit up and he shook my hand effusively. He had read my father's book; he had received an advance copy and had read it; a magnificent book; a great contribution. They talked some more, and then he went off to get something to eat.

"He's one of the greatest Talmudists in the world," Abraham Gordon said, watching him walk away.

Students kept passing by and greeting him, and occasionally one would stop to talk or simply to wish him Shabbat shalom. In the lulls between these encounters he talked to me about his trip to Washington, which he said had been very depressing because the city was under a pall of terror as a result of McCarthy, and about the book he was now writing in which he dealt with the problem of prayer, and about Rav Kalman's attack against my father. He kept referring to the attack as vicious and slanderous, and that surprised me a little—I had been upset enough by the directness of the attack but I hadn't thought of it as being vicious and slanderous—until I realized that he was talking about the second part of the article, which had been published in today's issue of the newspaper and which I had not yet seen. He was surprised at how carefully Rav Kalman had read my father's book and at how well he had understood its intricacies; he had not thought a man with an Eastern European yeshiva background could have understood so much about the technical aspects of Talmudic source criticism; but the attack was vicious and slanderous. I did not tell him how Rav Kalman had come by his understanding of my father's book.

We finished the meal and chanted the Grace and then went back up to his office. He sat alongside me at the table, his tall body curving forward in the chair. He asked me to tell him exactly what had happened on Sunday. I told him. He listened and was silent, his face grim. He had removed his skullcap immediately after we had chanted the Grace. His thinning hair lay combed straight back on his head.

"You know Daniel Saunders quite well," he said finally. "You probably know him better than anyone. Dr. Altman tells me he is an excellent student. You know, of course, that Dr. Altman is adjunct professor of clinical psychology at Columbia and that Daniel is in his class. You didn't know that? It was Altman who suggested that Daniel do his fieldwork at the treatment center. He is of the opinion that your friend is capable of doing original work in psychology." He paused for a moment. "Dr. Altman feels we ought to go ahead with Daniel's idea. My brother and his wife agree with him. But Ruth is absolutely opposed to it. How do you feel about it, Reuven?"

I told him I didn't know a thing about the process of therapy and had no way of evaluating the idea.

"I understand," he said quietly. "But how does one make a decision in such a situation? How does a person decide, for example, to accept a doctor's judgment that he requires surgery?"

I told him that the most important thing was to feel you trusted the doctor.

His gray eyes fixed on me intently. "Yes," he said. "I cannot think of anything more important than that."

I asked him what he thought of Danny's idea. He was silent a moment. Then he said he didn't know, he had not yet been able to make up his mind. "The notion of someone experimenting with my own son—" He shook his head. His huge body sagged against the back of the chair and he shook his head again. "It's strange," he murmured. "You raise a boy and you give him all the love you can, you play with him, you talk with him, you teach him to play ball and to swim, and he's healthy, and you know he loves you and you love him—and suddenly he's sick, and everything falls to pieces. I can understand a child being sick if his parents neglect him or bring him up with resentment or hate. But there was nothing of that." He shook his head again. "I don't begin to understand it." His eyes filled, and he looked away and was silent a long time. I could see his shoulders trembling. Then I heard him take a deep breath and he looked back at me.

"I trust Daniel Saunders," he said quietly. "I trust him totally and without reservation."

I did not say anything.

"That is the only reason I am even considering his idea. I trust him. That is why I wanted him in the first place. The genius son of a great rebbe who abandons the tzaddikate to go into psychology but doesn't abandon the tradition—that is a rare thing. It takes a remarkable young man to do that. And when you meet him and discover his sensitivity, his soul, you really begin to understand how remarkable he is. I needed someone I could trust. After the debacle with those three therapists, I needed someone I could trust absolutely and without the slightest reservation. I trust Daniel Saunders. I think I am going to let him go ahead. If I can convince my wife. It is going to be very difficult to convince Ruth. I don't know what else we can do. I'm afraid—I'm afraid Michael may hurt himself one day."

He fell silent then and sat rigidly, staring down at the table.

"I know how you feel about Michael," he said, still staring down at the table. "What does your instinct tell you we ought to do?"

I told him I didn't know what to say. I was really an outsider and didn't feel competent enough to decide one way or the other.

"An outsider?" He seemed quietly astonished. "You're less of an outsider than my brother. You brought us to Daniel Saunders. You're the only one Michael talks to without having to be prodded. No one considers you an outsider."

I was quiet for a moment. Then I asked him what Rachel thought of Danny's idea.

He waved the question away. "Rachel is in no position to judge anything of that sort now. The two of them are so crazy in love they see nothing but perfection in each other." He said it as if it were a piece of information he took for granted I had known about all along.

I sat very quietly on my chair and was silent a long time. Then I said, speaking softly and trying hard to keep my voice under control, that I trusted Danny, that Dr. Altman apparently also trusted Danny, that there did not seem to be much point in going on and on with Michael getting nowhere with normal therapy, that there really was no alternative, and that I had talked about Danny's idea with my father and he also felt that a person ought to gamble when the alternative was disaster.

He gave me a sudden sharp look and his broad shoulders stiffened. "Gamble," he muttered softly, his voice shading into quiet bitterness. "Yes ... Gamble." He seemed to think of something then and a peculiarly bright look came into his eyes. He sat there, nodding slowly, as if he were engaged in some kind of interior dialogue with himself. Then I saw him smile sadly and he looked at me and said, "Almost everything of importance that a person does is a gamble, isn't it? Every crucial decision is a gamble." He smiled wryly and was silent again, his gray eyes turned inward. Then he shook his head slowly and came back from wherever he had been. "All right. I am going to gamble on Daniel Saunders. I will let him experiment on Michael. I will have to convince my wife that we have no other choice." Then he lapsed again into silence, his eyes staring at me but not really seeing me.

We sat still for a moment, and then he got slowly to his feet and thanked me for coming. "We'll have you over for dinner yet," he said with a smile. "I'll have to show you the scrapbook I keep of attacks on me over the years. You won't feel so bad about Rav Kalman and your father." We were at the door to the office. He shook my hand, gripping it firmly and warmly. "Give your father my very best regards. And tell him that the introduction to his book will be required reading in my courses here from now on."

I took the elevator downstairs and stood outside a long time, staring up at the sunlight on the building. Then I walked to the bus stop. There was a newsstand on the corner and I bought a copy of *The Jewish Guardian*. The bus came and I got on and sat down and read the second part of Rav Kalman's article. I sat there, thinking of Abraham Gordon's last words and reading Rav Kalman's article and feeling the anger rising up in me again.

It was vicious, all right. Last week he had questioned my father's right to offer interpretations of the Talmud that ran counter to the accepted interpretations of the medieval commentaries; by what authority did my father dare emend the text; did he consider himself as great as the Rishonim or the Vilna Gaon; how could he dare give an interpretation to a Mishnah—the Mishnah is the vast written compendium of rabbinic oral law; the Mishnah and the Gemara together comprise the Talmud—how dare my father give an interpretation to a Mishnah that contradicted the interpretation given in the Gemara? He had used examples from my father's book, and in some of those examples I had recognized words that I had used as I had explained various parts of the book to him during our after-class sessions together. But now he had broadened his attack considerably. He was writing about the implications of my father's method, and he had turned vicious and sarcastic. What were some of the insidious implications of this method of study? he wrote. If one accepted the possibility of changing the text of the Talmud, then what might happen to the laws that were based on these texts? Did one change the halachah—"halachah" is the word for Jewish law—every time one discovered a law based on a text that was thought to be incorrect? And where would such a system of study end? If one permitted oneself the right to emend the Talmud, then why not go on and emend the Five Books of Moses as well? Why not change the text of the Ten Commandments or the various other legal passages? What then would happen to the sanctity of the Bible? How was one to regard the Master of the Universe if one could simply go ahead and rewrite the Bible? How was one to regard the Revelation at Sinai? The entire fabric of the tradition would come apart as a result of this kind of method. It was a dangerous method, an insidious method; it could destroy the very heart of Yiddishkeit. And it was dangerous not only to Jews but to all religion. The gentile world also had sacred texts. What would happen to the religion of the gentiles if they used such a method upon their texts?—I was amazed that Rav Kalman should feel it necessary to use the sacred texts of the gentiles in order to point up the dangers of my father's method of study; then it occurred to me that he was probably trying to add a note of sophistication and universalism to his argument. I continued reading. A method of this kind made man superior to God because it made the sacred texts subject to man's tiny understanding; what he did not understand, he changed. A scholar who used such a method was committing heresy; he was destroying not only Yiddishkeit but also the very essence of religion—the belief that the sacred texts were given by

God to be *studied* by man, not to be *rewritten* by him.
Those who feared God were forbidden to study such
works of scholarship; they were forbidden to let their
children study them. Had Jews suffered two thousand
years for a tradition based on texts that were filled with
scribal errors? What kind of scholarship could promulgate
such an idea? Dangerous scholarship! Malicious scholarship!—His hysteria was reminiscent of Reb Saunders's
attitude toward modern political Zionism, which he regarded as the spawn of Jewish secularists; there is a
numbing sameness to the way religious zealots express
themselves. Such scholarship should have no place in a
yeshiva, he wrote. Our children must never be exposed to
this kind of heretical handling of texts that were the very
heart and soul of the tradition!

I was sick with cold rage by the time I was done
reading it. I came off the bus. A middle-aged Hasid in a
long dark beard and a dark overcoat bumped into me
heavily as I walked beneath the sycamores. The brown
paper bags he held in his hands tumbled to the sidewalk,
spilling out oranges and apples and cans of fruit and
vegetables. He apologized loudly in Yiddish and I barely
heard him as I helped gather everything up off the
ground. He thanked me and went rushing off, holding
tightly to the bags. I went up the front steps of the
brownstone and into the apartment.

My father was not home. Manya was in the kitchen
over the stove. I could smell the Shabbat food all through
the apartment. I went into my room and sat behind my
desk for a while, then lay down on my bed, then went
back to my desk and tried doing some logic problems. I
played with the problems for a few minutes, then went
into the hall and called Danny. Levi answered. Danny
was not home yet. I could feel the phone trembling against
my ear. I wished him Shabbat shalom and hung up. I
went back into my room and stared out the window at the
sunlight on the ailanthus in our back yard. Then I lay
down again on my bed. A moment later I heard a key in
the front door and I went quickly into the hall and saw

my father come into the apartment. He said nothing to me as he put his hat and coat into the hall closet, but I knew by the look on his face that he had read the article. I told him I had read the article and began talking about how I felt. He stopped me with an abrupt and angry gesture of his hand. He did not want to discuss it now, he said. His voice was husky and he sounded as if he was coming down with another of his colds. He went into his study and closed the door.

I came back into my room and sat at my desk and did some more logic problems. The newspaper lay on top of a pile of books on my desk. I read the article again, then put the newspaper into a drawer. I sat there, working on the logic problems. Through the door that connected my room to my father's study I could hear my father shuffling papers and coughing, a hoarse, dry, rasping cough which with him could mean anything from a minor cold to a serious bronchitis or congestion of the lungs. This is going to be some Shabbat, I thought bitterly.

Danny returned my call later that afternoon and I told him what I had said to Abraham Gordon. He had had Michael in therapy that morning, and Michael had spent most of the hour talking disconnectedly about Rachel and giving Danny angry, knowing glances. In her visits with Michael, Rachel had been urging him to trust Danny and to talk to him, and Michael had apparently begun to realize why her voice was always charged with excitement each time she talked about Danny. Now he wanted to know how well Danny knew his cousin. Danny had been afraid of this all along. He was beginning to think he ought not to be doing any more therapy with Michael. He would discuss it with Altman on Monday. He kept saying over and over again that he should not have become involved with Rachel, that it would be a mess, that he had botched the whole thing, that the experiment was really a wild idea and who was he to try something like that, he was still only a student, he had no right to take a chance like that with someone else's life—and it occurred to me as I listened to him that Michael had always been more than merely a patient to him: Michael was his first attempt at self-vindication, the first in a long series of efforts he would be making to prove to himself that the pain he had caused his father at refusing to take on the tzaddikate, and the years the tzaddikate would ultimately take from his brother's frail life, was all worthwhile. He was frightened of making a mistake, frightened of failure—as much because of what it might mean to him as what it might do to Michael. I told him to calm down and stop being hysterical; I had had enough hysteria for one day from Rav Kalman's article, I said. He hadn't read the article yet, he said. He had just returned home. Well, it was a beauty, I said, and sitting across the desk from Rav Kalman next Sunday morning promised to be an interesting experience. Calm down, I said again. He had been trying to get Michael to talk by giving him Rav Kalman's article against my father. Maybe Michael would really talk if he found out about him and Rachel. I was trying to get him out of his black mood and was simply using whatever came into my head without really knowing what I was saying. There was a long silence on the phone during which I thought of what I had said and realized that it sounded rather ridiculous and waited for Danny to tell me to stick to Talmud and logic and let him do the planning about how to get Michael to talk. Instead, the silence continued. I asked him if he was still there. He said yes, he was still there, but it was getting late, he wanted to take a shower and get dressed. His voice was strangely calm. He wished me a good Shabbos and hung up.

That was not a good Shabbat—neither for me nor for my father. My father remained in his study until a few minutes before it was time to leave for the synagogue. He shaved and dressed hurriedly and we walked along the Williamsburg streets through crowds of Hasidim in long coats and fur-trimmed caps on their way to their various tiny synagogues. I listened to their Hungarian Yiddish. Walking to and from our synagogue every Shabbat was becoming an increasingly uncomfortable experience for me. It was like moving back through centuries to a dead world that came to life once every seven days. It was a strange enough experience being on those streets during the week. But on Shabbat, when I could feel them making the very air tremulous with exultation, when I could see them in their respective garbs, most of them in fur-trimmed caps, some in dark suits, some in white knickers, all of them walking quickly, sometimes in groups, sometimes alone, sometimes the father accompanied by a troop of male children—on Shabbat it was particularly strange and I felt myself to be an uncomfortable outsider who had somehow been transported to a world I once thought had existed only in the small towns of Eastern Europe or in books about Jewish history. They were my own people, but we were as far apart from one another as we could possibly be and still call ourselves by the name "Jew"—and I had never felt as distant from them as I felt that evening walking along Lee Avenue with my father on our way to the synagogue where we prayed.

My father said nothing to me as we walked. His cough seemed worse and inside the synagogue it was a quite audible counterpoint to the service. Many of my father's colleagues prayed in that synagogue and after the service they crowded around him, expressing their anger at Rav Kalman's article. I caught snatches of conversation that puzzled me. My father must not give in, someone said. He must not permit it to be withdrawn, someone else said. Names which I did not recognize were mentioned with tones of contempt. I stood aside and listened and wondered what was going on. As we walked back I tried to ask him what he was not supposed to give in on, but he would say nothing. We were not quite two thirds of the way home before I began to put it all together and realized that Rav Kalman's articles had not been upsetting my father nearly as much as what had been going on in his school.

"They want you not to publish the book," I said as we turned into our block.

He looked at me with annoyance and coughed raspingly. "They want," he said, his voice hoarse and filled with anger and contempt. "What they want and what I will do are two different things." I had never heard him so full of rage. "No one will ever dictate to me what I may and may not publish." He coughed again and wiped his lips with a handkerchief. It was night now, but I could see the rage in his eyes by the dim light of a lamp post. "No one," he said. "No one."

"What's going on?" I asked. We were walking up the front stairs of our brownstone.

"We will talk about it later," he said. "After the meal. I do not want to upset Manya."

We sat in the living room later that night and between ugly spasms of coughing my father told me that during the past two years four new Talmudists had been taken into the school. They had come from Europe after the war and had been hired by the new headmaster of the school, a man who had himself come from Bergen-Belsen. Slowly over the past few years the make-up of the faculty had begun to change. The original group of teachers was being replaced. The new ones were fiercely Orthodox. One of the new Talmudists had gotten hold of an advance copy of my father's book and had read it and shown it to the others and to the headmaster. There had been a furor. The book was dangerous. My father had been warned that its publication might jeopardize his position in the school. His old colleagues had lined up on his side against the newcomers. There had been meetings, plots, counterplots, bitterness, vituperation, insults in the corridors. And Rav Kalman's articles had served to fuel up the raging factions. The fight had come to the attention of the board of directors. There had been a meeting of the board last Sunday, and it too was split into opposing factions. The bitterness had been simmering quietly beneath the surface calm of the school during the past few years. My father's book had brought it all out into the open. And it was ugly.

"They can't fire you for the way you teach. You've got tenure in that school."

"Tenure," he said bitterly. "Reuven, do you know what

it is to teach in a school where people despise you? What does it mean to have tenure when the air you breathe is poisoned?"

"What are you going to do?"

He coughed and wiped his lips. "The book will be published," he said grimly. "No one will ever tell me what I may publish. Then we will see what *they* do?"

"But they can't fire you."

"No. But there are enough ways to make life unpleasant for a teacher so that he will leave without being fired."

"You're going to leave your school?"

"First the book will be published. Then we will see."

"You can't leave the school. They'll win if you leave."

"Reuven," my father said quietly. "They may have won already. It is impossible to argue with them or to attempt to convince them of another point of view. They know only the lives they led in Europe and the beliefs their families died for in the concentration camps. No one will change them. They are strong and inflexible and they will mold Orthodoxy to their own ways. They have probably won already." He was silent then, and his eyes regarded me intently from behind their steel-rimmed spectacles. "It is not a new quarrel, Reuven," he said softly. "I do not know if that is much of a consolation to you, but this is a quarrel that has been going on a long time. The Gaon of Vilna had a student called Menasheh of Ilye. This student was one of the greatest Talmudists of his time. He also studied mathematics and astronomy and philosophy and was even something of an inventor of new machines. But he taught Talmud in the method developed by the Gaon. No one would ever dare challenge the Gaon if he interpreted a Mishnah in a way that went against the Gemora or the Rishonim. But whenever Menasheh of Ilye attempted to teach in this manner, he was persecuted by sincere pietists—and sometimes by those who were not so sincere but were merely foolish. He was sent away from many teaching positions as a result of his method. And his method was not nearly as radical as mine. He simply did not have all the manuscripts of the text of the Talmud which we have today. He was an amazing man. He suffered terribly at the hands of others. So this is not a new quarrel, Reuven."

I told him it didn't make me feel one bit better to know that.

"I did not think it would," he murmured. "I merely mentioned it because I have always had a great affection for that man. I used to hear stories about him when I was young. He—his reputation had a great influence upon me. My father's father had been his student and talked of him often to my father. And my father talked of him to me. I feel I know him well. But I did not think I would ever be reliving a part of his life. That is the way the world is, Reuven. Each generation thinks it fights new battles. But the battles are the same. Only the people are different." He stopped and coughed into his handkerchief and wiped his lips and his eyes. "I am tired. Let us have some tea and go to sleep. You did not tell me what you and Abraham Gordon talked about today. Let us go into the kitchen and have some tea and not talk any more about my yeshiva and its quarrels. And do not look so gloomy, Reuven. The problems will work themselves out."

But he did not sound as if he believed the situation would resolve itself; he sounded grim, and the earlier anger was still in his voice, though considerably subdued now. He knew there would be a major conflict when the book was published, and he seemed quite prepared to do his share of the fighting. He was being challenged in the single most important area of his life—his scholarship and his writing—and he would fight.

We sat in the kitchen and drank tea and talked about my conversation with Abraham Gordon and then went to sleep. In the morning his cough was worse and I went to the synagogue alone. When I returned I found him in bed. He had no fever but the cough was very bad and I was afraid it would begin to affect his heart so I persuaded him to let me use the phone—something we did not normally do on Shabbat—and called his doctor. Dr. Grossman came very quickly and pronounced it a bad cold and told my father to stay in bed at least through Sunday. My father said he had a faculty meeting Sunday afternoon. The faculty would have to meet without him, Dr. Grossman said. Unless, of course, my father was interested in a good case of pneumonia. Was my father interested? He was not interested. Then he was to stay in bed. What was all this fuss about his book? Dr. Grossman wanted to know. He had seen a copy of *The Jewish Guardian*. Who was this Rav Kalman anyway? A guardian of the faith, I said. My father gave me a warning look. What a fuss he was making over the book, Dr. Grossman said, closing the bag and putting on his hat and coat. The bearded vigilantes were out in force these days. I said there were a few vigilantes without beards running around Washington. Politics and religion always brought out the best in people, Dr. Grossman said. I was to make sure my father remained in bed and to call him in case he developed a fever. He wished us a good Shabbos and went out of the apartment.

My father slept all afternoon. I tried reading a Hebrew novel for a while, gave it up, studied some Talmud and gave that up too, roamed through the apartment, stared through the front window at the Hasidim walking along the street, and then found myself in front of the bookcase in my room, looking at the section where I kept the English novels I owned. Then I was holding James Joyce's *Ulysses* in my hands. Then I was on my bed, reading the Ithaca section. I read until it was time for the Afternoon Service. After praying the service, I brought my father his supper on a tray and sat in the kitchen over some food and continued reading. Then I prayed the Evening Service, and my father chanted the Havdalah—he came into the kitchen for that, then into the living room to light the Hanukkah candles, and then went immediately back to bed—and afterward I sat at the desk in my room and went on reading. I had never quite understood that part of *Ulysses* until I read it that Shabbat. I was almost done with it when the phone rang.

It was Danny. Was I going out tonight? he wanted to know. I told him I wasn't going anywhere tonight, my father wasn't feeling well and I was staying home. Was it anything serious? he asked. No, it was a cold. Why? He wanted me to come with him to the Gordons. My head had been full of Ithaca until then and I had been talking and not really listening to him. Now I caught the panic in his voice. What happened? I asked. Something happened with Michael? Yes, something happened with Michael. No, he hadn't been hurt or anything like that. He would pick me up in a few minutes and we would go by cab to the Gordons. Rachel would be there with her parents. Could I be ready in a few minutes? Yes, I could be ready. He hung up.

My father was still coughing but he had no fever, so when I told him about Danny's call and listened to him urge me to go I did not feel too concerned about leaving him alone. I shaved and put on a fresh shirt and was knotting my tie when I heard the honking of an automobile horn outside. It was a cab. I told my father I was leaving and went quickly out. There was a cold wind and the branches of the sycamores swayed wildly. I slid into the back seat and heard Danny give the driver an Eastern Parkway address.

He was unshaven and his eyes blinked repeatedly and he looked as though he had not slept in a long time. He held a small overnight bag on his lap. He saw me looking at the bag.

"I went back to pick up my tefillin and some things," he said.

"Went back?" I stared at him. "You weren't home for Shabbat?"

"I've been at the treatment center since three in the morning."

"You went to the treatment center on Shabbat?"

He spoke very rapidly as the cab took us through the dark asphalt-paved Brooklyn streets. I listened in dread and with a sense of too much happening all at the same time, too much—why everything all at once like that? The cab dodged through traffic and lurched around corners. It was an old cab and it rattled and trembled and wheezed noisily. But it possessed a singular virtue for which I was grateful: a silent driver. I listened to Danny.

It had taken most of the day to reconstruct from Michael's disconnected words what had happened prior to Danny's arrival. At a quarter of one in the morning, Michael had opened the door to his room and looked carefully up and down the corridor. The child-care worker on night duty was in his room. The corridor was empty. Michael closed the door softly behind him. He was fully dressed and had on his knee-length coat. He walked quietly through the corridor and stopped at four other doors, tapping on each softly. Four boys came out of their rooms. They too were fully dressed. The five of them walked very quietly to the end of the corridor away from the main stairway that led down to the living room and the foyer. They went through the exit door and down the back stairway to the thick wooden double door that opened into the dining room and the kitchen. The door was locked. There were small rectangles of opaque glass in the door. Michael removed one of his shoes and with the heel broke one of the panes of glass and reached through and opened the door from the inside. He cut his wrist doing that, but it was a superficial wound and there was little bleeding. The sound of the glass falling onto the floor of the dining room had been indistinct even to the five boys immediately outside the door.

The dining room was dark but they did not need light to find their way into the kitchen; they ate in that dining room three times a day. In the kitchen Michael opened one of the drawers in the large wooden table on which meat was prepared. He distributed four long knives to the boys and took one for himself. They went quickly back through the kitchen and the dining room, then along the corridor past the offices and into the living room. The uniformed night watchman usually sat at the desk in the foyer. He saw them. He also saw the knives. He stood up very slowly. He was a big man, with a barrel chest and a heavy pink face and thick arms, but he moved slowly and carefully as the five of them came toward him with the long knives in their hands.

Michael told him to get out of the way. The guard asked him where they were going. Michael told him again to get out of the way. He couldn't do that, the guard said. They knew he couldn't do that. Why didn't they let him have those knives and then turn around and go on back to their rooms? He couldn't let them go out. They knew that. Why did they want to make trouble for him and themselves? The guard did not think they would do anything to him if he did not let them see how frightened he really was.

Michael turned to one of the boys, a short, dark-haired, thin-faced boy of thirteen with strange burning eyes and his tongue running constantly over his lips. Michael asked the boy if he thought the guard could keep them from going out. The boy looked at the guard and began to grin crazily. The guard then recognized the boy: a schizophrenic who was making excellent progress in therapy but had to be carefully watched. Certain kinds of schizophrenics are capable of doing anything with a knife if aroused. They can kill themselves or anyone near them; or they can go into a frozen panic and do absolutely nothing.

The guard moved slowly aside. Michael laughed in triumph. The boys unlocked the front door and ran from the building. The guard immediately called the child-care worker on night duty. Together they woke the rest of the staff, going quietly from room to room so as not to disturb the other children.

They could hear the five boys laughing and shouting and racing through the grounds. The outside lights were turned on. Two of the boys were spotted immediately and came forward meekly and surrendered their knives and were sent up to their rooms, each of them accompanied by a staff member. A few minutes later, a third boy was found near the school building. They had a little trouble convincing him to give up the knife, but he did, finally, and went into the house. Michael and the schizophrenic boy were discovered in the pagoda. Michael laughed when they told him to give them his knife. He laughed loudly and shrilly and said he would kill anyone who came near him, they were all liars and cheats and he hated them and he would kill them or they would have to kill him if they wanted the knife.

The cottage parents and one of the single child-care workers stood near the pagoda. One of them suggested that they call the police. But that would mean headlines the next day and more fear and bad feeling in the neighborhood. The decision as to whether or not the police should be called would have to be made by the treatment center administrator. The staff member on night duty said he had better call Dr. Altman and Dan Saunders. But at that point the administrator arrived. He was a tall, gaunt, bald-headed man and he approached the pagoda and ordered Michael to give him the knife. Michael cursed him, loudly, shrilly, his voice breaking. The administrator went quickly into his office and called Dr. Altman, who said he would be over immediately and told him to call Daniel Saunders.

There were three phones in Reb Saunders's house, all with the same number, one in Reb Saunders's study, one in the hall of the second-floor apartment where Danny's parents and Levi slept, one in the third-floor hall a few feet from Danny's room. The use of the phone on Shabbat is forbidden by Jewish law except in circumstances that constitute a clear emergency, and so the phones in that house almost never rang on Shabbat. On the rare occasions when they did ring they were ignored, because everyone assumed that the person at the other end had dialed a wrong number.

The phones in Reb Saunders's house began to ring at ten minutes past two that morning. Danny was immediately awake. He lay in bed in the darkness of his room and listened to the ringing of the phones echo through the house. After the seventh ring, the phones stopped. Then they started again. Danny was out of his bed and going down the stairs to the second floor when the phones stopped ringing the second time.

He found his father and brother in the hall of the second-floor apartment, both of them in robes and skull-caps. They were staring at the phone. Reb Saunders was about to say something to Danny when the phone started to ring again. He let it ring twice. Then he said to Danny in Yiddish, speaking over the noise of the ringing, "You think it is for you?"

Danny stared down at the phone and said nothing. He felt as if the sound of the phone were coming from somewhere inside himself.

"Who would ring at such an hour?" Levi asked in Yiddish. He held the robe tightly to his body as though he were cold.

"You think it is for you, Daniel?" Reb Saunders asked again.

"It's the wrong signal," Danny said. He had arranged an emergency telephone signal with the staff member on night duty: three rings, then stop, then ring again. That signal was to be used on Shabbat in case of an emergency with Michael. But the staff member did not know the treatment center administrator was calling Danny, and the administrator had no way of knowing the signal.

The phone stopped ringing. They stood there in the hall that had a single dim night light set in a wall socket, and waited. Almost immediately it began to ring again.

"It must be for you, Daniel," Reb Saunders said. "They are calling you."

Danny stared at the phone.

"Answer the phone, Daniel," Reb Saunders said.

Danny looked at his father.

"Answer," Reb Saunders said. "If it is a mistake, let the sin be on my head."

But Danny remained still. The phone continued to ring.

"Daniel," Levi said. "Our father tells you to answer the phone."

Danny lifted the phone and put it to his ear. He listened as the administrator, who of course knew of Danny's Orthodoxy, thanked him for answering and told him what was happening. Danny said if he did not call him back in five minutes it meant that he was on his way over, and hung up. He looked away from the phone and saw his father and his brother staring at him. Danny's face was white and he had to lean on the phone stand to steady himself.

"What is the matter?" Reb Saunders asked. "Daniel, what has happened? Levi, bring a glass of water. Daniel, tell me what is the matter."

Levi started out of the hall toward the kitchen, but Danny called him back. The three of them stood around the phone, Danny explaining, his father and brother listening. He spoke rapidly, in Yiddish. Had it been any other night of the week, he would have told them nothing. But this was Shabbat. He would be traveling on Shabbat. He had to tell them.

Reb Saunders listened until he understood enough to enable him to make a legal decision. Then he broke in on Danny's words. "Go!" he commanded. "Go quickly! Pickuach nefesh. Quickly! Quickly!"

"Take a taxi," Levi said urgently in Yiddish. "You will find one on Lee Avenue. And take money with you."

"Quickly!" Reb Saunders said again. "Quickly!"

Danny dressed and his father and brother accompanied him to the front door and he raced along his block beneath the naked sycamores and found a cab almost immediately on Lee Avenue. He told the driver it was an emergency. He was at the treatment center in less than half an hour.

He went directly to the pagoda. He found Dr. Altman and the administrator and a group of staff people standing among the trees, shivering in the cold and watching Michael and the other boy, who were sitting on the bench in the pagoda. He and Dr. Altman held a brief conference. The administrator listened, all the time keeping his eyes on the two boys in the pagoda.

"Michael has obviously hooked onto Jonathan's psychotic aggressions for his own needs," Dr. Altman said. He was a medium-sized, portly man in his late fifties, with

a kindly pink face, rimless glasses, and a graying
mustache. Jonathan was the name of the boy in the pagoda with Michael. "He will continue manipulating Jonathan. We must get Jonathan to decathect from Michael."

Danny said, speaking calmly and professionally and
trying to keep from trembling with the fear inside him,
that Jonathan was probably looking to be protected from
Michael's hostility.

Dr. Altman nodded soberly. "I will bet that with all his
aggression coming to the surface, Jonathan is terrified of
going any further and want the stops put in. He is beginning to sense what the reality risks are."

Danny said he would try to get through to Jonathan
and break the aggression-fear-hostility cycle. He came
over to the pagoda. The outside lights shone through the
trees and cast soft, broken shadows across the ground and
onto the pagoda. Michael and Jonathan sat close together
on the circular white bench, their faces ghostly in the light
of a nearby spot. The long knives glistened in their hands.

Michael rose quickly as Danny approached. Jonathan
remained seated, watching Danny, his tongue running
over his lips, his eyes bright and burning.

Danny stopped in front of the steps to the pagoda and
looked at Jonathan. About fifteen feet behind him the
staff people, the administrator, and Dr. Altman stood
bunched together, waiting.

"Jonathan," Danny said. His voice came out thin and
weak. He could feel the palms of his hands sweating in the
cold wind. "Jonathan," he said again, a little louder.

The boy stared at him and said nothing.

"You know you want to come down out of there,"
Danny said. "Come down and give me the knife."

The boy sat very still and stared and did not move.
Michael looked at Danny and laughed softly.

"You've come a long way in the past few months,"
Danny said quietly. "You don't want to slide back now."

The boy licked his lips, looked down at the knife, then
looked again at Danny. Slowly, he rose to his feet.

"No!" Michael said to him. "Stay with me!"

Danny did not look at Michael. "Come on, Jonathan," he said. "Come down out of there and let me have the knife."

"Don't listen to that cheat!" Michael shouted. "He's a liar and a cheat! Don't listen!"

Danny would not look at Michael. "He's using you, Jonathan," he said softly. "He's not freeing you. He's using you."

Jonathan stared at Michael. The hand holding the knife dropped limply to his side. He came forward, looking like someone who had just been saved from falling off a roof, and handed Danny the knife. One of the child-care workers came over and took him away toward the house.

"You bastard!" Michael was screaming. "You took away my friend! Just like you took away Rachel! You took everyone away from me! I don't have anyone left! You bastard!"

"Please come down from there," Danny said, and went up the steps into the pagoda.

"You stay away from me," Michael said menacingly, and made a wide slashing motion with the knife.

"Give me the knife," Danny said quietly, feeling the sweat and the panic, feeling Michael's terror, feeling the wind on his neck, feeling the leaves blowing against his shoes.

"I'll kill you!" Michael screamed, and made another slashing motion with the knife. His long, thin face was contorted with rage and his glasses were down on the bridge of his nose. His eyes bulged and his lips were stiff. "You took everyone away! I'll kill you!"

Danny took a step into the pagoda. Michael backed away, moving sideways, his legs against the white bench. The red beams and roof of the pagoda were dark in the artificial light.

"Give me the knife, Michael," Danny said again, taking another step into the pagoda.

"You'll take Reuven away too!" Michael screamed. The words echoed faintly through the darkness of the trees.

"No one can take Reuven away from you, Michael,"

Danny said softly, coming directly up to him. "You know that."

Michael stared. His shoulders twitched and a shudder went through his thin body and he lowered his head and broke into a sob and the knife fell from his hand and clattered dully on the wooden floor of the pagoda.

Danny bent slowly and picked up the knife. It was long and quite heavy, the wooden handle still warm from Michael's hand. He put his arm around Michael's shoulders. He could feel him trembling. "No one can take Reuven away from you," he said again, very softly, and led Michael from the pagoda into the house and brought him to his room and helped him undress and get into bed. Michael said nothing. He moved automatically and was silent. Then his nose began to bleed. It was a while before the bleeding stopped.

Danny spent the night in a nearby room. In the early morning Michael's parents were called. They came and sat awhile with Michael, who was awake but seemed dazed and would say nothing to them about the night. It was Shabbat, and Danny and the Gordons would not travel back to their houses, so they spent the day at the treatment center. Dr. Altman called, and a staff member relayed his message to Danny: an evaluation meeting was to be scheduled for nine o'clock Monday morning. Abraham Gordon was gray-faced with apprehension. Ruth Gordon somehow managed to convey an appearance of exterior calm. But once during the day she went off by herself and was gone a long time. When she returned, her eyes were red.

The story came out slowly during the afternoon hours the three of them spent with Michael. He had conceived the idea soon after his therapy session with Danny on Friday morning. He had spent the afternoon convincing the four boys to join him. He had especially wanted Jonathan. No, he did not understand why he had wanted Jonathan. He had felt he needed him. What had he expected to do once they were outside with the knives? He didn't know. He had just wanted to do something. Then he said he was tired, he wanted to sleep. They came out of his room and went downstairs.

It was Ruth Gordon who suggested that the family meet that night. And it was Abraham Gordon who requested that Danny call and ask me to join them.

They lived on the street floor of a five-story prewar apartment house two blocks from the Zechariah Frankel Seminary. There was a fenced-in lawn in front and plush chairs and gilt-edged mirrors in the lobby. We came through the lobby and climbed three marble steps and went down a carpeted hall. The nameplate on the door said, simply, Gordon. They were all waiting for us.

It was a solemn meeting, utterly unlike the last time I had seen them together when they had talked of the cab drivers of Naples and the back alleys of Rome and the rooted, aristocratic loveliness of Cambridge and Abraham Gordon's airsickness over the Alps and Molly Bloom recumbent and big with seed. I had not seen Rachel since the end of October, and her parents since they had left the resort area. Joseph and Sarah Gordon had not changed at all. But Rachel had let her auburn hair grow very long and there was a radiance in her face that made my heart turn over when I first saw her that night—and there was a sadness there too, a deep brooding sadness over Michael. She loved Danny. You only had to look at her as she gazed at him or listened to him talk to know how deeply she loved him. And Danny talked a long time that night. For they had all agreed within the first five minutes of their meeting that Danny's experiment was the only possibility left to them; but they wanted to hear again, and in very careful detail now, the manner in which the experiment would be conducted.

Danny spoke for almost an hour, describing the experiment and answering their questions. We sat in their living room, a large, handsomely furnished room—Persian rugs on the floor, odd little pieces of modernistic sculpture in the corners, a Steinway piano near the heavily draped front windows—we sat in that room and Danny talked. Rachel shared the sofa with her aunt and uncle. Danny sat closest to the fireplace, leaning forward, speaking softly, intently, his faintly nasal voice filling the large room.

On the ground floor of the treatment center, directly below the foyer, there was a small room which was now being used for storage. It had been a maid's room once when the building had been privately owned. It was about the same size as the foyer, perhaps a little smaller. The room had electricity and a small window set high in the wall facing the front of the house—high enough so that someone Michael's size would be unable to see through it. They would clean out the room and have it repainted. They would make certain it was properly ventilated and heated. A mattress would be brought into the room and placed on the floor. Then Michael would be taken into the room and left there alone with the door locked. He would be given nothing to read or see or hear. If sounds filtered through the window from outside, the window would have to be sealed or even boarded up. Michael would have nothing to focus on, except the silence and the loneliness and the bare walls. He would be fed regularly by staff people. He would be seen regularly by Danny. He would be checked regularly by a pediatrician. No one except Danny would be able to speak to him. How would he get to a bathroom? Joseph Gordon wanted to know. There was a bathroom with a toilet, sink, and shower directly across a small hallway from the room. He would be taken there regularly by staff people. The idea was, quite simply and honestly, to break Michael down so that he would want to talk to Danny, to make him so sick as a result of this radical therapy that he would want to undergo normal therapy.

Danny went into considerable technical detail about how he planned to organize the staff for this experiment: schedules, flexibility, contingency plans in case this or that occurred, the nature of his therapy sessions with Michael, what they would do in case Michael stopped eating, how they would handle possible hysteria, what their plans were in case he tried hurting himself in some way. Yes, Danny said in response to a question from Joseph Gordon. The chances were good that it would work.

Near the end of that hour, Ruth Gordon turned to me and said I had been so very quiet all night, what did I think, did I have any questions I wanted to ask Danny. I had a million questions, I said. It all seemed very strange to me, and I was sure it was a lot more technical and involved than Danny had indicated. But even if Danny gave us all the technical terms and the psychological theories that were part of this, would that really help us understand what this would do to Michael. The important thing was that I trusted Danny, I said. That was more important than anything else. I knew Danny for years, I said very quietly. We had grown up together. And I trusted him.

I had apparently given expression to their own deepest feelings. There were no more questions. Danny could go to the evaluation meeting on Monday morning and inform Dr. Altman that the Gordons favored going ahead with the experiment. Abraham and Ruth Gordon had canceled their sudden trip and would be home all week in case they were needed.

"It's a hell of a thing," Joseph Gordon said to me a little later, chewing on his pipe. The seven of us were sitting or standing around the room, talking quietly. "This is going to kill my brother if it doesn't work. He would have quit writing that new book if it weren't for Ruth pushing him to finish it. It's a hell of a thing." He gazed across the room at the couch where Danny and Rachel were sitting alone and talking. "That's quite a young man," he said, smiling faintly around the pipe. "Who would have figured Rachel falling in love with the son of a Hasidic rebbe? Rachel. My crazy, beautiful, sophisticated Rachel ... Go figure it," he said. Then he said, "We're meeting his parents next week."

I did not say anything.

"Go figure it," he said again in a tone of wonder and walked away, shaking his head.

I stood there, looking at Danny and Rachel. They were

sitting close to each other, not quite touching, and Danny was saying something and Rachel was leaning toward him, and I had the impression they were sealed off in a world of their own and had been talking only to themselves for all their lives. I looked at them and felt a rancid darkness inside me—and I turned my head away.

Sarah Gordon came over to me, looking handsome and slender—a lovely middle-aged version of Rachel. I ought to go into the marriage-broker business, she said. Then she said, seriously, "Tell me about Danny's parents. What are they like?" I told her Danny's mother was a gentle, sickly woman and Danny's father was—well, Danny's father was an experience. But the fact that he had consented to meet with them was a very good sign, I said. I thought there would be trouble over a Gordon-Saunders alliance, I said. She grimaced. There had been trouble, she said. There had been a great deal of trouble. Rachel had made some—compromises. I looked at her. No, Rachel would not cut off her hair and wear a Hasidic-style wig, she said. On that point Rachel had been adamant. But there were other things . . . I nodded and we let it go at that.

Danny was talking quietly with Abraham and Ruth Gordon, and Rachel was alone on the couch. I went over to her and sat down.

"It is as obvious as an Aristotelian syllogism that you have a slight crush on my good friend Daniel," I told her.

She smiled radiantly.

"It's good to see you again," I said. "It's good to see you like this."

She thanked me.

"Tell me something, my lover of county fairs and James Joyce. Why did you pick the Ithaca section of *Ulysses* to do a paper on?"

She looked at me curiously.

"Was there a special reason?"

"No," she murmured.

"I reread it today. No special reason?"

"No." There was a faint pink flush on her cheeks.

"Danny is contagious," I said with a smile. "Or am I reading something into it that isn't really there?"

She said nothing. But her eyes were moist.

"I'm very happy for you," I said quietly. "I really am. I mean that, Rachel."

She leaned forward and right there with everyone in the room kissed my cheek.

"Aha!" Danny said, grinning, as he came over to us and sat down on the other side of Rachel. "My friend. My best friend. I turn my back and suddenly my best friend reminds me I'm in the twentieth century."

"I'm practicing for the wedding."

"That's not the kind of wedding it's going to be, best friend."

"A Hasidic wedding," I said in a tone of mock despair. "I will have to dust off my caftan and fur-trimmed cap."

Danny and Rachel laughed.

"I will have to dust off my caftan and practice some dances and songs. It's been a long time."

"Yes," Danny said, suddenly serious. "For you. But it's my world, best friend. And I haven't seen anything outside that's better."

"Nothing?" I said.

"Nothing I can't use and still stay inside."

"As long as you take some of the good things."

"I'll see to that," Rachel said softly.

I left them there quietly together in the private world they were creating with their new dreams.

I sat down on an easy chair and was alone for a moment and found myself thinking of my father and his book and Rav Kalman and felt suddenly drained and hollow with the realization that the months of seesawing between the two worlds had finally ended for me this night with nothing but an awareness of how deep the separating chasm really was and how impossible it seemed to bridge it—unless you were a Danny Saunders and were rooted deeply enough in one world to enable you to be concerned only about the people of the other and not about their ideas. I was in between somewhere on a tenuous and still invisible connecting span, and I did not know how to make that span tangible to myself and to the inhabitants of both those other worlds. Maybe it could not be done. Maybe Rav Kalman was right. Maybe one had to take a stand and abandon one or the other entirely. I would enter Abraham Gordon's world if I was forced into taking a stand. The world of Rav Kalman was too musty now with the odors of old books and dead ideas and Eastern European zealousness. But it would be an unhappy choice. I did not think I could ever be comfortable with Abraham Gordon's answers. I found myself envious of Danny's solid-rootedness in his world—and discovered at that moment to my utter astonishment how angry I was at my father for his book and his method of study and the tiny, twilight, in-between life he had carved out for us. That awareness left me so frightened and shaken that it was a moment before I realized that Abraham and Ruth Gordon were standing in front of me and trying to get my attention. I got quickly to my feet. They were inviting me and my father over to dinner a week from tomorrow night. I accepted gratefully for myself and told them I would talk to my father and call them tomorrow.

"We'll want to see more of you from now on," Abraham Gordon said quietly.

"We're very grateful to you, Reuven," Ruth Gordon said. "Michael feels he knows you so well. We would like to know you too." She said it without any trace of hesitation or embarrassment. I did not know what to say to that, and so I said nothing.

"Perhaps we'll have an opportunity to talk about those answers of mine you say you don't care for," Abraham Gordon said with a smile.

"I'd like that," I heard myself say.

"We would all like that," Ruth Gordon said.

A few minutes later, Danny and I were putting on our coats and hats. Rachel and her parents were staying on awhile. There were some plans and things they still had to discuss, Rachel said. I noticed that Danny neither kissed her nor touched her when we left.

The night was bitter cold and I felt the wind through my coat. We hailed a cab and rode for a while in silence. Danny sat slouched against the back of the seat, his coat looking bulky around him, his face faintly luminous in the night light of the streets.

"Can a son hate a father and not know it?" I asked.

He was so startled by the question that I thought he would cry out. He became rigid on the seat and gaped at me. It was a moment or two before I felt him begin to relax.

"Yes," he said in a very tight voice.

"What would it do to him?"

"That depends," he said softly.

"Suppose he were all mixed up about a lot of other things. What would it do to him?"

"That still depends," he said, very quietly, looking at me, his eyes glittering behind his horn-rimmed glasses.

"Suppose he had just become an adolescent with all that that implies and had absolutely no one his age he felt he could trust and talk to and was afraid to talk to adults. What would it do to him?"

"Exactly what it's doing to Michael," he said.

We were silent the rest of the way home. I found my father asleep.

The church bells rang, and Rav Kalman entered the room. I sat in my seat, watching wisps of cigarette smoke spiraling slowly in the sunlight that fell across my Talmud—and thought about Michael. Rav Kalman did not call on me. But a moment before the end of the class he asked me to remain behind.

We were alone. He stood behind his desk, smoking and gazing down at me, a small chunky man, all of him dark, his clothes, his face, his eyes.

He said bluntly, "You are angry at me, Malter. Yes?"

The question took me by surprise and I did not respond.

"Tell me, Malter, who else should I have gone to in order to have your father's book explained to me? I did not want to attack your father for things he did not say. I wanted to understand clearly what he wrote. I went to his son because the son of David Malter understands his father's writings, and I know the son."

I stared at him and did not say anything. I wanted to get out of there. I was finding it almost impossible to be physically close to him. I had never in my life come across a man who was so zealous a guardian of Torah that he did not care whom or how he destroyed in its defense. I had never thought Torah could create so grotesque a human being.

"You have thought of what we talked about, Malter?"

I nodded.

"And?"

I told him I would prefer to discuss it another time.

"Another time," he said. "When?"

I told him soon.

"We have a lot to talk about, Malter. It should be very soon."

He dismissed me. At the doorway, I glanced over my shoulder and saw him sitting behind his desk, his head in his hands. I went out of there utterly despising him and took a bus home.

The following Sunday morning Danny and two child-care workers brought Michael into the small room below the foyer of the residential treatment center. Danny had told Michael only that they were going to let him stay alone for a while in a special room because they felt it would help him get well. Michael screamed that he hated to be alone in a room and fought them. They locked him in. Danny stayed outside the door for a while, listening to Michael's curses and screams, then went upstairs to his office.

Rachel was there with her parents and her aunt and uncle. Danny sat behind his desk and spoke to them reassuringly. Ruth Gordon wept quietly, making no sound, the tears flowing down her face. Abraham Gordon sat alongside her, his tall body bowed and his face ashen.

Danny grew silent. Then—as Rachel described it to me later—a strange thing happened. As if suddenly taking on a life of its own, Danny's right hand rose slowly to the side of his face, and with his thumb and forefinger he began to caress an imaginary earlock. His eyes were closed and he sat behind his desk, swaying faintly back and forth, and the thumb and forefinger moved against each other and then the forefinger lifted and made small circular motions in the air and then lowered and met the thumb again, moving across it, caressing the invisible hairs, softly, gently. Ruth Gordon stopped crying. The five of them sat there, staring as if hypnotized at the slow movements of Danny's fingers. Then Danny opened his eyes and became aware of his hand alongside his face and drew his fingers away and let his hand fall slowly to the pile of monographs on top of his desk.

BOOK THREE

All beginnings are difficult.

THE MIDRASH

Thirteen

And again there were the twilight weeks, a length of dark winter between January and March when I was unable to see Michael but could not stop thinking of him alone in a bare room on a mattress with only hate and rage for companions. The leaves were all gone from the streets now, blown away by the winds or reduced to dust beneath trampling feet, and there was the cold sun or the gray skies and only an occasional ghostly memory of the lake and the Sailfish and the water against the shoreline and the dock.

Michael haunted my dreams. They were dreams of horror, filled with distorted visions of him screaming his fears to the unheeding walls, and I would wake in the night trembling, with the sound of his thin voice still echoing in the darkness of my room. To convince myself of the scientific feasibility of the experiment, I spent most of January reading the literature I had seen in Danny's possession and a great deal of other material I had not seen earlier but which he felt I might want to read. I understood enough to realize that the experiment had a sound theoretical base. But it made no difference. Michael continued to scream in the dark nights of my room.

Others were screaming too in those twilight months of waiting.

Rav Kalman wrote nothing else about my father's book. After his second attack there were days when the

synagogue where we prepared for our Talmud classes
seethed with noisy arguments as students debated the
various points he had raised. To my surprise and anger
most of the students agreed with much of what he had
written: the method of study used by my father was dangerous to all religion; it was a threat to the sanctity of the
Talmudic text; it *did* endanger the structure of religious
law; it *did* make possible the specter of biblical emendation. There were students who sought to defend the method: it was intended to *better* our understanding of the text;
it was *not* a threat to religious law because once this or
that law had been decided upon it became independent of
any specific text; a clear and logical line *could* be drawn
between the Talmud, which had not been revealed and
therefore could be altered by scholars, and the Pentateuch, which had been revealed and therefore must remain untouched. But those students were few in number
and were invariably shouted down by the others. After a
few days I was no longer surprised and angry. This was a
yeshiva. I could not expect anything else from the student
body of a yeshiva.

On the Tuesday morning following the second attack
there was a sudden raging argument between Rav Kalman
and Rav Gershenson in the corridor outside the
synagogue. We heard their voices as we sat at the tables
and we came away from our studies and crowded the
doorways of the synagogue and listened in stunned amazement to what was going on. They stood in the middle of
the corridor, their faces pale with rage. I had never seen
Rav Gershenson angry; I had never heard him raise his
voice. But he was angry that morning. His long, pointed
gray beard quivered; his voice, which in class was often
barely audible, was now loud and rasping. And Rav Kalman, looking quite small next to Rav Gershenson's tall
frame, stood his ground and shouted back, his eyes glittering with almost uncontrollable fury.

"You want too much!" Rav Gershenson was shouting.
"You want to make them all into saints! You are destroying the Torah!"

"What do you say?" Rav Kalman almost screamed. "I am destroying the Torah? I?" He stood on the tips of his toes, his head tilted back, his dark beard jutting outward almost level with the floor, and I saw his hands clench into fists. He shook a fist in Rav Gershenson's face. "It is you who are destroying the Torah!" he shouted. "You!"

"It is a different world here! You cannot—"

"It is a corrupt world! I will not be changed by it!"

"You are destroying people with your religiosity!" He used the Yiddish word "frumkeit," hurling it at Rav Kalman as though it were an epithet. "Know that you are destroying people!"

The argument raged on a moment longer, and then as suddenly as it had begun it came to an end, and the two of them stormed away from each other, going in opposite directions along the corridor. None of us knew what had caused it, but it was the subject of awed conversation for weeks. The talk about my father's book died quickly in the wake of that argument.

On a Monday morning in the middle of January, the Dean called me into his office and asked if I intended taking the smicha examinations that spring. I told him yes, I intended to take them. He was a short, roundish, pink-faced man in his fifties, clean-shaven, double-chinned, a scholar turned administrator, with a reputation for fairness in his dealings with the students. We called him "The Peacemaker." He spent much of his time placating the various religious factions in the school. I knew, of course, that the examinations would be given by Rav Kalman and Rav Gershenson, he said; he would also be present, but merely as an onlooker, a representative of the school administration. I knew, I said. He had not had any negative reports about me from Rav Kalman, so he assumed there were no difficulties. Were there any difficulties? he wanted to know. I was quiet a moment.

"Ah," he said softly. "There are difficulties." He smiled in a kind and gentle way. "That is why I have these preliminary discussions. If there are difficulties, now is the time to discuss them."

I decided to tell him what had been going on in the class the past year and a half. He listened, a paternal smile on his face. Then he shrugged.

"I know all this. It is his style of teaching. A student must accustom himself to all kinds of teachers. You are upset that he attacked your father?"

"Yes."

"It was his right. He is defending Torah. He was not of those who believed in going willingly to the crematoria. He was with the partisans and killed German soldiers for Torah. Now he defends it with words. I do not agree with everything he says. But it is his right." He brought the tips of his fingers together, forming an arc over his vest. "Reuven, that is all that is troubling you?"

I hesitated for the briefest of seconds, then said, "Yes."

He smiled and nodded. "You see? It is good that we discuss our difficulties. We expect that you will do very well in your examinations. You are one of the best students we have here."

That was the week my father's book was published. We thought at first that it had suffered the fate of Hume's first work and had fallen stillborn from the press. But by the end of the month we began to hear that reviews of the book were being written for many important scholarly journals, and that the reviews would be quite laudatory. My father was happy when he learned of that—but not as happy as he might have been. The publication of the book had intensified the quarrel in his school.

My father's school had always been one of the finest yeshivoth in Brooklyn, a model of enlightened teaching, both of Jewish and secular subjects. And so it did not take long before the quarrel spilled out beyond the walls of the school and I began to hear of it from different people— from students in my class who had younger brothers in that yeshiva; from Rav Gershenson, who stopped me in the corridor one day as I was leaving Rav Kalman's shiur and asked me if what he had heard about my father's yeshiva was true, and when I told him yes, it was true, went away, looking angry and shaking his head and muttering darkly about frumkeit; and, one day in the last week of January, from Abraham Gordon, whom I had begun to see regularly now, in his office, in his home, in the dining room of his school, and once in Prospect Park where he had asked me to meet him just so we could walk and talk; he just wanted to walk and talk and thought I might not mind being the other half of his conversation. We walked and talked for three hours on the afternoon of the last Sunday in January. And then he took me to his apartment, and Ruth Gordon served up a magnificent meal—after which we all sat and talked for another three hours, and Abraham Gordon kept coming back to the subject of my father's quarrel with his school. How serious was it? He had only heard what he had to assume were wild rumors. Were they really threatening to revoke his tenure? How could they possibly do that? He could take them to court. My father wouldn't take his own school to court, I said. No he wouldn't, Abraham Gordon said quietly. Not your father.

I double-dated with Danny and Rachel on the first Saturday night in February, and we went to a movie theater in Manhattan and saw *Death of a Salesman*. My date was the Brooklyn College friend who had first told me about Rachel last spring. Her name was Eileen Farber. She was a dark-haired, vivacious girl, and I had gone out with her a few times in December and January. She and Rachel had been friends for years.

Rachel came out of the theater with her eyes red and her face pale. She had put on her glasses for the movie and had forgotten to take them off, and, walking along the street, I reminded her she was still wearing them but she did not hear me. Danny walked silently beside her, his hat tilted on the top of his head. A few minutes later, as we sat around a table in a crowded dairy restaurant on a side street off Broadway, Rachel began to talk about the structure of the plot, the development of the characters, and the way Arthur Miller had gone about proving his argument that it was possible to write tragedies for the contemporary stage and that the proper hero of such tragedies was the common man. I asked her what she had thought about the way this particular common man had cheated on his wife and his sons, and she said that's what life was all about, the way we cheat and hurt each other and still try to live together somehow. Danny went into a lengthy psychological analysis of Willy Loman's delusions and talked about how crucial it was to be able to distinguish between reality and fantasy. The two of them sat there, discussing the movie, and I drank my coffee and ate my pie and listened and saw Eileen looking fascinatedly at Danny. She had known about Danny, of course, from Rachel, but she had met him for the first time earlier that night, and now she seemed a little awed by him. Then Danny stopped his psychological analysis of Willy Loman and began to talk about what it must mean for a man to see everything he worked for cracking apart, his life suddenly rubble, his dreams suddenly smoke—and I stopped drinking my coffee and eating my pie and stared at him. He was looking down at the table but I saw Rachel glance at me, then glance quickly away. "I can't think of anything more agonizing than that," Danny said softly, "except a long dying. A person can do one of two things in that kind of situation, assuming that he isn't a Willy Loman but is capable of making a decision. He can stay inside his world and try to reshape it somehow, or he can leave it and make his life over again elsewhere. Either choice involves further suffering, but it would be a creative suffering that might ultimately give rise to something worthwhile. It would not be Willy Loman's delusional wallowing. He could, of course, try to destroy his world and then attempt to build a new world out of the rubble. But it probably wouldn't work. No modern revolution ever really succeeded. They all substituted one tyranny for another."

"The Jewish Marxists of the twenties and thirties should hear you talk," I said.

"My father says most of those Marxists are real-estate salesmen now in California," Eileen said. We laughed.

A few minutes later, Danny and I sat alone at the table. The girls had gone off together—"to powder our noses," as Eileen had put it.

"We must be reading the same books," I said.

"How is your French?" he asked.

"Pretty good."

"Read *L'Homme Révolté* by Camus. It came out last year. You can get it in French.

"We are reading the same books," I said. Then I said, "Not everyone who resorts to violence is a fool. Remember the story of Abraham lopping off the heads of the idols."

"Yes," he said. "I can understand violence if a person makes a rational decision that his world is utterly evil and irredeemable and that nothing in it is worth saving."

"Not many people can make a decision like that rationally."

"They ought to read some good books."

"Marx read a lot of good books."

"Marx was full of rage. Books don't do much good when you're that full of rage."

"We're all full of rage. That's something I've begun to think about these days. Who isn't full of rage?"

"Yes. But most people manage in one way or another to handle it."

"Why are people so full of rage? How would your friend Freud answer that?"

"With a lecture on sex and repression, and by drawing you a model of the id, ego, and superego."

"Would it help?"

"To some extent. It would begin to teach you how to become aware of yourself. That's what the soul is, I think. Self-awareness."

"The soul," I said.

"The crust is self-delusion. The soul is self-awareness."

"And if you're rebelling and are full of rage and don't have that self-awareness—what then?"

"You become a Marx or a Michael."

I looked at him. "Michael is rebelling?"

"Yes. That's what it's all about, I think."

"What is he rebelling against?"

"I don't know."

"Does Michael?"

"No. He won't know until he's able to talk about it."

"How is he getting along?" I asked.

"Michael is right now probably still smashing his fists against the door trying to get out of that room. He broke a knuckle on his right hand two days ago."

"My God. Do his parents know?"

"His parents are told everything."

"How long do you think it will take?"

"Weeks. Maybe months."

I did not say anything.

"He was in a trembling panic when we first put him in. He kept screaming that we were throwing him into a toilet. Now he's raging against it. I think he'll start experiencing hallucinations and nightmares soon."

"You think."

"Yes."

"That material you gave me to read made the experiment sound as if it had a solid theoretical base."

"It has. But we're dealing with a human being, not with one of your deductive systems."

I asked him some of the questions that had occurred to me as I had read the material and he warned me that his answers were going to have to be a little technical. I told him I was ready to be impressed, and he hesitated a moment, choosing his words, then began to speak. "Most disturbed children are able to respond to normal therapy," he said, "unless they are very disturbed. Those in a treatment center setting who resist normal therapy usually manifest this resistance by manipulating their therapy sessions, by organizing members of their peer group in order to resist adult authority, by indulging in destructive behavior. They might use any or all of those forms of resistance. Am I describing someone you recognize? Yes ... Now we become a little technical. When we have a boy like Michael, whose acting out is clearly destructive and with whom we cannot develop a workable therapeutic relationship, we can do one of two things. We can send him away—and in Michael's case that would mean institutionalization, because he's dangerous to himself and to others—or we can experiment. We're experimenting with a radical intervention technique. We're depriving him of his peer group so he'll no longer be able to channel his resistance to adult authority into and through his peers; and we're controlling his environment and showing him that his omnipotent defenses and magical thinking—which almost invariably occur in severe character disorders—are really ineffective. And now I'll become very technical. A state of deprivation not only brings on regressive disorganization but also promotes a constructive reorganization of deeper resources within a person. It breaks him down so that, sometimes with help—in Michael's case, the help would be normal therapy—he can then build himself back up. The regression it induces is utilized by the person in the service of renewed ego development. Regression in the service of the ego. How's that?"

"I'm impressed," I said.

He looked around the crowded, noisy restaurant. "The girls are taking a long time."

"Girls usually do. Does your father know about the experiment?"

He gave me a queer look. "Of course not."

"How did the meeting of the parents go?"

"There were—problems. Hello. Here come the girls."

I looked across the restaurant. They were threading their way slowly through the crowd. Rachel was still wearing her glasses.

"Lovely lady," I said to her a few minutes later as we came out of the restaurant, "how is it possible for a girl to powder her nose and not see her glasses?"

She looked astonished and quickly put her hand to her glasses.

She smiled shamefacedly and removed the glasses and slipped them into her purse.

"How was the gathering of the parents?" I asked.

She looked puzzled.

"The Gordon-Saunders convention."

"Oh," she said. "It was—all right."

"I'll bet it was," I said, and was about to ask her what she had thought of Reb Saunders when Danny came over. We went along the side street. There was much traffic and the sidewalk was crowded and, a block away, I could see the garish lights of Broadway. It was a cold night but there was no wind. Eileen took my arm. Danny and Rachel walked slightly ahead of us, their heads inclined toward one another, talking. I noticed that Rachel did not have her hand in Danny's arm.

"Your friend is fascinating," Eileen said excitedly.

"Really? Why?"

"My father says Hasidim are medieval. He's not at all medieval. I didn't think Rachel would find someone who was medieval."

"Not Rachel."

"Do you find that really brilliant people are scary sometimes?"

"Sometimes."

"He scares me."

"Yes? Good."

She gave me a quizzical look.

"I mean it's good to know I'm not the only one he scares."

We took the subway home.

That Friday afternoon I had an appointment with Abraham Gordon—he was going to show me some rare medieval manuscripts of works in Jewish philosophy— and I came into the lobby of the Zechariah Frankel Seminary and there was Rachel.

"Hello," she said, smiling at my surprise. "My uncle told me you would be here."

She had on a brown coat and her auburn hair was long and her eyes were bright and she looked radiant—and I did not know what to say. So I said something about it being a happy surprise to see her.

"Walk outside with me, Reuven. Let's walk and talk."

"Let's walk and talk" was an expression Abraham Gordon liked to use.

We went outside. It was cold but there was a bright sun and the sky was blue and without clouds. We walked beneath the trees. She was silent.

"We're walking," I said.

She said nothing. The sun was on her face and hair.

"But we're not talking," I said. Then I said, "What did Danny's father tell you?"

She looked at me quickly, surprised.

"What did he tell you? Is there a problem about your uncle and that ridiculous excommunication?"

"No. I don't think so. Danny said he would take care of that with his father."

"Then what is your problem, lovely lady?"

"Danny's father wanted to know how I would raise our children."

"And you said?"

"I said I would raise our children to be educated Jews."

"And that didn't satisfy him."

"He kept looking at Danny and asking me how I would raise our children."

"What did he say to your parents?"

"He was very cool and polite. He acted as if we were stealing Danny from him."

"You're not a member of the fold," I said. "That's the problem. How did your parents feel?"

"My father was annoyed. My mother was a little hurt."

"And you were frightened."

"Reuven," she said. "What does it mean to bring up a son in silence?"

"Yes," I said. "I was waiting for that. I've been waiting for that for months now. Do you see that bench on the island across this street? I want to sit down on it. My legs are suddenly heavy with memories."

We crossed to the island and sat on the bench, and there was the traffic in the center lanes of the wide parkway and the sun in our eyes.

"Who told you about the silence?" I asked.

"Danny."

"What did he say?"

"That he was brought up in silence."

"That was all he said? Nothing else?"

"He wanted me to know about it. He said to trust him. He didn't want to tell me any more than that."

"It scares you."

"Yes."

"It scared hell out of me. It's a form of nonverbal communication. Danny will explain it all to you."

"I don't understand." Her eyes were wide and moist and frightened.

"Rachel, listen. You love him."

"Yes."

"Then trust him. He'll never hurt you. He is incapable of hurting anyone unless it's a hurting in order to help. That's what the silence did to him. He'll explain it all to you. And it doesn't mean you'll *have* to raise your children that way. Danny was a very special case, and Reb Saunders raised him in a special way. Hasidim don't raise their children in silence. It's something that's done by only a very few Hasidic families—and then only in extraordinary circumstances. There's no magical hocus-pocus about it. Danny is using a variation of it on Michael. But I doubt that Danny would ever use it to raise a son. So be scared. But don't be too scared. Danny will explain the whole business to you."

She looked at me, her eyes brimming. "I was so frightened."

"I know."

"I thought—"

"You don't have to say it."

"I love him." There were tears rolling down her cheeks now, jeweled in the sunlight. "I was so—so—" She could not go on.

"You love him and you thought suddenly here was something weird and medieval that affected not only you but your children. You could take it if it affected only you, but not if it affected your children. So suddenly you wondered if you might have made a terrible mistake. Yes?"

"Yes . . ."

"Love him," I said. "You haven't made a mistake. And neither has he, that lucky genius." I reached over and wiped the tears from her cheeks with my fingers. "Your cheeks will freeze in this cold with all those tears. We can't give our Danny a frozen-cheeked bride. How did you do it? How did you get him to go out on a date with you? Hasidim consider dating an absolutely dangerous and lustful activity."

She smiled through the sheen of tears in her eyes.

"The wily female in pursuit. You kept bumping into him at the treatment center. You kept calling him on the phone to ask about Michael. Then, while talking about Michael, you would bring up this and that, and before anyone knew it you somehow managed to get him to ask if you might perhaps by any chance be interested in seeing a very fine movie which he heard had been well-reviewed and—"

"Reuven, don't make fun of it. Please."

"I'm not. I didn't want you to think I was."

"I love him. I saw him in the summer and drove him to the house and back and talked with him in the car—and I loved him. Me. Rachel Gordon. Twentieth-century sophisticate. Daughter of college professors. Did you know I read D. H. Lawrence with my father when I was sixteen, and he explained what it was Lawrence was doing? We had a smuggled copy of *Lady Chatterly's Lover,* and my father went over the erotic passages with me and explained their presence in the book from the point of view of literary necessity. We read a lot of books that way. I grew up free and sophisticated, with my parents trusting me to take care of myself. And I am in love with Danny Saunders. Isn't that crazy? I love him. He's so gentle and tender and kind and so deeply and honestly religious—and so clumsy with certain things but so eager to learn. And so stubborn too about—well, about some things. He won't touch me. He won't hold my hand. The second time we dated he asked me outright—but in a beautifully gentle way—if I was a virgin. He did it in such a way that I wasn't even embarrassed. I've never known anybody like him. I was so afraid about the silence. I thought—I thought—"

"When will you be married?" I asked.

"In June. Reb Saunders wanted us to be married right away. He doesn't approve of the dating. But it will have to be June. I graduate in June."

"A June bride," I said. "Does the lovely lady feel better now?"

"Yes. I'm grateful . . ."

"For the walk and the talk? Yes. You don't have to tell Danny that we walked and talked. Let it be between us. All right?"

"Yes."

"Listen, let's walk and talk our way back to the seminary. Your uncle is sitting alone with some rare manuscripts worrying about me."

"I told him you would probably be a little late."

"I really ought to go up there now."

"Yes." She leaned forward toward my cheek but I moved back and stood up. She looked at me in surprise. Then she nodded slowly. After a moment she got to her feet and thanked me and I wished her Shabbat shalom and watched her walk quickly away, her auburn hair shining in the sun. Then I went up to her uncle.

We spent over an hour together, comparing the different manuscripts and discussing the implications of some of

the variant readings we discovered, and just before I left
he invited me to his home on Sunday. The galleys on the
first part of his new book had arrived the other day and
he was wondering if I was interested in having a look at
them. I told him I was very interested. His round face
grew flushed. He made no attempt to conceal his pleasure.
Two o'clock at his apartment, he said. We could spend the
entire afternoon together. If the weather was nice we
could go out for a while, and walk and talk. Two o'clock
was absolutely fine, I said.

I was there at exactly two o'clock. That was the day
Abraham and Ruth Gordon began to talk about themselves.

An icy wind blew powdery snow through the gray
streets, and so we did not go outside but remained in the
apartment all that afternoon. We sat in Abraham Gordon's study, a huge room which was really a combination
library-workroom-study, with floor-to-ceiling bookcases,
small writing desk in front of heavily draped windows,
and a long worktable on which were piled galleys, sections
of manuscript, white and yellow sheets of blank paper,
legal-sized yellow pads, long editorial scissors, paste, and a
variety of pens and pencils. The table was against the wall
opposite the door. Above it was a large chart which
showed the stages of the various parts of Abraham Gordon's current book. The cart was tacked to a cork bulle-
tin board on the wall behind the table. Abraham Gordon's
current book had been completed some weeks before and
was now undergoing final revision. The first part had
already been revised and was now in galleys. According to
the chart, the second part needed "minor rephrasing" and
the third part needed "major rephrasing." Expected dates
of completion were noted alongside each part. There were
various notes concerning the stages of the bibliography,
index, and the book's two appendices. It was all very
efficient and thorough—and it was all being done by Ruth
Gordon.

She sat at the long table, wearing brown slacks and a

plaid woolen shirt, with her hair falling across her shoulders and her eyes fixed intently upon a page of the manuscript. She had on a pair of dark-brown horn-rimmed glasses, which she used only for reading; when she was not reading but was still at the worktable, the glasses were pushed up high on her head so that they lay on top of the chestnut hair like two sightless lenses waiting for eyes. She smoked a great deal and hummed softly to herself as she worked—a melody I did not recognize, though it sounded like an Eastern European Yiddish tune. She worked with a soft lead pencil. Most of the time she made her corrections in silence. On occasion, she would interrupt her husband, who sat at his desk reading the galleys, and ask him about a certain word or phrase or sentence he had used, and there would be a brief conference and almost invariably he would tell her to use the new phrases or words she had suggested, and she would make the corrections. Twice that afternoon some major rewriting was required, and Abraham Gordon left his desk and stood alongside his wife, a hand on her shoulder, bending over the passage, and they worked it out together and then he went back to his desk and the galleys.

What I read in those galleys fascinated me. The book was about prayer, and the part of it that I read that afternoon was a moving and poetic account of what prayer had once meant and why it could no longer mean that today. And once again I found myself agreeing with all of Abraham Gordon's questions and none of his answers.

Later, we came out of the study and sat in the living room in front of a fire and saw the dry snow against the windows and heard the wind blowing against the building, and Abraham and Ruth Gordon talked freely and openly about their lives and about their anguished bewilderment over Michael. Ruth Gordon had served us hot, spiced wine—reserved only for cold Sunday afternoons, she said —and now she sat next to her husband on the couch, and they talked. They seemed to need to talk about themselves now. I sat in an easy chair near the fireplace, and listened.

The Orthodoxy in which Abraham Gordon had been raised by his parents in Chicago became a riotous mockery to him about one year before he entered the university. He never really rebelled against his religion. He simply stopped taking it seriously. Rebellion, said Abraham Gordon, is a conscious act of the will directed toward the remolding of ideas or institutions whether by force or by persuasion. Turning one's back upon ideas or institutions is therefore not an act of rebellion but an act of disengagement. The old is considered dead.

All through college he considered the old dead. And yet, strangely enough, he found it impossible to abandon the rituals of the tradition. The entire theological structure upon which those rituals were based had disintegrated into a joke: creation in six days, the revelation, miracles, a personal God—all of it. But the rituals—particularly prayer, kashruth, the Shabbat, and the festivals—had intrinsic value for him; and so he continued to observe the rituals while no longer believing in the theology, all the time gambling that he would one day develop a new theology for the old rituals. But by the time he was done with graduate school all of it was a joke, including the rituals. He went off to Europe for two years to do postdoctoral work in logic with some of the Vienna Circle positivists, met Ruth in the American Express office in Paris, where he had come to pick up some mail and where he suddenly discovered—that's right—he had misplaced his passport. They were both on their way home then; she from a year at the Sorbonne, where she had done postdoctoral work in French literature, and he from Germany, which he had visited for a month after finishing his work in Vienna. So they met; they discovered they were traveling home on the same boat; they fell in love; four months later they were married. While still in Europe, Abraham Gordon had been offered an assistant professorship by Harvard. But during the trip back, he decided he would rather be a professor of Jewish thought than of gentile logic, and entered the Zechariah Frankel Seminary. He had seen Germany. "I could smell the smoke of the crematoria even before anyone knew what a crematorium was," he said. "I did not think there would be much left of European Jewry before Hitler would be stopped. So I gambled. I gambled that there was enough strength and depth in the tradition for me to be able to make it into more than Sunday-school Bible stories. I had no stomach for fundamentalism. I wanted American Judaism to become something an intelligent person would have to take seriously and be unable to laugh at and want to love. No one laughs at what I write. They may hate it. But they don't laugh at it." He jumped to his feet and went out of the room and came back a moment later with a huge scrapbook which he placed on my knees. "I call it the scrapbook of hate. There's more than a decade of vilification pasted to those pages. It's grim reading. But no one laughs at what I write." He was silent then, sitting on the edge of the couch, his body bent forward over his knees, his eyes staring moodily at the carpeted floor. "A few of the articles in here were written by some of the graduates of the seminary. But they aren't vicious pieces. Most of the vicious ones were written after the war. A lot of them are in Yiddish. Their coming here made a big difference. But how can I be angry at them after what they suffered?"

Ruth Gordon recalled her husband's struggles over his first book—"Philosophers sometimes write with the grace of an elephant," she said—and how they had slowly created the method by which they worked together. They had tried to interest Michael in helping them, but they had a difficult time thinking of things for him to do and he cared little for the things they did think of—so nothing much ever came of that. On Sunday afternoons he would come into the study and stay with them awhile, watching silently, and then go back to his own room. They were under the impression that he liked the times he was with them, watching them work together.

They had always spent a great deal of time together as a family. Ruth Gordon had no doubt that he loved them deeply. She simply could not understand why he was ill.

It had happened so suddenly . . . She put out her cigarette. I saw her lips tremble and her eyes fill, and she rose from the couch and went quickly out of the room, tall, beautiful, regal with dignity and self-control. She returned some minutes later, her eyes red and puffy.

"May I bring you some more wine?" she asked with a quiet smile.

"Yes."

Abraham Gordon went out to replace the scrapbook and his wife went to the kitchen. I was alone for a moment and I sat back on the easy chair and gazed into the fireplace, feeling the warmth of the flames on my face. Then I closed my eyes and found myself thinking of Rav Kalman and found too, somewhat to my surprise, that thinking about him no longer caused anger. At that moment there was the feeling that I could walk away from Rav Kalman and his world with infinite ease and with no regret.

Abraham Gordon came back and sat down. "There are two other scrapbooks filled with praise and serious evaluations," he said, smiling. "But we won't show you those. 'Let a stranger praise you, and not your own mouth,' " he quoted in Hebrew.

Ruth Gordon returned with more wine and filled our glasses. The wine was hot and spicy and was making me deliciously light-headed. She sat down next to her husband and gazed at me thoughtfully.

"Do you intend taking a pulpit after your ordination?" she asked.

"I don't know. I may go on for a doctorate in philosophy and then take a pulpit."

"I wanted to take a pulpit," Abraham Gordon said. "Ruth talked me out of it."

"He would have put all his energy into the pulpit and left nothing for his writing," Ruth Gordon said. "I couldn't have that."

"Very strong-willed, my Ruth."

"You would not have enjoyed the pulpit," Ruth Gordon said softly.

"I don't know. Sometimes I wonder."

"You would not have enjoyed it," she said, her voice quiet.

"You would have hated it."

"Yes," she said, smiling. "You're quite right."

"I might have liked it. Helping people. Being part of their sorrows and joys. I might have liked it very much."

"You could not have done your writing."

"Not as much of it anyway."

"It would not have had the same quality."

"Perhaps."

"Not perhaps. There's no perhaps about it." Her voice was gentle but edged with conviction.

"All right," he said. "There's not much point to discussing it now."

"Shall we have dinner soon? Reuven, will you stay for dinner?"

I told her I would be very happy to stay for dinner. Then we were silent for a while. Abraham Gordon took his wife's hand. I saw her smile at him, her blue eyes very bright. She had removed her glasses and she sat with her long legs folded beneath her, leaning back against the couch. She seemed deeply content now, as if the long afternoon of work with her husband's manuscript had added to her reservoir of comfort and strength. We sat there, listening to the fire and the wind and watching the dervish dance of the snow outside the windows.

At the dinner table she said to me, "I read your father's book. He writes beautifully."

"I'll tell him you said that. He'll be pleased."

"Did you help him at all?"

"Only with the footnotes and the variant readings."

"Checking the galleys in the manuscript room got Reuven into trouble with his school," Abraham Gordon said.

"With my Talmud teacher," I corrected.

"Don't be so charitable," he said. "If your Dean knew

you were friendly with Abraham Gordon, you would have questions to answer."

"I find most of them quite detestable," Ruth Gordon said quietly, a sudden hardness entering her voice. "They have cobwebby minds, and I find them dangerous and detestable."

"How is your Rav Kalman these days?" Abraham Gordon asked.

"The same."

"Have you read any of his books?"

"Yes."

"Have you read his book on ethics?"

"That was the first one I read."

"I had occasion to read it a few weeks ago. I had no idea he was a student of Finkel. If you read the book you know about the rebellion in the Slobodka Yeshiva."

"Yes."

"What rebellion was that?" Ruth Gordon asked.

"Finkel was head of the Slobodka Yeshiva. In 1905 the students rebelled. He excommunicated those he couldn't subdue and had them thrown out of town."

I saw her shoulders stiffen beneath the plaid shirt she still wore. "They are rather detestable," she murmured.

"Finkel established quite a few yeshivoth where musar was taught," Abraham Gordon said placidly. "He refused to accept the recognition and support of the Lithuanian government in 1921 because it meant having to add secular studies to the curriculum."

"Medieval cobwebs," Ruth Gordon said.

"Not entirely," Abraham Gordon said. "Some excellent ideas were taught in those musar yeshivoth. Love of man, obedience to God, honest self-criticism and criticism of others, sincerity in the performance of the Commandments. Those were some beautiful ideas."

"They were nice people as long as you agreed with them," I said.

"That's the way it is with most people, Reuven."

"Well, Rav Kalman is Rav Finkel at his worst. He's a permanently angry Rav Finkel."

"No," Abraham Gordon said very quietly. "He can't be."

"Why?"

"He cannot be the same as Rav Finkel."

"Why?"

"Rav Finkel never experienced Maidanek." He paused, eyeing me intently. "You might want to think about that, Reuven."

Ruth Gordon looked uncomfortable.

A few minutes later Abraham Gordon said, "You know, it's strange. I can't get it out of my head how strange this all is. I sit here and talk and eat, and my son is locked in a room, suffering . . . But I don't know what else I can do . . ."

"There is nothing else we can do," Ruth Gordon said gently.

"Sometimes I wish there *were* a personal God," Abraham Gordon said moodily.

"Would you pray to Him?" his wife asked with a thin smile.

"I would have someone to shout at."

"Are you having tea or black coffee, Reuven?" she asked.

"Black coffee," I said.

Later, as I was putting on my coat, he said to me, "What do you think would happen if Rav Kalman discovered you were seeing me?"

"I don't know."

"Would he refuse to give you smicha?"

"He might. I really don't know."

"I would not like to be the reason you did not receive smicha."

I looked at him.

"If next Sunday is a nice day, let's meet at two in Prospect Park at the lake, and walk and talk. All right?"

"Yes."

"Good night, Reuven," Ruth Gordon said. "It was very good to have you with us."

"Is there still much of a fuss at your father's yeshiva over his book?" Abraham Gordon asked.

"Very much of a fuss."

He nodded slowly. "Good night, Reuven. You are good to talk to and to have around."

We shook hands and I went home.

My father was in his study. I put away my coat and hat and tapped on his door. He told me to come in.

He sat behind his desk, his black Waterman's pen in his hand.

"I don't want to interrupt your writing, abba."

"I was grading papers, Reuven. This is the last paper. Sit down and give me a moment."

I took the chair next to the desk and watched as he read the paper carefully and made an occasional correction, then graded it with the words "very good" in Hebrew and placed it on the pile of papers he had already read. He screwed the cap back onto the pen and sat back in his chair.

"Did you have a good day, Reuven?" he asked.

"Yes."

"They are very fine people."

"He asked what was happening in your school."

He looked at me and blinked his eyes. Then he smiled sadly. "I do not recognize my school these days. I am afraid that the good reviews of the book that are beginning to appear now in the scholarly journals have added to the anger of my opponents. The shouting drowns out the learning. The school has become almost—intolerable." He spoke softly. I had expected raging anger to accompany those words. Instead he seemed strangely at ease. His next words jarred me. "I will probably be leaving my school," he said quietly. "I am too old and too tired to continue teaching in such an atmosphere of repression."

I stared at him, and again there was the feeling of a world coming apart and rage against silent walls.

"Inquiries are being made in my behalf," he went on with a smile, his eyes twinkling suddenly behind their steel-rimmed glasses. "You will be surprised when I tell you."

"What inquiries?"

"Hirsch University is planning a graduate department in rabbinic studies. I was informed by telephone this morning that there are those who are interested in having me on that faculty."

I felt amazement and the sudden steep mounting of joy. "At *Hirsch?*"

My father laughed. "Yes," he said.

"With Rav Kalman around?"

"Your Rav Kalman is not the only voice at Hirsch."

"I don't believe it. I can't believe it. A graduate department in rabbinics with Rav Kalman around."

"It will be a very small department. But they want to begin in September."

I was so overjoyed that I sprang from the chair and made a quick circle of the study. There was happiness and, deep inside me, a sense of vengeance too. What incredible irony! My father teaching at Hirsch University! I sat back down again and stared at my father.

He laughed again, softly. "It is all very secret and only at the very first stages of negotiation. We will see. It will be interesting to see what can be done at your school with modern Jewish scholarship. Now, will you join me for a glass of tea, Reuven? I think I would enjoy a glass of tea."

That was the first night in weeks that I slept deeply and without dreams.

Two days later, Rav Kalman asked me to remain behind after class. He waited until everyone was gone, then lit a cigarette and sat down behind his desk. I sat across from him, waiting, feeling uncomfortable and eager to get away.

"It has come to my attention," he said, "that you have been seeing Gordon."

I was surprised at how calm I felt as I told him yes, I had been seeing Professor Gordon.

He stroked his beard. "You are aware of my feelings toward Gordon?" he asked quietly.

"Yes," I said.

"I have told you that Gordon is in cherem." His voice had risen. But he seemed to be making an effort to control himself.

I did not say anything.

He stared down at his closed Talmud. His short, thick-shouldered body seemed suddenly to shrink into itself. I thought I heard him sigh.

"You will continue to see Gordon?" he asked.

"Yes," I said, very quietly.

He regarded me in silence a moment, his eyes dark. "You are seeing Gordon for—personal reasons?" he asked.

"He is a friend," I said.

"And the cherem means nothing?"

I told him I did not consider the cherem valid. He began to stiffen. I could see his mouth fall open and his eyes flashing with sudden anger. Speaking very softly, I added that there were also medical reasons involved. My decision to disobey the cherem had been based on a medical reason, I said. I was giving Rav Kalman the legal sanction found within Jewish law that permits one to disregard the strictures of excommunication.

The anger died away immediately. "A medical reason?" His eyes narrowed. "What do you mean?"

I told him I could not discuss it.

"I have heard that the young son of Abraham Gordon is ill. You are involved with the son?"

I told him again that I could not discuss it, and wondered where he had heard about Michael.

He nodded briefly. I glanced at my wristwatch. He sensed my impatience but ignored it.

"Malter," he said quietly, "you are planning to leave the yeshiva?"

I looked at him and realized I was no longer frightened of the truth and told him that I had not yet made up my mind.

He seemed to cringe at that. His dark beard quivered and he closed his eyes a moment, then opened them quickly.

"You are reading the books of Gordon?" he asked.

"I read them last year."

"You told me you have not read them."

"I did not tell you the truth."

He blinked his dark eyes. "Why?"

"I was afraid."

He blinked his eyes again. "You are no longer afraid?"

"No."

He smiled at that. He actually smiled. I saw his lips curve upward behind the dark beard. He seemed pleased.

I glanced again at my wristwatch and shifted impatiently on my chair. But he would not let me go.

"Malter," he said quietly. "You are influenced by the books of Gordon?"

"No," I said. "I don't like his answers."

"And the questions?"

"I ask the same questions."

"You have answers?"

"No."

"Where are you looking for answers?"

"Everywhere."

"In the books of the goyim too?"

"Yes."

He seemed about to say something but the door to the classroom opened and closed quietly and I turned to see who had come in and it was Danny. I stared at him and closed my eyes and opened them again, but it was still Danny. He had on his coat, and his hat was tilted backward on his head, and he gave me a brief smile across the length of the room and came quickly toward us. I sat frozen to my chair and when I turned back to Rav Kalman I saw he had gotten to his feet and was standing behind his desk, a respectful look on his face as he gazed at Danny. That look on Rav Kalman's face surprised me almost as much as Danny's sudden presence in the room. I felt dazed and cold and found myself unable to do or say anything except sit there and watch what was going on in front of my eyes.

They shook hands, Rav Kalman nodded and smiled and seemed a little tense as he asked Danny to sit down.

"Excuse me for being late," Danny said to him in Yiddish. "A teacher kept us longer than usual."

Rav Kalman glanced at me, then looked back at Danny and asked him again, in a respectful tone of voice, to have a seat. Danny nodded, but waited. Rav Kalman sat down behind his desk. Then Danny sat down alongside me. His coat was still cold from the outside air. I could feel the cold coming off it and moving against my face and hands.

"How is your father?" Rav Kalman asked quietly.

"My father is well, thank you."

"And your mother and brother?"

"They are as well as one can expect," Danny said.

They were talking as if I were not in the room.

Rav Kalman's cigarette had been reduced almost entirely to a smoldering stub of gray ash. He put it out in the ashtray and lit another cigarette immediately. I could see Danny watching him closely. Rav Kalman put the match into the ashtray. His voice was soft and respectful when he spoke.

"Nu, Rav Saunders. You said on the telephone you wanted to speak to me about the son of Gordon and your friend Malter."

I stared at Danny. But he did not look at me. He was sitting on the chair, still wearing the coat and hat, his eyes looking very calm but alert. Rav Kalman had addressed him as Rav Saunders because a year and a half ago Danny had received his smicha from the Hirsch Yeshiva. But I had never heard him called by his title before, and I had an uncomfortable sensation for a moment, because I thought he had been called by his father's name—Reb Saunders.

"The son of Gordon is very sick," Danny said quietly.

"It is permitted to ask what is the matter with him?"

"I am only able to tell you it is not a physical sickness."

Rav Kalman's eyes opened very wide and his face paled. "How do you know this?" he asked, his voice quavering.

"I know because I am treating him."

Rav Kalman stared. "You are treating the son of Gordon?"

"Yes."

"He is very sick?"

"We have failed with everything we have tried until now. We are now experimenting with a new way to help him."

Rav Kalman stiffened. The fingers holding the cigarette went rigid, pinching the cigarette flat between them. "Experimenting?" he said in a loud, hoarse voice. "Experimenting?"

"Yes."

"You are experimenting with the son of Gordon?"

I stared at him. His face was ashen and his body was quivering.

"He is very sick," Danny said. "There is no choice but to try this new way."

"Master of the Universe," Rav Kalman breathed. "Master of the Universe." His eyes closed. I thought he had fainted. But he opened his eyes immediately and put the cigarette into the ashtray with an abrupt gesture of his trembling hand.

"Reuven Malter knows this boy," Danny went on softly. "It is important for the health of the boy that he continue to see the father."

"You know this?"

"Yes."

"You are sure of this?"

"Yes."

"You are telling me this as a doctor?"

"Yes."

"Experiment," Rav Kalman breathed. "Master of the Universe, what do you want from us?" He was staring down at the closed Talmud on his desk.

There was a momentary silence. Outside a bus went by, its tires loud on the asphalt-paved street.

Then Danny said, speaking gently, that in his judgment the cherem could not apply in my case and therefore he had not attempted to dissuade me when he had learned I was planning to see Abraham Gordon. He cited a passage of Talmud from the tractate *Moed Katan,* quoting it by heart. Rav Kalman nodded and said hollowly, "I know, I know." Then Danny cited a passage in *Sanhedrin* about one of the Rabbis of the Talmud who had been excommunicated and had become seriously ill, and Rav Kalman nodded again. Then Danny quoted some passages from Maimonides about the laws of excommunication, and Rav Kalman quoted a passage from the code of laws written by Joseph Karo—and then the two of them became involved in a lengthy and involved discussion about the laws of excommunication and under what circumstances they could be abrogated, and at one point Rav Kalman said that a law Danny had referred to had been used elsewhere in the Talmud to make a point in an altogether different situation, and they went on from there to something else, and soon they were moving all through the vast span of Talmudic and post-Talmudic literature, discussing, debating, arguing about a complex variety of subjects that had nothing to do with excommunication or anything even remotely related to it. I sat and listened and remembered another time and other Talmudic discussions between Danny and his father, and it seemed the years had vanished and it was Reb Saunders sitting behind the desk, and then Rav Kalman was quoting from a passage of Talmud and I saw Danny smile and shake his head and say no, he had not quoted the passage accurately, and Rav Kalman stared at him as Danny repeated the passage and indicated Rav Kalman had given the version found in one of the early medieval commentaries, and Rav Kalman smiled and nodded, looking very happy to have been caught in an error, and I stared at him and found myself strangely and deeply relieved to see the grief and the sadness gone from his face. I listened to the seesawing dialogue between them, and realized that the excommunication issue was over with now, they were no longer bothering with it at all, it had been resolved, and I felt a weight of darkness fall from me, and sat watching them, hearing their voices fill the room. They went on like that for a long time, and then I saw Danny lean forward and give me a glance and nod, as if to say, "Now, listen!" and he waited until Rav Kalman finished giving his explanation of a very difficult passage in a Mishnah and then said quietly that the explanation seemed to him a little difficult because there was another Mishnah that appeared to contradict it, but he thought the following explanation was something worth considering. I knew that Mishnah and its difficulties and I also knew how tortuously—and, it seemed to me, unsuccessfully—the Gemara had attempted to resolve them, but Danny's explanation was simple and brilliant, and ran absolutely counter to the words of the Gemara. In a traditional Talmudic disputation you never offered an explanation of a Mishnah that contradicted the Gemara. Nothing could contradict the Gemara. Rav Kalman looked astonished. But before he could say anything, Danny added that he had offered the explanation given by the Vilna Gaon. Rav Kalman's mouth fell open. He smiled. Yes, yes, he knew of that explanation. Now that the son of the Dubrover—he was referring to Reb Saunders by the name of the Russian town Dubrov where he had once served as rebbe before bringing his people to America—now that the son of the Dubrover mentioned it, he remembered the words of the Gaon; but he did not really think the Gaon's explanation went against the Gemara—and he launched into an involved and hopeless attempt to reconcile the two explanations. Danny listened and nodded and smiled and said nothing. With that, the discussion came to an end.

Rav Kalman sat behind his desk. In the year and a half

that I had been in his class I had never seen him so happy. I was astonished by the look on his face; he seemed suddenly alive.

Rav Kalman got to his feet. Danny rose quickly. And I rose too.

"Nu," Rav Kalman was saying, "it was good to sit and talk Torah with the Dubrover ilui." "Ilui" is the term attributed to one who is young and has a phenomenal knowledge of Talmud. "It was a joy. I thank you for coming." He was holding Danny's hand, shaking it, seeming to be reluctant to part from him. Danny was tall, a little taller than I. Rav Kalman looked quite short next to him. He stood with his head tilted upward, and he was smiling and beaming and seemed not to know how to express his happiness to Danny. "In Vilna," he was saying, "in Vilna, with my students, with one student especially, there were hours, days, when we sat and studied Torah, and—" He stopped, his face darkening. He lowered his eyes. "Nu," he said quietly. "That was a dream . . ." He was silent a moment. Then he looked at me. "I give you my permission to see Gordon." Then he said, softly, "But, Reuven, do not become a goy."

He dismissed me with a barely perceptible nod of his head.

I got my coat and hat and came out of the school with Danny. The two of us stood on the street in the winter sunlight.

"Thanks," I said.

"Thank Professor Gordon," he said. "He told me to call Rav Kalman."

I looked at him. The lines of his face stood out sharply in the bright sunlight. We started along the street.

"How did you know he would respond like that?" I asked.

"I'm not a threat. He knows who I am."

"He would have gone up the walls if I had used that explanation by the Vilna Gaon."

"You think so?"

"I know so."

"Only because you would have used it against him as a weapon."

I said nothing. We walked in silence.

"How do I show him I'm not a threat?" I asked.

"Aren't you?" he said.

I was quiet.

"If you're not, you'll know how to show him."

"Psychology is also a weapon," I said.

"It's not a weapon. It's a tool to heal people with. When it's used as a weapon it's ugly, and the people who use it are ugly."

"Where are you going now?" I asked after a moment.

"To the treatment center."

"How is Michael?"

"Nightmares and hallucinations. Yesterday morning his mother came through the walls to kill him."

I stared.

"Whatever it is," he said, "it's beginning to surface." Then he said, very quietly, "Thanks."

"For what?"

"For talking to Rachel." He looked at me and his eyes blinked. "Thanks," he said again. Then he turned and went toward the subway, walking quickly, tall and lean even in his coat, with the hat still tilted back on top of his head.

I told my father all about it that night, and he said, "When your world is destroyed and only a remnant is saved, then whatever is seen as a threat to that remnant becomes a hated enemy. I can understand Rav Kalman. I can understand his colleagues in my yeshiva."

"That's why he attacked Abraham Gordon."

"Yes."

"That's why he attacked you."

"Yes. And he is right. We are both threats to his way of life."

"That doesn't mean you should both stop writing."

"No, of course not. But it is different when you understand it. There is less of the—hatred."

"How do I convince him that the way we study Talmud is not a threat?"

"But it is a threat, Reuven. I just told you it is a threat. In the hands of those who do not love the tradition it is a dangerous weapon."

"Everything is dangerous in the wrong hands. How do I convince him that we're not a threat?"

"I understand what you are asking. Let me think about it, Reuven. We will spend Shabbat talking about it."

Later, I went into my room and took a book from a shelf of my bookcase and sat at my desk. It was a book about the concentration camps. I read the section that described what had gone on in Maidanek. I closed the book and put it back on the shelf and sat at my desk, staring out at the ailanthus in the back yard, and thinking of Rav Kalman's reaction to the word "experiment."

That Thursday he asked me to stay behind after class and we sat alone in the room and talked.

"Tell me," he said. "You have seen Gordon since Tuesday?"

"No."

"You will see him again soon?"

"On Sunday."

He shook his head slowly. "I do not understand it. How can a man not believe in the Master of the Universe and write books asking Jews to remain good Jews? I do not understand it."

"He loves his people," I said.

He looked at me, bewildered. "And the Master of the Universe? He has no care for the Master of the Universe?"

"He can't love what he doesn't believe in."

"I do not understand it."

"He tried to find something else."

"I know what he found." His voice edged into contempt. "He found an idea. When we went to our deaths to sanctify the Name of God, we died for an idea? How can such a thing be, Reuven? My students died for an idea? You can pray to an idea? I do not understand it."

I was quiet.

"Tell me," he said. "How is his son?"

"Very sick."

"There is no improvement?"

"No."

He sat hunched forward on his chair, staring down at the closed Talmud and stroking his dark beard.

"Do not let him make you into a goy, Reuven," he said. Then he dismissed me.

That Shabbat my father and I sat in his study. Piled high on the desk were half a dozen different tractates of the Babylonian Talmud, as well as the huge volumes of the Palestinian Talmud and a variety of critical editions of other ancient rabbinic texts. In careful detail, using texts as examples, we reviewed together the various techniques of the critical method and spent a great deal of time on the pioneering work done in this field by the nineteenth-century Eastern European Talmudist H. M. Pineles. We talked about the theoretical base that underlay each step of the method. I had grown up with this method of study, had always taken it for granted, and had never bothered to justify its use. We studied together all Shabbat afternoon and, because I had made no date for after Shabbat, we continued to study far into the night.

The next day I met Abraham Gordon at the lake in Prospect Park. We walked and talked.

It was cold and there were very few people in the park. The trees stood stiff and silent in the windless air, black-barked against the dead, brown earth. Overhead the sun shone like a white disk through a film of high clouds. The lake was silvery, its rim frozen to thin ice. We could see horses trotting along the bridle paths, the riders leaning forward in the saddles. A group of horses passed close to us, going very fast, the steel hooves sending up sprays of earth. Abraham Gordon ignored them.

"I did not want your choice affected by your relationship

to Michael," he said. "I am very glad we've cleared that matter up with your Rav Kalman." He was hatless, his coat collar up around his neck, his face ruddy with cold. His breath vaporized in the air as he spoke. "It was rather tactless of Ruth to ask you to have dinner with us in front of Michael. I understand that you could not refuse." He looked at me, smiling. "I would like to think that Michael is not the only reason you are seeing us now."

"He isn't," I said.

"When are you required to take your smicha examinations?"

"Anytime in April or May that I tell them I'm ready."

"Will you take them?"

"I—think so. I'm not sure."

He was silent a moment. Then he said, walking with his eyes on the ground, "I would like to have you as my student, Reuven. I would like that very much. I've never quite met an Orthodox boy like you. You might even talk me into changing some of my views." He looked at me then and smiled faintly. "You would have to work hard to do that."

I did not say anything.

"But don't abandon it until you're certain you have no alternative. First be absolutely certain you're in an intolerable situation and that you cannot alter it. Otherwise you'll be torn the rest of your life. That's free advice."

We walked on awhile and passed a horse and rider that had raced by us some minutes ago. They were standing on the bridle path, the rider, a woman in her thirties, sitting forward with her elbow on the pummel, the horse sweating and steaming faintly in the cold air. It snorted as we went by and the rider patted it gently on the neck.

"He doesn't understand my concept of God," Abraham Gordon murmured. I had told him earlier what Rav Kalman had said. "I don't understand his. A God who worries about every human being, every creature. I find it an incomprehensible notion in the face of what we know about the world and about evil. A primitive concept. What do I do with the truth, Reuven? Evolutionary theory and astronomy and physics and biblical criticism and archeology and anthropology—they present us with truths. What do I do with the truth? I cannot ignore the truth. So I try to make it serve me. But don't leave unless you are absolutely certain. If everybody who had brains and doubts left Orthodoxy, we would be in a great deal of trouble. Still," he added, "I would like you as a student."

We walked and talked a long time, making a wide circuit of the lake.

"Of course, that's the problem," he said to me once. "How can we teach others to regard the tradition critically *and* with love? I grew up loving it, and then learned to look at it critically. That's everyone's problem today. How to love and respect what you are being taught to dissect."

We came to one of the roads that ran through the park. The sun was only a few minutes away from setting. I saw Abraham Gordon stop by a tall sycamore alongside the road and put a skullcap on his head and pray the Afternoon Service. I prayed with him. When we were done, he said, "Come on home with me, Reuven, and let's have dinner together. I've walked enough for one day. I did not put on my long underwear and I'm freezing." He grimaced. "I don't listen enough to Ruth. I should listen to her more."

Outside the park we hailed a cab and rode to the apartment.

She served us hot, spiced wine and made a fire and we sat around awhile in the living room, and then Abraham Gordon excused himself for a few minutes and Ruth Gordon and I were alone. She wore dark slacks and a yellow long-sleeved blouse and her face was drawn with fatigue and concern. She stared into the fire, her fingers playing with strands of her chestnut hair.

"Has Daniel told you about Michael?" she asked softly.

"Yes."

She nodded and continued staring into the flames. I

could see the reflection of the flames on her face, the smooth skin gold and bronze.

"It is the strangest coincidence, you know," she said suddenly. "Your name being Malter. When I was in graduate school I came across Henry Malter's work on *Ta'anit* and read the introduction. I had never quite realized that Jewish scholarship could be so sophisticated and challenging." She looked at me. "What do you make of a coincidence like that, Reuven?"

I told her I didn't know.

She looked back into the flames. A moment later she said, "It was all lies, you know, the way I was taught by my parents. The parting of the Red Sea and voices from mountain tops and the sun standing still. You cannot ask of a person that he respect intellectual nonsense." She looked at me again, the flames dancing in her eyes. "You see, for a long time it was all nonsense to me and quite abhorrent. People ought not believe such nonsense in this century." She gazed into the fire and sipped slowly from her glass of wine. "It can be made to have sense," she said. "If one has the courage . . ."

Abraham Gordon returned and sat down on the couch next to his wife. Ruth Gordon looked at me.

"May I get you some more wine, Reuven?"

We sat and talked and had a fine meal and did not mention Michael once. We did not have to mention Michael. We could see him everywhere.

The next day Rav Kalman asked me to remain behind after class.

"How is the son of Gordon?" he asked.

I told him there had been no change.

He sighed and stroked his beard. He was no longer tugging and pulling at it now, but stroking it, his hand with the misshapen fingers moving across it in a rough but not angry caress. "Tell me, Reuven," he said, leaning toward me. "What is the experiment with the boy? Are you permitted to describe it to me?"

I was not sure whether or not I ought to, but I decided

to tell him about it anyway, thinking that there could be no harm in it. I described it.

I saw his mouth drop open as though he had been slapped. "Alone?" he said, sounding as if he were choking on the word. "In a room, alone, by himself? Master of the Universe! Rav Saunders knows what he is doing?"

"Yes."

"But alone! Master of the Universe! Alone!" He seemed to be writhing in pain and I was frightened for a moment. But he grew quickly calm. He lit a cigarette. His trembling hand showed plainly how agitated he still was, though he gave no other outward indication of his feelings.

"Alone," I heard him say softly, speaking more to himself than to me. "Master of the Universe, if only one of them had been spared, I would have had someone to talk to. Only one ... Was that too much to ask? One ... We could have talked about what happened ... But there is no one to talk to ..." He became aware then of his words and sat up straight, trying to compose himself. His dark eyes were wet. He looked at me and opened his mouth to say something but could not. He dismissed me with a wave of his hand.

I asked around the next day and one of my classmates told me he lived by himself in a small apartment in the Borough Park section of Brooklyn. Why hadn't he remarried? I asked, and was answered with a shrug. There was talk that something had been done to him in Maidanek, he said.

That Thursday he stormed into the classroom and placed his books on the desk and without opening his Talmud began pacing back and forth, his face wild with rage. He tugged at his beard and paced and smoked and went into a violent and almost incoherent tirade, his arms waving, his eyes bulging, the words coming out in a torrent of raging sarcasm. He had heard there were plans being made for a department of rabbinics in the graduate school where modern methods would be taught. Rabbinics! He uttered the word with shrill contempt. There would be no such department! Not while he was in this school! Rabbinics! They would not defile the Torah as long as he was still within the walls of this yeshiva! What kind of a yeshiva permitted the teaching of rabbinics? He went on like that for about a quarter of an hour. I sat very still and watched him. I had been expecting it and wondered why it had taken him so long to find out. I sat and listened and felt no need to do a logic problem in my head.

When I told my father about it that night, he said quietly, "They will establish the department. I have been told that is now definite. The only question is whether I wish to teach in a school filled with quarrels. It will be oppressive. It will be my own yeshiva again, but on a higher level."

I asked him if he had any other choice.

"There are other choices," he said. "But first I will want to think about Hirsch University."

I told Abraham Gordon about Rav Kalman's tirade the next Sunday afternoon as we walked through Prospect Park, the sky thick with clouds and the feel of coming snow in the air. He reacted in almost the same way my father had about two weeks earlier after I had told him of Danny's sudden appearance in the classroom.

"He is trying to save what is left of his world. I can't blame him. I wish it could be otherwise. I wish—Ah, what difference does it make what I wish? The concentration camps destroyed a lot more than European Jewry. They destroyed man's faith in himself. I cannot blame Rav Kalman for being suspicious of man and believing only in God. Why should anyone believe in man? There are going to be decades of chaos until we learn to believe again in man." He stared at the cloud-filled sky. "I have no one else I *can* believe in," he said quietly. "But I can understand your Rav Kalman."

A few minutes later, I asked him how Michael was coming along.

"He sits."

I stopped and looked at him.

"Daniel calls it an intensification of resistance. He has

been the same now for days. He sits on his mattress and stares and is quiet." I saw his lips quiver. "I find it hard to imagine Michael sitting for days and days, and not—" His voice broke. He turned quickly away from me and his hands brushed across his face.

Two days later Rav Kalman came into the classroom and, together with his books, he carried a copy of *The New York Times*. He put the *Times* away in a drawer of the desk and conducted the shiur. A moment before the end of the class he asked me to stay behind.

He removed the *Times* from the drawer and placed it on top of the desk. He was upset and a little frightened and his face was almost the color of the starched white shirt he had on. He pointed a finger at a headline on the front page.

"What is it?" he asked querulously. "They will die?"

I looked at the story. I had not yet had a chance to see the *Times* that day. The newsstand where I boarded the bus had sold out its copies very early.

The story reported that the death sentence of the Rosenbergs had been upheld by a higher court. The Rosenbergs had been tried for spying against the United States and had been sentenced to death in the electric chair.

"They will die?" he asked again, his voice tremulous.

"Probably," I said.

"Because they are Jews?" He was really frightened.

"No," I said. "Because they're spies."

"Spies? Only because they are spies?"

"That's enough," I said.

"Reuven, there will be—trouble?" His voice was tense with fear.

"What kind of trouble?"

"For Jews."

"No. There won't be any trouble for Jews." Then I realized what was disturbing him. "It doesn't work like that," I said, very gently. "There will be no pogroms because of the Rosenbergs."

He looked at me in disbelief. He had been in the country about two years and he still didn't understand what it was really all about. He was unable to put aside his blood-filled parcel of memories.

"No pogroms," I told him. "Do not worry. No pogroms."

"A strange land," he murmured, shaking his head. "So much goodness and so much ugliness all in one land . . ." He looked at me sharply. "You are sure?" he asked.

"Yes."

"How can you be sure?"

"I'm sure," I said. "I grew up here."

"A strange land," he murmured again. "How does one learn to live in such a land? . . . It is difficult to know what to like and what to dislike . . . A strange land . . ." He shook his head in bewilderment.

Irving Goldberg was waiting for me near the coat racks in the synagogue, looking his usual round and solemn self.

"What do the two of you do in there?" he asked.

"We talk."

"You talk? All those times you're in there, all you do is talk?"

"What do you think we do?"

"I don't know."

"We talk."

He looked awed. "You and Rav Kalman, you just talk?"

"That's right."

"Maybe the Messiah has come and no one knows it."

"Sure," I said.

"What do you talk about?"

"Dybbuks," I said.

He gaped at me.

"I'll see you tomorrow," I said.

It snowed that Shabbat and my father and I remained home all day and studied Talmud together. It snowed all day and into the night, and the next morning the city lay

like a crippled giant beneath almost five inches of snow.
On Sunday afternoon we began to hear the snow trucks
moving through the streets and that evening my father and
I walked carefully through the snow that had drifted high
against the houses and stores on Lee Avenue. We turned
into the block were Reb Saunders lived and by the time
we were halfway down that block we were caught up in a
steady stream of dark-clothed, bearded, fur-capped Hasidim, all of them going to Reb Saunders's synagogue.

It was my father who had urged me to make Danny my
friend during the days I lay in the hospital hating him for
turning the baseball game into a war between our teams and
for sending that ball into my eye—and my father had never
yet been inside that synagogue. Some weeks before the
game, he had met Danny on the third floor of a public
library, had watched him reading novels, books on psychology, Darwin, a boy dressed in the garb of a Hasid
reading forbidden books, hungrily, swiftly, as if he were
swallowing the pages. Then Danny had hesitantly approached my father and asked him to recommend more
books for him to read, and they had sat in the library and
talked—and my father discovered that Danny was able to
remember by heart every word he read. He told no one, not
even me, of Danny's visits to the library—until the day
they had both come to see me at the same time in the
hospital. That had been more than seven years ago. In all
those years my father had never met Reb Saunders. Now
we were going to Reb Saunders's synagogue. We had been
invited to participate in the celebration of the tenaim,
the ceremony that would mark the engagement of Danny
and Rachel.

About ten feet away from the stone staircase that led up
to the brownstone where Reb Saunders lived, we were
stopped by a solid wall of jostling Hasidim. I started to
push my way in, then stopped. I did not want my father
to have to move through that crowd. My father looked at
me and saw my concern and was about to say something
when I felt a tug on the sleeve of my coat. A young Hasid
in his late teens stood alongside me. He had on a dark

coat and a black hat and his pale face was covered by a scraggly black beard.

"You are Malter?" he asked in Yiddish.

I nodded.

"Come with me," he said, and proceeded to elbow his way gently but firmly through the crowd, opening a path that enabled us to move with some ease and that closed behind each step we took. We were swallowed by Hasidim. Holding onto my father's arm, I wondered how the Hasid had been able to find us in the crowd, and then realized he had simply been told to look for two people in ordinary clothes. We came up the crowded staircase and into the crowded hallway and then into the packed synagogue where it seemed no one could get through the mass of Hasidim jamming the chairs and the aisles and the benches—but we kept moving behind the young Hasid, somehow the crowd kept parting and we kept moving until we were seated in a front row of seats facing a long table and chairs that had been placed in the middle of the synagogue. The rows of seats formed a rectangle around the table and chairs. Beyond the seats to my left was the podium and beyond that was the Ark. Along the walls in the rear of the synagogue there were long tables and chairs. Between the back row of seats to my right and the long tables was an open space that was filled with Hasidim. There were no women in the synagogue, only men and boys. The women were in another room somewhere with Rachel and her mother, celebrating by themselves. I thought of Rachel and her mother surrounded by Hasidic women. Rachel and her passion for James Joyce and county fairs surrounded by Hasidic women. I couldn't picture it.

The noise inside the synagogue was loud, almost deafening, a crescendo of joy accompanied by faces that seemed frenzied with happiness. It moved in huge waves between the walls of the synagogue, ecstatic, pulsing, and my father and I sat quietly, watching, listening, and I felt the joy of the night move through me as something quite tangible and was suddenly struck with peculiar bitter-sweet force by the thought that Danny—Danny!—was becoming engaged. I must have had a strange look on my face for I saw my father gazing at me and smiling somewhat sadly. I was about to ask him how it felt to be in the midst of the holy of holies—my father cared very little for the frenetic zealousness of Hasidism and even less for the tzaddikim who were its leaders—when I saw him notice someone sitting in the row of seats on the other side of the long table and raise his hand in greeting. I looked and saw Abraham Gordon. He was seated in the second row across from us, surrounded by caftan-garbed, dark-bearded men. He wore a dark suit and a white shirt and dark tie, and I had not seen him earlier because of the crowd that kept milling around the table. He saw my father and his face broke into a smile and he returned the greeting with a wave of his hand. I wondered who had brought him inside. I wondered if a young Hasid had been instructed to meet him too in the crowd in front of the brownstone and to ask him, "Are you Gordon?" My father seemed deeply moved to see Abraham Gordon there. I saw him smile to himself and nod his head, and was surprised to discover that he appeared not all uncomfortable in the midst of this tumultuous, jostling, liquid crowd. I caught glimpses of Abraham Gordon; he sat very still, gazing straight ahead of him, a pale smile on his face. There was a small, dark skullcap on his balding head. His heavy shoulders and tall body stood out quite sharply against the shorter caftan-garbed men who surrounded him.

Then someone said "Shah!" loudly, once, and the synagogue was suddenly silent, and I got to my feet along with all the others and craned my neck and saw Reb Saunders coming slowly through the crowd, which moved back for him, somehow finding the room to make a wide path. He wore a dark satin caftan and a fur-trimmed cap, and his beard was white and he walked slowly, supported on his right hand by Danny and on his left by Levi. Danny too wore a dark satin caftan and a fur-trimmed cap and looked tall, lean, and quite majestic I thought. There was a smile on his face and he nodded his head in acknowledgment of the hushed greetings uttered as he went through the crowd, and his eyes were luminous, blinding, as if filled with a light borrowed from one of Michael's stars. Levi looked thin and frail, but he walked very straight alongside his father, and some of the men touched him gently as he went along, touched the dark satin of his caftan as though to acknowledge his coming sovereignty over them. Behind Reb Saunders and his sons walked Joseph Gordon, dressed in a dark suit and looking a little dazed. Behind him there followed more than half a dozen elderly men, all in dark caftans, all bearded, all in fur-trimmed caps, except one, who wore an ordinary black hat and seemed younger than the rest. I recognized most of them from descriptions or from photographs I had seen or heard over the years. They were tzaddikim of the various other Hasidic sects of Brooklyn.

The crowd around the long table had melted away into the seats, and I thought Reb Saunders would go directly to the chair at the head of the table. Instead, as he began to pass by my father, he stopped and turned. His dark, watery, tired eyes gazed at my father. I saw Danny give me a smile. Reb Saunders stood there, looking at my father. In all the years that I had known Danny this was the first time Reb Saunders was actually seeing my father. He stood gazing at my father, and I thought I saw his lips quiver in the tangle of his long white beard, and then he moved very close to my father and reached out with his right hand and took my father's hand and then put his left hand over my father's hand and just stood there, holding my father's hand in his two hands, just holding them for what seemed a very long time, and I saw my father nod and smile, and then Reb Saunders released my father's hand and raised his arms and brought them around my father's thin body and embraced him and I could hear whispers move like a sudden wind through the synagogue. "Who is that?" "Who?" "Malter?" "Which Malter?" "David Malter?" "The Talmudist David Malter?" "The one who—?" "The book?" *"That* Malter?" "Look at the rebbe!" "He is kissing him!" "Which Malter did you say?" *"The rebbe is crying!"* "Shah!" "Let there be silence!" "Shah!"

Reb Saunders stepped back. Danny and Levi took his arms. Danny did not look at me. My father's face was flushed. His eyes were wet. Reb Saunders moved to the chair at the head of the long table and sat down. Danny took the chair to his left, Levi to his right. Joseph Gordon sat down next to Danny. The other Hasidic rebbes took seats around the table. There was a faint shuffling of feet and scraping of chairs as everyone in the synagogue sat down. The silence continued. Everyone sat staring at the table.

The ceremony was brief: the two fathers signed the document containing the terms of the betrothal agreement; two men at the table who appeared to be the oldest of the tzaddikim signed as witnesses; a handkerchief was produced and each of the two fathers held a corner of it, performing the kinyan, the legal formality which binds both parties to the terms of a written agreement; the document was read aloud by the rebbe in the dark hat; another rebbe then produced a plate and broke it against the top of the table, an act that symbolizes the destruction of Jerusalem—and the ceremony was over. Someone in the crowd shouted, "Mazel tov!" and the words were picked up by the others until they became an ecstatic din. A moment later there was silence once again. Everybody stared tensely at the table, waiting.

Reb Saunders sat in his chair, swaying faintly back and forth, his right hand playing with an earlock. I noticed Abraham Gordon staring at him intently, his face expressionless. Then Reb Saunders began to speak. His voice was thin and frail, a shadow of what it had once been. It quivered and trembled and he had to stop from time to time to gain control of himself. He spoke for only a few minutes on a passage of Talmud in the tractate *Nedarim*. Then Danny rose and spoke for half an hour on a very difficult passage of Talmud which he explained brilliantly, moving briskly and with flawless ease through a dozen tractates and a host of medieval commentaries as he spoke. The crowd sat enraptured. Levi gazed up at him in awe. My father smiled with pleasure. Abraham Gordon stared in disbelief. And Joseph Gordon continued to look dazed.

Then Danny was done. He sat down. I saw Reb Saunders bend over to him and whisper something in his ear. Danny's face broke into a joyous smile and he nodded at his father. Levi was saying something to him. He seemed to be talking loudly but I could hear nothing. For the crowd inside the synagogue had exploded. That is the only way to describe what happened. It exploded. Chairs were picked up, tables were moved away from the walls, food was brought in. The young Hasid who had led us into the synagogue suddenly materialized by my side and took us to a table; there was the ritual washing of the hands, the blessing over the bread, and we were eating and singing, and then I was dancing, wildly, ecstatically, the hand of an old Hasid on my right shoulder and of a young boy in his teens on my left, whirling and dancing and singing, and there was Danny and I grabbed a chair and pushed it under him and others helped me and I took hold of the legs of the chair and we raised Danny over our shoulders and danced with him on the chair, Danny high on the chair, and the songs loud and the hands clapping and the feet stamping and the joy like a wildness all inside me and around me. I was exhausted and sweating when we were done, and Danny came off the chair and looked at me and said nothing and suddenly I felt his arms around me and my arms went around him and the satin of his caftan was smooth against my fingers and then we separated and he smiled, his blue eyes moist and brilliant, and someone grabbed him for another dance and he was gone.

I started back to the table and saw that the chair in which my father had sat was empty. I looked around. He was standing against a wall of the synagogue, talking quietly with Abraham Gordon. I sat down and had something to eat. When I turned around again I saw that both my father and Abraham Gordon were gone. A few minutes later my father came back into the synagogue and was on his way to the table when an elderly Hasid in a long gray beard stopped him. My father nodded and accompanied the Hasid to the table where Reb Saunders sat together with the other rebbes. He sat down in Danny's empty seat. Reb Saunders leaned forward. The other rebbes moved their chairs closer to Reb Saunders. Levi and Joseph Gordon were in the crowd somewhere. The rebbes and my father sat around the table. Reb Saunders was talking. The others listened, nodding their heads. My father was there a very long time before I saw him get to his feet. There was a smile on his face. He made his way slowly through the crowd to the table and sat down.

"What did you talk about?" I asked.

"Torah," he said.

"You didn't produce that Yerushalmi." The Yerushalmi is the Palestinian Talmud.

He looked at me, puzzled.

"The passage in the Yerushalmi that would have solved Danny's problem."

He laughed loudly. "No, Reuven. I did not mention the passage in the Yerushalmi." He laughed again. "You are more of a scholar than I am. In the midst of a celebration like this you can remember a Yerushalmi!"

"That Yerushalmi could have saved Danny a lot of trouble."

"Why do you consider it trouble? The people who listened to Danny considered it trouble? Can you see them listening with joy to the critical method?"

"No," I said. "I can't see that at all." A moment later I said, "Did Abraham Gordon leave?"

"Yes. He has to fly to Chicago early tomorrow morning."

"He doesn't look well."

"He has reason not to look well. Michael has not moved in days."

Levi came over and asked me to join him in a dance. I got up and entered a circle of Hasidim with Levi at my side, and danced. We danced around Danny, who stood clapping his hands and singing, and I looked at Danny and felt a part of myself slide out of the dance and look coldly at what I was doing, and heard it telling me how strange it was to be dancing with Hasidim, whose way of life I disliked, whose ideas were so different from mine, whose presence was destroying my world. I continued dancing, but for the rest of that night that part of me remained outside it all, watching.

Sometime later, the dancing and singing ceased and we all returned to our chairs for the Grace. It was almost midnight when my father and I said good-bye to Reb Saunders and Danny, and left. The crowd inside the synagogue had resumed dancing. We could hear the singing and the stamping of feet as we walked carefully through the snow beneath the dark sycamores, and could still hear it, coming faintly through the night, when we turned into Lee Avenue. The wind and the cold had crusted the surface of the snow into a thin, hard film, and I could feel it breaking beneath my feet. Lee Avenue was dark and deserted, the lights of the lamp posts faintly smoky in the powdery snow blown through the air by the wind. I held my father's arm as we walked. We went along in silence for a while, the singing and dancing still echoing in my ears.

"He told the others how I had influenced you to become Danny's friend," my father said. "He told them how I had guided his son's reading and prevented him from leaving Yiddishkeit. He thanked me before the others for helping him to raise Danny."

We walked on a while longer.

"He is a remarkable man," my father murmured. "They are remarkable people. There is so much about them that is distasteful to me. But they are remarkable people."

"I wish they weren't so afraid of new ideas."

"You want a great deal, Reuven. The Messiah has not yet come. Will new ideas enable them to go on singing and dancing?"

"We can't ignore the truth, abba."

"No," he said. "We cannot ignore the truth. At the same time, we cannot quite sing and dance as they do."

He was silent a moment. "That is the dilemma of our time, Reuven. I do not know what the answer is."

We turned into our block. The wind was loud in the winter branches of the sycamores. I turned to my father.

"Is Abraham Gordon talking to you about teaching in the Frankel Seminary?"

He stopped and looked at me in astonishment. Then he laughed and shook his head. "How—?" He broke off and shook his head again. "You are remarkable," he said, smiling broadly. I could see his eyes very bright in the lights of the lamp posts.

"Is he?" I asked.

"Yes."

"Will you do it?"

"I do not know."

"What happened to the offer from Hirsch?"

"I have told them I want a little time to consider it."

I did not say anything.

"Will you be upset if I accept a position at the seminary?"

"I don't know."

We went up the stone stairs and into our brownstone. As we were putting away our hats and coats, he said, "Will you take your smicha examinations?"

"Yes."

"How will you take them?"

"Exactly the way you taught me."

He nodded soberly. We stood in the hall of the apartment. I looked at the phone. For some strange reason I almost expected it to ring. I saw my father smiling at me.

"It has been a long and happy night, Reuven. But I am still cold from the walk. Would you like to have some tea? Come, let us drink tea and take the cold from our bones before we go to sleep."

It was after one o'clock when we finally went to bed. I lay awake a long time with the sounds of the singing and dancing in my ears before I was able to fall asleep.

"You are still seeing Gordon?" Rav Kalman asked me the next day after class.

"Yes."

"How is the boy?"

"There's no change."

"You are going to take your smicha examinations?"

"Yes."

"You have informed the Dean?"

"I'm going to do that now."

"So," he said. "You have made your choice."

"Yes."

"Where do you stand now, Reuven?"

"I'll have to show you."

His eyes narrowed.

"At the examinations," I said.

His face darkened. "What do you mean?" he said.

"I can't tell you my choice. I'll have to show it to you."

His lips grew thin and he tugged at his dark beard. "I will not give smicha examinations to someone—" He stopped. "I will not give you smicha examinations until I know with certainty where you stand."

"Then I can't take the examinations," I said very quietly.

He stared at me from across the desk. The hand with the misshapen fingers trembled quite visibly on the closed Talmud. There was a long silence.

"What will you do at the examinations?" he asked softly. "You will use your father's method?"

"Yes."

"I know the method. I do not need you to show me that method."

I did not say anything. There was another long silence.

Then he said, "What will you do if I refuse to give you smicha?" He spoke softly.

"I don't know."

"You will go to the seminary of Gordon?"

"I don't know."

"You are very clever, Reuven. You are forcing me to make the choice, yes? That is what you are doing."

I was quiet.

He tugged at his beard. He seemed to be controlling himself with enormous difficulty. There was anger on his face. But it remained on his face, soundless this time. "I do not know what to do with you," he muttered. "I have never had such a problem." I remembered him using those same words weeks ago. But there was quiet pain in them now. He closed his eyes. His fingers drummed noiselessly on the Talmud. He opened his eyes.

"When will you take the examinations?" he asked softly.

I told him.

He nodded his head once. "Tell the Dean I will give you the examinations." His face was weary, expressionless. He dismissed me. At the door of the room I turned and saw him sitting behind the desk, staring fixedly at the Talmud, looking small and lonely and forlorn.

I arranged to take the examinations in the first week of April.

I saw Abraham and Ruth Gordon the following Sunday in their apartment. We spent some time together in the study, and I helped him read the galleys of his new book. Then we sat by the fire in the living room and drank hot, spiced wine and talked about the engagement celebration. Ruth Gordon had been with the women, together with Rachel and her mother. There had been singing and dancing, and the women, all of them in wigs and long-sleeved, high-necked dresses, had been sweet and kind and Old-Worldly, and Ruth Gordon had found it all very quaint and primitive and crude. She did not like the medieval subservience of Hasidic women. She did not like the meekness with which they accepted their secondary roles. She did not like the patriarchal aura of the Hasidic family. She despised their blind unwillingness to accept twentieth-century reality. She could understand someone objecting to opinions and half-formed ideas. But facts—

how could anyone born in this century reject facts! She had grown up in Canada in the midst of blind Orthodoxy—this was the first time I was hearing that she had not been born in America—and had despised it and broken with it and now found herself incapable of comprehending it. What difference was there between Jewish Orthodoxy and Catholicism? she asked. What difference was there between the blind belief of Hasidism and that of the Catholic women who climbed the stone steps of the new church in Montreal that was being built when someone claimed to have seen a vision of Joseph—climbed those steps on their knees, saying a prayer on each step? There was no difference, she said. None at all. It was the same blindness, the same absurd rejection of facts. She could not understand Rachel marrying a Hasid, even a Hasid like Daniel Saunders. She grew quite heated and her eyes became bright with anger and her voice filled the room with her scorn.

Abraham Gordon pulled at an ear lobe and sat listening to her patiently. "The attraction of opposites," he said finally with a smile.

"That is nonsense!" she snapped. She was really angry. I had the feeling Rachel's coming marriage to Danny was presenting her with some kind of bewildering challenge.

"I would wager," Abraham Gordon said quietly, "that Rachel is attracted to Daniel's God, and Daniel is attracted to Rachel's twentieth century. Is that nonsense, Ruth?"

"It is inconceivable to me that Rachel finds anything sensible in Daniel's God."

"There is a great deal of beauty in that sort of faith," Abraham Gordon murmured.

"I find no beauty in nonsense," she said coldly.

"Only because you don't believe in it. Nonsense is often that in which a person cannot believe. But you once believed in literature, Ruth. You found beauty in literature. You said so yourself. You believed in and loved the esthetic quality of French literature." He was silent a moment. "Is it impossible for two people to fuse two separate commitments into a single purpose?" He spoke softly, gazing at his wife. "I seem to recall talking to someone about that once."

She looked at him, her blue eyes suddenly narrow.

"I have a vague recollection of a conversation along those lines," he said.

She was very quiet.

"A boat in the middle of the Atlantic and a long walk and talk on the deck. A man and a woman suddenly in love. The man wanted to write about certain ideas and was rather clumsy with words, and the woman was excellent with words and wanted to know about those ideas. Where could I have heard that?"

I saw a crimson flush spread slowly across her features.

"Where could I have heard that?" Abraham Gordon murmured, looking at his wife.

She smiled then. It was a hesitant smile at first. Then it broadened, and she laughed softly. For the first time since I had met her, I saw the cool, regal composure in which she clothed herself melt away, and I caught a glimpse of what she was really like when she no longer felt it necessary to show she was all mind, all molded and formed by the century in which she had been born and in which, during a passage across the dark waters of an ocean, she had given away her freedom and joined herself to the destiny of a man whose deepest dreams she would help bring to life.

I did not see Abraham and Ruth Gordon again until the last week in April.

Fourteen

The twilight winter ended for me that second week in March. I began to study for my smicha examinations. And much of the time I was able not to think about Michael.

I locked myself into the world of the Talmud, lived in it even during the hours when the texts were not open in front of me, saw the shapes of its printed pages everywhere, on bus rides to and from school when I closed my eyes and silently recited whole sections of it by heart, on walks beneath the sycamores when I juggled complicated commentaries in my mind, on shopping expeditions to the stores on Lee Avenue when, surrounded by dark-clothed, bustling Hasidim, I would gleefully but soundlessly emend texts and go on mental safaris for parallel passages and search out contradictions within the Babylonian Talmud, a forbidden pleasure because such contradictions, according to very Orthodox Talmudists, could not exist since the Babylonian Talmud was regarded by them as a coherent unit. But they existed, all right, and I found them and would recite them to myself while waiting to be served by the red-bearded Hasid from whom we bought meat, or the black-bearded Hasid from whom we bought our vegetables, or the pale, gray-bearded, wizened old Hasid from whom we bought our bread and rolls. Going home from the stores, I would sometimes review passages out loud, and once I passed a group of Hasidic boys playing stoopball two houses away from mine and barely noticed them and went on talking to myself, and I heard one of them

say in Yiddish, "Who is that?" and heard another answer,
also in Yiddish, "The son of Malter," and heard the first
one respond, "Malter, the goyische Talmudist?" to which
the other said, "Huh." I thought to stop and go back to
them and tell them—tell them what? I did not know what
I could tell them. They were boys mouthing things they
heard in their homes. I continued walking, but it was a
while before I was able to return to the Talmud. I had
borrowed from my father some of the scholarly Talmudic
works he had in his study library, books by Solomon Luria
and Yerucham Fishel Perlow and H. M. Pineles and J. N.
Epstein, and also the writings of Joshua Krokovsky on
Maimonides, and often I would read as I walked—and one
day I bumped heavily into a sycamore and bruised my
knee. But the book I was reading remained undamaged
and I walked more carefully from then on, but continued
reading. I lived in a world two thousand years in the past,
in a time when sages had been remarkably unafraid of
new ideas, and I sat on the earthen floors of ancient
academies, listening to lectures on the Mishnah, listening
to the discussions that followed, and sometimes a sage
would take my arm and we would go into a silent grove of
trees, and walk and talk.

Twice during those weeks I traveled to the Zechariah
Frankel Seminary and sat in the library and spent hours
checking variant readings in medieval manuscripts of the
Talmud. The second time I was there I went up to the
fifth floor and knocked on Abraham Gordon's door. But he
was not in and I went home.

And so the weeks of March went by, and only on the
days when I felt myself sweating a little in my coat did I
realize that the sharp edge of winter was gone from the
air. I saw nothing of Danny during those weeks and spoke
to him only occasionally on the phone. There was no
change in Michael. He sat on the mattress and did not
move. He was visited hourly by a child-care worker and
daily, sometimes twice a day, by Danny, and at least two
or three times a week by Dr. Altman. He was spoon-fed;
he was checked periodically by a pediatrician; he was

helped to the bathroom; his clothes were changed regularly; he was bathed. He was completely docile; he responded to nothing and to no one; he did not talk; his face was stonelike, devoid of even a flicker of emotion. He sat and stared and was silent.

Danny told me in the middle of March that he had anticipated a reaction of this sort from Michael and was not concerned. But as the weeks went by and Michael continued motionless, Danny began to waver. In the last week of March I was on the phone with him for almost an hour. He was in one of his black moods of self-doubt, and all I could do was tell him that if Dr. Altman felt the experiment should be continued, then it should be continued. I did not know what else to say to him, but somehow hearing me say that about half a dozen times helped him a little, and much of the fear and uncertainty were gone from his voice by the time he hung up the phone.

Most of the time I studied alone. On occasion, when I felt myself too entangled in the complexities of source criticism, I would go into my father's study and ask for his help. But I was reluctant to disturb him. He was working hard on another article. And he was constantly meeting with his colleagues. There was a curriculum battle going on in his school; the newcomers wanted the hours for secular Hebrew subjects—poetry, prose, history—reduced, and the time allotted to the study of religious law expanded. My father was not even certain he would be in the school next year. But as long as he was a part of it, he would fight to keep it the kind of school it had been before the appearance of the newcomers. So he fought. Between his writing and his fighting I had little opportunity to study Talmud with him.

The book, we were informed by the publisher, was doing quite well. The attacks had aroused curiosity. Reviews of the book were still appearing in scholarly journals, and they were all uniform, and occasionally even impassioned, in their praise of my father's scholarship. To our complete amazement and joy, the book was also reviewed in a popular national literary magzine: the technical chapters were intended for scholars, the reviewer said; but the introduction could be read by any intelligent layman and was "a model of clearly presented ideas about a method of scholarship that has radically altered man's understanding not only of the Talmud but also of the great texts of the ancient world." My father told me that one of the newcomers in his school had gone into a rage over that review and had called the reviewer an am ha'aretz. "Am ha'aretz" is the Hebrew term for ignoramus. The man who wrote the review was the same man I had met in the Frankel Seminary dining room in December, the person Abraham Gordon had referred to as one of the greatest Talmud scholars in the world.

In the third week of March another attack against the book appeared in a popular Orthodox magazine. The reviewer followed Rav Kalman's line of reasoning almost point by point—but his words were rather quiet in tone. There were a few other attacks in obscure Orthodox newspapers and newsletters. But most of the Orthodox press did not even bother to mention the book and treated it as if it did not exist.

In the middle of March Rav Kalman came out with two tirades in one day, both of them about the projected graduate department of rabbinics. But he continued to ask me to remain after class. Both of us knew that the tirades were also aimed at my father. Yet he seemed perfectly able to dissociate his oblique attacks against my father from the after-class conversations we were having. He never mentioned my father during those conversations. He would ask me if I was still seeing Abraham Gordon; he would ask about Michael; he would point to a newspaper article and inquire about this or that section which had puzzled him. He wanted to know what I thought of Senator Joseph McCarthy, and I told him. He wanted to know whether McCarthy's two young assistants were really Jews, and I told him. He was pleased by a photograph showing Mayor Impellitteri shaking hands with Mayor Shragai of Jerusalem during the latter's visit to New York early in March. He was shocked by the vehemence with which a

critic dismembered a Broadway play and its author. Slowly over the course of those weeks a subtle change occurred
in our relationship: he remained my teacher during each
shiur and became my student afterward.

It was quite apparent that he was very concerned about
my visits with Abraham Gordon for he was constantly
asking me whether I was still seeing him. I kept telling
him no, I was studying for the smicha examinations. By
the end of March he no longer mentioned Abraham Gordon. But he always began our conversation with a tense
inquiry about Michael. "How is the son of Gordon?" he
would ask, and I would say there was no change, and he
would be silent for a moment, smoking, his fingers drumming soundlessly upon the Talmud, and then we would
talk.

There was a grimness about him, a wall of stiff, humor-
less rigidity, an unbending quality of mind that placed
everything it came into contact with into immediate and
fixed categories of approval or disapproval where I knew
they would remain forever. And his criterion of judgment
was a rather harsh and inflexible version of Eastern European Orthodox Jewish law, which he applied to everything.

All through March he kept asking me to remain after
class so we could talk. I had the feeling sometimes that I
was the only link he had to the bewildering American
world into which he had suddenly been plunged.

Then, in the first week of April, there was another
raging tirade against the graduate department in rabbinics,
and the next day he was absent and someone came into
the class from the Dean's office and told us to study by
ourselves, Rav Kalman was ill. He was gone the next day
too, and then the next, and we began to hear rumors that
he was refusing to teach until he received an absolute
assurance that there would be no graduate department in
rabbinics and that if this assurance would not be given
him soon he would resign.

He was still out of the school the week I was supposed
to take my smicha examinations. When I talked to the

Dean about it, he gave me a diplomatic smile. I should come back tomorrow, he said. It would all be straightened out by tomorrow and he would assign a new date for the examinations. I returned the next day and was told to come back the following week.

We heard only the faintest echoes of the fight that was going on behind the closed doors of the Dean's office during those weeks. Rumors flew wildly about the synagogue; there had been a furious argument between Rav Kalman and Rav Gershenson; each had threatened to resign if the other remained; Rav Gershenson favored having the department in rabbinics; Rav Kalman stated he would not continue to teach in the school if the department were established; there had been loud, angry words, some of which one would hardly associate with teachers of Talmud. Then Rav Kalman had actually resigned and word of this had somehow gotten out to certain very Orthodox circles, and there were phone calls and letters, and cables from as far away as Israel—the full force of Rav Kalman's enormous influence and reputation hurled itself at the Dean and the school administration. Rabbinic arbiters were called in; some kind of compromise was reached; Rav Kalman was asked to return.

We had no way of knowing what that compromise was. But on the Sunday before Passover Rav Kalman entered the classroom accompanied by the ringing of the church bells, placed his books on the desk, lit a cigarette, and proceeded to teach as if nothing at all had happened, as if more than a week of muted chaos simply did not exist. He even asked me to remain after class and we talked about an article he had read that morning in the magazine section of the Sunday *Times*. Before he dismissed me, he told me to go to the Dean and arrange for another examination date.

The smicha examinations at Hirsch were always given on three consecutive days, two hours each day. They began at three thirty in the afternoon and ended at five thirty in the evening. Because of the oncoming Passover festival, there were only two schooldays left in that week.

I arranged to take the examinations after Passover in the last week of April.

When I returned home from school the next evening I discovered that my father had been informed earlier in the day that the department in rabbinics would definitely be established but that the offer made to him to teach in it would have to be withdrawn—for reasons he was unhappily not able to discuss, the president of the school had said.

Danny phoned the next night and wanted to know why I hadn't told him about the results of my smicha examinations. I told him about the postponement, then asked him if there had been any change in Michael. There had been a brief change that morning, he said. One of the child-care workers had gone in to feed him and Michael had muttered something to her about knowing what he had to do but it was too hard—and had returned to his frozen silence. Yes, Danny had seen him later. But Michael had said nothing. He had sat on the mattress, staring blankly at the floor, and Danny had been unable to get him to say a word. Danny had immediately informed his parents. Ruth Gordon wanted the experiment stopped. But Abraham Gordon insisted that it be continued. Danny sounded exhausted. There were moments when I could barely hear his voice over the phone. He wished me a kosher Passover and hung up.

It was a grim Passover. My father had invited an old colleague of his to the first Seder. He came with his wife—his children were all married and lived in distant parts of the country—and we chanted the Haggadah and then Manya served the Passover meal, and all through that meal my father and his colleague reminisced about the early days of the school, the struggles they had experienced in establishing it, the months during the Depression when they had gone unpaid because there were no funds for teachers' salaries, the headaches and the heartaches, and the joy of seeing the school firmly established—and then the advent of the newcomers. My father's colleague grew quite bitter about those newcomers. He was a man in his late sixties, with a shock of white hair and myopic eyes behind thick, rimless glasses, and he kept saying that he could understand my father wanting to leave the school now but that his going would seriously weaken the ranks of those who were trying to hold back the influence of the newcomers. His wife, a rather loud and sharp-tongued woman, contributed a few choice expressions of her own on the subject of the newcomers. It was an unpleasant time.

Another of my father's colleagues was his guest at the second Seder the following night, an old and kindly man who was retiring at the end of the term and was being replaced by a young European-trained rabbi who had survived Dachau. The talk was an almost word-for-word repetition of last night's conversation. I sat and listened and saw how torn my father was, and said nothing.

During the intermediate days of Passover I worked sporadically on the thesis I was doing for a Master's degree in philosophy. Most of the time I studied Talmud. Then came the final two days of Passover. The following Sunday I returned to school.

The next afternoon, at exactly three thirty, I walked into the small room on the second floor of the yeshiva where the smicha examinations were to be held. The room contained a long, polished black-wood table and some chairs. At the head of the table sat the Dean, looking small and chunky and uncomfortable. To his right sat Rav Gershenson and Rav Kalman, separated by two empty chairs. The walls of the room were painted a light green and were bare. The table was bare too, except for an ashtray. Overhead a light bulb burned inside a ceiling fixture. There were no windows.

The door closed behind me with a loud click. I sat down opposite Rav Gershenson and Rav Kalman. The Dean brought the tips of his fingers together and rested his hands over his vest. He smiled at me, his pink face looking a little tense. Then he cleared his throat softly and said in Yiddish, "Let us begin."

Fifteen

There were no preliminaries. Rav Gershenson smiled behind his gray beard and in a soft voice asked me a question having to do with a point of law found in the *Yoreh Deah,* which is a medieval work on Jewish law and which I was required to know together with the Talmud tractate *Chullin* and any other tractate of my choice. I was also required to know the various important commentaries on these works. I was required to know it all by heart. No other kind of knowing was recognized.

I answered Rav Gershenson's question, speaking quietly and slowly. It was a simple question and I gave it the terse and simple answer it needed. He asked me another relatively easy question from the *Yoreh Deah,* and I answered it in the same manner as before. He nodded and smiled, then asked me a somewhat more complicated question, also about the *Yoreh Deah,* and I cited a number of differences of opinion among various medieval authorities about the case he had referred to, then gave the accepted and final legal decision.

This went on for about thirty minutes, the Dean sitting in his chair with his fingers over his vest, Rav Gershenson asking questions on the *Yoreh Deah,* and Rav Kalman absolutely silent, looking morose and grim and, I thought, a little tense. Sometime during the first ten minutes of Rav Gershenson's questions, he had lit a cigarette. He was on his third cigarette now and still had not said a word.

The questions and answers continued. I was having no

difficulty at all and was actually beginning to feel as if I were alone in the room with Rav Gershenson. Rav Kalman seemed uninterested in what was happening. He smoked and tugged occasionally at his beard and frowned and stared down at the polished table top. He seemed impatient; he squirmed; I had the feeling he wanted to get up and pace back and forth. But he sat there, smoking and frowning, and said nothing.

Three quarters of an hour later I was still answering questions on the *Yoreh Deah,* and Rav Kalman still had not said a word, and the Dean was beginning to give him uneasy and embarrassed glances, his pink face looking apprehensive. Rav Gershenson asked me one more question and I answered it, and then he sat back and nodded and was quiet, apparently satisfied that I knew the *Yoreh Deah.*

There was a brief silence. The Dean stared at Rav Gershenson, then at Rav Kalman, then back at Rav Gershenson. He looked at his wristwatch. He cleared his throat and shifted uneasily on his chair.

Then, with his eyes still on the table and his face quite grim and a cigarette between the thumb and forefinger of his right hand, Rav Kalman asked me to explain a passage from *Chullin.* I recognized it immediately. It was one of the passages he had asked me to read months ago, a difficult passage with obscure words which he had insisted over and over again I explain clearly. I cited the passage, explained it, cited some of the commentaries, and explained them. He asked me again to explain the words. He did not understand how the words could have the meaning I attributed to them, he said quietly. I told him that was the meaning most of the Rishonim had attributed to them. He said, his voice rising a little, that he knew what the Rishonim had said about the text, but was *I* satisfied with the meaning I had given the words. I told him yes, I was satisfied. It was a difficult though not an impossible text and I did not know what I could do to improve it.

There was another brief silence. Then Rav Kalman cited a statement in one of the Rishonim I had quoted earlier, a statement that contained a reference to another tractate in which there was a word similar to one of those we had been discussing, and he asked me to explain the passage in that tractate. It was not the tractate I had chosen to take the examination on. I saw Rav Gershenson give Rav Kalman a sharp look. The Dean's mouth opened slightly and a hand came off his vest and he was about to say something when I began to answer Rav Kalman's question. The Dean looked at me and his mouth dropped a little further, then he sat back in his chair, shaking his head. Rav Gershenson smiled into his beard, and listened as I cited the passage and began to explain it.

It was one of the passages I had been waiting for. There were others like it scattered all through the Talmud. Sooner or later I would have managed to steer us onto one, or we would have come across one by ourselves. Now I was in it and explaining it and knowing exactly what words I would use and seeing it all half a dozen steps in advance like a chess game.

The passage was from a Mishnah. There are sixty-three tractates of the Mishnah. Orthodox Jewish scholars believe that together with the giving of the Written Law on Mount Sinai—the Pentateuch—there was also given an oral law; the latter is an amplification of the former and was handed down by sages through the generations together with the teachings of the Written Law. Both are sacred; both comprise what is referred to as Torah. Thus there is one Torah, and this Torah has two sources: the word of God committed to writing, and the parallel system of law transmitted orally by the sages of the tradition. This oral tradition was first set down in writing in the second century of the Common Era by a great sage of the Talmudic period. The early written oral tradition is called the Mishnah, which means, study or oral law, in contradistinction to the Mikra, which means reading and is the term applied to the recitation of a text of Scripture. The Rabbinic discussions of the Mishnah which took place in the various Jewish academies in Palestine and Babylonia are called Gemara, which means completion—the complete mastery or study of the Mishnah. The oral discussions on the Mishnah were ultimately set down in written form. Those oral discussions which took place in the Palestinian academies were set down in written form, together with the pertinent texts of the Mishnah, at about the beginning of the fifth century of the Common Era. This is the Palestinian Talmud. The discussions that occurred in the Babylonian academies were set down in final written form, also together with the pertinent texts of the Mishnah, in the sixth century. This is the Babylonian Talmud. In matters pertaining to Jewish religious law, the Babylonian Talmud is regarded as the more authoritative of the two because its teachers lived later than those mentioned in the Palestinian Talmud and because it was the first of the two Talmuds to reach the Jewish communities of the Western world. Many Orthodox Jewish scholars believe that the printed version of the Babylonian Talmud is the fixed and final depository of the oral tradition and that its teachings are identical in date, origin, and sanctity to the teachings which are derived from the interpretation of Scripture itself.

This was a position which my father and I found impossible to maintain. There were too many variant readings, too many obvious scribal errors, too many emendations and substitutions of texts even within the Talmud itself for us to believe that text was frozen. We saw the Talmud as containing almost a thousand years of ideas and traditions that had been in flux; we saw the text of the Talmud as fluid, alive, like a body of rushing water with many tributaries leading into it and from it. And the Mishnaic passage which Rav Kalman had just led me to was one example of the nature of that fluidity.

I recited the passage by heart, then went on to discuss at great length the many difficulties that the Amoraim, the Rabbis of the Gemara, saw in that passage. The resolution of these difficulties was rather difficult in itself, and the medieval commentaries struggled to make it clear. I cited the commentaries, showed how they had attempted to clarify the discussion, and concluded by saying that the commentaries were themselves difficult to understand. Then I was silent. I knew what would come next. But I was silent, and waited.

Rav Kalman leaned across the table and put out his cigarette. Rav Gershenson sat very quietly, his hands on the table, looking at me intently and smiling. The Dean had been nodding his head all through my long review of the passage. He was still nodding.

In a very quiet voice, Rav Kalman asked me if I thought I could add anything to our understanding of the passage. I told him it seemed to me that the text was very difficult to understand. I did not say it was wrong; I said it was very difficult to understand. But I used the word "text."

The Dean stopped nodding and opened his eyes very wide. Rav Gershenson did not move. The smile froze a little on his face.

I emended the text.

There was a long silence in the room. I could feel the silence. It was electric with sudden tension.

Rav Kalman lit another cigarette, the two misshapen fingers jutting sharply outward from his hand. He put the cigarette between his lips and stroked his dark beard. On what did I base my emendation? he wanted to know. He used the English word "emendation," and there was sarcasm in his voice.

"On the correct text."

"Yes?" His voice shook a little. "Where is it found?"

I cited the version of the text as it appears in another tractate of the Babylonian Talmud. This version was clear and precise and made the entire Amoraic discussion on the previous text unnecessary.

The Dean squirmed in his chair. Rav Gershenson sat very still and said nothing.

"The discussion in the Gemora is over a wrong Mishnah?" Rav Kalman said sharply. "You are telling us the Amoraim wasted their time discussing a wrong Mishnah?"

I told him they hadn't wasted their time; they had been

trying to understand the version of the original text that had been transmitted to them, and had done the best they could with it. It was a minor change, I said, and was supported by internal evidence in the Talmud itself. Texts had been corrected in this manner by Talmud scholars all through centuries, I said. I saw no reason why I could not do it if it helped clarify a difficult passage. I only used it when it would help me understand a passage that was otherwise unclear, I said. I spoke quietly and respectfully, and wondered from which of the three the explosion would come. But they sat there, staring at me, and were silent.

A moment later the Dean rose to his feet and the first of the three examinations came to an end.

I went home in a trembling sweat. At the supper table that evening I went over the passage with my father and he told me he had absolutely no doubt that I had emended it correctly. He also told me that he had received a firm offer of a professorship in Talmud that afternoon from the Zechariah Frankel Seminary.

I came into the little room the following afternoon and encountered the grim faces of the Dean and Rav Kalman. But Rav Gershenson sat looking very relaxed, smiling occasionally, his pointed gray beard moving slowly back and forth as it accompanied the nodding of his head. Each time I answered a question he nodded and smiled. Once we spent twenty minutes on a point in *Chullin* and he tried to dissuade me from an interpretation I had given a certain passage in the Gemara and in the end I relented, realizing that he was probably right, despite the fact that his understanding of the passage contradicted that of some of the early commentaries. A few minutes later we were deep in a passage of Mishnah and when I cited the variant reading and said it was found in the Jerusalem Talmud, Rav Kalman suddenly jumped to his feet, almost upsetting his chair. We stared at him. I could feel my heart beating.

"I know that Yerushalmi," he almost shouted. "The

Mishnah is not as you say it is. I will bring it and show you." He stormed out of the room.

The Dean squirmed some more in his chair and threw me angry looks. Rav Gershenson sat quietly, smiling. We waited in tense silence.

Rav Kalman returned with one of the huge volumes of the printed Jerusalem Talmud. He had it open to the Mishnah. He put it down on the desk and, standing over it, read quickly. The text was an exact duplicate of the one found in the Babylonian Talmud.

"Nu?" he said in angry triumph. "Where is the Mishnah different? How is it different? It is the same!"

"It's been corrected," I said.

He stared at me.

"That's the Vilna Edition. It was corrected according to the Bavli." "Bavli" is the Hebrew term for the Babylonian Talmud.

"Reuven," Rav Gershenson said softly. "Is the reading you speak of found in the old Venice Edition of the Yerushalmi?"

"Yes."

Rav Kalman straightened and stood stiffly behind the table, staring first at me, then at Rav Gershenson, then back at me. He closed the volume of the Talmud and went with it out of the room.

There was another tense silence.

The Dean looked at me, opened his mouth to say something, then changed his mind, and was quiet.

Rav Kalman returned. There was a look of bewilderment on his face. He said nothing about the Venice Edition of the Yerushalmi, which he had no doubt checked for the variant reading. He sat down and asked me to explain a passage in *Sanhedrin*, which was the tractate I had chosen to be examined on. I explained the passage. We went from one passage to another in *Sanhedrin*, and then we were in the Mishnah which lists ten differences between cases concerning property and capital cases, and I recited the Mishnah by heart and instead of going directly to the Gemara that followed the Mishnah, I jumped a few pages to where an Amora questioned the number of items listed in the Mishnah, claiming that he saw only nine differences. The Gemara resolved the difficulty, but unsatisfactorily as far as I was concerned.

"The second Amora did not have the exact same Mishnah as the first Amora," I said, and then was silent, waiting.

The Dean's face went from its normal pink to very red. Rav Kalman's face was pale above the starched white collar of his shirt. And Rav Gershenson looked at me narrowly.

"Where is the other Mishnah found?" he asked softly. "It is not in the Bavli and it is not in the Yerushalmi."

"No."

"Where is it found?"

"In a manuscript."

"A manuscript," Rav Gershenson echoed.

"You saw this manuscript?" Rav Kalman asked loudly.

"The manuscript appears in the Napoli Edition of the Mishnah," I said.

"The Napoli Edition of the Mishnah," Rav Kalman repeated, staring at me. His entire world of learning was being challenged. All the mental gymnastics to which he would have subjected that passage of Talmud had been turned into smoke by a variant reading found in a fifteenth-century edition of the Mishnah.

"Where did you see this edition of the Mishnah?" the Dean asked abruptly, his voice a little high pitched.

"In the Frankel Seminary Library," I said.

He gaped at me. I heard a thin sigh escape from between his lips. He sat back heavily in his chair and said nothing. But his face was now a deeper shade of red than before.

Rav Gershenson said quietly, "You found this manuscript by yourself, Reuven?"

"Yes."

"You studied the Gemora and thought there might be a different Mishnah and you went and found it?"

"Yes."

He nodded heavily. He was no longer smiling. He did not mind emendations that were supported by internal evidence in the Talmud itself. But to appeal to a reading that was not found anywhere inside the Talmud—that was dangerous. That sort of method threatened the authority of the Talmud, for it meant that the Talmud did not have all the sources at its disposal upon which laws could be based. He shook his head slowly.

Rav Kalman sat stiffly on his chair, his eyes very dark. He seemed not to know what to say or do.

I decided then to go all the way. I had planned to do this tomorrow, for I was working in stages—first emending a text on the basis of a reading found within the Babylonian Talmud, then clarifying a text on the basis of a reading found outside the Babylonian Talmud but within the Palestinian Talmud, and finally showing that texts existed which were not found in either Talmud but which nevertheless had been used by the Amoraim in their discussions. Now I would show them that there were contradictions even within the existing text of the Bavli, that the text as we have it could not be regarded as a unity, a coherent whole.

I started with an apology. It was not my intention, I said, to cause anyone unhappiness or pain by what I was doing. Nor was it my intention to defame the Talmud. I was defending the Talmud, not defaming it. I was trying to add to my understanding of it by going to the original sources of the many statements it contained. I understood that this method had dangerous implications, I said, but it was the only way I knew to study Talmud. I quoted from the works of Luria and Perlow and Pineles and Epstein in support of my position. I cited a passage in the tractate *Pesachim* where the statement of one Amora is quoted in order to contradict the words of a second Amora and is then brushed aside by the Gemara with the word "beduta"—foolishness, a rather strong word, which carries the implication that the Amora did not know what he was saying. The Gemara itself did not know what to do with the contradiction, and so it called the apparently unsupported words of the first Amora foolish. But they were not foolish at all, I said, and cited a text in another tractate upon which I felt the Amora had based his statement. The ones who had brushed that statement aside obviously had had no knowledge of the text upon which it had been based. The Amora had not been foolish. He had used a legitimate text which had been unknown to the ones who had later discussed his words. I wanted to defend this Amora, I said, speaking very quietly and respectfully. I wanted to show that he had not been foolish at all. Then I cited two Talmudic discussions in the Gemara of the tractate *Ketubot*. They dealt with similar problems; but it was obvious that neither Gemara knew of the other: one based law A upon law B, and the other based law B upon law A. Yet both discussions used virtually identical words. How was it possible for two separate discussions to contain the same words? Only if the discussions originated from the same source, a third source, which originally had contained both discussions in itself—and I reconstructed that third source.

I was aware of the presumptuousness of my words, for they implied that I knew more than the Gemara had known. So I kept saying over and over again that I was not trying to be disrespectful to the Gemara but was only trying to better my understanding of it.

They sat there, staring at me in stonelike silence, not moving, not saying anything, just staring.

I was quiet. My hands were sweating and I could feel beads of sweat on my back. The silence lasted a very long time.

Rav Kalman sat on his chair, swaying slightly back and forth. He had closed his eyes. Rav Gershenson looked down at the table. The Dean stared at them, glanced at his wristwatch, then stared at them again.

Rav Kalman opened his eyes. "Malter," he said quietly. "You will teach Gemora this way to others?"

"Yes," I said.

He closed his eyes again.

"You use this method on the Five Books of Moses too?" Rav Gershenson asked softly.

"No," I said.

"And on the rest of the Tanach? On the Prophets and the Writings?"

I did not answer. I was torn over that question and did not yet have an answer to it. But I did not have to answer it. These were questions of theology and they had no place a smicha examination, and they all knew it. So I remained silent.

Rav Kalman opened his eyes. "I have no more questions," he said.

The Dean looked at Rav Gershenson. "No more questions," Rav Gershenson echoed in agreement.

"We will meet again tomorrow," the Dean said.

"No," said Rav Kalman. "I have no more questions." He looked at me as he spoke. "It will not be necessary to meet tomorrow."

The Dean stared at him. Then he looked at Rav Gershenson.

Rav Gershenson shrugged. "A meeting tomorrow is unnecessary," he said, very quietly.

The Dean asked me to leave the room. I rose and very respectfully thanked them for listening to me and for giving me the examinations. Then I went to the door. As I opened the door, I looked over my shoulder and saw the three of them sitting fixedly at the table. I closed the door behind me and went home.

The smicha examinations marked the conclusion of my academic year and I no longer had to attend Talmud classes. I spent my time writing my Master's thesis. The decision as to whether or not a student had passed his examinations always came in the mail two or three days after the last examination. Four days passed and nothing came in the mail. On the afternoon of the third day, Friday, Danny called to tell me that Michael had come out of his trancelike state and had asked to see me, and then had gone immediately back into his silence. No, Danny did not want me to visit Michael yet. He wanted Michael to talk to him, not to me. He wished me a good Shabbos and hung up.

That night, after the Shabbat meal, my father told me that he had decided to accept the offer of the Zechariah Frankel Seminary to join its faculty as a professor of Talmud. He would leave the school he had helped create.

I was not surprised—but again there was the feeling of old worlds crumbling to pieces.

"I would have preferred to remain with my yeshiva," he said quietly. "But it would mean spending the rest of my life fighting. I do not know how many years I have left, Reuven, but I do not want to spend them fighting. I am too tired now for fighting. This past year of fighting has been too much . . ." He blinked wearily. "Fighting is for those who are young and have strength. The young who wish to change the world should stay and fight. I do not have that strength . . . you are disappointed in me, Reuven?"

I was proud of him, I said. A professorship in the Frankel Seminary was something to be proud of.

"I would have enjoyed teaching in the Hirsch graduate school," he said. "I would have enjoyed that very much. Still, it is a great privilege to be able to teach in the Frankel Seminary."

He had made his decision. But it would be a long time before he would reconcile himself to the fact that he was abandoning a school and a world he loved. He was moody and silent all the rest of that Shabbat and kept wandering through the rooms of the apartment and sighing softly to himself.

On Sunday morning I called the office of the Dean and was informed that the matter of my smicha was still under discussion. Was it true that my father had accepted a position at the Frankel Seminary? the Dean asked. Yes, it was true. He hung up.

That afternoon Danny called and asked me to stay near the phone as much as possible. Michael and he had talked for almost five minutes that morning, and Danny wanted me to be immediately available in case I was needed. I asked him what he could possibly need me for. Just be available, he said. I told him I would stay near the phone.

It was a dismal day, wet with rain and gray with fog. Outside the window of my room I could see the ailanthus in the back yard, dripping rain, its buds beginning to open, tiny green shoots appearing on its branches.

A few minutes before supper that night the phone rang. I answered and heard Rav Kalman's voice and sat down on the chair next to the telephone stand. He wanted to see me in his classroom after the shiur tomorrow, he said. I was trembling. All of me was shaking and trembling and cold. He must have heard the trembling in my voice because he said quickly that I should not worry, they were giving me smicha, but he wanted to see me tomorrow. I felt my heart surging and the blood beating inside my head and I told him I would be there at exactly three o'clock and hung up the phone and let out a whoop of joy that brought Manya racing from the kitchen in a fright and my father rushing from his study, his eyes wide, and I told him and we embraced and I do not remember too much of what else happened that night, except that I think the three of us did a dance in the hall and that I called Danny to tell him the news and he was very happy and asked me again to stay near the phone as much as possible. I went to sleep wondering why Rav Kalman wanted to see me.

I was there at exactly three o'clock. The room was already empty and I saw none of my classmates in the corridor. He had apparently dismissed the class early.

He rose to his feet as I entered the room and waited behind his desk while I moved toward him through the classroom. Then he offered me his hand. His palm was cool and hard, and I could feel the misshapen fingers, and I remember wondering for the briefest of seconds how many German soldiers he had killed with that hand. It was the strangest thought to associate with a scholar of the

Talmud, and I did not know why it had suddenly occurred to me.

He told me to sit down. Then he asked me about Michael.

I said that Michael seemed to be improving slightly.

"Yes?" he said, as if he were clutching at the news. "Are you permitted to tell me what is happening?"

I told him as much as Danny had told me. He nodded.

"You broke the cherem for a good reason," he said. "I am glad." He was evaluating Michael's situation from the point of view of his understanding of Jewish law. He had satisfied himself that his granting me permission to see Abraham Gordon had been a wise decision.

"Tell me, Reuven, you have seen Gordon lately?"

"No."

"You will see him again?"

"Yes."

"Even though his son is better?"

"Yes."

"You are a good friend to Gordon now?"

"Yes."

He nodded. "I disapprove," he said. "But I can no longer stop you."

I said nothing.

"Your father will teach in the Frankel Seminary?" he asked then.

I nodded.

"I did not want to give you smicha," he said quietly. "My teacher would not have given you smicha, Reuven. He would not even have let you take the examinations. But he did not see—he did not live through—" He broke off and passed his hand across his eyes and was silent for a moment. "I did not want to drive you away from the yeshiva. I did not know what to do ... The others ... they prevailed upon me ..." He stopped and gazed at me. "It is different hearing and seeing your father's method than merely reading about it ... A voice ... It needs a voice to give it life ... You understand me, Reuven?"

"Yes."

"I still do not approve of it. I will fight you when you teach it . . . But it is different when one hears it . . ."

I said nothing.

"Once I had students who spoke with such love about Torah that I would hear the Song of Songs in their voices." He spoke softly, his eyes half closed. "I have not heard the Song of Songs now for—for—" He blinked. "I did not hear the Song of Songs in America until I heard your voice at the examinations. Not your words, but your voice. I did not like the words. But the voice . . . Do you understand what I mean, Reuven?"

"Yes."

" 'My sons have conquered me,' " he said softly, quoting in Hebrew. Then he said, "Do you know why it is different when one hears it?" He did not intend for me to answer. He went on himself. "Your father's method is ice when one sees it on the printed page. It is impossible to print one's love for Torah. But one can hear it in a voice. Still it is a dangerous method. And I will fight you if I learn you are using it too much in your classes."

I was in something of a daze and was not quite listening to everything he said, so I did not fully grasp the meaning of his last words.

"I will be able to keep my eyes on you here," he said. "I could not have influenced your father. But you I can influence. Why should I give you to Gordon when I can keep you here? I have lost too many students. Too many . . . I will take a chance on you, Reuven. I have given you my smicha and will keep my eyes on you to watch how you teach. We will have many fights. But they will be for the sake of Torah." He saw me staring at him and seemed surprised. "You have spoken to the Dean?" he asked sharply.

"No."

"He has not asked to speak to you?"

"No."

"He is a better scholar than he is an administrator. Go speak to the Dean."

I got shakily to my feet.

"Reuven," he said.

I looked at him.

"You will use your method on the Prophets and the Writings?"

I did not say anything.

"You will give approval to those who use such a method on the Prophets and Writings?"

"Do not ever dare to do that. I will fight you in print if you do that. I will fight you the way I fought your father. Now go speak to the great administrator."

I went to the Dean's office and was informed by him that I was a troublemaker. He had better things to do with his time than run back and forth trying to make peace between Rav Kalman and Rav Gershenson, he said. He did not go into details about that fight, but I gathered from him that Rav Gershenson had gone to the president of the school and there had been a long and angry meeting and Rav Kalman had finally agreed to give me smicha on the condition that I never be permitted to teach Talmud in the yeshiva. The president had agreed—and then had suggested that the graduate school might want to make use of my Talmudic abilities. He understood Rav Kalman's refusal to let me teach in the rabbinical school of the yeshiva where smicha was given, but the graduate school ... That had precipitated another quarrel, but in the end Rav Kalman had yielded. He could hardly threaten to resign over my appointment to the new department of the rabbinics when he himself had just agreed to give me smicha. I did not have to give them my decision right away, the Dean said. "Go home and think about it. Source criticism in a smicha examination! Go home and call me later in the week." He was angry but he shook my hand.

My father smiled with pride and delight when I told him. "You should accept it, Reuven. It is a great honor. I wish—" He stopped. "You should accept it," he said.

"Malter versus Kalman. I feel like I'm back where I started. Constant battles with Rav Kalman."

"No, Reuven. You will be fighting him from within.

That is the only effective way to fight a man like Rav Kalman. Will you accept it?"

"Yes," I said.

He looked at me, his eyes wet. "Rabbi Malter," he said. "Rabbi Malter."

Manya called us in to supper.

I took a long walk later that evening through the dark streets of Williamsburg. The streets were filled with Hasidim, and I walked among them, listening to their Yiddish and watching their gestures, and thinking of the boy who had called my father a goyische Talmudist. It was a cool, clear evening, and I could see stars in the sky and I thought about Michael and then forgot Michael as I peered through the front windows of some of the shops that were still open and watched the buying and the selling and still felt out of it all, only remotely connected to it by a shared history. I read the Yiddish signs on the storefronts and listened as three elderly Hasidim passed by talking in awed tones about their rebbe. I did not understand them and they did not understand me, and our quarrels would continue. But I was part of the chain of the tradition now, as much a guardian of the sacred Promise as Rav Kalman and the Hasidim were, and it would be a different kind of fight from now on. I had won the right to make my own beginning. And I thought I might try to learn something from the way Rav Kalman and the Hasidim had managed to survive and rebuild their world. What gave them the strength to mold smoke and ashes into a new world? I could use some of that strength for the things I wanted to do with my own life.

I walked a long time through the cool April night, and when I returned to the apartment I found a message near the phone. It was in my father's handwriting. Abraham Gordon had called. Would I please call back?

"Congratulations," I heard him say into the phone. "Rabbi Malter."

I thanked him.

"Ruth and I want to know when we'll see you again."
His voice sounded dull with fatigue.

I told him I could come over the following evening.

"Michael asked for you again today," he said. "He
spoke to Daniel for about half an hour."

Had they seen him? I asked.

"No," he said. "Daniel won't let us near him."

I came over the next night and we talked and they were
both genuinely pleased that I had passed the examinations.

"This young rabbi won't smash at me the way the Rav
Kalmans do," Abraham Gordon said to his wife. He was
trying hard to sound cheerful, but his face was drawn and
he seemed very fatigued. He sat with his huge body
slumped back on the couch, his feet on the coffee table.
Ruth Gordon sat next to him, smoking quietly. "We have
an ally in the enemy camp, Ruth."

She smiled wanly. She was making no attempt to
maintain her pose of regal coolness tonight. She looked
like a badly frightened mother.

I asked him about the book.

He had stopped working on it, he said. He couldn't
concentrate on it any more. He couldn't concentrate on
anything any more.

Ruth Gordon asked me if I would like a cup of coffee
and I said yes, I would, and she went out.

"She's not even urging me to finish the book," Abraham Gordon murmured, staring after his wife. "Neither of
us has any stomach for that book." He looked at me. "It
will be very good to have your father at the seminary," he
said. "You at the yeshiva and your father at the seminary.
Strange," he said softly. "Usually it's the other way
around."

Ruth Gordon came back with the coffee and we talked
awhile longer. There was no particular purpose to their
having asked to see me. They seemed simply to want me
around, to talk to me, to someone, anyone, and I was, or
had been, the closest one to Michael—and so they wanted
to be near me.

"I really would have liked you as a student," Abraham Gordon said to me at one point. "But I'm glad you're remaining where you are. God help us all if Orthodoxy becomes dull-witted with fundamentalists like Rav Kalman. We'll never be able to talk to each other. But I don't envy you the fights you'll have on your hands."

"There are fights everywhere," Ruth Gordon said.

"Yes," Abraham Gordon said, nodding. "Indeed there are." Then he said, "It took courage for you to do what you did. I would not have thought Rav Kalman would give you smicha."

"He almost didn't. The others had a difficult time convincing him."

"That's not why he gave you his smicha. You can't convince someone like Rav Kalman to give smicha to a person he feels doesn't deserve it. You know what smicha is to people like him? It's the link between them and Moses at Sinai. And that business about the Song of Songs—that wasn't the reason, either."

"What was?"

"Maidanek," he said.

Before I left, Ruth Gordon asked me if I would have dinner with them the following Sunday. I accepted. She shook my hand warmly.

The next day I arrived at the yeshiva at five minutes before three and waited outside the door to Rav Gershenson's classroom. Rav Kalman dismissed his shiur first, and my classmates came out and crowded around me, loud with their congratulations. Irving Goldberg's solemn face beamed as he shook my hand and pounded my back. Even Abe Greenfield, the shy and suddenly explosive rebel of months back, found the courage to say a few nice words before he retreated back into his silent world. Then I saw Rav Gershenson's students beginning to leave their room, and I went quickly inside.

There was the usual group of students around Rav Gershenson's desk. But he saw me and asked them to leave. A moment later, we were alone.

He took my hand in both his hands. Then he asked me

to sit down. He sat back in his chair and peered at me and smiled and shook his head.

"I do not know how many smicha examinations I have given in this yeshiva," he said. "But I have never given an examination like that one. Tell me, Reuven, did you know the chance you were taking?"

"Yes."

He shook his head again. "You came close to losing. You even almost lost with me when you began to talk about—nu, what difference does it make? It is all over. But we had a very difficult time with Rav Kalman. Tell me, Reuven, will you write articles on the Gemora using this method?"

"Yes."

"I am not sure Rav Kalman will like that."

I did not say anything.

He smiled. "It is hard for an old tree to bend, Reuven. Be careful in your articles. Be very careful. Do not be afraid to write." He smiled sadly. Years ago, I had looked up his name in the English and Hebrew catalogues in the school library and discovered he had never published anything. "No," he said. "You should not be afraid to write. But be careful that you know what you are saying. Rav Kalman and others like him are—difficult opponents. They would be impossible to bear if they were not such great scholars. Nu, I am glad you succeeded. Give my regards to your father. Tell him—tell him it would have been a pleasure to have both Malters in our school. But I am grateful for winning at least half a victory."

And again he took my hand in both his hands and held it a long time.

I went home and spent the rest of the day working on my Master's thesis. I finished it that Friday, half an hour before it was time to begin to prepare for Shabbat.

The phone call from Danny came four days later, on Tuesday morning in the first week of May. He wanted me to come immediately to the treatment center. His voice was soft and very tight. He needed my help, he said. It was very important that I come immediately. Could I come? Sure I could come. Michael's parents would be there too, he said. I was to give my name to the person at the desk in the foyer and someone would take me downstairs to the isolation room. He was expecting me to be there in about three quarters of an hour, he said. I took a cab to the treatment center.

Sixteen

The guard at the gate recognized me. He was the one who had helped me stop Michael from setting fire to the leaves in the pagoda. He nodded as I went by. There were tiny green leaves on the trees now and I heard the warm wind in the branches. I could see the pagoda through the trees. Its slanted red roof gleamed in the sunlight.

I went quickly up the wide stone stairway and into the foyer. The man behind the desk spoke briefly into the phone after I gave him my name. A moment later another man came through the living room. He wore a tweed suit and horn-rimmed glasses and looked to be in his thirties. He asked me to go with him. We went into the living room and along the corridor past Danny's office and then through a heavy metal door at the end of the corridor and down a flight of stairs to another corridor with a cement floor and cinder-block walls. An overhead bulb burned dimly from an old ceiling fixture. Near the end of the wall to my right was a door. The man tapped on it softly. It opened and Danny came out and closed it immediately behind him. The man nodded at Danny and went away.

Danny took my arm and led me away from the door back to the staircase. He seemed exhausted. His eyes were rimmed with dark circles of sleeplessness and there were beads of perspiration on his forehead and upper lip.

"Thanks," he said.

"Are you all right?"

"I'm tired. But I'm all right. Listen, I want to talk to you before you go in there."

"You said his parents would be here."

"They're inside."

"How are they?"

"Very badly shaken."

"Is Michael talking to them?"

"Michael isn't talking."

I looked at him.

"We had a fine session yesterday and he asked to see them. I finally got him to ask for them." He was tense and nervous and his eyes blinked repeatedly. "Early this morning he was fine. Now he's back into one of his catatonic withdrawals and has stopped responding. I want you to go in and visit with him as if he were upstairs in his own room."

"Catatonic?" I heard myself say. "Michael is catatonic?"

"He's been in and out of it for weeks. All I want you to do is go in and talk to him the way you did before."

"What do you want me to say?" The news that Michael had been catatonic all these weeks had filled me with horror. I was trembling inside. "I don't know anything about all this. What should I say?"

"Say anything. Treat it like a normal visit. Say anything that comes into your head. I have no idea what will finally get him to talk. He has got to be able to tell his parents what he told me or it won't mean very much. So say anything." His voice was tight. He ran a finger across his perspiring upper lip. He had not had a haircut in a long time. His sand-colored hair was thick along the back of his neck and over the tops of his ears. "He'll hear you. A catatonic hears and sees and remembers everything that goes on around him." He stopped and looked at me. "I have got to get through to him," he said, softly, urgently. "Altman is beginning to have his doubts about this whole thing. I have got to get through to this boy." There was desperation in his voice and a plea for help. "Come on," he said. "And don't worry about the way he looks. He's lost some weight, but he's physically all right."

"Can I say anything to his parents."

"Say whatever you want to anyone you want. Just be yourself."

"I'm scared," I said.

He gave me a grim look. "I've been scared for weeks," he said. "Come on."

We went back along the corridor to the door. It was a heavy wooden brown door with large brass hinges, a brass knob, and a small circular key insert that was flush with the wood. Danny took a key ring from the pocket of his jacket. The keys jangled softly in the silence of the corridor. He selected a key and inserted it into the lock. There was a soft click. He pushed the door slightly open and held it for me and I stepped inside and he came in and I heard the soft click of the door as it closed behind us.

We were in a small dimly lit room. The walls were white and bare. The wooden floor was a dark brown. Set high in the wall opposite the door was a small narrow window. It was closed and the panes had been painted white. The ceiling was white. Silence, utter silence, filled the room, dense, thick, pressing against the window and the walls. I could feel it, I could actually *feel* it pushing against me. Directly below the window, Michael sat on a mattress, his legs folded Indian-fashion beneath him, his back to the wall. A white sheet and a brown blanket covered the mattress. He sat on the mattress and stared at the floor. He wore dungarees and a pale-blue polo shirt. His hands lay limply across his thighs. He had lost a great deal of weight. He seemed reedlike now, gaunt, his face almost as white as the sheet, his dark-brown hair thick and wild, falling across his forehead, his blue eyes wide and blank behind the glasses that had slipped down along the bridge of his nose, his narrow face devoid of expression. I looked at him and felt a shock of terror move through me. A few feet to his right, Abraham and Ruth Gordon sat on chairs near the wall with the high window, their coats across their laps. They looked at me as I went slowly toward Michael, their faces tortured, bewildered, white with fear and pain. They said nothing. Ruth Gordon held a handkerchief in her hands. She twisted it slowly. I saw her twisting it slowly on her lap, twining it around her fingers and twisting it. Abraham Gordon sat very still, his huge body curved forward on the chair, his round face and balding head covered with perspiration. I stood in front of Michael and looked down. I could see the top of his uncombed hair and the glasses on the bridge of his nose and the arms limp on his thighs and the curve of his shoulders and back, all of it very still, frozen, matching the dark silence of the room. Danny was alongside me. I glanced at him and he nodded briefly. I removed my coat and hat and put them on the floor in front of the mattress. I sat down on the floor. Danny sat down beside me. I sat there, staring at Michael and did not know what to say. I listened to the silence. It moved against me like something alive, and I found myself trying to reach beyond it for a sound, any sound, the tick of a clock, the tapping of shoes on a floor, the soft clearing of a throat, the wind in the branches of a tree, the skittering of leaves across the ground, anything. But there was nothing—only the silence, like a giant hand around the room. I was trembling and sweating. Danny sat beside me, gazing at Michael, and there was on his face a look of pain and anguish and suffering, as if he were somehow inside Michael, peering out at me through Michael, and I had come to talk to him in his entombing silence.

We sat in that silence a long time and then I began to feel myself choking and drowning in it, felt a need for a voice, and I heard myself say, softly, "Hello, Michael. Mr. Saunders said I could visit you and I came right away." The words sounded inane. But I did not know what else to say.

Michael sat very still on the mattress, his eyes staring fixedly at the floor. He did not move. He said nothing.

"You've lost more weight," I said.

Michael said nothing.

"You'll be able to gain it back this summer," I said.

Michael said nothing.

"You'll visit your aunt and uncle and we'll do some more sailing."

Michael said nothing.

"Would you like that?"

Michael said nothing.

"You've really lost an awful lot of weight," I said. Then I said, "Don't you want to talk to me any more?"

Michael said nothing.

"We had some good talks. Do you remember the time we went sailing and we tied up in the cove and you told me what the clouds looked like? Do you remember that?"

Michael said nothing.

"Do you remember the roller coaster ride and the nose-bleed and that old man?"

Michael said nothing.

"Michael," I said. "Please, Michael." My God, I thought. He's dead. There's nothing there. He's turned to stone. What have they done to him? They've killed him with silence. At least before there was something there. He's dead. He's alive and dead and they'll take him out of here and put him into the back ward of an asylum some-where and he'll be alive and dead the rest of his life. What have they done to him? What has Danny done to him with his crazy silence? They've killed him inside. He's breathing but he's dead and they've killed him. I looked at Danny. His eyes were fixed on Michael. I looked at Abraham and Ruth Gordon. They were staring at Mi-chael in terror. Say something, I thought, looking back at Michael. Say something. Do something. Anything. Blink your eyes. Move a finger. Talk. Scream. Cry. *Anything!*

Michael said nothing.

I panicked then and heard myself begin to babble. I did not really know what I was saying, but I talked. I talked on and on, quietly, my voice shaking, using the words to push away the silence and fill the room with something that was truly alive, with words, driving out the silence with words, beating against the silence with words, pouring the wind and the lake and the memories of the summer into the emptiness of the room. I talked about the first time we had gone sailing together and how frightened he had been but how quickly he had learned to handle the balancing of the Sailfish. I talked about the way we had overturned and the trouble he had had with the center board. "Those center boards warp sometimes in the water," I said. "Do you remember my saying that? Do you remember, Michael? And we lay in the cove and talked about Rachel, and your father's books, and all the attacks against your father, and Rav Kalman, and the students in your school. Rav Kalman is an angry person," I said. "But he suffered. He lost his whole world and people who are suffering sometimes take out their suffering on others. They defend what the ones they loved died for. They become angry and ugly and they fight anything that's a threat to them. We have to learn how to fight back without hurting them too much. We can talk about that next summer. We'll sail again and talk about it," I said. "But you have to tell us you're all right. Tell me you hear what I'm saying. We'll sail again and you'll read some more clouds for me. Or maybe you won't have to read the clouds any more. But tell me you hear what I'm saying. Michael. Please. Michael. I know what it's like to be inside a small room, fighting. I was inside a small room too. But I talked. I fought back. You have to learn to talk and fight back. You have to learn how to do it even if it hurts people you respect or love. You're not anything unless you can learn to do that. I fought them but I respected them and I won and I'm getting my smicha and I'll be teaching at Hirsch next year and when I get my doctorate in philosophy I'll take a pulpit but I'll be able to continue teaching. Do you hear me, Michael? I fought them and I won. You can win too if you learn how to fight. You have to talk if you want to fight. I fought Rav Kalman and he's giving me smicha. I tried not to hurt him too much. I fought with words, Michael. And sometimes you have to fight even if it means hurting people terribly. Sometimes you have to hurt a person you love if you want to be yourself. We can talk about that too in the summer. We can go sailing and you can take the tiller and the mainsail and we—"

"You're getting smicha from Rav Kalman?" Michael said.

"—can talk about that and about—"

I had barely heard him. I was all caught up in the flood of my own words and had barely heard him. I stopped and felt as if a sudden surge of electrical current had come up from the floor and gone all through me and into my head. My hands tingled. I felt the top of my scalp and the back of my neck suddenly hot with shock. Michael had raised his head and was looking at me over the top of his glasses.

"You're getting smicha from Rav Kalman?" he said again, his voice thin and faintly trembling, his eyes narrow with hate.

"Yes," I said. I did not look at Danny or Michael's parents. I kept my eyes on Michael.

"He attacked your father and he's giving you smicha?" Michael said in a high, thin voice. "You're accepting his smicha?" He was sitting up very straight now, his gaunt body stiff, his hands clenched into fists. There was a crimson flush on his face. He seemed to be going into one of his rages. I stared at him and was afraid and did not know what to say.

"Go away," Michael said.

I said nothing.

"Go away," Michael said again, clenching and unclenching his fists. "You liar, you cheat, you bastard. Go away!"

I heard a soft gasp from Ruth Gordon. I did not look at her.

"You bastard," Michael said, digging his knuckles into his thighs. "You cheating bastard." His voice was rising and there was rage in his eyes. He trembled with the rage. It poured from him. "You're all the same. Leave me alone!"

I said nothing.

"Get out of here!" he shouted. "Leave me alone!" His

voice beat against the bare walls. "Leave me alone! Just leave me alone! I like it here alone! Go away!"

I sat very still and felt the words pounding at me and said nothing.

"Michael," Danny said softly.

Michael looked at him, blinking, his hands clenched, the knuckles digging into his thighs.

"Why should Reuven not have accepted smicha from Rav Kalman?"

Michael said nothing.

"Because Rav Kalman attacked his father?" Danny said.

Michael said nothing.

"Do you think Rav Kalman is an evil person?"

"Evil," Michael said. "Ugly and evil. Evil evil evil."

"Why is he evil?"

"Evil evil evil evil—"

"Michael," Danny said softly, gently. "Did you know that Reuven wanted smicha? He wanted it almost more than anything else in the world. It's a very great honor to receive smicha from the Hirsch Yeshiva. Did you know that, Michael?"

Michael said nothing.

"Did you know that Rav Kalman almost didn't give him smicha?"

Michael said nothing. He kept digging his knuckles into his thighs and said nothing.

"He disapproves of the method Reuven uses to study Talmud."

Michael said nothing.

"Do you know where Reuven learned that method?"

Michael said nothing.

"He learned it from his father." Danny paused for a moment. Then he said, leaning forward slightly, "Would you have wanted Reuven not to have gotten smicha and to hate his father?"

Michael's mouth opened slightly. I heard someone stir on one of the chairs but I did not look up. I kept looking at Michael. His mouth was open and he had suddenly stopped digging his knuckles into his thighs and he was staring at Danny.

"Is that what you wanted, Michael?" Danny asked softly. "Did you want Reuven to become like you so you could share something private and secret with him?"

Michael stared and I thought I saw his eyes glaze over and was afraid he had gone back into his dead world. Then I saw his hands begin to clench and unclench again on his thighs. He closed his eyes and opened them again and pushed his glasses back up along the bridge of his nose with the knuckles of his right hand and continued staring at Danny.

"Don't you have a secret you want to share with him?" Danny asked quietly.

Michael ran his tongue over his lips. He had opened his hands. They lay palms down on his thighs. He said nothing.

"Don't you?" Danny said softly.

"I'm afraid," Michael said in a very small voice.

"Yes," Danny said. "I know you are. We're all afraid of such secrets. You hated Rav Kalman for hurting Reuven and his father but deep inside you were also happy. Isn't that right, Michael?"

Michael looked wildly around the room, as if searching for an escape. He saw his parents staring at him in dread, and he jerked his head away from them and looked back at Danny.

"Isn't that right, Michael?" Danny said again, very gently.

Michael nodded and began rubbing the palms of his hands up and down against his thighs. His eyes were wide and rolling. He had the look of a terribly wounded animal.

"You wanted to tell it to someone," Danny said. "But you were all alone and afraid and you thought you could tell it to Reuven once he felt that way too. Am I right, Michael?"

"I needed someone," Michael said hollowly. "I needed someone to—" He stopped. His shoulders sagged. He

kept rubbing his palms up and down against his thighs.
Then he began to sway slowly back and forth, the upper
part of his body moving back and forth. "He would have
understood," he said. "We could have talked. I needed
someone. We could have talked and talked and talked. I
needed someone. I didn't want him not to get smicha and
to have his life ruined. But I needed someone." He looked
at me then. "I'm sorry," he said. "I didn't want to hurt
you. I'm sorry. But I needed someone. I didn't want to
hurt you, Reuven." His lips were trembling. All of him
was trembling and he kept swaying back and forth and
rubbing his hands against his thighs. "You would have
hated him and we could have talked but I didn't want you
to hate him because I knew you loved him. You would
have loved and hated him and we could have talked.
Reuven, I'm sorry. I'm sorry. I'm sorry. Oh God, I'm
sorry. I don't want to talk any more. I'm afraid. Oh God,
I'm afraid. Make me stop talking. I don't want to talk.
Reuven, make me stop. Please. Make me stop. Oh God
make me stop. *I don't want to say any more!* How can
you love and hate a person at the same time? How can
you love and hate anything at the same time? You would
have understood me, Reuven. Oh, I'm sorry. I didn't know
what I was thinking. I'm sorry. Please, Mr. Saunders,
make me stop. I'm afraid. I didn't want you to be hurt,
Reuven. I only wanted you to be able to understand. I
hated it. I hated it. How can you love anything that does
that to human beings?" He was swaying faster now, back
and forth, back and forth, swaying. "How can you—how
can you—how can you love a religion that does that to
human beings? How can you love a religion that makes
people hate other human beings? I hated it. God, God,
God, I hated it. I wanted to crush it. I wanted to burn it. I
wanted to tear it to pieces. I hated hated hated hated it.
And my father is trying to teach it. He loves it. Reuven, he
loves it. You know he loves it. You know that, don't you?
He loves it. But I hate it. I hate it. I hate anything that does
that to human beings. He loves it. But I don't understand.
I don't understand. How can he love it? How? How? Tell

me how, Reuven. I love my father. And I—and I—*I hate him!*" I heard a loud gasp from Abraham Gordon. Michael trembled visibly with the force that had pushed those words from him. It was as if something had exploded inside him somewhere and had expelled itself through his open lips. "I hate him," he said in a choked voice. "I hate him. You would have understood that, Reuven. We could have talked about that. I hate him. I love him and I hate him. I hate him for what he made me go through. It wasn't only *his* name they attacked. Did you see the scrapbook, Reuven? He sent me to a special school to learn Yiddish and I read that scrapbook one day. It wasn't only *his* name they attacked. *It was my name too!* Gordon. Gordon. They almost never said Abraham Gordon. They said Gordon. And the students in my class said Gordon. And sometimes I could hear people in the street say Gordon. Gordon destroys Judaism. Gordon is a heretic. Gordon will be punished with Hell after he dies. Gordon is an apostate. Gordon is a deliberate sinner." He used the Hebrew words for apostate and deliberate sinner. "Gordon. It was Gordon they hated. No one ever asked *me* whether he should write those things. No one was interested in how *I* felt. He just wrote. I hated those books. Everytime one of them came out it would mean more attacks. I loved him. And they attacked him. And I felt hurt because he was attacked. It hurt me to see him suffer. God, how it hurt me . . . Oh God, how I suffered . . . God, what he made me go through. I hate him . . . And my mother—she helped him to write. I would sit in the study on Sunday afternoons and watch her help him. She urged him to write. And everytime one of those books came out, there was an attack. Why didn't she see how I was suffering? A mother is supposed to see that. A mother is *supposed* to—to comfort a son. Isn't a mother supposed to comfort a son? I love my mother. And I hate her." I heard a soft moan and turned my head and saw Ruth Gordon with her hands across her eyes, the lips below the hands open and wet and trembling, and Abraham Gordon holding her close to him, his face a mask of horror. "I love her," Michael said in a hoarse, choked voice, "and I hate her, and I don't know what to do any more. I don't know what to do. What can I do, Reuven? I don't know what to do. Help me know what to do . . ." He lowered his head. His body continued swaying, slower now. He kept rubbing his hands against his thighs. Then, suddenly, he stopped swaying and looked up, all of him rigid, his eyes wide, bulging, staring at me. "I didn't—I didn't want to hurt them. I was—afraid. God, I'm afraid. I don't want to—hurt them. I hate them. *I hate them!*" I saw his head stiff, and the veins standing out on his thin neck. I saw his head trembling, shaking and trembling. I saw him turn it in a single sudden motion toward his parents. *"I hate you!"* he screamed, the words lashing at me, cutting at me, cutting the walls and the window, flaying at his parents who stared back at him in frozen horror. "I didn't want to tell you!" Michael screamed. "They made me tell you! I hate you! I could—*I could kill you!* What have you done to me? Oh God, I didn't want to tell you. I can't help it. I can't stop it. I hate you!" He was trying to get to his feet. I saw him push himself up with his hands. "I hate you both!" he was screaming. I thought Danny would stop him. But he did not move. He sat very still, watching Michael intently. I had not looked at Danny all the time Michael had been talking. Now I saw him watching Michael rise weakly to his feet, still screaming his hatred, and was astonished at the look on his face. The sculptured lines had softened. He seemed suddenly deeply calm. He sat there as Michael's screams filled the room, watching Michael move slowly toward his parents. "Abba," I heard Michael say. "Imma. I didn't want— They made me! They forced me! I was afraid. They forced me. Abba, I didn't want to hurt you! Imma, I didn't want to hurt you! I didn't—" Then his voice cracked and a loud animal wail, a cry of tearing pain, broke from him. *"Oh God, I love you so much!"*— and he was on them, almost flinging himself on them, his father's chair tilting dangerously backward but straightening immediately as Abraham Gordon moved forward and took his son in his arms and

Ruth Gordon leaned across Michael's shoulder and covered him with her body and buried her face in his neck and I could see Michael's arms around them, clutching at them, hungrily, and hear his sobs, loud, gasping, and the soft, muted sobs of his parents—and I looked away and found I was hot and cold and shaking as though with a fever and the room swayed and spun and seemed suddenly dark and I put my hands on the floor to steady myself and heard Danny ask me if I was all right. I nodded and took a deep breath and heard talking going on somewhere inside the room but could not make out the words and the room tilted and swayed and spun around again and I thought I would have to lie down. I took another deep breath and felt my palms hard against the floor and began to push myself to my feet but could not get up. They were talking softly near me and I thought I would have to ask Danny for help and I looked around, feeling dizzy and frightened, and saw Michael standing with his parents away from the chairs, talking, gesturing, crying, and Ruth Gordon with the handkerchief covering her lips and Abraham Gordon's hands over his eyes and Danny on a chair against the wall near the mattress, reaching up to the window. I saw him pull at something and then the window fell inward and hung suspended on a chain and immediately there was a rush of warm wind and I felt it on my face, felt it moving silkenly across my face and I took deep breaths of it and the room slowly stopped spinning. Danny got down off the chair and came over to me.

"Are you all right?" he asked anxiously.

I nodded.

"You looked like you were going to pass out. Let me help you up."

I felt his hand on my arm as I rose to my feet. Michael and his parents were still standing together. They were not talking. They were simply standing together, looking at one another.

"Wait outside a few minutes," Danny said quietly to me. "I need to talk to them alone. It'll only be a few minutes."

He opened the door and I stepped into the corridor and then he closed the door and I was alone. I found it difficult to stand. I went through the corridor and sat down on the stairs. I was feeling very cold and I put on my hat and coat. I closed my eyes and was back inside that room and opened them again quickly. I sat very still, with my eyes open. I sat and stared at the cement floor and the cinder-block wall and the ceiling fixture and saw cracks in the cement and the cinder blocks and let my eyes trace their jagged lines and then the door opened and Danny came out with Abraham and Ruth Gordon and they moved toward me through the corridor. I got to my feet. We went up the stairs through the door and along the corridor to Danny's office. Outside the office we stopped and Abraham Gordon said quietly to Danny, "I'll call you tomorrow morning," and Danny nodded. Then Abraham Gordon turned to me and said, "I can't quite begin—" and stopped. Ruth Gordon said nothing. Her eyes were dark and wet and filled with bewildering pain. Then they went along the corridor, walking very closely together, Abraham Gordon's hand in Ruth Gordon's arm, each seeming to be supporting the other, and turned into the living room and were gone.

"Come inside a minute," Danny said. "I want to talk to you."

We came into the office and sat at the desk.

"How do you feel?" Danny asked.

"I don't know. Very tired."

"Have you had lunch? I have a sandwich we—"

"I'll eat at home."

"Do you want some water? You look—"

"No," I said.

He nodded. Then he said, "You should have been a psychologist."

"Thanks," I said.

"You did it for me."

"I didn't do anything. I didn't even know what I was saying."

"No," he said. "You knew what you were saying."

I looked at him. There was a brief silence.

"I'm really tired," I said. "I want to go home."

"Do you understand what happened in there?" he asked.

"I—think so," I said. Then I said, "You took quite a chance. He could have stayed catatonic. What would you have done?"

"Altman would have stopped the experiment. He would have come out of it."

"Why didn't Michael tell his parents what they were doing to him?"

"I don't know," he said. "We'll have to work that out in therapy. I would guess that in a way he was enjoying his rage. Sometimes a person who feels helpless seeks power by manipulating the pain-giver into giving more pain. Or he acts erratically and causes the pain-giver pain as a way of avenging himself. He might even get some kind of sexual pleasure out of his rages. Yes . . . Even that. I don't know. Michael has a long way to go. But I think he's ready now."

"You knew all along," I said. "You knew what it was about all the time."

"I guessed."

"You didn't guess. You knew."

"Yes," he said quietly. "I went through some of that myself a while ago." He closed his eyes and after a moment I saw him begin to sway back and forth behind his desk. Then he raised his hand and with his thumb and forefinger began to caress an imaginary earlock.

I left him there and closed the door softly behind me and went home.

For a very long time my father sat at his desk, staring at me in disbelief. Then he tried to say something but the words would not come out and he cleared his throat and coughed.

"I would not have hated you that way, abba," I said. "We would have talked about it."

"You are sure, Reuven?"

I nodded.

"You would have told me how you felt about me if the things that were most precious to me had ruined your life?"

"Yes."

"Haven't you hated me during these past months?" he asked softly.

I hesitated. "It wasn't really—"

"Why didn't you tell me, Reuven?"

I looked at him and did not say anything.

"What a chance we take when we raise children," my father murmured. "What a terrible chance."

Rachel called me later that day and we talked for a while. She and her parents had spent part of the afternoon with her aunt and uncle. They had looked shattered. Her aunt and uncle had just sat together on the couch, broken and shattered. But they were grateful to me. They wanted to see me again, she said. Especially her aunt. They hadn't thanked me properly. They wanted to thank me. I told her they didn't have to thank me. I had learned a few things myself, I said. They didn't owe me anything. Bloom had his son back, I said. He didn't need Dedalus. She was silent a moment. Would I see them anyway? she said. Yes, I said. I had the impression that she had been talking all along through tears.

I went over to their apartment the following evening. They had recovered somewhat, but they were both subdued. Abraham Gordon looked pale. He was trying to get back into his book, he said. Ruth Gordon said very little. But she cried easily and made no effort to conceal her tears.

I saw Michael a few times during the next weeks. They had taken him out of isolation and he was back in his old room. Danny was seeing him in therapy three times a week. They thought he might be able to leave the treatment center at the end of June, he told me. But he would have to continue in therapy for a long time. And they would be sending him to a special school next year, and if that worked out he could return to his regular school the year after.

We walked beneath the trees on a day in the second week of June and there was sunlight on the leaves and on the red and white pagoda. We sat on the circular white bench and looked through the trees at the sky. He had put on some weight but his hair was still uncombed and he seemed tense and a little dazed. I saw him take his eyes from the trees and look around at the pagoda.

"I think I might have killed him," he said softly. "I remember—I remember I was so angry I wanted to hurt somebody." He seemed frightened by his words. "But he said no one could take you away from me and I knew you were my friend and I didn't want to hurt you by hurting him." He was silent. A breeze stirred the leaves. Then he looked at me. "He's a nice person. Even if he is so religious. I wish—I wish Rachel hadn't fallen in love with someone so religious."

The following Sunday I received my Master's degree in philosophy and a week later, in a long and joyous ceremony attended by dozens of rabbis and a variety of dignitaries from all over the country, I was given smicha. Later, sitting in my seat during a particularly lengthy speech, I unrolled the parchment and read the words and saw his signature alongside that of Rav Gershenson. It was a strong, spiky scrawl. The letters stood out sharply, his title, his name, and the name of his father. They seemed to glitter in the bright lights of the huge auditorium.

I was standing with my father at one of the tables in the reception hall when I saw him come toward us, looking small but stately in his tall black skullcap and starched white shirt and dark knee-length jacket. He shook my hand and I felt the misshapen fingers against my palm.

"Your son has chutzpah," he said to my father. "I have never had a student with such chutzpah." Then he smiled thinly. "And with such derech eretz." "Derech eretz" is the Hebrew term for respect and good manners.

I watched as the two of them shook hands, coldly,
guardedly. Then he walked off and disappeared into the
crowd and I saw my father grimace and shake his head.
They would be opponents all their lives. I did not for a
minute think he had heard the last of Rav Kalman. For
that matter, I did not think I had either.

Danny and Rachel were married on the last Sunday in
June. It was a lavish, tumultuous, Hasidic wedding in a
hall in Williamsburg. Men and women sat separately.
There were Hasidic musicians. There was dancing and
singing and the radiant face of Rachel and Danny's eyes
shining as he danced and Abraham Gordon standing
against a wall and watching and Ruth Gordon's face cold
and contemptuous and Joseph and Sarah Gordon looking
distressed and uncomfortable and totally unable to reconcile themselves to the world their daughter had forced into
their lives. Reb Saunders danced briefly with my father
and a group of tzaddikim and there were lengthy discourses
on passages of Talmud and at one point as an old rebbe
wound his way tortuously through a labyrinth of Talmudic reasoning I remembered a Yerushalmi and solved his
problem for him with a variant text but I sat there listening anyway, fascinated by the look on his aged face and by
the gestures of his hands. Then Danny spoke and he was
very good and I did not need to do anything to the text he
used. Sometime during that wedding Abraham Gordon
came over to me and told me he had finished his book and
he and Michael and Ruth were going off on a vacation for
a while, and Joseph Gordon chewed on his pipe and asked
me how in God's name anyone could think in all this
noise, and Rachel, beautiful Rachel, told me she and
Danny had found a small apartment near Columbia and
she would be going to graduate school for a degree in
English literature until—she stopped, and I said, Until
Rachel became big with seed, and she blushed and
laughed and went off. From time to time I glanced over at
the table where Michael was sitting with his father and

saw him staring at the dancing Hasidim, his face pale, his eyes wide. Then he was gone from the table and I looked around and found him standing near the door and I came up to him and asked him how he was feeling. His nose had begun to bleed a little, he said. But he was all right now. Then he looked at me through his glasses. "We're going away for a few weeks," he said. "The doctors told my parents it was all right. We might see the observatory in Palomar. Have you ever seen that observatory?"

"No."

He was silent for a moment, gazing moodily at a circle of dancers. "I really hurt my parents," he said. "I really hurt them."

I did not say anything.

"They're not over it yet," he said. "I can feel they're not over it. I wish it hadn't happened. I wish you hadn't made me do it. I wish—I wish—" His thin body sagged slightly. "I'm tired," he said. "I want to sit down."

He went off in the direction of his table.

Danny came over to me and said, "You're not dancing."

"I'm resting. I don't have the strength you Hasidim have."

"Will I see you this summer?" I asked.

"I'll be working on my dissertation this summer."

I asked him what the topic was.

"Michael," he said.

I looked at him.

"It was Altman's idea."

"I think it's a fine idea."

"We may come up to see you in August."

"I'd like that."

"Come and dance with me, Reuven. I want you to dance with me."

He took my hand and we broke through a circle and did the handkerchief dance and I heard them singing and clapping and stamping their feet and the room shook to the rhythm of the music. The whole wedding was like that. It was—it was a splendid wedding.

I did not see any of them again until the middle of August.

Joseph and Sarah Gordon spent all of July and the first two weeks of August alone in their summer home by the lake. My father and I moved into our cottage in the first week of August and a few days later I went over to see them. I found Joseph Gordon on the dock with a new book about Hemingway and Sarah Gordon on the patio, flinging paint onto a canvas. I was with them for an hour or so and we had a pleasant enough time and they told me that Rachel and Danny were coming up to spend two weeks with them. Rachel had talked Danny into taking off for a while. They were expecting to see me, she said, daubing paint on the canvas and stepping back to gauge the effect. She would call me when they came.

Those early weeks of August were warm and quiet and restful. I was able to do some swimming and sailing, but mostly I sat with my father at the wooden table on the screened-in porch of our cottage. We were preparing our lectures for the classes we would be teaching in September.

Danny and Rachel came up in the third week of August. They looked the way all newly married couples look: radiant, somewhat shy, and filled with the quiet amazement of discovery. I asked Danny if he had heard from Michael and his parents, and he said yes, he and Rachel had received a card from them and they seemed to be enjoying their trip. He would be seeing Michael again in therapy when they returned. He was really only at the beginning of things with Michael. There was still a long way to go.

I found Rachel on the dock late one morning, sunning herself and reading a Hebrew book, and when I asked her what it was she handed it to me and I saw it was a Hasidic book about the concept of the holiness of the family. Danny came down and we sat on the dock and talked, and later I watched Rachel trying to teach him how to swim and he was as awkward as a finless fish in the water. I took him out in a sailboat one afternoon but he could not get the feel of it and I did not take him out again. That was the afternoon Rachel asked if we might go to the county fair in Peekskill. She had checked it out and it was really a fair this time. Did it have a carnival? Danny asked. Yes, she said. But it was a very small carnival and we could ignore it and see the exhibits. Danny said he would feel uncomfortable in a place like that and did not want to go. But Rachel insisted and we went and the old man was not there and we had a good time.

A few days later Michael and his parents arrived for the weekend and on a warm and windy Sunday morning I crossed the back lawn and went past the old maple and through the woods and around the lake to the Gordon home. I found them playing volleyball on the lawn beyond the patio, Michael and his parents forming one team and Danny and Rachel and her parents forming the other, and I stood on the side for a while and watched. Danny was playing volleyball the way he had once played baseball, with an intense, hungry eagerness to win. He played wildly, his long body everywhere on the court, his small skullcap attached to his hair with a bobby pin so it would not fall off, one of his ritual fringes falling out of his polo shirt and flapping against his leg as he ran about.

Abraham Gordon saw me and called me over to join his team. "We need help," he said.

"Nothing will help," Joseph Gordon laughed.

I went over to Abraham Gordon's side of the court. He was bare to the waist and sweating profusely. He shook my hand.

"Where did that Hasid learn to play ball like that?" he asked.

From the other side of the net came Rachel's laugh and Joseph Gordon's loud and happy challenge. "It won't help. We'll even use the Geneva Conventions. But it won't help. We've got ourselves a powerhouse here."

"How was Palomar?" I asked Michael.

"It was great," he said, smiling happily. Then he said, "Can we go sailing in the afternoon, Reuven?"

"Absolutely," I said. "This wind is perfect for sailing."

"Your friend plays a rather frenzied game," Ruth Gordon said.

"Yes," I said. "Always."

The three of them seemed rested and relaxed and I joined them and did the best I could, but with Danny on the other side we lost anyway and at the moment the final point was scored Rachel shouted with joy and in front of everyone planted a kiss on Danny's lips. I saw his eyes above the curve of her cheek, wide, startled, and his face a sudden flaming crimson. He was going to have quite a time of it with Rachel's twentieth century.

I went back to the cottage to have lunch with my father and later that afternoon I took a Sailfish across the lake to the dock and then Michael and I sailed toward the middle of the lake. There were many clouds in the sky but they were not blocking the sun. There was a strong wind and Michael held the tiller in one hand and the mainsail sheet in the other and I sat near the center board, balancing the boat. We sailed to the rhythm of the water and the wind and then Michael headed the Sailfish past the house and the dock toward the cove and I pulled up on the center board and felt it move smoothly through the slot and we tied up to the branch of a tree that lay in the water.

"Do you want to swim?" I asked.

"Sure."

"I'll race you to that rock."

We swam for a while then we lay on the Sailfish and I saw Michael looking up at the sky. He looked up at the sky a long time.

"Sometimes I still see faces," he said.

I asked him what he was seeing now.

"Clouds," he said.

About the Author

CHAIM POTOK was born in New York City in 1929. He graduated from Yeshiva University and the Jewish Theological Seminary of America, was ordained as a rabbi, and earned his Ph.D. in philosophy from the University of Pennsylvania. He is currently editor of the Jewish Publication Society of America. His first novel, *The Chosen,* published in 1967, received the Edward Lewis Wallant Memorial Book Award, was a nominee for the National Book Award in fiction, and was a number-one bestseller. His most recent novel is *My Name Is Asher Lev.*

Dr. Potok lives in Philadelphia with his wife, Adena, and their three children.

MODERN CLASSICS

☐ THE ASSASSINS—Oates		23000-7	2.25
☐ WONDERLAND—Oates		22951-3	1.95
☐ MARRY ME—Updike		23369-3	1.95
☐ A MONTH OF SUNDAYS—Updike		C2701	1.95
☐ THE CHOSEN—Potok		22878-9	1.75
☐ IN THE BEGINNING—Potok		22980-7	1.95
☐ WOMAN ON THE EDGE OF TIME—Piercy		23208-5	2.25
☐ GILES GOAT BOY—Barth		2483	2.25
☐ CHIMERA—Barth		23152-6	1.95

PRIZE-WINNING NOVELS

☐ **THEM**—Oates   22745-6   1.95
☐ **THE CENTAUR**—Updike   22922-X   1.75
☐ **TALES OF THE SOUTH**   X2757   1.75
   PACIFIC—Michener
☐ **THE KEEPERS OF THE HOUSE**—Grau   23031-7   1.50
☐ **ANGLE OF REPOSE**—Stegner   C2717   1.95
☐ **CHIMERA**—Barth   23152-6   1.95